# Haven's Joy

### Third in the Haven's Series

*Tia Austin*

authorHOUSE®

*AuthorHouse™*
*1663 Liberty Drive*
*Bloomington, IN 47403*
*www.authorhouse.com*
*Phone: 1 (800) 839-8640*

*Published by AuthorHouse  04/30/2018*

*ISBN: 978-1-5462-3988-8 (sc)*
*ISBN: 978-1-5462-3986-4 (hc)*
*ISBN: 978-1-5462-3987-1 (e)*

*Library of Congress Control Number: 2018905206*

*Print information available on the last page.*

*This book is printed on acid-free paper.*

# ~ Contents ~

# ~ 1 ~

**B**race ran a sleeve across his brow, keeping one hand on the wooden ladder to steady it. He peered up into the rafters, where Daris stood perched on the highest rung of the ladder.

"Can you reach it from there?" Rudge asked him, standing at Brace's side.

"Yes, I've got it," Daris replied, leaning forward and reaching, careful not to lose his balance. Coming down a step, he handed Brace the tight jumble of twigs he held in his palm.

It was a bird's nest, Brace could see easily enough. He pushed the tiny broken eggshells around with his fingertip, then picked up a small red feather. So soft, it almost felt like *nothing* as he let its curved shape slide over the end of his thumb.

"You were right," Brace commented as Daris came down to stand with the rest of them. "It is a bird's nest."

"This one's all set, then?" Brodan asked, peering up at the underside of the roof.

"Looks ready to me," Rudge commented.

In the more than two years since the Day of Light, as it had come to be called, the steady work of repairing Haven's blue-gray stone houses had been underway, readying them for new inhabitants. Nearly sixty, in fact, had since either found their way to Haven or had been brought back with a returning search mission.

Much to everyone's surprise, the first to arrive were three of the four surviving soldiers who had been sent by King Oden to try and take control of the city. Jair had sent them back to Glendor's Keep with a small piece of lightstone, protecting them from attack by night screamers. King

1

Oden needed to be warned of the dangers of sending anyone to attack the city. Brace had certainly been surprised when, just over a month after the soldiers had departed on foot, they returned —three of them, at least— Farris, Alban, and Korian by name — bringing wives or children or a father, a brother. They had expressed their deep desire to leave the rest of the world behind and call Haven their home, and had been welcomed in. There was no longer any reason to fear anyone with impure motives or malice in their heart ever passing through Haven's high, crescent-shaped stone entrance gate.

The city would *know*, the light would *know*, Jair had told them, what was in each person's heart, and would only allow in those whose hearts held no ill will.

The arrival of the soldiers and their families had been followed by a group from Roshwan, of all places. The country north of Dunya was far distant enough that it had taken the nine travelers nearly six months on horseback to complete their journey. Fortunately, the woven cloth bearing their map to Haven had led them on a path north of the mountains, and they had managed to avoid the high, rocky pass altogether. They had been thin, dirty, and tired when they arrived, but unharmed.

When questioned if they'd had any trouble with night screamers, the looks on their faces had said yes.

The "*khala bhuta*," one of the men called them. Tall, thin, with long dark hair and tattooed markings on his neck and arms, the young warrior Bahadur had told them they'd heard and seen the mist-shrouded beasts almost every night for the past twenty days, and they had only managed to keep them away by burning branches all through the long hours of darkness.

The two children in particular, Hoden and Aneerah, had looked as though they'd had more than enough of the frightening creatures, almost more than they could bear, and were beyond relieved at finally arriving in safety, even as their mother had wept for joy at seeing Haven at last.

Over the past few years, there had been many successful search missions, initially led by Dursen, who had then turned over his leadership role to Gavin when he and Nerissa were married and settled in as caretakers of Haven's animals and farmland.

Young as Gavin was, he had quickly proved himself to be an efficient leader, with Stanner and Berrick joining him. Traveling throughout the country of Dunya, the three of them had brought many more newcomers, generally a handful on each mission, at times only one or two.

And finally, only six months ago, another group had arrived from the far south of Danferron. A middle-aged man called Brannock, a descendant of the ancient remembrance keepers, had gathered together his family and a few friends, and the eight of them had arrived in mid-autumn with even more news about the increasing presence of night screamers, as well as the decreasing amount of sunlight to be seen each day.

The constant expectation of new arrivals, never knowing how many there would be or when they would come, kept everyone busy restoring Haven's empty homes. The thick stone walls were solid enough, but from time to time, surface cracks were found which needed mortaring. More often than not, the thatch roofs were in need of repair, and every house required basic cleaning, sweeping out dust or removing birds' nests. There was no sense in waiting for more people to arrive before they made a place ready for them to live.

Today, Brace had joined Rudge, Kalen, Daris and Brodan in completing the work on two more homes in the area near the border of Haven's Woods. The early spring weather provided perfect conditions for working, but wasn't the weather in Haven always perfect?

"Hello there!" a friendly voice called out. "Are you all still out here?"

Brace looked up, and Daris smiled, giving him a nod.

Looking over his shoulder toward the open doorway, Brace called out an answer. "We're still here!"

A shadow passed through the doorway momentarily before Jair entered after it. "How is everything coming along?" he asked with a quick, easy smile.

"Well enough, lad," Brodan replied, pulling the ladder away from the wall and balancing it on his shoulder. "Another one ready to be moved into."

"Fantastic," Jair remarked, gazing up at the newly repaired roof.

Brace glanced up into the rafters before letting his gaze fall on Jair's face. At fifteen years, Jair was on the far edge of boyhood. His straight, smooth hair had darkened to an almost chestnut brown, and his arms were beginning to show a hint of muscle. His voice had deepened over the past year as well, and now, when he stood beside Brace, there was a mere three inches' difference in height between the two of them.

Though Jair had grown considerably, physically and in confidence, Brace was grateful that Jair's heart remained much the same —caring for others, always wanting light to win over darkness. Always searching for the good in every situation, in everyone he met, always holding onto hope for what tomorrow might bring.

"Yes, we've got the roof fixed," Brodan was telling Jair now. "Everything else feels solid enough."

"Now we'll just see how long it takes for someone new to show up at the gate," Kalen spoke up.

"Might be sooner than you'd think," Brace commented.

"You've done great work here," Jair told them. "Thank you."

Brodan nodded, leaving through the open doorway, the ladder trailing behind him. Stanner chuckled.

"Someone ought to tell Brodan not to talk so much, heh?"

His comment brought smiles and light laughter, for everyone knew that beneath Brodan's quiet, gruff manner was a fiercely loyal heart. There was never any doubt that, once a friendship with the man had been established, he would be the first to rise up in your defense if the need arose.

Jair watched as Brodan went on farther down the road, then turned toward Brace.

"What's this?" he asked, looking down at Brace's hands.

"Oh, it's a bird's nest," he replied. "Daris found it up near the roof."

"Looks like a good one," Jair commented, peering at it more closely.

"Think Dorianne might want it at the school?" Brace asked. "The little ones could enjoy seeing it up close."

"Sure," Jair replied, taking it lightly in his hands. "I'll bring it to her on my way back."

"Thanks," Brace told him, brushing flakes of straw from his palms.

"Well," Daris spoke up, "since we're all through here, I think I'll be heading for home."

Brace nodded, waiting with Jair near the open doorway as the others left.

"Did you attend classes today?" Brace asked lightly, running his fingers through his hair as they stepped out into the full light of day.

"Nah," Jair replied, wrinkling his nose. "I haven't been going as much.

I have other things on my mind. Things I'm learning that Dorianne could never teach me."

"Oh, really?" Brace asked. "Things such as?"

Jair smiled. "More about Haven, of course. Isn't it always?"

Brace laughed. "Sure enough, it is. What is it this time? What mysterious truth about our fair city have you been woken up to now?"

"I'm not exactly sure," Jair admitted. "It's still cloudy. I'll need to look into it more."

"Let me know when you've put it all together, will you?"

"Of course I will."

Brace elbowed him, and he laughed.

"You'd better go on, then. Tell Ovard hello for me."

"I will." Jair hesitated. "How is Tassie?" he asked, his eyes growing solemn. "Is she doing any better?"

Brace rubbed pensively at the back of his neck. "Somewhat," he replied. "She still doesn't quite seem her usual, confident self. But she's getting there."

"She doesn't blame herself for Lomar's death, does she? It wasn't her fault. It was just his time to go."

"I'm not certain," Brace answered. "Actually, I think she does blame herself, at least a little. She always believes she could do more than she does. But I think, really, it's just more the strain of having seen him die. That, and the realization that death still happens. Even in this perfect place."

*If only that was all that weighed on Tassie's mind these days*, Brace thought. But Jair couldn't know, not all of it. Tassie had made Brace promise he wouldn't tell him, or Ovard, or anyone.

Jair nodded somberly. "I know what you mean," he agreed, his voice low. "I think I'd been holding on to some hope that we'd never need to see anyone die, here in Haven."

"Well," Brace thought aloud, gazing up at the sky full of dense white clouds, "at least he got to see this place for himself before he went. What more could anyone ask for?"

Jair managed a smile. "Not much else," he agreed. He sighed. "Well, I'd better be off. Tell Tassie I hope she's well."

Brace nodded. "I'll do that." He lingered, standing at the edge of the lightstone wall, watching as Jair disappeared around the corner.

He knew he should get home, and most of him wanted to. But there was part of him that hesitated, the part that was tired, helpless, not knowing the right thing to do or say to help Tassie. She wasn't in this alone, for just as she had so often been pulled into Brace's struggles, now he was a part of hers, and he was affected almost as deeply as she was.

A handful of small, white birds flitted in and around the Fountain Court as Brace entered it, alighting on the stone rims of the bowl-shaped tiers of the fountain and sipping from the glinting, cascading water as it flowed into the basin.

*Little bits of joy around every corner*, Brace thought to himself, remembering the words that Essa had spoken once. Haven was full of unexpected joys. What joy could he bring Tassie now, today? If only she'd been here with him at this moment, to watch the birds darting all around. They might have made her smile.

A patch of bright color drew his attention. Nerissa had been planting flowers here and there around the city, and just like the crops, they were growing profusely.

*A few of them surely won't be missed*, Brace thought, and he stopped to gather a handful of the tall, red blossoms, admiring their ornately-shaped petals. They weren't yellow, but they were flowers, and they would surely bring Tassie a bit of cheer, small though it may be.

When Brace neared the house, he could see at once that Tassie wasn't there. The cloth banner bearing the medic insignia hung on the front door told him she was at the clinic. Brace sighed. He would have preferred to see her here at home, but so be it. He left without going in, taking the flowers with him.

As soon as Brace opened the door to the clinic and stepped inside, he was flooded by the sound of children crying – one nearly wailing while the other whimpered. He grimaced. If there were moments when he envied Tassie her deafness, this was one of them.

He glanced around the room, trying to put together what might have happened. Tassie stood beside the bed near the center of the room, with eight-year-old Trystan seated on it, crying loudly. Yara stood nearby, her hands resting on the shoulders of another boy who, if Brace remembered correctly, was only slightly younger than Trystan. *Shale*, that was his name. The son of Farris, one the king's former soldiers.

Brace and Yara's eyes met briefly, and she smiled and shrugged.

"What happened?" Brace asked over the noise of crying children.

"It was an accident at the school," Yara replied. "The boys were playing outside, and Trystan got hurt."

"I see."

"I'm sorry, Trystan," Shale whimpered, wiping tears from his face with his long sleeve. "I didn't mean for you to get hurt."

"Stop crying, Trystan," Tassie admonished him, holding a wet rag on his arm. "You're not even bleeding any longer. Do you see?" She lifted the rag away and Trystan looked down, blinking through his tears.

"Do you see?" Tassie asked again. "You'll be all right. Don't cry any more, you are making your friend sad."

"I didn't mean to knock him down," Shale asserted. "It was an accident."

"Of course it was," Yara told him, resting her hand on his head. Tassie turned from where Trystan sat and caught sight of Brace standing near the door. She half-smiled at him before going to the supply shelves for a jar of ointment and a small rolled bandage.

"You're going to be perfectly fine," Tassie informed Trystan as she treated and wrapped his arm.

The room was finally quiet as Trystan slid down from the bed and stood, wiping away his last remaining tears.

"All through?" Yara asked, stepping forward, and Tassie nodded.

"He will be all right."

"Thank you," Yara replied, holding Shale's hand and giving Trystan a gentle push toward the door. "I think these two have had enough. I think I'll take them home."

Tassie nodded, crossing her slender arms over her chest.

Yara grinned awkwardly at Brace on her way out, and Brace nodded, lifting a corner of his mouth in a half-smile.

The two of them had managed to build something akin to friendship, but it still felt a bit strained. When they had first met in Erast, they had been attracted to each other, causing Brace to struggle with temptation for the first time since his marriage to Tassie. Not to mention the fact that Yara's father had given Brace a beating, from which he still had a scar on his lower lip. Brace had tried simply avoiding Yara, but he was learning that real solutions came from facing your troubles, not running from them.

Brace gently closed the door after Yara and turned toward Tassie. Alone now, they stood facing each other. Brace couldn't remember ever feeling so awkward around Tassie. He cleared his throat, searching for something to say. "I brought you some flowers," he said, holding them up for her to see.

She smiled in return, a slow, tired smile.

"Thank you," she replied, coming over, leaning to breathe in the musky fragrance, closing her eyes as she did. "Are these from the Fountain Court?" she asked, gathering them into her hands.

"Yes," Brace replied.

"They're very nice." Tassie tucked her loose hair behind her ear. "I'll go and put them in some water."

"Wait," Brace told her, catching her hand. She looked at him curiously before he pulled her close to wrap his arms around her.

"I'm all right, Brace," she lightly scolded him, giving him a quick hug before stepping back. She forced a smile. "I'm fine, really. I should get these flowers in some water or they'll wilt."

Brace nodded. "All right." He watched in silence as Tassie filled a vase from the large stone basin, arranging the flowers and setting the vase on a shelf.

"So," Brace spoke up when Tassie looked his way. "There was a bit of an accident at the school, hmm?"

"Yes, just some boys playing too roughly," Tassie replied. "Nothing to worry about."

Brace nodded. "Do you want to head for home, then? Are you through here for the day?"

Tassie glanced around the room. "I think so. Just … let me get things cleaned up first."

She turned and gathered a handful of rags, some blotched with Trystan's drying blood, putting away the few medicinal jars she'd used. Brace stepped up close behind her, resting his hand on her back.

"Let me help you."

"It's all right, Brace. I can do it. It will only take a moment."

"If I help, you'll get done quicker."

"Really, Brace, I'm fine. I can do this." She sighed. "I need to get past Lomar's death. I need to do things the way I always would. It will help me get beyond thinking about it."

Tassie turned away, but Brace stepped forward and caught her arm.

"This isn't about Lomar's death, Tassie," he told her when she looked at him. "You know what I'm getting at. Having lost the baby... I don't want you to tire yourself out. I just, well, I just don't want you to push yourself too hard."

Tassie lowered her gaze. "It's been over a week," she said quietly, then looked up. "I'm perfectly fine."

Brace slowly shook his head. "You're *not*."

Tassie sighed, and Brace could see the fight go out of her. She stepped closer and allowed Brace to hold her close.

"I don't understand," Tassie spoke against his shoulder. "I know how to take care of myself. I'm young, and I'm healthy. I've been eating Haven's crops, drinking Haven's water. What could I be doing wrong?"

Tassie wasn't really expecting an answer, Brace knew, and he didn't have one to give her. He rested his chin on her head and let out a breath. They weren't doing anything wrong, he was as certain of that as he possibly could be. It had been more than a year past when he and Tassie had decided they were ready to have a child, and after so much time had gone by with no results, they had begun to think it would never happen.

When Tassie at last realized she was pregnant, she'd been so full of joy, as had Brace, though he'd finally come to understand at least a bit of Arden's insecurities at the idea of becoming a father.

Tassie had been six weeks along when Lomar passed away, and a week later, she had lost the baby.

Few knew of it. Only Brace and Tassie, and Ronin and his small family, to whom Tassie had gone for help when she'd realized something was wrong. Tassie had been adamant that she wasn't ready to tell anyone, particularly her uncle Ovard, nor Jair. She couldn't bear the thought of them pitying her, or seeing the sorrow on their faces after they had shared her joy at the news she'd been expecting.

It was true, Tassie knew well enough how to take care of herself during her pregnancy. She'd certainly studied enough medical literature throughout her years of training. Brace had begun to wonder, early on when Tassie couldn't get pregnant at all, if it was somehow his own fault. As far as he knew, he had never fathered a child. Not that he had stayed around long enough anywhere he'd lived to find out about it if he had.

Finally, Tassie stepped back and looked up. "I don't think you're doing anything wrong," Brace told her.

"What, then?"

"What if it isn't you? What if it's *me*?"

"How is that?" she asked, frowning slightly.

"Well, we both know what my life was before I came here. All the wrong I did. What if this is some sort of punishment?"

Tassie shook her head firmly. "*No*, Brace. I don't believe that. Not for one moment, I don't. We're here in Haven to have a safe and peaceful place to live, not to be punished for our past mistakes. And *I'm* the one who wasn't able to keep the baby, not you. It is no fault of yours."

"It's no one's fault, then," Brace told her. "It just happens, you know that better than I do."

Tassie nodded, her expression resigned to the hard truth.

"Well," Brace went on, wanting the conversation to end. "Will you let me help you clean up here, or not? So we can get home?"

Tassie managed a smile. "Yes, you can help me," she replied. "I'm sorry I was being so stubborn about it."

Brace smiled, giving her hand a squeeze. "That's all right," he told her. "I'm sure you picked that up from me."

# ~2~

The sound of Denira's laughter bounced off the high stone walls all through the Fountain Court. Her pale golden hair, tied with ribbons, flounced as she raced around the burbling fountain's wide stone basin. Zorix watched her from a distance, glad that for now at least, she was not chasing *him*.

"I've got you!" Jair exclaimed, hurrying around the other side, cutting off her path. Denira squealed and turned, giggling, to run the other way, but Jair snatched her up and set her down on his shoulders.

"Hold on tight," he told her as she giggled, and she grabbed onto tiny fistfuls of his hair.

Jair winced and peered up at her out of one eye. "That's good and tight," he commented, and Denira laughed.

Cheerful notes of music drifted through the air as Ovard and Eridan played together on their flutes. The young woman had come to Haven from Dunya with a search mission nearly a year and a half ago, and now it was difficult to imagine life there without her. Her constant smile, shining eyes and easy laugh lifted everyone's spirits, and her joyous attitude about life was quite contagious.

"Mammy! Dadda!" Denira called out, releasing her grip on Jair's hair.

"Don't fall off," Jair warned her, keeping hold of her feet.

"I've got her." Arden rose from the stone bench to lift her off Jair's shoulders.

Denira laughed as Arden held her high above his head. "Dadda!" she squealed. "Down, Dadda!"

Arden laughed and lowered her into his arms for a quick hug until she squirmed to be let down.

"I'm not going to try and keep up with her any more," Jair commented, raking his hair down with his fingers. "She's getting faster on her feet."

"She is, isn't she?" Arden agreed. Denira hurried over to grab onto Leandra's legs momentarily before she wandered off again.

"I'll watch her," Kendie volunteered. She stood and brushed the bread crumbs from the skirt of her sky blue dress. "Denira!" she called out. "Sissie's coming to get you!"

Brace watched her as she hurried away, her single braid of dark hair bouncing against her back as she ran. Thirteen years old now, Kendie had developed a healthy sense of confidence, and it showed. The years she'd spent with Arden and Leandra had been good for her. Quite a change from living with the likes of Rune Fletcher.

She still enjoyed singing, and had in fact written the song that was Haven's anthem, now well-known by its citizens and recorded in one of its newly-bound leather books.

Jair sat beside Brace on the corner of the large woven blanket, spread out on the courtyard floor. The two exchanged a friendly smile just as the music from the flutes drifted away into silence.

"That was beautiful," Shayrie told Ovard and Eridan. "Thank you."

"Always my pleasure," Ovard commented, smiling.

"And I'll join you any time," Eridan spoke up, biting into a ripe piece of fruit gathered from Haven's thriving orchard. "I love to play."

"We love hearing you," Leandra joined in, keeping her eyes on Kendie and Denira.

"How's your head?" Brace asked Jair in a teasing voice, tugging at a few strands of his hair.

Jair chuckled. "It's fine." He glanced past Brace at Tassie, who was silently eating small strips of roasted elk. Jair nudged Brace with his elbow, a subtle movement. "How is she?" he asked under his breath.

"Tassie?"

Jair nodded. "She seems so quiet. I know when she has something on her mind, that's all."

*Believe me,* Brace thought, *I know exactly what you mean.*

12

"She's all right," he answered softly. "She's better than she has been, at least."

Jair nodded, and Brace strongly wished he could tell him the truth about what troubled her. But he had promised to keep quiet about it until she was ready, and that was that.

"Today is the perfect day for this," Eridan thought aloud.

Nevin chuckled. "Isn't it always?"

"The weather, you mean?" Eridan asked with a laugh. "You're right about that. But I meant that this just feels so wonderful, gathering here like this together. There are days when that's *exactly* just what everyone needs – a little bit of rest, something to eat, and time with friends. I don't know about you, but it does my heart good."

"That it does," Tassie agreed, looking in Eridan's direction, able to read her lips. "It's done my heart some good as well."

Jair glanced at Brace, one eyebrow raised doubtfully. Brace shrugged. Maybe it had, whether it showed in Tassie's mood or not.

Eridan tucked her flute into the wide sash belt around her waist, and sat gazing up into the sky overhead. "*That day in June,*" she quoted the age-old poem, "*was fair at noon when Bern called on his love. A maiden fair with flowing hair, and sweeter than a dove. 'Twas on that day they stole away, our Bern and his true love. They had no fear, as birds sang clear like blessings from above.*"

"I know that one," Kendie spoke up, leading Denira back by the hand. "It's about one of the King's men from a long time ago, who had fought in so many battles and done so many brave things, and then one day he ran off with the girl he loved."

"That's right," Eridan replied with a smile.

"I always wondered if it was a true story." Kendie picked up Denira and deposited her into Leandra's waiting arms.

"It could have been, well enough," Ovard told her. "I've read other tales of Bern, though who his lady was, I've no idea."

"He was supposed to have been a very brave man," Arden added.

"I don't know how brave it was for him to have left his duty to the King and run off the way he did."

Persha's voice took them all by surprise as she approached, with her brother Gavin beside her.

"There are different ways to show bravery," Arden told her, his voice pensive. "Having to choose between love and duty is not an easy thing."

Brace watched Persha to catch her reaction, but she only nodded – slightly, almost imperceptibly. He knew how much respect Persha had for Arden, as a man of *harbrost*, and as the one who had helped her hone her archery skills. Not to mention the fact that he was now her commander – she was second under him on the hunting parties as well as on the team of gate watch.

At eighteen years of age, Persha was still as independent and strong-willed as she had been from the day she'd first set foot in Haven. Something, however, seemed to have tempered her fierceness to a degree. It showed now in her silence.

"Mammy," Denira said, tugging at Leandra's hand.

"What, sweet?"

"You happy?"

"Yes, I'm happy," Leandra replied with a laugh.

"Happy?" Denira asked again, gesturing out toward the group who had gathered there.

"Yes, Denira, everyone is happy. Why?" Leandra asked. "Why are you asking?"

Denira sat quietly for a moment, then smiled. "Happy," she said firmly.

"She's a funny little thing, isn't she?" Eridan asked kindly.

*Ironic of her to say that*, Brace thought to himself with a smirk. Eridan was much like Denira herself; the two of them were always full of joy and laughter.

"I'm glad you're happy," Arden told Denira, tugging at her hair ribbon.

"No, Dadda, no," she protested, giggling. She flung her little arms wide. "Big happy!"

Beside Brace, Jair chuckled. "What about you, Gavin? Are you '*happy*'?"

Gavin smiled a little. "Sure enough. Why not?"

"You're awfully quiet," Jair pointed out, and Gavin tipped his head slightly.

"Not worried about the next search mission, are you?" Shayrie asked her son.

Gavin shook his head. "No sense worrying about that, I've learned. Just take it as it comes."

14

"What, then?" Jair asked casually.

Gavin glanced quickly at Persha, then shrugged. "Nothing, really."

Brace could see easily enough that Jair didn't believe Gavin, not completely. He cleared his throat awkwardly, then Shayrie spoke into the uncomfortable silence.

"Why don't you young people head out to the orchard and bring back some fruit?" she suggested. "I'll make you a pie. How does that sound?"

"For a pie?" Jair asked, grinning. "Sure, I'll go and get some fruit for you."

"This is a good time to end our meal, at any rate," Leandra added, holding Denira on her lap. "It's time for this little one to have her afternoon nap, I think."

"No nap," Denira whined.

"Yes, nap," Arden told her, standing and lifting Denira into his arms.

"This was a splendid afternoon," Eridan commented airily. "We must do this again."

Nevin and Shayrie rose from their seats as everyone began packing away their things.

"I'm heading home," Shayrie told Gavin. "You'd better go and get that fruit. I'm sure I'll have the pie crust made by the time you get back to the house."

Brace turned to face Tassie. "Are you feeling all right?" he asked her quietly.

"I'm fine, Brace," she replied, slipping her slender hand into his. "Will you walk to the clinic with me? I have a bit of inventory to do."

Brace nodded. "I'll walk you there," he said, grinning, "if you let me help you."

Tassie shook her head and smiled slightly. "I will."

～

Jair stood beside Gavin in the Fountain Court as he watched everyone clear away. Persha lingered for a moment, then flexed her shoulders.

"I would go with you," she told them, "but I'm next on duty watching the gate."

Gavin nodded, his dark hair falling over his forehead. "See you tonight, then."

"Right," Persha replied, nodding respectfully to Jair and her brother before turning to leave.

The boys started off at a leisurely pace toward the front of the courtyard, but Jair paused when he caught a glimpse of Kendie from the corner of his eye. Would Kendie want to go to the orchard with only two young men for company? Shayrie had said *"you young people,"* hadn't she? That included Kendie. It would make sense to invite her along.

Jair looked back over his shoulder. "Are you coming, Kendie?"

She smiled broadly. "I'm coming." She hurried to walk beside them, pushing her long black braid over her shoulder.

Jair glanced at her, the top of her head level with his ear. He could see that she was more than glad she'd been included, and he smiled to himself.

"So, Gavin," Jair said, turning toward his friend, "If you haven't got the next search mission weighing on you, what is it?"

Gavin raised an eyebrow.

"Come on now," Jair scolded him lightly. "You know as well as I do that you're not acting like yourself."

"I noticed it too," Kendie added gently.

Gavin sighed in resignation. "Well…" he began hesitantly. "I'll tell you, but you both need to promise that you'll *absolutely* not say anything to anyone."

"I promise," Kendie said quickly.

"I promise," Jair echoed.

Gavin nodded. "It isn't about me. It's about Persha."

"Persha?" Jair asked in surprise.

"Yes … well, she actually confided in me," Gavin admitted.

"Are you sure you should be telling us?" Kendie asked him.

"You might actually already know most of it. It's about her and Bahadur."

"Right," Jair replied. "She *likes* him, doesn't she?"

"She does," Gavin answered. "Quite a lot."

"But," Kendie began hesitantly, "they argue all the time, don't they?" Knowing Jair still had some interest in Persha, Kendie had mixed feelings.

She herself, for the last two years at least, had wanted Jair to notice her the way he noticed Persha, but to no avail.

Kendie had been confused when Persha and Bahadur began spending so much time together. After all, Persha had said more than once that she didn't need a man, that she could take care of herself. Confused, but glad – Kendie had thought that now, if Jair realized Persha had feelings for Bahadur, maybe he wouldn't think about her so much.

Now, having heard the words she'd just spoken – about Persha and Bahadur's frequent arguments – she wished she had kept her mouth shut. If Jair thought Persha and Bahadur's relationship wasn't working out, he might start thinking about her again, and Kendie wouldn't have a chance. So she said no more. Instead, she watched Jair's face to see what his reaction might be.

"They do argue," Gavin agreed, and Jair's expression remained neutral. "They're both just so stubborn, you know? They are different in a lot of ways, but they're both the same in that."

Different, yes. It was true, and easy to see, that the two of them were different. Dark-skinned, dark-haired Bahadur, and Persha with her hair of deep honey gold. But they were both brave, bold, warriors at heart, and yes, stubborn and strongly opinioned.

"You're right," Jair told Gavin. "I knew about all of that. So, what did Persha tell you? None of this is anything new."

Gavin hesitated a moment. "Well, Persha told me she felt like she might be changing her mind about not wanting to be married. She said Bahadur is just the sort of man she would want – strong and brave – and he really knows how to see her, she told me. Like he really knows who she is, and accepts her."

"Persha might want to marry Bahadur?" Kendie asked in surprise. "But if she thinks he's so wonderful, what is it they are always fighting about?"

"Just opinions, really. Neither of them is very good at backing down when they think they're right about something."

"Well," Jair said as they entered the dappled shade of the orchard, "if she thinks she wants to marry him, they're going to have to find a way around that."

Kendie was surprised to not hear any trace of sadness in Jair's voice. Maybe he had gotten over his attraction to Persha, as Leandra had said he would? Trying to hide a smile, Kendie picked up a broken twig and feigned interest in its leaves. If Jair was no longer drawn to Persha, maybe it would be easier to draw his attention to herself.

"Right," Gavin agreed with Jair's statement. "She feels sort of confused right now. She is falling in love with him, she says, like she never really thought she would. So on one hand, there's love, but on the other hand, there's the fighting. She's just trying to figure things out."

Jair nodded.

"So, you promised not to say anything, right?" Gavin asked the both of them.

"Of course not," Jair replied nonchalantly, gazing up through the trees.

"No, I won't say anything," Kendie told him earnestly, shaking her head.

"Thanks."

The orchard trees nearest the heart of the city had recently been picked clean, and new blossoms were just beginning to open up. Farther on up the grassy hillside, Kendie could see plenty of ripe fruit weighing down the branches.

She glanced at Jair, but he was standing still, his eyes fixed on something in the distance.

"Jair?" Kendie asked him softly. "What are you looking at?"

"Hmm?" Jair asked, blinking. "Oh – nothing. Sorry."

"Was Haven trying to tell you something?" Gavin asked him. "Like that day you found the lost key to the white room?"

Jair smiled at the memory, then shook his head, his expression growing pensive. "I'm not sure. Maybe it is. I was just starting to get a sense of *something*."

"And I interrupted," Kendie said glumly. "I'm sorry."

"It's all right. I'm sure it will come to me again. It always does."

"Right," Gavin spoke up, waving his hand. "Come on. Let's go pick some fruit so my mam can finish that pie."

# ~ 3 ~

T he shifting of misty white vapors, swirling in slow-moving patterns, never ceased to make Brace hold his breath in amazement. They filled his vision, fading away as the view beyond the gate began to take shape, filling the expanse of wall before him.

Pure white light shone all around him, from the walls, the tables, the benches. From the carved, hooded figures, their hands held out before them.

He found himself glancing over his shoulder, struck by the notion, yet again, that the city was alive, as Jair insisted. Hadn't Haven been speaking to the boy for years? Hadn't Jair been able to communicate with Haven in return?

Though he knew he was alone in the White Room, Brace always felt as though he was being watched. The tall figures carved into the walls, though their faces were hidden, gave Brace the impression that they were alive, aware of his presence. And it could be that they *were*.

Brace let out a breath and studied the viewing wall. Everything was clear, as he had come to expect it to be. Turning away, the nearest carved figure fully caught his attention. *Such pure light*, Brace thought. Everything in the room was so pure and clean. Looking at his own hands, his own clothing, all varying shades of brown, he felt dirty. As though his presence there might somehow taint that sacred place.

And it was not only light, but life that flowed through the walls, Brace knew that beyond all doubt. He'd seen it himself.

He had long ago stopped wondering if the things he'd witnessed were even possible; he had been awed by too many miracles to doubt the city's mysterious living power. The only question still plaguing him was *how?*

19

How did the light come alive and destroy the king's invading army? How did Haven's crops, and the fruit in the orchard, and the red vine fruit continue to grow through every season? How did the water in the stream give renewed strength and how did the red vine fruit heal injury or disease?

And the biggest question of all – how did Haven *tell* Jair anything? How did it tell him where to find the fruit, or the water, or most recently, the key to the door leading down here to the White Room?

Brace chuckled. No more need to pick the lock.

He flexed his shoulders, trying to shake off the unnerved feeling growing inside him. Despite his misgivings, he was honored to serve on the gate watch. There were six of them now, sharing this duty. Two shifts each day, so that each team only served once every three days: Arden and Farris, Alban and Persha, Brace and Ben-Rickard. It was a position of honor, one he in no way deserved, no question about it. He was certain he would never take it for granted.

Brace turned when he heard the familiar sound of footsteps coming down the narrow hallway.

"Come in," he called out when he heard a light knock at the heavy double doors.

Ben-Rickard entered the room, a friendly smile on his face.

"Had a quiet morning down here?" he asked, setting down a short, fat candle and straightening his dark green vest.

"Yes," Brace replied. "All quiet as usual. How are things way up there?"

Ben chuckled at the question. It had become somewhat of a joke between them, referring to the ground level as "the top" or "way up there."

"Just another day," Ben replied. "Everyone off doing what they're doing. Eridan is collecting another batch of honey today."

"Mmm," Brace replied, recalling the taste of the last jar he and Tassie had received. "Has she got anyone helping her?"

"Yes. Jordis, and whoever else is brave enough, believing she knows how to keep the bees calm so they won't sting."

"You're right there," Brace agreed.

"Well, my friend," Ben said, giving Brace a friendly clap on the shoulder, "you should get up there and enjoy the sunlight. I'll take over down here."

"Thanks," Brace replied, picking up the candle. "I will. If that's all,

I'll get going. I don't want to spend one second longer in the hallway than I need to."

Brace always found it hard to breathe in that close, narrow hallway leading to the White Room. He would feel himself tense up, on the verge of panic. Getting to the end of it was always a relief.

Ben laughed. "You'd better be off, then."

One foot in front of the other, keeping his eyes on the end of the dark hallway, Brace hurried on and up the stairs, grateful to push open the door and emerge out into the large meeting room of the Main Hall. Only when he stood firmly on the stone-paved floor and had let the door fall closed did he let out his breath.

Looking up, Brace noticed Jair sitting at the long table alone, gazing out into the room as though deep in thought.

"Hello there?" Brace asked him, stepping closer and blowing out the candle.

Jair looked over quickly. "Oh – sorry. Hello."

"Anything wrong?" Brace asked.

Jair shook his head. "No, I'm all right. Just thinking." He paused, running his finger along the edge of the table. "Thank you, Brace."

"For what?"

Jair shrugged. "For everything. For being part of the gate watch, even though you hate small spaces. You're always willing to do whatever needs done, to help." He shrugged again. "Thank you."

Brace smirked and mussed Jair's hair. "Anything for you, little brother."

Jair smiled at the remark, though he quickly reached up to smooth his hair back into place.

～

A brief walk through the Fountain Court and a turn to the right brought Brace to the door of the clinic, where he knew Tassie and Ronin would be continuing their training of Kendie and Ona as future medics.

He hesitated, wondering what spirits Tassie would be in. That morning, she had been quiet, subdued. Brace missed her smile, he missed the humor that would flash in her deep green eyes. He even missed the scolding gaze she still gave him at times.

He was doing all he could to try and be strong for her, but he was still hurting as well. Would things ever go back to the way they had been?

Brace sighed, gathering his resolve, as he pulled open the heavy wooden door and stepped inside. Tassie was busy, as he had suspected. Kind-hearted, dark-haired Ronin stood beside her at the work table, along with Kendie and Ronin's fourteen-year-old daughter, Ona. Open books were sprawled across the surface of the table. Only Ona saw Brace enter, and she smiled.

"Hello, Brace," she greeted him lightly. Ronin and Kendie turned in his direction, and Tassie followed.

"Off duty?" Ronin asked with a smile.

"Yes," Brace replied with a nod. "How are things here?"

"Confusing," Kendie replied.

"Amazing!" Ona exclaimed. "Our bodies are amazing things. Did you know that you can find out about the health of your lungs by pressing on part of your foot?"

"Or stop someone from gagging by pressing on their palms?" Kendie added, shaking her head. "It doesn't really make sense to me."

Brace glanced at Tassie while the girls went on about something in one of Ronin's books. She hadn't yet said a single word, and Brace could see from her posture that her mind was elsewhere.

"It doesn't have to make sense," Ona told Kendie forcefully. "You just need to remember what's what."

Brace's eyes met Ronin's, and Ronin nodded, giving him a knowing look.

"All right, girls," he said, turning toward them. "I think that's plenty for today. You'll need to study on this for a while, and then I'll test you on how well you've learned it."

Kendie groaned in protest as Ona gathered all of the books into a stack.

"We're going, Tassie," Ronin told her, lightly resting a hand on her arm.

She nodded. "All right. Will you come again tomorrow?"

Ronin hesitated. "We shall see. Come on then, Ona, Kendie," he told the girls, heading toward the door, stopping to shake Brace's hand. "Have a good evening," he said sincerely, slightly tipping his head in Tassie's direction. "A quiet evening."

"I will," Brace replied. "Thank you."

"Goodbye, Tassie. Goodbye, Brace," Kendie said as she followed the others outside.

"Yeah, goodbye," Brace replied absentmindedly. The door thumped closed, and there they were, just the two of them.

"How are the girls doing?" Brace asked.

"Well enough," Tassie replied. "They are eager to learn. That's important."

Brace nodded. "And how are you?"

The corner of Tassie's mouth lifted, almost a smile, but it quickly faded. She opened her mouth to speak, but shook her head.

"I don't know," she answered, her voice full of emotion. "I think I'm all right. I'm just ..." She almost turned away when Brace reached out to her, but she allowed him to gather her into his arms and hold her tightly. "I'm just so tired," she finished. "I'm just tired."

Brace made no attempt to reply. He simply stood there, enjoying the softness of her hair against the side of his face.

After a moment, Tassie moved so she could look up at him. "It isn't the work that's tiring," she told him. "It isn't the girls."

"What, then?"

"I..." she paused, searching for the words. "I have to carry it around with me every day. I start to think I'm ready to tell Ovard what happened, but the thought of saying the words makes me shiver. I feel like I already *knew* the baby, Brace. I feel like it was someone I'd already met, and now they're gone, and they never got the chance to really become *real*. I never got to see his face."

Tears welled up in her eyes, but Brace was at a loss. What could he possibly say to comfort her?

"I feel," Tassie went on, "like my arms are empty but they shouldn't be. I should be holding our baby. I feel almost haunted by him, like he's somewhere around me but I can't touch him."

A tear escaped and she quickly pushed it away.

"I know, Tassie," Brace told her. "I know, I feel that way too, maybe not as strongly as you do, but I *do* feel it. But what can we do about it? What can we do, but wait for that feeling to fade?"

"It isn't fading," Tassie protested. "I dream about the baby. It wants me to come and find it, but I can't."

"I know, Tassie."

She sniffed, wiping at her face. "You know?"

Brace nodded. "Sometimes I can't sleep. At night, it really weighs on me, too. I can't sleep, and I see you. I can see that you're dreaming. I've tried to wake you a few times, but you turn over and fall back to sleep."

"What are we supposed to do, Brace?" she asked desperately. "I don't want to feel like I need to cry every day. This shouldn't be happening, not to us. It shouldn't happen to *anyone*. Not here."

"Stop, Tassie," Brace pleaded. "Stop thinking about it. Stop wondering *why*. It isn't helping either of us."

She nodded, wrapping her arms around herself. "I just wish I knew what we should do."

Frustrated, Brace ran his hands through his chin-length hair. "Let's just go home," he suggested. "Right now, we should just go home."

He held out his hand and waited for Tassie to take it.

"All right," she said quietly, holding his hand tightly. "Let's go home."

Though the day was bright and cheery, a heavy silence hung over them as they went back to the house, a silence that continued even after they had gone inside.

Brace stood by and watched as Tassie filled a mug with water from their basin. Sighing deeply, he turned to gaze out through the window. He had to do *something*. Things couldn't go on like this. But what was there to do? In the years before he had ever heard of Haven's existence, he had known exactly what to do when life got hard. Run away, start over. There was always another city to run to.

*Start over…*

Turning away from the window, he saw that Tassie was watching him.

"Maybe we *can* do something," he suggested, with only a small flicker of hope that it might do them some good.

"What?" Tassie asked, exhaustion in her voice.

"Maybe we can start over."

"What's that?"

"Start over," he repeated. "We've gotten into this so deep. We need to be able to breathe." He shrugged, lowering himself onto the cushioned window seat. "I know we can't forget what's happened," he went on, "but we can put it aside, can't we? Could we… just go back to the way we were?

*Way* back, I mean," he explained, seeing Tassie's frown. "Back to when we were still trying to find Haven. When we were getting to know each other. Can we do that for a time?"

Brace noticed when a bit of understanding and relief showed in Tassie's eyes.

"Yes," she said carefully. "I think we could do that."

Brace forced a smile, patting the seat beside him. Reservedly, Tassie came to sit on the window ledge, leaning back against the wall. She gazed out the window for a long moment before turning her eyes toward Brace.

*I can see I'm going to have to get this going myself,* Brace thought. *Well, it was my idea, after all.* He took a breath, trying to release some tension. Pulling his feet up off the floor, he sat cross-legged, facing Tassie.

"So," he began, searching for the right words. "It's pretty great here, isn't it?" he asked, trying to act as though he hadn't a care in the world. "The weather's always perfect, and it never rains. Doesn't get much better than that, does it?"

Slowly, a smile came across Tassie's face as she realized what Brace was doing.

"I never much minded the rain," she told him. "I liked the smell of it. But I'm glad it doesn't get cold here. I can't stand the cold."

Brace shook his head. "Neither can I. Or the desert heat. I've been in both."

"We're so far away from city life here," Tassie went on. "Do you miss the excitement of it?"

"Not a bit," Brace replied with a wave of his hand. "I'd much rather lie in the grass by the stream."

"Sounds nice," Tassie replied, absently running her fingers through her long, wavy hair. "What's a favorite memory of yours?" she asked.

Brace's expression darkened. "What's one of yours?" he asked, feeling unwelcome tension. She had to know that most of his memories were bad ones.

"A childhood memory?" she asked, unfazed.

"Sure."

Tassie thought a moment before answering. "I must have been … eight years old, not much more. My Uncle Ovard took me to a place outside of town, where there were a lot of trees, and flowers. I remember climbing up one of the trees – it wasn't very high. I looked down at him and he was smiling. The sun was so bright, and there were flowers everywhere. He picked some of them for me, and had me smell them. They were so strong and sweet. I don't think I'll ever forget that smell."

Brace grinned, knowing the answer to his next question before he asked it.

"What color flower is your favorite?"

Tassie smiled. "Yellow," she replied. "What about you, Brace? You must have a good memory from your childhood. At least one."

Brace leaned his elbows on his knees, thinking. "Well," he began hesitantly. "I do remember one thing in particular. I don't know how old I was. Eleven years, maybe. I had run away from the farmer I'd been working for. I hadn't been on my own for long, but I'd been running the whole time, afraid he would find me. But one night, I'd finally gotten far enough away, and enough time had passed, and I felt like I was safe. Like I just somehow knew he had stopped looking for me. I was alone, in a field or something, with a few trees and high grasses all around me. I was lying down that night, on the ground, and looking up at the sky. It was so black, and so full of stars. I'd never seen so many. And I remember thinking, it felt like the whole world belonged to me, right then. Like the world didn't own me anymore, but that I owned it. Does that make any sense?"

Tassie smiled. "Of course it does."

Brace sat, unmoving, gazing at Tassie, caught up in the joy of the moment. He wished he could make it last.

"I felt so free," he added.

Tassie tipped her head. "Were you, then?"

Brace considered the question. "I felt like I was," he answered. "I know I could have fallen into a trap at any moment. The farmer could have found me, or I could have been caught, making trouble. Here, now, I know I'm free. Here, I'm not trapped by anything." He chuckled. "Only by things I want to be trapped by."

Tassie's smile deepened. Brace sighed and glanced through the window.

"Well," he said, tugging at his boot laces, "I don't think I need to keep wearing these. I think I'll stay for a while, if that's all right with you."

Tassie leaned back in her seat. "I don't know about that," she replied as Brace let his boots fall to the floor. "I'm not sure it would be proper."

Brace smirked. "It will be, only if your boots are off as well."

"How brash!" Tassie said in mock embarrassment.

"Allow me?" Brace asked, holding out his hands.

Finally, Tassie nodded. Brace easily loosened her laces and slid them from her feet, letting them fall to the floor beside his own.

"You have beautiful feet," he told her, pulling off her stockings as well.

Tassie wrinkled her nose. "No one has beautiful feet."

"You do."

"Well," she replied, "if you get to look at my feet, then I should get to look at yours."

"I don't think they're worth seeing," Brace mildly protested, but she was already pulling off his stockings.

"Satisfied?" Brace asked with a laugh. "They're ugly things, aren't they?"

Slowly, Tassie shook her head. "I've seen them plenty of times. Nothing of yours is ugly to me."

All of the playful humor had gone out of Tassie's voice, Brace noticed. He took her hand in his, admiring yet again the way they matched one another – tattooed with the same ornate lines that seemed to flow like water across the backs of their hands, circling their wrists. They were forever bound to each other. There was no erasing it.

He stretched out his legs across the window seat, pulling her feet up over his so they rested on his knees.

"I'm glad you're mine, Tass. Do you know that?"

Tassie nodded slowly. "I do."

"We will always belong to each other," he went on, absently running his fingers along the side of her foot. "No matter what happens. Isn't that what really matters? Isn't that what we promised each other?"

"Yes," she replied quietly.

Brace paused to consider his words before going on. "Maybe all of this has been happening because we've been trying too hard to change things."

"Maybe," Tassie agreed, fingering the hem of her dress.

"So," Brace continued, "maybe we should stop trying. Just let it go for a while."

Tassie let out a slow breath, then nodded. "Maybe you're right."

"We just need to forget everything that makes us anxious. Just enjoy the quiet and the peace of life here for a while."

Tassie's smile was solemn, almost defeated. "All right."

"We can go out to the orchard tomorrow," Brace suggested. "You always love it out there. The lake, the trees, the stream. Would you like to do that?"

"Yes." She sat forward and rested her hand on his. "Thank you," she told him.

"I love you, Tassie."

"And I love you."

"We're going to be all right, you know."

Tassie nodded. "We will be."

~ 4 ~

Zorix pawed impatiently at Leandra's wide, loose-fitting breeches as everyone gathered in the square courtyard outside the Main Hall. "I know, I know," she told him, balancing Denira on her hip. "This won't take long."

Zorix huffed at her, and she smiled. "I know you're hungry. We'll eat soon."

Sighing, Zorix wrapped his long tail around himself, his fur taking on an orange hue, revealing his nervous state. He would never get accustomed to being in a crowd.

It was by no means a *large* crowd that had gathered there today. Send-offs for the search missions were now a common occurrence, so generally only family or close friends came to see their loved ones off on their journey. Today, Gavin was accompanied by his family, his parents looking proud but concerned, while Persha seemed distracted. Brace was glad to see that Alban and Korian had come to see Alban's brother Landers off on the mission. They were quite fortunate to have the former king's men as citizens of Haven.

While everyone conversed quietly among themselves, Denira leaned over, reaching toward Zorix.

"Don't do that, sweet," Leandra scolded, shifting Denira to her other hip. "You'll pull me over."

"Bwace, Bwace!" Denira exclaimed, pointing, when she saw him approaching, Tassie beside him.

"Yes, we see him," Arden told her. "Don't make a fuss, now."

But Denira paid him no heed, struggling in Leandra's arms until she let her down. Denira ran to Brace, holding out her arms. He laughed under his breath, giving Tassie an apologetic glance before letting go of her hand to pick up the little girl.

"Oh, you're getting heavier," Brace commented as he settled Denira in his arms. She laughed and playfully poked at his chin.

"Are you being a good girl today?" Brace asked her.

"Deniwa good," she replied casually. Brace chuckled and glanced over at Tassie. The look in her eyes caught him off guard. So full of longing – he should have known better than to hold Denira. It was a blatant reminder that he and Tassie had no child of their own to hold.

Brace cleared his throat nervously. "Maybe you'd better go back to your mammy now."

"Come here, sweet," Leandra said to Denira, holding out her hands, and Denira obediently went to her. Leandra gave Brace a look; she'd seen the unease on his face. Brace turned away, straightening his faded roughspun shirt and taking Tassie's hand once again. She forced a smile, then turned toward Arden.

"Is everyone here?" she asked.

"It seems so," he replied. "We're sending off five today – Gavin, Berrick, Landers, Halyard and Eridan."

"Quite a group," Brace commented.

Arden nodded again, a breeze tossing his long tail of pale hair over his shoulder. "They're going north all the way to Pran's Helm," he explained. "They plan to stay at least four days."

"They'll be gone for a month, then, won't they?" Tassie asked, concerned.

"About that," Arden replied while Leandra tried to keep Denira occupied with her cloth doll.

Brace held Tassie's hand tightly, and she looked over at him. "They'll be fine," he told her, and she nodded.

"Thank you, everyone, for coming today," Ovard addressed the small crowd, with Jair standing beside him. "Let us have a few last words, and we'll send them off, shall we?"

Everyone gathered in closer, the five members of the search mission dispersed among them. When the courtyard grew silent, Jair stepped forward.

"Does anyone have any last words of advice or encouragement?" he asked, as was customary.

Jair stood, respectfully silent, along with his team of advisors, as well as Avi, the wise older man who'd come with the group from Roshwan over two years ago. Avi's wisdom and insight had gained him Jair's unflinching respect, and he would soon be formally accepted into his team of advisors as well.

Nevin finally broke the silence. "It's the same as it's always been," he said. "Be there for each other. Remember that you are a team, and though you are five, you should act as one."

Cayomah leaned in closer to Eridan, who was ready to travel with the others, and the two women exchanged a quick smile. Brave, gentle Cayomah had only arrived in Haven from Danferron six months ago, and the two women had quickly become close friends. It was the two of them who had decided that it would be wise to have a woman along on the search missions, and Jair had agreed with them. Eridan and Cayomah had been trading off since then, one of them being a part of every search team that went out.

"Thank you, Nevin," Jair said as Gavin nodded in response to his father's advice.

"Remember why you're going," Brannock added. "There are people out there who need you, who need Haven to be their home. Your visit to Pran's Helm might be their only chance. Keep your eyes and ears open."

Brodan coughed to clear his throat before speaking up. "Don't forget that we're all here, thinking of you every day. Take care of yourselves, and come back to us."

"We will, Brodan," Berrick told his friend. "Thank you."

Jair allowed a moment or two to pass in silence before he spoke again.

"Well, if that's everything, we'll move on." He turned toward Ovard, who handed him an ornately carved stone goblet filled with sweet red wine.

"Search team, come in closer," Jair instructed them, and they moved in to form a small circle, everyone gathering in close behind them.

Brace watched the ceremonial sharing of the cup, remembering the first time he had been invited to participate in such an event. He had not yet laid eyes on Haven at the time – in fact, he had just begun to believe that it might be a real place after all.

It hadn't been wine in the cup then, only tea, but the meaning had been the same. They were all of one mind, one heart – all one for the cause. Apart from his marriage to Tassie, this was the most sacred thing that Brace had been a part of, and he enjoyed watching the search team members partaking of it with each other.

After the cup had been passed around, Jair took it once again and held it. The entire courtyard was silent, even Denira. Could she possibly understand the significance of the day?

Finally, Jair looked around and smiled, particularly at his friend Gavin. "It's time you all were off then," he told them. "Let's have some last goodbyes, and we'll see you to the gate."

A low murmur of conversation filled the courtyard once again. With hugs and handshakes going on all around him, Brace was glad to simply stand by and hold Tassie's hand. He was glad he wasn't part of the group that was leaving. He knew what an important task, but he had done it four times, and he could honestly say he did not miss the world beyond Haven's gate. The world had not been kind to him, and he no longer wanted any part of it. What more could he want, aside from what he had right here, all around him, right beside him?

Brace glanced over at Tassie, and when he caught her eye and smiled, she sighed.

"Are you all right?" Brace asked, concerned.

Tassie nodded slowly. "I think I just want to go back to the house, or to the clinic. There's just too much going on here."

Brace nodded, frowning. Tassie had never before been bothered by coming to these events, not that he knew.

"All right, we'll go," he told her, but before he had a chance to turn away, Eridan was there, warmly embracing Tassie, who hugged her in return.

"Take care of yourself," Tassie told Eridan, speaking into her long, loosely gathered hair.

Eridan pulled back so Tassie could see her face. "You do the same," she told her. "I miss laughing with you, Tassie. I think I'll be gone about a month. When I get back … well, I hope this extra bit of time brings you more healing." She paused, taking Tassie's hand in her own. "It's been nearly a month since Lomar passed. I'm not saying you shouldn't still be grieving. I just miss you, Tassie. The *real* you. I miss your laugh, your teasing, your strength. That's all."

Tassie nodded wordlessly. What could she possibly say to her friend, her dear friend? Eridan had no idea about any of it. How could she tell her now, as she was leaving? Tassie looked over at Brace, her eyes asking for his help. Brace stepped forward, though he knew little how to handle the situation.

"She'll be all right, Eridan," Brace told her kindly. "We will miss you, but Tassie will be all right here. Just come back safely, and keep your spirits up," he added with a grin. "It wouldn't do the rest of us any good if you let worry rob you of your joy."

Eridan smiled. "Don't worry about that. It takes a lot to bring me down. It's springtime, in here and out there in the wide world. I love the springtime. And I'll be back before you know it."

Halyard stepped up beside Eridan, shrugging a small pack onto his shoulders. "Are you set to go?" he asked her. "The horses have all been readied, and our supplies are loaded up."

"Sure," Eridan replied with a nod. "I'm ready."

The pair of them smiled and waved as they departed, Eridan giving Tassie another quick hug before leaving.

"Sorry about all that," Brace told Tassie after they'd gone.

"I'm all right," she replied. "But thank you. It was uncomfortable," she went on, her voice almost a whisper. "I think I'm going to need to tell people soon, about what happened."

Brace nodded. "All right," he replied, feeling heaviness at her words, yet at the same time, relieved at her decision. "Can you go on here a little longer? We should see Gavin off before he goes."

"Yes, it's all right," Tassie replied. "One more quick goodbye."

"Right," Brace agreed, taking Tassie's hand, moving through the slowly emptying courtyard toward the small group that remained gathered around Gavin, Jair, and Ovard.

"You're not too worried about it, are you?" Jair was asking.

"No," Gavin replied with a light shrug. "It's made things more complicated out there, that's certain, but we've managed, haven't we?"

"What's all this about?" Brace cut in.

"Oh, it's just what King Oden's been doing," Jair answered. "Spreading lies about Haven, that it's a bad place, a dangerous place. It's been making it harder for the search missions to talk to people, never knowing what they'll say. I don't like putting anyone in danger."

Gavin shook his head. "No, it's all right," he insisted. "People always respond in one of three ways, I've seen lately. One," he said, counting off on his fingers, "they tell us to go away and not to bother them, believing what Oden's been saying; two, they still believe the old stories about Haven and are eager to come with us; or – believe it or not – some people still insist that Haven isn't a real place at all, despite what happened to King Oden's men. They say it was something else entirely, and Oden is simply trying to cover up a dreadful mistake of his by blaming the whole thing on a myth."

Kendie shook her head, her eyes wide. "I don't see how anyone can just *not* believe that Haven is a real place," she said in a serious tone of voice.

"Some people still don't, until they've seen it," Gavin told her.

"Even though they come back here with you?"

"Yes."

"Why would they come if they didn't believe you?" Kendie asked, incredulous.

Gavin shrugged. "What have they got to lose?"

Brace couldn't help but smirk at Gavin's comment. "That's how I felt, Kendie," he told her. "When I first decided to stick with Ovard and everyone, I wasn't sure I believed in it."

"Don't try and get it all figured out," Arden told Kendie. "It all works out in the end. Whoever is supposed to be here, will be here. We're just the messengers, so to speak."

"Does that make sense to you?" Jair asked her.

"I think so," Kendie replied, crossing her arms over her chest.

"Mammy," Denira spoke up from Leandra's arms, "awe they weaving?"

"Yes, they're leaving," Leandra replied. "They're going to find us some new neighbors."

Denira was quiet a moment, taking in Leandra's words, then a tiny smile grew on her face, and she kissed the palm of her hand, waving it out toward Gavin, who laughed.

"Are you blowing me a kiss?" he asked.

"Kisses!" Denira replied firmly.

"Thank you," Gavin said, still laughing. "Now I *know* we'll have a safe trip. Don't grow too much while I'm gone, little thing."

Denira giggled and hid her face against Leandra's neck.

"Well," Gavin said, turning toward Jair to shake his hand. "I guess I'll be off then. Take care."

"Take care yourself," Jair replied. "We're all safe here, you know that."

"Right." Gavin took in the faces of those still gathered around. "So long."

Shayrie stood close beside her husband, her arms wrapped around herself. "I don't think I'll ever be able to stop worrying about him," she commented.

Nevin put an arm around her shoulders. "You wouldn't be a true mother to him if you could."

"Gavin will be fine," Persha spoke up. "He has the lightstone pieces to keep the screamers away. That's the only real danger they'd expect, and that's taken care of."

"Right, so it is," Jair agreed weakly.

"Let's go home now, Brace," Tassie said, resting a hand on his arm.

"Of course," he replied.

"Is everything all right?" Leandra asked.

"Yes, thank you," Tassie replied. "I've just got some things I need to take care of at the clinic."

Leandra nodded. "You both should come over to our place soon for a visit," she suggested, as Denira popped her thumb into her mouth.

"That sounds fine, thank you," Tassie replied. "Come over tomorrow, will you, and we can plan something?"

"Of course."

Arden and Brace nodded to one another as they parted ways. Brace could always see something deeper in those pale blue eyes of the archer's, he thought to himself. Arden was certainly not skilled at keeping his thoughts from showing, and Brace had picked up on a hint of concern at that moment. He felt it touch all the way into his heart, the knowledge that he and Tassie were so cared for. That they had these few companions who were so close, they could tell each other anything, and share every joy or sorrow that came into their lives.

*Anything,* Brace thought ruefully. *We could tell them anything, but we didn't, did we?*

He sighed as he put an arm around Tassie's shoulders. What could he do about it now, but let it be? One thing he had learned over the years, was that truth always found some way out into the light. He would deal with it when it happened.

~

Jair watched as everyone left the courtyard, heading off into the small area of Haven that had become their home. There was so, so much more of the city, he had been learning, taking small journeys farther and farther out, with Gavin in his company. The two of them had been adding to the maps of Haven they'd begun putting together for quite some time, and the city was proving to be larger than anyone had expected.

*Another search mission gone*, he thought to himself. Who knew what to expect when they returned? In the meantime, he would be missing his friend.

"Are you ready to head inside?" Ovard's voice broke the almost-silence.

"Not quite yet," Jair told him. "I think I'd like to have a moment to myself, if that's all right."

"Of course," Ovard replied. "But don't dwell on things too heavily. Remember you're not alone in any of this. You've got the lot of us here to help you," he told him, giving his shoulder a light squeeze.

"I know, thanks. I remember."

"Well, you know where to find me," Ovard said kindly as he turned to follow Brannock and Jayla toward the Main Hall.

"I won't be long."

Ovard nodded and smiled a wise smile as he left.

Jair stood in the quiet air of late morning, with only birdsong and an occasional insect's hum reaching his ears. He tried to look around at the white and blue-gray stones of Haven's walls and structures as if for the first time, trying to recover some of the initial awe he'd felt so long ago. Had he become so familiar with it all that he was beginning to take it for granted? Was that why he was having such a hard time grasping what the city seemed to be trying to tell him? Was he supposed to find something new? He felt sure that was part of it, but there was more. There was most certainly more.

The sound of voices interrupted his thoughts, taking him by surprise. Hadn't everyone left?

He took a step or two forward, turning his head toward the sound, then stopped. *That's Persha!* He thought, and felt his heart miss a beat. Yes, there was no mistaking Persha, even from this distance, nor was there any mistaking Bahadur, who stood nearby, facing her.

Jair could hear their voices, but couldn't make out the words they spoke. He took a step back, hiding himself from their line of sight, he hoped. Leaning a little to see beyond the edge of the lightstone wall, he watched them.

Persha was beautiful, Jair had never stopped seeing her that way. But the truth had long ago settled into his mind – there was no possibility of the two of them ever being together. He was simply too young for her. And now here was Bahadur, who at twenty-two years, was the perfect age for Persha, only four years older. Not to mention the fact that he was dark, quiet, and mysterious.

And *his* markings, Jair noted resentfully, he had chosen for himself. Tribal markings, a warrior's markings. Not directions to an ancient city that had been put there by his parents before he had been too young to remember.

There was no doubt that Persha was falling for Bahadur, despite their consistent squabbling. Jair watched them now, noticed the way they stood close, the way their hands touched as Bahadur gave Persha a gift. What sort of thing could he be giving her that would touch her heart? Jair wondered. Persha wasn't like other girls. She wasn't moved by flowers or lace or silver chains.

Jair continued to watch them, his interest piqued, as the muffled sounds of their voices carried toward him. Bahadur lifted – whatever it was – out of Persha's hands and reached up to the side of her head, just above her ear. *Something to put in her hair?* Jair wondered. *As simple as that?* Maybe the gift itself didn't mean so much as the heart of the giver.

Jair felt his face redden when Persha leaned forward to receive the kiss Bahadur gave her as well. It was no quick, light kiss. No, it kept going, and Jair quickly decided he'd seen enough.

Turning away, he strode through the courtyard toward the Main Hall, then stopped abruptly at the sight of Kendie.

"You're still here?" he asked in surprise.

"Well, yes," Kendie replied awkwardly, sitting on one of the benches. "It's just so nice and warm out," she said simply, *lamely*, she thought. "I didn't feel like hurrying to get home."

"What about classes?"

"They teach reading in the mornings, for the younger ones," she told him. "I don't need to be there for a while yet."

Jair shrugged. "All right."

"What about you?" Kendie asked, searching for something more to say. "Why are you out here alone?"

Jair rubbed at the markings on the side of his face, as though he might be able to wear them away.

"Just thinking."

"What about?"

Jair shrugged slowly. "Something I've been trying to figure out, that's all."

"Did you?" Kendie asked enthusiastically. "Did you get it solved?"

"No," Jair admitted. "I – I got distracted."

Kendie nodded. "I saw you were looking at something. Or, at least it seemed like you were."

"It was …" Jair hesitated. "Well, do you remember what Gavin said about Persha?"

"I do."

Jair glanced back over his shoulder, but the road leading from the Main Hall was now empty. "Well," he went on, "that was Persha I saw back there. And Bahadur."

"Oh?" Kendie asked, trying to sound nonchalant. She hadn't wanted the conversation to go in that direction – why did things always need to be about Persha? Couldn't she simply have the chance to talk to Jair? *Just her and Jair?*

"Well," Jair went on, "they definitely love each other."

Kendie had to admit she was glad, for more reasons that one. Persha deserved to find someone she could love; she was an amazing person, always brave and wanting to be of help. Kendie's *other* reason was not such a selfless one – as long as Persha was with Bahadur, Jair might have less reason to think of her. Now, if she could only get Jair to notice *her* instead …

*What to say?* Kendie wondered. "I'm glad for them," she finally managed.

Jair's face was a blank slate. Kendie couldn't help but notice that he was avoiding looking at her.

"Right," Jair commented. "Well, I should be heading inside. Don't be late for your schooling."

"I won't be," Kendie replied, feeling like she was being shrugged off. "I'll see you later, then?"

"Sure," Jair answered, finally looking in her direction with a bit of a grin. "See you later."

Kendie sighed to herself as she watched Jair disappear into the Main Hall. The sun still shone, and the birds still sang, but suddenly, she felt dejected.

She sat alone on the bench a moment longer before pulling herself up and slowly heading for home, her thoughts – and her stomach – churning all the way.

~ 5 ~

assie seemed ill at ease, Brace thought, watching her from across the room. Peering at her face yet again in the small mirror, running her fingers through her long waves of hair. It was only Leandra and Arden they would be visiting, Brace thought, not King Oden himself. Was she so concerned about her appearance?

Brace thought Tassie was beautiful, as always, in her long, pale blue dress, the sleeves rolled up at the elbows. The fabric was light and airy – she couldn't be too warm. Why was her face flushed? He cleared his throat.

"Tassie?" he asked, but there was no response. Of course – she had her back to him. He stepped closer, lightly touching her elbow, and she flinched.

"Tassie?"

She let out a quick breath. "You startled me," she scolded him.

"I'm sorry," he replied. "I just thought you might be ready to leave. You've checked yourself in the mirror three times now. You look fine."

Tassie managed a thin smile. "I know, I just..." She shrugged.

"Try to leave your worries behind," Brace told her. "We're just sharing a meal with friends. Right?"

She nodded in self-reproach. "Right."

"We're trying to make our lives feel normal again," Brace went on. "Just like this, spending time with Arden and Leandra." He smiled, a lop-sided grin. "You've known them longer than I have."

Tassie nodded again, smoothing her hands along her dress. "You're right," she replied, putting on a brave face. "Life is still happening, isn't it?"

"It is," Brace answered. "It's what you want, isn't it? You want life to go on for us?"

"I do. I'm sorry, Brace. I'm sorry I've made our lives stop."

Brace shook his head. "Forget about it. I understand. It's over now. We're starting over, remember?"

Tassie nodded, trying to smile.

"Come on," Brace said, taking her hand. "Let's go."

The two houses of blue-gray stone were close neighbors, so it was only a short stroll before Brace was knocking at Arden's door.

"I've got it!" he heard a voice call out, and he turned toward Tassie with a smile. "Kendie's coming to the door," he told her, and she nodded.

In a moment, the door was pulled open and they were greeted by Kendie's smiling face and the smell of seasoned meat and vegetables.

"Hello," Kendie welcomed them. "Come on inside, everything's almost ready."

Brace was surprised when Tassie stepped forward, going into the house ahead of him. He followed her, resisting the urge to tug playfully at Kendie's braid the way he used to. Surely she was at an age now where it wouldn't make her laugh. Instead, he held out his hand for her to shake it.

Kendie smiled, ignoring his offered hand and giving him a firm hug instead. "Don't be silly," she scolded him.

"Tassie, Brace, you're finally here," Leandra told them, coming around the table toward them. "Come in, make yourselves at home."

"I hope you're hungry," Kendie added. "We cooked up a whole deer. Arden brought it back from hunting yesterday."

Brace noticed Zorix sprawled out comfortably on the window seat, gnawing at a large piece of meat all his own.

"It smells great," Brace commented, and Arden nodded in response, settling Denira into her seat at the table.

"Would you like some water?" Kendie asked Tassie, "or tea?"

"Water, please," Tassie replied. "That would be fine."

"Kendie, you're not waiting on tables at an inn," Leandra chided. "Let them sit down. We can talk while the sauce is heating."

Kendie grinned, shrugging off Leandra's comment as everyone gathered around the heavy wooden table.

"Bwace! Tassie!" Denira called out, waving, a twinkle in her bright blue eyes.

"Hello there, little one," Brace responded, seated across the table from her, with Tassie beside him.

"Dadda, sit!"

"Mind your manners," Arden told Denira. "You need to say it nicely."

"Dadda, sit *pwease*."

"That's better," Arden said with an amused smile as he lowered his tall form onto the wooden bench beside his daughter.

"Here's your water, Tassie," Kendie said as she brought her a glass. "Would you like some, Brace?"

Brace hardly had time to nod in response before Kendie turned toward Leandra. "I don't mind serving them," she asserted. "I *like* helping."

Leandra shook her head in mock frustration. "Well, will you bring me some tea while you're at it?"

Kendie smiled. "Of course."

Leandra came to the table with a small, steaming bowl of sauce, resting her hand on Tassie's arm. "How are you?" she asked.

"I'm doing well, thank you," Tassie replied in such a way that even Brace was convinced.

"I'm very glad to hear it."

"Is everyone ready to eat?" Arden asked as Kendie returned to the table with the water and tea.

"Sure, any time," Brace told him.

"Food, Dadda!" Denira exclaimed. *"Pwease."* She smiled innocently.

"That's better," Arden told her, tapping her nose and making her laugh.

"Let's eat then," Arden went on, standing and using a pair of large two-pronged forks to separate portions of the meat.

"This is very good," Brace commented, starting in on his plate without hesitation.

"Thank you," Leandra replied. "We all had a hand in it."

"Except Denira, of course," Kendie added, grinning. Brace looked across the table at her, but the little girl seemed to be deeply concentrating, picking bite-sized pieces of meat off her plate and nibbling at them.

"Well, she'll be helping out soon enough," Leandra pointed out. "She's growing fast. No need to rush things."

Moments passed in contented silence as everyone enjoyed their meal. Tassie was, to Brace's surprise, the next one to speak.

"How is your schooling going, Kendie?"

"It's all right," she replied. "I'm keeping up with reading and mathematics. Sometimes Dorianne has me helping the younger girls with their lessons." She paused to chew another bite. "We're also learning words in Haven's language, and some music, and sewing, and farming. Things like that."

"Her writing is improving," Leandra commented, scooping grilled vegetables onto her plate from a large bowl in the center of the table. "She's been working on an idea for another song."

Kendie's face reddened. "I'm just getting started on it," she murmured.

"Well," Tassie spoke again, "Kendie's medic training is coming along. Hers and Ona's both. I'm glad to be able to work with the girls."

"Ona's better at it than I am," Kendie stated, wrinkling her nose.

"But it's something you want to do, isn't it?" Arden asked. "To be a medic?"

"Very much!"

"Then don't give up on it. Don't tell yourself it's too hard, or that you aren't good enough. Some learn faster than others. If you really want it, you'll get there. I know you've got the determination in you," he told her. "I saw that in you from the first. I knew you wouldn't let anything get in your way, or get you down."

Kendie smiled and shrugged.

"How was gate watch this morning?" Arden asked Brace, dipping a chunk of deer meat into the rich brown sauce.

"Same as it has been," Brace replied. "Quiet. It gives me a lot of time to myself, to think. Sometimes too much."

Arden nodded. "What's got you thinking so much?"

Brace glanced at Tassie, and her eyes met his. *Don't say anything*, they silently pleaded.

"Just life," Brace answered, looking back at Arden. He shrugged. "You know me."

"Are you still second-guessing yourself?" Leandra joined in.

"Honestly?"

"Yes, of course, honestly."

"At times, I still do," Brace admitted. "But doesn't everyone? I mean, no one can always be doing everything just perfectly, can they?"

"Not always," Arden told him. "But you don't need to worry yourself unless you feel inside that something really isn't what it should be."

Brace raised an eyebrow.

"You'll know," Arden explained, "if you feel unease about something in your life and you know you could be doing it differently."

"As long as it matters to you," Leandra added. "Caring about those things is the first thing, the most important thing. *Wanting* to do what's right is the first step toward actually doing it."

"I don't know everything about everything," Arden went on, "but I'm here if you ever feel inclined to ask for advice."

Brace nodded. "I know that. I'll never forget it. Thank you."

Arden nodded, grinned, then spooned more vegetables into his mouth.

Leandra turned toward Tassie and was about to speak, when she was interrupted.

"*Fiew!*" Denira exclaimed suddenly. "*Fiew*, Mammy!"

"Fire?" Leandra asked. "Where?"

Denira sat still a moment, then started sucking on her fingers.

"What fire, Denira?" Arden asked firmly. "Where?"

Denira lifted her free hand in a shrug.

"What's going on?" Tassie asked. "Did someone say 'fire'?"

"It was Denira," Brace replied, shrugging. "I think she was just playing."

"No pwaying," Denira protested, pulling her fingers out of her mouth.

"What is she talking about?" Kendie asked with worry in her voice.

"I don't know," Leandra answered as Arden rose from his seat to look out the window. Zorix leaped from his seat on the far window ledge, scurrying to Arden's side to look as well.

"I don't see any smoke," Arden commented, craning his neck to look upward through the window.

"We had a fire going to cook the meat," Leandra added, "but it's nearly out now."

"Is that what you meant, Denira?" Kendie asked. "The hearth fire?"

"*No*, sissie," Denira answered. "No hawf fiew."

Satisfied that he had seen no sign of trouble, Arden came back to the table. "What fire, Denira?" he asked, perturbed. "Why did you say *fire*?"

"Donno," Denira replied quietly, sucking on her fingers nervously.

"Well, you frightened us," Arden scolded. "Don't say that word unless you mean it."

"*Sowwy.*"

"Don't scare people, sissie," Kendie chided. "You scared me."

"*Sowwy,*" Denira repeated softly.

Leandra pushed herself up, away from the table. "I think I'll have more tea. Anyone else?"

"I would like some," Tassie spoke up.

"So would I," Kendie added.

"Brace?" Leandra asked. "Arden?"

Arden shook his head, his mouth full of food.

"No, thanks," Brace answered. "Water is fine."

Leandra crossed the room, pouring two heavy mugs of steaming tea while the rest of them sat eating in silence.

"Thank you," Kendie said when Leandra placed one of the mugs on the table in front of her, handing the other to Tassie.

"Is there honey in it?" Kendie asked.

"Of course," Leandra replied with a smile as she went back for more. "I know the way you like your tea."

"Thank you," Kendie said again, wrapping her hands around the mug, feeling its warmth.

Denira seemed to have decided she was finished eating, playing with a bit of her meat as she hummed a lively, off-key tune.

"Denira, don't play with your food," Arden scolded. "It's meant for eating."

"Done," she announced, holding the meat out at arm's length in Arden's direction.

"Do you want me to eat it?"

"Yes, Dadda eat."

Arden plucked the bit of meat from Denira's hand and popped it into his mouth. Denira laughed.

"Dadda funny!"

Leandra chuckled. "Dadda is *hungry*. It's hard work going all the way out into the Woods to hunt, then coming all the way home again, carrying the meat with him."

Denira gazed up at Arden's face and smiled, as though no one in the world had ever been more proud of him in that moment than she was. Arden looked over at Leandra, smiling and winking at her.

Leandra grinned in response, then rose from her seat. "Will anyone want any more of this?" she asked, lifting the stoneware platter holding what remained of the seasoned meat.

"No, thank you," Brace replied.

"I've had plenty," Tassie added.

"Good," Leandra commented. "Then we can bring out the pie."

"Pie?" Brace asked as Zorix scurried toward Leandra, his large ears pointing straight upward in anticipation.

"Yes," Kendie spoke up. "We made a pie with the fruit from the orchard."

"Pie, pie!" Denira exclaimed as Leandra brought the dessert to the table, setting it down with a heavy thump.

"Eat up, everyone," Leandra encouraged, cutting wide slices of fruit pie and placing one on each plate. A smaller piece was cut for Denira as well, and she stared at it with delight.

"*Pie*," she said wistfully before pinching off a piece of syrupy fruit and biting into it.

Kendie laughed. "She *loves* desserts," she commented, drawing light laughter from around the table. Denira paid them no heed, intent on enjoying what remained on her plate.

Brace glanced sideways at Tassie, but her eyes were on her plate as well. She seemed to only be poking at it with her fork, and not eating it. He gently nudged her with his elbow.

"Everything all right?" he asked, trying to sound nonchalant.

"I'm fine," Tassie replied with a flat smile. "I think I've just about eaten all I can for one night."

"Why don't you take it home with you?" Leandra suggested. "It will keep until tomorrow."

"Thank you," Tassie replied. "I think I will." She set down her fork and rested her hands on her lap, her long brown hair cascading over her shoulders, held in place on one side by the leather starflower that Brace himself had made for her before they were married.

She was so beautiful, Brace thought. Why did she need to bear this sorrow? What could she possibly have done to deserve something like this? Where was justice?

He realized after a moment that he was staring at her, and he made himself look away. His eyes met Kendie's and she smiled at him. Brace tried to smile in return, failing miserably, then stuffing another forkful of pie into his mouth.

"I taught Denira how to sing a song," Kendie announced cheerfully. "It's called 'Love in the Lilies'. Should I see if she'll sing it with me?"

"You can try," Arden replied, "if you can get her to forget about her food long enough."

Determined, Kendie sat her fork down on her plate with a clatter. "Denira, will you sing with sissie?" she asked.

Denira eyed Kendie, sucking sticky fruit juice from her fingers.

"Can you sing 'Love in the Lilies' with me?"

Denira smiled, pulling her fingers out of her mouth. *"Wove in the wiwies,"* Denira sang, and Kendie, laughing, joined in. "Love in the lilies, in the fairest of spring, two hearts united, a bird on the wing …"

Brace looked in Tassie's direction once again, and noticed that her shoulders were slightly hunched forward, her eyes on the table in front of her. He frowned, concerned, when he noticed a tear slide down her face.

Reaching out, he took hold of her hand. "Tassie, what's wrong?"

She shook her head, pressing her hand over her mouth as more tears came. "I'm sorry," she muttered.

Kendie stopped singing abruptly, and Denira's voice lingered alone for a moment before she was silent as well.

"Tassie?" Leandra asked in alarm, seeing that she was crying. "What happened? Are you all right?"

"I'm sorry," Tassie repeated, wiping away her tears. "I didn't mean for this to happen."

Leandra sat close beside Tassie, putting her arms around her. Brace pulled back slightly, watching them. He glanced across the table at Arden, who was looking back at him with concern written all over his face.

"Tassie, what's wrong?" Leandra asked. "I know something's been bothering you, more than just Lomar's passing. Will you tell me what it is?"

Tassie glanced around the table; everyone's eyes were on her, including Zorix's. She looked over at Brace for reassurance.

"You should tell them," Brace said with resignation in his voice. "I think it's what you need to do."

When Tassie nodded, Brace felt a wave of relief sweep over him. Finally! No more keeping the secret – at least not from everyone.

"I'm sorry I didn't tell you," Tassie said to Leandra. "I just – well, I couldn't bear the thought of saying it, not for a long time. I lost the baby shortly after Lomar died." She shook her head. "I didn't tell *anyone*. Only Brace and Ronin and his family know. I've been trying to leave it behind me and just go on, but sometimes it's just too much."

"I'm so sorry, Tassie," Leandra told her. "I was afraid it had been something like this. You don't need to try and pretend that everything is fine, Tassie, when it isn't. We're your friends. We want to be here for you when you need us."

Tassie nodded, trying to stop her tears.

"Why Tassie cwying?" Denira asked innocently.

Leandra took a breath. "She'll be all right, Denira. She's just feeling sad."

"Do you want me to take her into the other room?" Kendie asked meekly.

Brace could see that everyone in the house was deeply affected by Tassie's words, himself included.

"Yes, Kendie," Arden spoke up. "Why don't you go and get her cleaned up? She's a mess."

Kendie nodded, then stood and held out her arms toward Denira. "Come with sissie," she said, her voice heavy. "Come and have your bath."

Denira glanced around the room, then looked at Arden, seeking reassurance.

"Go on," Arden told her gently. "Everything's all right."

Obediently, wordlessly, Denira allowed Kendie to gather her into her arms and carry her out of the room.

"I'm so sorry," Tassie apologized again. "I've ruined the whole evening."

"Don't be sorry," Arden told her as Leandra wrapped her arms around her again. "It couldn't be helped."

"You can't hold on to things like this," Leandra said, looking into Tassie's eyes. "They only get bigger if you do. You know that."

Tassie nodded, leaning into Leandra's embrace as Zorix slunk across the floor to sit at Tassie's feet.

Brace sat by helplessly until he felt Arden's hand on his arm. "Come on," he said, tipping his head toward the door. "Let's give them some time."

Brace nodded, though it was with hesitation that he rose from the table and followed Arden outside. They stopped just outside the house, Arden pulling the door shut softly behind him. Brace leaned against the outside wall, crossing his arms over his chest, and Arden joined him.

The archer stood a head taller, and Brace felt somewhat dwarfed standing beside him, though he was no longer intimidated by him. At least, most of the time.

At that moment, Brace was glad he was there.

"I *am* sorry we didn't tell you until now," Brace commented, and when Arden said nothing in response, he went on. "I'm sorry things turned out the way they did tonight. Tassie's been trying so hard to just go on. But Leandra said she'd suspected something was wrong? Did she talk to you about it?"

"She did," Arden replied.

"Why didn't you say anything?"

"If you had wanted us to know, you would have told us."

Brace nodded, clenching his jaw in frustration. "I don't know if I'm doing *anything* right," he grumbled.

Arden looked over at him, raising an eyebrow. "I thought we'd already gone over this."

"No, I don't mean my life as a whole," Brace told him. "I mean with *this*. What's happened with Tassie, and the baby. I have no idea what on this earth I should be doing. Tassie said she didn't want anyone to know, so I didn't tell anyone. But was that the right thing to do? Ovard doesn't even know! Is it right to keep things like this from your own family?"

Brace leaned his head back against the wall and let out a breath. "It's taken time," he went on, "learning to re-think my life and make wise choices. It hasn't been that hard, not really. Not until now. I have no idea what I should be doing. I know Tassie's hurt, but so am I. How can I be strong for her when I don't even know what to do with myself?"

Arden hesitated before speaking. "Are you asking me for advice?"

"I don't know. Maybe I am. But don't tell me about *harbrost*, Arden. That's not the answer for every situation."

"You're angry."

"Yes, I'm angry! This shouldn't be happening."

The two men stood side by side, a heavy silence settling over them. Finally, Arden spoke. "It is hard to act with courage when you don't know what road you should take," he admitted. "It seems that now, you only need the courage to keep going."

"What do you mean?"

"To not give up. To do the right thing, whatever that may be. If one thing isn't working, try something else. You'll find the answer."

Brace sighed, long and deep. "That's all I *can* do, isn't it?"

"It is. But remember this – a burden is always lighter when it's shared. We're both here for you if you need us."

Brace felt divided. It would be so easy for him and Tassie to just shut themselves in their house and not come out again for days, it seemed. Sleeping, eating, and mourning. Let life go on for everyone else, and let it pass over them. Just forget about trying to act normally. Maybe it would help, but maybe it wouldn't. Maybe he should go and tell Ovard what had happened, whether Tassie wanted him to or not. Maybe Tassie needed to stop trying to run from her feelings about what had happened and just let herself face them. Maybe she needed *him* to make the right decision for *her*.

*A burden is always lighter when it is shared.* If nothing else, Brace knew that much was true. He already felt his own burden lifting, if only slightly. At least now he didn't need to feel alone in all of it.

Finally, he raised his eyes from gazing at the street to look over at Arden.

"Thank you."

Arden reached out and rested his hand on Brace's shoulder. "Always, my friend. Always."

"It is positively *gray* here," Halyard commented, gazing out at the city of Pran's Helm from the back of his sorrel gelding.

"It doesn't look like a very friendly place," Eridan joined in. "Does it?"

"No," Gavin agreed, "but don't let its appearance be discouraging. First impressions can fool you."

"I hope that's the case here," Halyard said in a heavy tone of voice. "Even the buildings seem to be telling us to go away."

Only the sounds of impatient horses could be heard as foreboding thoughts settled over the group.

"Come on, everyone," Gavin spoke again at last. "Keep up your courage. Remember why we're here. And remember what Jair has said — whoever is destined to come to Haven, will. Our only duty is to find them."

"And we *will* find them," Landers agreed with a brash smile, a breeze flowing across his shoulder-length hair. "Why are we hesitating? Since when do we let a bit of *gray* keep us from our duty?"

"I agree," Stanner spoke up. "Let's keep on. The buildings can't do us any harm, after all. Even if they do look like they're frowning."

Gavin heeled his horse onward into the city, the others following him.

The stretch of Royal Road leading into Pran's Helm was wide and flat, and nearly as gray as the city itself, as was the sky above it. Guards clad in dull metal armor kept watch at the outer wall, eyeing the travel-weary group entering on horseback, but saying nothing.

Gavin let out a breath of relief. One obstacle overcome — surely that would be the most difficult part, entering the city? He prayed there would be no disturbances at their mention of Haven – Oden had created so many lies that were spreading all around Dunya.

The chaotic rhythm of life inside the city swallowed them up. All around were loud voices, the rattle of iron-rimmed wheels on cobblestone roads, and the clanging of metal smiths in their work shops.

Their horses snorted uneasily at the commotion and constant movement. Gray roads, gray stone buildings, gray armor of the watchmen. Gray *sky*! Gavin missed the colors of the wildlands just outside of Haven. Lush green grasses, wildflowers of untold colors, and the deep blue of the vast sky overhead. Here, more than just the wet cloud cover of spring blocked out the expanse of blue. Gavin thought at times that he could feel it in the air, whatever it was obscuring the light of the sun. It was, if nothing else, completely unnatural.

Landers' horse tossed his head fearfully as a large, heavy wagon clattered past, and he tried desperately to calm it.

"Easy now, Flecks," he said as he stroked the horse's neck. "I know you're used to the quiet of the open country. Easy, now, easy!"

The horse shook its long mane, taking several steps backward, until a loud clanging sound stopped it in its tracks, and it spun around, neighing in fear.

"Grab his reigns!" Stanner called out to Halyard, who was nearest the frightened animal.

"Watch out now!" A female voice reprimanded them.

Gavin looked over his shoulder to see a young woman struggling with a small metal cart she'd been pulling. "Your beast nearly knocked the whole thing over," she snapped.

"Sorry about that," Landers apologized. "He isn't used to all the noise."

"Let me help you," Eridan offered, sliding off her own horse and handing her reigns over to Gavin.

"Thank you," the woman replied shortly as she and Eridan steadied the cart on its low wheels.

"What all have you got in there?" Eridan asked disarmingly. "Feels like a full load."

"Yes," the woman replied, straightening her short, smooth dark hair. "It is full. It's all towels and soaps and things for the bath house."

"Bath house?"

"Just there," the woman replied, gesturing to the nearest building at her left.

"Do you work there?" Gavin asked.

"I do," she replied defensively, then softened. "Are you all in need of a hot bath? Have you journeyed far?"

"Plenty far enough," Landers spoke up.

"Well, I'm sure we can get you all in there. We've got a lot of space." Finally, the woman smiled. "My name is Noora Hayes. Forgive me for being rude. But the owner wouldn't like it much if all of the new towels ended up sprawled out all over the street."

"No, I'm sure he wouldn't," Eridan replied. "I'm glad to meet you, Noora. My name is Eridan, and this is Gavin, Stanner, Halyard and Landers. I think we could all use a bit of cleaning up. Don't you?" she asked, looking up at her traveling companions, still atop their horses. It was true enough, they were all in need of a good bath. The dirt from the Royal Road, stirred by the horses' footsteps, had left them all looking quite dusty.

"Well, as long as it doesn't take too long," Gavin relented. "We can have a short rest before we go on."

"Where are you headed, if you don't mind my asking?" Noora pulled the cart along toward the nearby bath house as she spoke.

"Here, actually," Eridan told her. "We've got important work to do here."

"Really?" Noora asked in interest. "Such as?"

Eridan looked up toward Gavin, who led her animal beside his own. Her eyes met his, silently asking him just how much he felt she should say to Noora.

Gavin cleared his throat, drawing Noora's attention. "We've come from a city to the south," he told her, "from beyond the mountains. We've come to invite people to return with us. Maybe you've heard of it? It's called *Haven*."

Noora stopped pulling on the cart and looked up at him, her dark eyes wide. "Haven?" she asked. "Do you mean it's a *real* place?"

"What have you heard of it?" Eridan asked her.

"What have I heard?" Noora asked, surprised. "All my life, I've heard of it! But I thought it was only a story. Then King Oden started sending messengers telling everyone it was dangerous. I had no idea what to think of *that* news. Most of the people here have just been ignoring it. I don't think they believe it's even real, not at all."

"No, it's a very real place," Eridan told her. "It's meant for all of us, anyone wanting to live in peace and safety. It's meant for *you*."

Noora glanced at each of them, then looked around nervously. "I want to hear more," she said, "but not here. We need to be careful. Come to the bath house, everyone. Get cleaned up. I need to find my sister – she works there too. Then we'll talk."

Gavin looked over at Halyard. "Is this mission going to be as easy as that?" he dared ask.

"It seems that way," Halyard replied, keeping his eyes on passersby who eyed them with suspicious curiosity. "But don't let your guard down. Trouble is more likely to come when you're not expecting it."

Gavin nodded in agreement as Eridan turned to smile up at him. "Do we follow her?"

"I can't see any reason not to. Stanner?"

"I'm all for it," he replied. "At the very least, we can have a bath. I feel coated all over with dirt."

Landers chuckled, guiding his horse toward the bath house. "You *are* coated with it."

⁓

The horses were tethered, and hot baths were enjoyed in the semi-privacy of the bath house. Men and women came and went continuously over the hour that followed, but very few of them gave any of the travelers so much as a second glance.

Finally feeling clean – why had he taken it so for granted? – Gavin pulled his long-sleeved roughspun shirt on over his head, wishing it was as clean as his skin. Slipping his feet into his boots, he stuffed his travel clothing into his leather sack. He headed out of the small, steam-filled room into the main hallway, where he could see once again that the bath house was almost as squat and gray inside as it was out.

Water dripped from Gavin's hair as he went along, working his way toward the front doors. The main attendant, one the few men Gavin had seen working there, barely gave him a nod as he left. What a strange place

Pran's Helm was, Gavin thought. Nothing at all like Meriton, where every public place seemed to be competing with all of the others for patronage, going out of their way to give visitors whatever they needed or wanted, trying to make them all feel like honored guests. What little Gavin had seen of the people working in Pran's Helm gave him the impression that they cared not at all about welcoming any guests into their establishments. Maybe they felt no need to – Pran's Helm was smaller than Meriton. Maybe they had no competition to concern themselves with.

Well, it was all the same to him. He wasn't here for himself. He was here for people like Noora, who wanted to hear about Haven.

Stepping outside, Gavin felt the chill of the afternoon air hit him after becoming accustomed to the warm, stuffy air of the bath house, and he shivered.

Eridan stood waiting at the corner of the building, and she smiled a tight smile as Gavin approached, her damp hair tied back haphazardly in a wide strip of white cloth, the ends hanging long down her back.

"Feeling refreshed?" she greeted him.

"Better, yes. You?"

Eridan nodded, her smile fading. The door to the bath house opened, and they turned to look expectantly. The man leaving the building was unknown to them, however, and they only watched him for a moment before turning away.

"What's wrong?" Gavin asked Eridan. "You don't like it here, do you?"

"Not too much," she admitted.

"Neither do I. Let's just find Noora and see how things go. Maybe we can leave sooner than we planned. Is everyone out?"

"All but Stanner," Eridan told him. "They're around back, with the horses."

"Let's wait there with them," Gavin suggested, turning again to look when the door opened once more. Stanner stepped out into the pale light of the afternoon, followed closely by Noora and a younger woman who could only be her sister.

Gavin lifted his hand to catch Stanner's attention, who nodded, gesturing for the dark-haired sisters to follow him.

"Are you through for the day?" Eridan asked Noora, and she nodded.

"Finally, yes! I told Lida what you'd said, that you came from Haven. You've got to tell us more. Tell us all about it!"

"It is a real city, after all?" young Lida asked, her black eyes wide.

"Very real," Eridan told her. "And we'll be glad to tell you everything. Come with us, we'll get something to eat and we'll talk."

"Come to our house," Noora insisted, rounding the corner to where the others waited.

"Are you sure about that?" Gavin asked. "There are five of us..."

"Please come," Lida joined in.

"The rest of your family won't mind?" asked Eridan.

"There is only the two of us," Noora informed them as they joined Landers and Halyard.

"Well," Gavin spoke up. "If you're sure it's all right, it would be our pleasure to eat with you."

"You can leave your horses here," Lida said quickly. "They'll be all right. We live just down the road a bit."

Gavin smiled. Lida and Noora both were anxious to hear about Haven, that was clear. Whatever stories they'd been told about the ancient city, now they had the chance to hear about it from someone who had actually *been* there.

It was a quick walk to the small house the sisters shared, and with the food the group had brought with them and what was stored in the kitchen's larders, there was plenty to go around.

"There," Lida said, setting a platter of breaded mushrooms on the table. "Now tell us about Haven, please!"

Landers laughed at her straightforward, earnest enthusiasm – she sounded so much like himself.

"Well, it is a real place," he began. "I don't know what all you've heard, but it's the ancient city of our ancestors, where everything is peaceful and safe, and full of light."

Noora and Lida leaned in closer, eager to hear more.

"The city is meant for everyone," Gavin went on. "Anyone who wants to come back there and live in peace is welcome."

"What does it look like?" Noora asked.

"It's an enormous city," Stanner told her. "The streets are wide and smooth, with walls made of stones like glass. There are homes to live in, and buildings that we use for meetings, or a clinic, or a school. The sun *always* shines there, and no evil can ever enter it."

"We grow our own food there," Eridan added. "And there is a courtyard with a beautiful fountain, and an orchard, and a lake with pure, clean water that gives you strength when you drink it, and vine fruit that heals injuries when you eat it. It's ... enchanting."

"It's time now for everyone to come back there," Gavin spoke up. "The city has been empty for generations, but there are people living there now, and there's plenty of room for everyone who wants to join them. The city was *made* for us to live there. It's for you, Noora, and Lida. It was *made* for people like us, like you."

The two sisters exchanged a glance.

"But why is King Oden spreading the word that it's dangerous?" Lida asked.

Gavin's face grew solemn. "Well," he began, "Just over two years ago, the king sent troops of his men to come and try to invade the city. They were destroyed."

"Destroyed?"

Gavin nodded. "The light came out of the stone walls, and then the men were gone. Just *gone*. It shouldn't have happened. No one can ever enter the city wanting to do harm. The light of Haven ... it senses what's in men's hearts. It destroyed them."

"There were a few who survived," Landers joined the conversation. "My brother was one of them."

"*How?* How did they survive?" Noora asked in amazement.

"They were simply following orders," Landers explained. "My brother had no desire to take control of the city, or to harm anyone inside. He and three others survived, and all but one of them now call Haven home as well."

"What about the fourth?" Lida asked. "What does he do?"

Landers smirked. "He drinks," he replied glumly. "He doesn't want to face what happened. Or maybe he's come to believe what Oden has been saying. I really don't know."

"But believe me," Stanner cut in, "Haven is *not* an evil place. It's what is out *here* that is turning too quickly to evil. That's why we've come. To bring people out of it and back to the city that they *should* call home."

Noora nodded slowly as understanding came over her. "So," she began, "no one has the right to stop us from leaving, do they?"

"No," Gavin told her. "Though they may think they do. We need to be careful. We don't know who we can trust."

Lida's eyes filled with concern. "You want to go back with them, don't you?"

"I do," Noora replied firmly.

"What about Eaton?" Lida asked. "What about Mica, Corben and Drayus? We can't leave them behind!"

"Are they friends of yours?" Eridan asked.

"More than friends," Lida replied. "They're the only family we have."

"Do you think they would want to come back with you?" Gavin asked.

"I'm not sure," Lida answered. "Most of them would, I think. They know what King Oden's been telling everyone, but if you came with us to tell them the truth, we might be able to convince them."

"How long are you planning on staying here?" Noora asked.

"Four days, at least," Halyard replied.

Noora turned toward her sister. "That's enough time for them to make up their minds, I think."

"It is," Lida agreed, "if we tell them *today*."

The hesitation in Noora's eyes was difficult to miss.

"Come on, Noora!" Lida scolded. "If we've been given the chance to get out of this place, we've got to tell the rest of them. Why wait?"

"Why indeed?" Noora agreed, a smile playing on her lips. She turned toward the others. "Will you come with us? Some of you with Lida, others with me? They'll be more likely to believe it's true if they hear it from you."

"I'm willing to go," Gavin replied, and the others quickly agreed. Only moments later, the two groups had been arranged so that Gavin and Halyard would accompany Lida to find Eaton and Corben, and Stanner would find rooms at an inn while Eridan and Landers joined Noora in search of Drayus and Mica.

"They've probably already gone to the *Iron Moon*," Noora said as she cleared away what was left of the food. Lida pulled Stanner outside, pointing out the route he should take to the nearest inn, where they would also be able to stable their horses for the night.

"The *Iron Moon*?" Gavin asked.

Noora looked up at him. "The ale house," she explained. "We all gather there at the end of the work day. Nothing else to do here," she muttered.

"There won't be any ale houses in Haven," Halyard informed her lightly, and she smirked.

"Do you think that matters?" she asked, her dark eyes shining.

"Let's not waste any more time!" Lida exclaimed, coming inside and grabbing hold of Gavin's arm. "Come on! Let's go and tell Eaton the news. He might still be working. It isn't far. Come with me!"

"All right, we're coming!" Gavin laughed. "We'll all meet back here when we're through, then we'll head to the inn together."

"Take care!" Stanner called out as the two groups parted ways. "Best of luck, and we'll see you again later tonight."

"Does the inn close its doors after nightfall?" Gavin asked as he hurried to keep up with Lida.

"No, no, don't worry about that," she replied carelessly, flipping her long dark hair over her shoulder.

"Where exactly are we going?" Halyard asked her.

"To the blacksmith's," she told him. "It's not far."

"Doesn't your friend Eaton go to the ale house with the others?"

"When he can," Lida replied, looking back at him. "The smith makes him work long hours."

"What does he do?" Gavin asked, nearly stumbling over an uneven stone on the cobbled walkway before Halyard caught him. "Thanks," he muttered.

"He re-shoes the officials' horses, keeps the fires going, and cleans the place up, along with everything else," Lida answered his question, only pausing for a moment while Gavin regained his footing. "He demands the best, the smith does, Eaton's told me, but nothing anyone does is ever quite good enough. If *anyone* would want to leave this place, Eaton will. I'm sure of it."

The walks along the streets of Pran's Helm were full that evening, and Gavin suspected they always were. Everyone seemed to be in a hurry to get somewhere, not paying any heed to anyone else around them. The only reaction Gavin drew from those who passed him was an occasional scowl if he got in their way.

"I thought you said we weren't going very far," he called out toward Lida.

"It's right over there," she replied, pointing across the street.

The blacksmith shop was the same stony gray as everything else, set apart only by the wide opening in the main wall that served as a doorway. Too much heat would build up otherwise, Gavin knew, from the fire that continuously burned in the back of the deep, square room.

"I don't see anyone inside," Halyard commented as they approached.

"No," Lida replied. "The smith would have gone home by now, but the fire's still going. Eaton must still be there. Follow me."

Gavin obeyed, with Halyard close behind him, as they entered the dark, low-ceilinged room, heat closing in around them.

"Eaton?" Lida called out as they made their way toward a far corner, weaving their way around rickety wooden shelves and stacked, empty crates. "Are you here?"

"I'm here," a quiet voice answered from the back of the room. Gavin peered through the dim light and saw a young man straighten up from some task, running the back of his arm across his forehead.

"What extra work has the smith got you doing now?" Lida greeted him.

"Just fixing the buckle on this harness," Eaton replied, lifting it up in his fist, at an odd angle, for her to see. Glancing past Lida into the darkness of the shop, Eaton realized that she wasn't alone.

"Who are they?" he asked in surprise.

"You would *never* guess," Lida replied. "They've come from Haven, Eaton! *Haven!* It's a real place, and they've come to tell us that we can go back with them and live there too. Isn't that completely amazing?"

"Well, she certainly didn't waste any time, did she?" Halyard commented with a chuckle.

"Wh – what?" Eaton asked, setting down his metal tool and pushing his wheat blond hair away from his face.

"This is Gavin and Halyard," Lida introduced them. "They came from the city of Haven! You know, the one King Oden's been warning people about? It isn't a bad place. It's a perfect place, and we've been invited to come and live there!"

Eaton looked over at Gavin, an eyebrow raised, questioning.

"It's true," Gavin replied slowly, trying to make up for Lida's excited rambling. "I've lived there for over two years myself."

Eaton clumsily hefted the leather harness and placed it on the scarred wooden table beside him, peering through the dimly-lit room, getting a better look at the strangers Lida had brought with her.

"Don't worry at all," Halyard told him. "We are not lying, not in the slightest. We have come from Haven, and we are inviting anyone to come back with us. It's all true."

Eaton's raised eyebrow slowly settled back into place as he became more accustomed to the news. He rested his hands along the edge of the table, sweat glistening on his face and neck. Gavin studied Eaton even as he studied them. He was young; likely close in age to Lida, who couldn't be more than a few years older than Gavin himself. Eaton seemed to want to say something, but had no idea what, given the strangeness of the situation, and he ran his palms along the wooden surface of the table, gathering his thoughts.

Now, Gavin couldn't help but see why Eaton had had difficulty handling the leather harness - he was missing the last two fingers on his left hand. Gavin's curiosity mixed with empathy as Lida moved around to Eaton's side of the table and took hold of his sleeve. "Noora and I are going," she told him, "and we want you to come with us. You'll never have to work for that horrible blacksmith another day!"

Eaton only started at Lida, dumbfounded. "You're leaving?" he asked. "Just like that? They say they are telling the truth, but how can you know for certain?"

He looked back toward Gavin, his eyes full of doubt. Gavin searched his thoughts for some bit of proof, then he remembered.

"Can I show you something?" he asked, stepping closer.

Eaton looked him over from head to toe, then nodded tentatively.

Gavin slowly reached up and tugged on the leather cord he wore, holding the broken fragments of lightstone. The continuous light they gave off shone brightly in the dark room, and Eaton and Lida both blinked in surprise.

"There are so many walls made from this stone, back in Haven," Gavin explained. "The light is everything that is good, and it keeps away everything that is evil. We bring it with us on every journey. It keeps us safe from the night screamers."

"What are *they*?" Lida asked, suddenly fearful.

"Haven't you heard them after sundown?" Halyard asked. "We don't often see them, but their shrieks are hard to miss."

Eaton nodded slowly. "I have heard them recently. And quite often. Why? Where do they come from?"

"It's hard to explain where they come from," Gavin answered, "but they are the only true enemies of Haven. They *are* darkness, just like these stones are light. The screamers can't harm us as long as we have the lightstones."

Eaton looked at Lida once again, incredulous.

"They're going back in four days," she told him. "That gives you time to think it through. But I'm leaving, Eaton. And I *so* want you to come with me. I'm willing to take a risk for this. Aren't you?"

Silence filled the room, broken only by the snapping of flames in the fire pit nearby.

Eaton swallowed, looking from Lida to Gavin and Halyard and back again, his posture tense.

"If you come with us to Haven," Gavin spoke up, "you won't need to work like this. We haven't got a blacksmith in Haven. We've only recently gotten horses, and we don't ride them often. If you enjoy this work, you could be a blacksmith there, and you wouldn't be taken advantage of. You wouldn't need to work such long hours, and everyone would care more about *you* than the amount of work you're able to do."

Eaton nodded, his expression softening. "I …" he began, glancing around the large, cluttered room. "I don't know what to say."

"Say you'll come with us," Lida urged. "At least you can close up for the night. We're going to talk to Corben next, if he hasn't already gone to the *Iron Moon*."

Eaton shook his head. "I'm sorry, I can't. I need to finish this harness first, and I'm responsible for making sure the fire's put out, and for pulling the gate closed."

"Will you think about it, then?" she asked. "Think about Haven? Please? We're not leaving for a few days."

"I will," Eaton replied earnestly, glancing around the blacksmith shop with sudden distaste.

Lida stood on her toes and leaned in to kiss Eaton's cheek, and he reacted in mild embarrassment.

"Good," Lida told him. "I've got to go now, I've got to try and find Corben. I'll see you again soon."

Eaton nodded, eyeing Halyard and Gavin with deepening curiosity.

"It was good to meet you," Gavin told him.

"Come on!" Lida called out, already heading for the door. "It's dark out there already! Corben's probably already at the *Moon*. Let's go and meet your friends there!"

Eaton nodded farewell, and Gavin did the same, stepping out into the gathering darkness of the streets of Pran's Helm once again.

The lanterns outside the ale house were already lit when Noora led Landers and Eridan up to the front doors. There, she paused and looked back. "You've all been inside an ale house, haven't you?" she asked.

"I have," Landers replied, and Eridan nodded.

"Once or twice."

"All right, then," Noora said with a nod. "You know things can tend to be a little rough. Just follow me. Drayus and Mica should be here. I'll take you to where we usually sit."

"We're right behind you," Eridan said with a confident smile.

Inside the building, the constant din of voices and clattering of glasses, not to mention the overwhelming smell of spiced ale, assaulted their senses. Landers leaned in closer to Noora's ear so she could hear him speak.

"It's hard to imagine nice girls like you and your sister spending much time in a place like this."

Noora gave him an amused smile, obviously taken in by his inviting appearance and spirited ways, as people often were.

"We don't get into any trouble," she informed him, weaving her way between the full tables. "The truth is, there just isn't anything else to do in Pran's Helm, not really. We work, then come here to try and get rid of the frustrations we've carried with us throughout the day. None of us would really make it here," she added, "if we didn't have each other. That's why it's so important that I tell them about Haven. I just couldn't leave here without giving them a fair chance to decide if they want to come with us."

"But you made up your mind so quickly," Eridan pointed out. "You knew right away you wanted to see Haven for yourself."

Noora smiled. "Lida and I aren't like most people. We're dreamers. My friends, I'm afraid, will take a bit more convincing. There they are," she added, pointing to the far side of the room. "Follow me."

Eridan obeyed, holding her head high, trying to shrug off the leering glances she'd seen directed at her by more than one of the *Iron Moon's* male patrons.

"There you are!" a cheerful voice called out, catching Eridan's attention.

"Hello, Drayus," Noora replied, approaching a table where a dark-haired man sat beside a young woman with sunset-orange hair and full, rosy cheeks. "Hello, Mica."

"Where have you been? Where's Lida?" Drayus asked her as she sat in one of the empty chairs, gesturing for Landers and Eridan to join her.

"She's gone to see Eaton," Noora explained. "And I'd like you to meet someone. Drayus, Mica, this is Eridan and Landers. They have something amazing to tell you about."

"What's that, now?" the young woman asked. "Something like what?"

"Have a seat," Noora instructed the visitors, who remained standing.

"Do you mind if we join you?" Landers asked politely.

"We don't own the place," Drayus replied, sipping from his glass of golden ale. "You're free to do what you like."

Wordlessly, each of them pulled out a well-used wooden chair and joined the others at the table.

"So what is it you've got to tell us?" Drayus asked, an amused expression on his sharp features, a playful glint in his eyes.

"You both know what's been said," Noora began, "about the place called Haven?"

"That place where all of the king's men were killed?" Mica asked.

"Yes, that place," Noora answered. "Well, the king's story isn't completely true."

"How so?" Drayus asked.

"Well …" Noora began, then looked over at Landers.

"The king's men *were* killed," Landers admitted. "But they were not innocent victims. The king sent his men to take the city by force in his name, and the city wouldn't allow it."

"What do you mean, the city wouldn't allow it?" Mica asked, frowning.

"It's difficult to explain," Eridan spoke up, waving away the server who offered her a drink, "but the city is alive. It's a miracle, really. I can't see any other way to put it. The city is alive and it stopped those soldiers from taking over. It was protecting the people who live there."

"Wait a minute," Drayus broke in, shaking his head. "You're telling me that this *Haven* place is really there, and all of the king's men were killed by it? It's not just some crazy story?"

"No, it's not just a story," Eridan told him. "The city is real, and people are meant to come and live there. Just, no one who wants to cause trouble or take it for themselves. Everyone who wants to live there peacefully is welcome."

"My grandmother used to tell me stories about Haven," Noora told her friends. "She said it was a place full of light and peace, and that a long time ago everyone left because they wanted to go their own way. They left the light behind, she told me, and when they did, the darkness started to grow. And it's been growing ever since. I know you've seen it. In the sky, and in the people all around us. I see it here every day. No one cares for others as much as they do themselves. I've always dreamed of Haven being a real place, and now I know that it is!"

"How do you know that, really?" Drayus asked pointedly.

"These two say they've come from Haven themselves," Noora explained, "and I believe them. There are three others who came with them. They're here in the city as well."

"You mean you've seen the light city with your own eyes?" Mica asked, looking in Eridan's direction.

"I have," Eridan replied. "Haven is my home now. It can be yours as well. You're both more than welcome to join us."

Mica smiled while Drayus simply stared at her in disbelief.

"Hey there," a new voice spoke as a tired-looking young man in worn cottager's clothing came up to the table. "Is there still room here for me?" he asked in surprise, casting curious glances at Landers and Eridan.

"Of course there is," Drayus replied, indicating an empty seat on his right.

"What's going on?" the new arrival asked, joining them at the table. "Who are these two?"

"They're saying that *Haven* place is for real," Mica informed him. "They said they live there and we can come to live there too."

"*What?*"

"Corben," Noora interrupted, "did you see Lida out there? She was going to look for you."

"No, I didn't see her," Corben replied. "Why isn't she here?"

"She went to talk to Eaton," Noora explained. "You see … well, I've decided that I'm going to leave here and go to Haven. Lida and I both are. And we want you all to come with us."

Drayus' dark, heavy eyebrows arched in surprise. "You're leaving?"

"I am," Noora told him, almost apologetically.

"Just like that?" Mica asked.

"I'm sorry," Noora told her friends. "It's just that this isn't something I can forget about. This might be my only chance. Our only chance. Lida and I want you to come with us."

A silence settled over the table, the only quiet spot in the whole room, it seemed.

"You don't need to decide tonight," Noora spoke again. "There's still time. Not a lot of it, but there is time."

Drayus gazed at the near-empty glass in front of him, while Mica stared at her friend in disbelief. Corben sat looking out across the room, his eyes not focused on anything in particular.

"I know this seems completely crazy," Noora admitted. "But I've made up my mind. It would grieve me to leave any of you behind. You're my family. You know that, don't you? Mica? Corben? Drayus?"

Corben at last let his gaze settle on Noora's face. "How can I just pack up and leave?" he asked her. "I've been working so hard to get where I am now. You know this is something I've wanted for so long, Noora. And now it's right there in front of me. I was finally able to make a sword all on my own. Did you know that? It's one of the last stages in my training. I've worked hard for this for *years*. Commander Blackwood was here from Glendor's Keep, and he saw my workmanship, told me he was impressed by it. I think I might finally get the chance to start forging blades all on my own for the king's men to use. How can I just forget about all of that?"

"I understand," Noora told him. "It's just that you're one of my dearest friends, and I would be leaving a piece of my heart behind if you didn't come with me. Haven is going to be so wonderful," she went on, looking at each of them in turn. "More wonderful than even I can imagine, I'm sure, and I've tried to picture it in my mind countless times. Please promise me you'll seriously consider it? For yourselves, and for me and Lida?"

Corben chewed thoughtfully at his lip while Mica and Drayus looked at each other.

"Well," Mica finally said, "the two of you really are going, aren't you?" She shook her head. "I don't know if I can live like you and your sister. Just up and leave because you're struck with the desire to. I don't know, but ... I *might* like to go with you." She lifted her shoulders in a shrug. "I'm not sure, but I *think* so."

Noora smiled, then looked over at Drayus, who sighed. "I just don't know about any of this," he told her. "I suppose I'll consider it." He shook his head, drumming his fingers on the side of his glass. "This really is crazy, Noora. You know that?"

"It isn't crazy," Eridan spoke up. "I know I've only just met Noora, but I can see she isn't crazy. I'm sure you know that. She's just ... Well, she's being brave. She's taking a big chance, but I can tell you it's more than worth the risk."

Drayus raised an eyebrow at her, then nodded, downing what remained of his drink. "I think I've had enough for tonight," he commented.

"Meet me here again tomorrow," Noora told him as he stood to go. "I'll bring Lida."

Drayus nodded once again, then turned toward Landers and Eridan.

"I still think this sounds crazy," he informed them, "talking about just up and leaving. But it doesn't seem like you're lying. Maybe I'd like to hear more about it tomorrow night."

"That will be no trouble," Landers replied. "We'll be glad to tell you whatever it is you'd like to hear."

"Right. Tomorrow, then." Without another word, Drayus left them – Corben sitting in contemplative silence, Mica gazing at Noora wistfully. The idea of Haven's existence had struck each of them differently. While Corben and Drayus seemed troubled, the thought of Haven had lit a spark inside of Mica that wouldn't easily be put out.

# ~ T ~

"Trystan, pay attention," Dorianne scolded. "School isn't over yet."

"Sorry," Trystan muttered, looking up at her.

Kendie glanced at her younger classmate before looking back at Dursen and Nerissa, their guest teachers for the day. Dorianne was frowning – Trystan often daydreamed during classes – but Dursen wore an amused smirk.

"Anyway," he went on undaunted, "as I was sayin', when we plant the seeds, we make sure they're deep enough for the roots to take hold, but not too deep so they're smothered."

"What do you do with the gardens after you plant the seeds?" nine-year-old Marit asked with interest.

"Nearly nothing," Dursen replied with a smile. "Just plant them, water them, and when the crops are ready, we harvest them."

"How do you know when to do that?" Marit spoke up again. Her eagerness was easy to see; the girl was enthusiastic about almost everything, but the subject of farming had particularly caught her interest.

"I can show you that myself," Dursen replied, "when the next crops are ready. Won't be too long till then."

"Who planted them?"

Dursen looked to Nerissa, his eyebrow raised in a question.

"I think this time it was … Adivan, Dorn, and Worley," she replied, holding tightly to the rope she'd tied around the neck of her goat, Spice, who she had brought to show to the children.

"Yes!" Aneerah spoke up. "My dadda *is* one of the ones who planted."

"That's right," Dursen agreed, turning back toward the class.

"Everything grows so fast here in Haven," Kendie joined in.

"It does," Dursen told her. "And it surprised us all. It grows fast, and it grows plenty. No one in Haven will ever need to go without."

"How do you know when the crops are ready to be harvested?" Marit wondered aloud, causing Trystan to roll his eyes.

"Well …" Dursen paused, considering the question. "Why don't you come to the garden and I can show you?" he suggested. "Then you can see for yourself."

"Can I?" she asked, her eyes bright.

"It's all right with me if it's all right with your mam and dad."

Marit smiled. "I know they'll say yes."

"Thank you, Dursen," Dorianne spoke up, Yara standing beside her under the bright afternoon sun, the blue-gray stone wall of the school house at their backs. "And thank you, Nerissa, for showing us how you milk your goat. Kids, say thank you to our guests."

There were words of thanks in varying degrees of enthusiasm, and Kendie wasn't sure who was the more bored of the two younger boys – Trystan or Shale. The only thing those two ever seemed to want to do was *play*!

"We were glad to come," Nerissa told the class. "Thank you for listening so well. Maybe we can come again and talk about how to care for the chickens."

Spice bleated loudly, and several of the children laughed. Kendie found the animal amusing enough, but her heart was still heavy. Having learned of Tassie's troubles only a few days past, she bore a heavy burden, unable to tell anyone. Only Brace or Tassie had a right to say anything.

At least Ona already knew.

"Children!" Yara spoke up above the restless chatter that had begun, "It's almost time for the school day to end. You all did well, so we're going to let you go home early."

"Wahoo!" Trystan exclaimed, and was immediately hushed by Dorianne.

"One last thing before you leave," Yara continued. "Everyone keep up with your reading and memorize the list of words in Haven's language that we gave you. You'll be tested on them next time we meet."

As though by some unspoken cue, the children seemed to all turn as one and hurry into the school house to collect their belongings. Kendie followed after them at a slower pace, Ona walking along beside her. By the time the girls reached the school, Shale and Trystan were already coming back out, shoving the doors open and running toward the nearest road.

"Sorry!" Shale called out as he raced past Kendie, nearly knocking into her.

Kendie watched them go, offering no response.

"Are you all right, Kendie?" Ona asked, concerned.

"I'm fine," she replied. "I've just got something on my mind, that's all."

"Is it about Jair?" she whispered.

Kendie felt her face redden. "No!" she exclaimed. "Well, not so much, not today. I mean, I have been thinking about him, but there's something else too."

"Tassie's doing all right, really," Ona told her gently, and Kendie nodded.

"I know it. I just feel so badly for her."

The girls gathered up their papers, which were few. Paper was expensive to buy, and heavy to carry, and they hadn't yet been able to begin making their own in Haven, so it was used sparingly.

"Goodbye, Kendie," eight-year-old Aneerah called out, following her twelve-year-old brother Hoden toward the door.

"Goodbye," Kendie replied. "See you again soon."

"She's cute, isn't she?" Ona asked, and Kendie nodded.

"Her eyes are so dark, they're almost black, aren't they?"

"Yes," Ona agreed, pushing open the door and stepping outside. "Hoden's, too. So," she went on with an air of authority. "So, you still like Jair? I mean really *like* him?"

"I do," Kendie muttered.

"Does he like you back?"

"I don't know," Kendie sighed. "Last time I tried to talk to him, he seemed like he didn't even want to be around me."

"Didn't you say he was trying to figure something out? Maybe he just had a lot on his mind."

"*Maybe.*"

"He's probably at home now. Why don't you go over to see him? Just to say hello, of course," she added, seeing the surprise on her friend's face.

Kendie considered the idea for a moment, playing out possible outcomes in her mind.

"Well?" Ona pressed. "Why don't you?"

"I suppose I could," Kendie replied. "But what would I say to him?"

"Just say *hello*," Ona told her. "Why not? That's not so strange, is it? Just stopping by to say hello?"

"No..."

"He won't be working at the Hall or at the library," Ona pointed out. "Just go on. You've known him for *three years*, Kendie. It isn't as though you've only just met, for pity's sake."

"You're right," Kendie replied, trying to gather her resolve and determination. She pushed her long braid over her shoulder and held her school papers close. "I will go over and see him. I'll do it."

Ona smiled. "Don't get all nervous," she advised. "Just be yourself, or he'll think you're acting strangely."

~

By the time she parted ways with Ona, Kendie had begun to feel more at ease about seeing Jair. He hadn't been trying to shrug her off last time, she had almost convinced herself. He had only been distracted.

Approaching the home Jair shared with Ovard, Kendie could see at once that he was there, sitting outside on an old stone bench, cutting away at an uneven block of wood with a small, sharp knife. She smiled to herself. That was just like him. He'd always enjoyed whittling, even if it meant sharpening a stick for roasting meat over a fire.

Kendie took a breath, keeping up her courage, then stepped closer.

"Hello, Jair," she called out, and he looked up in surprise.

"Hello," he replied, blowing wood shavings off his hands. "Are classes done for the day?"

"Yes, they let us go home early."

Jair smiled, and Kendie felt a rush that she hoped wouldn't show in her face.

"That's nice," Jair commented.

"Hmm?" Kendie asked. "Oh – school. Yes, it is nice to get out early."

She paused, searching for more to say. "It must be nice for you, not having to attend classes at all, if you don't want to."

"Well," Jair shrugged, running his knife along the length of the wood, "it's not so much that I don't want to. I've just got so much else to do."

"Like what?" Kendie asked earnestly.

Jair looked up from his work. "There are so many old books, Kendie," he told her, "from Haven's past. You wouldn't believe it. Some of them are so old that I can't even read the writing, but most of them are all right. We're re-writing them, though, Ovard and Jayla and I. And everyone reports to me about how things are going. Arden tells me about the hunting trips or the gate watch, Rudge about all of the repairs, Dursen about the crops, Tassie and Ronin about medical supplies, Dorianne about the school -"

"She reports to you about the school?" Kendie interrupted.

"Yes," Jair replied, smirking. He shrugged. "So, I have to make sure that everyone has everything they need, and if they don't, I'm the one who has to figure out how to get it. And…"

"And what?"

"Well," he went on, chipping away at the wooden block, "there's still something that Haven is trying to tell me. I can feel it. I'm just not sure what it is." He pushed hard with the knife, sending a large splinter of wood flying out to the ground past his feet.

"That must be frustrating," Kendie sympathized, sitting beside him on the bench. "But you'll find out what it is. You always do."

"Thanks," Jair replied, not sounding too convinced.

The silence that lingered felt awkward to Kendie, though Jair didn't seem to mind at all.

"What is that you're making?" Kendie asked, nodding toward the ragged block of wood.

Jair wrinkled his nose. "It's supposed to be the deer. Haven's deer – the one on the wall in the Main Hall. I don't think this piece is tall enough, though."

"Don't give up on it too quickly."

Jair shrugged, turning the piece over in his hands. "Maybe."

He set the wood and his knife on the ground near his feet, dusting wood shavings from his breeches. A far-away look came into his eyes, suddenly distracted. "When Gavin comes back," he commented, "we're going to start mapping the city again. It's so much bigger than we'd ever thought."

Kendie nodded. She desperately searched for the right thing to say, wanting to re-direct the conversation without seeming too obvious about it. She knew there was no way she could come right out and tell Jair the real reason she'd wanted to come and see him. She glanced at her shoes, her school papers, then her hands, and she subconsciously pulled her long braid over her shoulder.

"Do you think my hair is getting too long?" she asked.

Jair blinked and looked over at her. "Your hair?"

"Yes," she said, shrugging. "Leandra keeps hers shorter, just at her shoulders. Do you think I should cut mine too?"

Jair let out a bit of a laugh. "I don't know. Whatever you want to do with it."

Kendie felt heat rising in her cheeks. *How silly*, she scolded herself. What did she expect him to say in response to such a question? *No, Kendie, don't cut it, I think your long hair is beautiful??*

She shrugged, trying to make it seem like it didn't matter at all.

"I know, you're right."

*Awkward, awkward silence!*

"You said Dorianne reports to you about the school?" Kendie asked.

"Yes," Jair replied. "Either her or Yara."

"Do … Do they ever say anything to you about how the students are doing?"

Jair smiled. "They say that Trystan and Shale are daydreamers, and that it's hard to get them to see why it's important for them to learn what they're teaching."

Kendie nodded. "That's true. Do they ever say anything about me?"

Jair frowned slightly in thought. "Not that I can remember," he told her. "But you're a good enough student, aren't you? You try hard and you care about the lessons."

"I think I'm good enough, most of the time."

"That's what really matters then, isn't it?"

"Sure," she replied, smiling.

Again, Jair settled into what must be for him a comfortable silence.

Couldn't he see that she wanted to *talk* with him? She fingered the corner of the paper on her lap, considering what to say next.

"Do you ever get any time all to yourself?" she asked.

Jair shrugged. "Yes, a little. Like right now."

"Do you like to go out walking in the Woods?"

"Sure, sometimes," Jair replied casually.

"So do I. I don't go very often because Arden says he doesn't want me to go out there alone."

Jair nodded. "It is safer to go with someone."

Kendie stifled a frustrated sigh. Well, if she had to come right out and say it...

"Maybe you and I could go out there together. I'm sure you've gone out farther, and seen more of the Woods than I have."

"Yes, maybe we could," Jair agreed. "I don't know when exactly, but some time." He leaned forward to pick up his knife and the choppy block of wood. He stared at it for a moment, turning it in every direction.

"I don't know about this one," he commented. "I just can't see it. It's not tall enough."

"You can do it, Jair. Don't give up. If it's not that piece of wood, another one will work. Do you know what I think?"

"What?"

"I think you've never failed at anything. Not in the whole time I've known you. You always succeed, eventually, no matter what it is you're trying to do."

Jair shook his head, wrinkling his nose. "Not everything," he protested. "This doesn't really matter, anyway. It's just a piece of wood. There are a lot more important things I need to think about."

"I'm glad you're our leader, Jair. Ever ..." Kendie paused, hesitating. Should she say it? "Ever since I met you, I could always see that you were different. And I don't mean the markings on your face. I could see that you would do great things. You don't give up easily. And I ... I really like that about you."

"Thank you," Jair replied, tipping his head away as he always did when he was embarrassed.

With a sigh, Jair stood. "Sorry, Kendie, but I think I should go."

"Do you need to do *more* work?" she asked. "I thought you were done for the day."

"I am, but I've got a lot on my mind. I'm sorry. Maybe we can talk again another day."

Kendie stood up beside Jair, gathering her papers into her arms. "All right," she said dryly. "I'll see you later, then."

Discouraged, she turned and left without another word. Jair obviously didn't feel the way about her that she did about him. If he had, he would have *made* the time to talk to her because he wanted to. He would have *wanted* to go walking in Haven's Woods with her. She could see that he really didn't want her to hang around, and since that was so, she would just leave.

Jair watched Kendie march down the street without looking back, and he frowned. What had caused her to leave so suddenly? She'd seemed to be in good spirits when she'd come to the house. Hadn't they been talking more just now than they'd had a chance to, for a long time?

*How can I help it*, he wondered, *if I don't have time to attend classes with the rest of them?*

Kendie had said she was glad he was the overseer – if he was going to be efficient at it, he had to put in the time and effort that it took to accomplish what needed to be done, and to discover what the city was trying to tell him. He'd been glad to see Kendie coming to the house. With Gavin away on a search mission, Kendie was the only other young person in Haven that he really considered a close friend.

What had he said or done to make her so upset, to leave so abruptly? She'd said she liked to walk in Haven's Woods, and hadn't he said that was something they could do together? Hadn't he said that they could talk again soon?

Jair groaned as he turned toward the house. The last thing he wanted to do was hurt Kendie's feelings. Didn't she know how much he cared for her? Maybe she cared for him too – she had seemed to.

"*Girls*," Jair muttered in complaint as he pushed open the door and went inside.

Kendie's legs were beginning to ache by the time she reached home, she had been walking so fast, but she didn't let up until coming inside and shutting the door behind her. She wasn't in the mood to talk to anyone else but Leandra.

She quickly glanced around the front of the room, setting her school work on the table.

"You're home early," Leandra commented, sitting near the window with Zorix by her side, Denira playing on the thick woven rug at her feet.

"Sissie!" Denira exclaimed, dropping her rag doll and running to Kendie. "Up, sissie, up!"

Kendie managed a smile and hefted Denira into her arms, joining Leandra near the window.

"Yes, I'm early. Dursen and Nerissa were there talking about how to milk goats and harvest crops. When they were done, Dorianne let everyone leave."

Denira planted a messy kiss on Kendie's cheek, then squirmed to be let down. Kendie watched the little girl playing with her dolls and humming to herself, until she realized that Leandra was watching *her*.

"What?" she asked self-consciously.

"You've got something on your mind. I know that look. What is it?"

Kendie sighed as she sat beside Leandra. "Is Arden here?"

Leandra shook her head. "Not for a short while longer. What's got you thinking?"

"Jair," Kendie admitted sheepishly.

"Again?"

"*Still.*"

"I thought we'd been through all this a long time ago," Leandra gently scolded.

"I *know*," Kendie replied, almost whining. "I just can't help it. And I'm older now. I'll be fourteen years next month. And I *really like Jair.*"

"Why are you so intent on growing up so quickly?" Leandra challenged. "I was already twenty-five years myself when I married Arden. You know that, don't you?"

"I do."

"So, why do you want to seem older than you are? You're still so young."

Kendie nervously tugged at the sleeves of her dress. "Well," she began in a quiet voice, "a lot of the other servers at the Wolf and Dagger used to say that when girls were my age, they were already a woman, really. So, aren't I?"

Leandra shook her head solemnly. "Please don't tell me you hold to the kinds of things those women told you. You *do* remember what it was like, living at the inn? You saw enough of those women to know what kinds of lives they lived. Don't ever try to be like them, Kendie. Promise me you won't?"

"No, I don't really want to be like them," Kendie replied. "I just … well, I want to be beautiful. And I don't want people to think of me as a child any more. I'm not a *child*."

Leandra smiled again, taking Kendie's hand in her own.

"No, not so much," she agreed. "But you're not quite a woman yet either. You're somewhere in the middle, and it's a confusing place to be, isn't it?"

Kendie nodded glumly.

"But Kendie," Leandra added intently, "you *are* beautiful. Don't think you're not. You're very beautiful, what others can see of you as well as what only *hearts* can see. And that is where true beauty lies. You know that, don't you?"

"I know." Kendie paused, her thoughts jumbled up and fighting one another. "So," she continued hesitantly, "what *should* I do about Jair?"

"What about him?"

"Well, the last few times I tried to talk with him, he acted like he didn't want me around. We've always been friends. Why would he all of the sudden not like me any longer? I don't understand."

"Oh, Kendie," Leandra sighed. "My belief is that most girls start to think seriously about these things before the boys catch up with them. I can't say I know what's going on in Jair's mind, but it could be he's just not ready for this sort of thing. Just be a friend to him, Kendie. Don't try to push anything else on him. Show him that you care about *him*, and don't try to get him to notice *you*. And don't expect anything from him. You can only truly love someone when you're willing to love them even if they don't give you anything in return. Do you think you can love Jair that way?"

"I think I could. It might hurt, though."

"Love can hurt sometimes."

Kendie sighed in resignation. "I know."

Leandra sat closer and put an arm around Kendie's shoulders, kissing her lightly on the side of her face. "Will you at least try and take to heart the things I've told you? I know I'm not really your mam, but I don't think I could love you any more if I was. I'm only thinking about what is best for you."

"I will," Kendie replied. "I promise. I know you want the best for me. I'll just be Jair's friend and try to forget about the rest … for a while."

Leandra smiled. "That will have to be good enough, won't it?"

Kendie sighed again, resting her hands on her knees. "Why does love have to be so *confusing*?"

# ~ 8 ~

Brace poured the fresh goat's milk from the stoneware pitcher into the small clay bowl until it almost reached to the rim, then stopped, a few drops falling to the surface of the wooden table. Ignoring the small mess that was slowly growing into a larger one, he set down the pitcher and poured the small bowl of milk into a larger one, over the heap of broken eggs and finely-ground grain, mixing them together with a large wooden spoon.

He was not an accomplished cook, something he was sure by now he would *never* be, but he knew how to light a hearth fire, and he had learned how to bake a loaf of bread. Yes, that much he could do, and he found a sense of pride in it.

The dough was still a sticky mass clinging to the sides of the bowl when Tassie wandered into the kitchen from the back of the house.

Brace looked up when he saw her, pausing in his work. The sunlight streaming in through the window shone brightly on her cascade of dark curls, which showed not the slightest hint of being out of place.

"Hello there," Brace greeted her tentatively.

Tassie crossed her arms over her chest and leaned her shoulder against the nearby wall. "You let me sleep the morning away," she told him.

Brace nodded slightly, fearing a reprimand. "I did."

Surprisingly, Tassie managed a smile. "Thank you."

Brace felt relief sweep over him. So she *had* needed the extra sleep.

"I thought you might enjoy it," he explained, scraping the sides of the bowl with the wooden spoon. "At least for one day."

Tassie nodded in reply. In the two weeks since their dinner with Arden and Leandra, Tassie had finally worked up the courage to tell the truth to Ovard and Jair. Though Brace had been by her side, it had been a difficult thing to do, and it seemed to have wearied her. She had been carrying her own sorrow, but bringing that sorrow into her family had been the last thing she had wanted to do. There had been some tears, but in the end, Jair and Ovard both had thanked her for telling them the truth.

The full night's sleep she had finally gotten had done much to improve the look about her. The heaviness that had clouded her features had started to lift once again, and she almost, Brace thought, *almost* looked as though her heart had healed completely.

"I did need the rest," she told him, coming up to the far side of the table. "Thank you. What is this you're making?"

"Bread," he replied, spooning the dough into a heavy iron loaf pan.

"Did you spread butter along the sides first?" Tassie questioned.

"I did," Brace replied, sliding the bread pan onto the makeshift rack over the fire, then turning back toward Tassie. He started to run his hands across the front of his shirt, but stopped when he realized they were dusted with flour and felt sticky.

Tassie grinned crookedly, wetting a small rag in their wash basin and cleaning Brace's hands with it. "What would you do without me?" she asked lightly, but Brace frowned.

She shook her head. "Don't take that to heart, Brace. I was only making light of the mess you've made."

Brace managed a smile. "I wouldn't know what to do with myself."

Tassie washed the last of the flour from Brace's hands, then lightly dropped the rag onto the table. "Do you ever wonder," she began, "what our lives would be like if we had never met?"

Brace's expression darkened. "Maybe it's crossed my mind." He shook his head slowly. "But I might not even be alive right now if I hadn't met all of you in the wilds. Do you realize that?"

Tassie pondered the question, then nodded. "I do."

"What about you?" he asked, changing the subject. "You'd be just fine without me."

"I would be alone."

"You don't know that. Besides, you have Ovard. You have Jair."

"But they're so busy," she pointed out.

"You are as well. You're a medic. You help take care of everyone. That's what you've always wanted, isn't it?"

"Yes," she replied, "but haven't you noticed, Brace? I haven't made use of most of what I've learned since we came here. Most everything that's wrong with our bodies can be healed just by eating the vine fruit. Most of the time, people here don't really *need* a medic."

"You helped Leandra deliver her baby," Brace reminded her. "Vine fruit can't do that."

"Well, yes. That's true."

Brace pulled Tassie closer. "Are you disappointed in your life here? I know how much you've wanted to be a medic. It isn't the same here in Haven, I know, as it would be out there. Do you feel like you're not needed enough?"

"Sometimes."

Brace's disappointment was easy to read on his face, and Tassie saw it immediately.

"I'm sorry," she told him. "It isn't as bad as all of that, really. It's more like what Arden once said, about not feeling fulfilled. All his life, he wanted to be the best archer he possibly could. A man of *harbrost*, giving all he could to defend his own. It's the same with me. I want to heal people. I want to help them. I don't feel unwanted. It's just ... it's not what I thought my life would become."

"You wouldn't ever leave Haven, would you?" Brace asked her. "Would you leave, to help people out there?"

Tassie gazed out through the clear glass window. "Leave?" she asked. "No, I can't say that I would. But there are people out there who need healing, and I might have been able to help them. I want to do something important, something that makes a difference to someone else."

"You've made a difference for me," he told her, and she smiled.

"I know."

*There she is*, Brace thought, seeing that familiar confidence in Tassie's deep green eyes. *That's the woman I fell in love with.*

"I was infatuated with you, did you know that?" he asked. "From the first time I saw you, I couldn't get you out of my mind."

Tassie nodded slightly. "Yes, I could see that."

"I couldn't really figure you out," he admitted. "Not for the longest time. But those little smiles of yours – I couldn't get enough of them."

Tassie laughed at Brace's comment. "You've always been such a flirt."

"I'm not the only one guilty of that," he pointed out, and Tassie laughed again. Brace smiled. "It's good to hear you laugh," he told her.

"It feels good," she replied. Slowly, her smile faded and she grew solemn.

"We will be all right, Brace. This..." she shrugged. "This won't last. And I'm sorry about what I said, not feeling like I'm doing enough. I shouldn't have made it seem like I'm not happy here. Or that it's not enough for me, just being here with you, with our friends. Because really, it is."

"There must have been some truth in it, though. In what you said about wanting to help people. I know you have a heart for that, more than most."

Tassie nodded, wrapping her arms around herself. "I do want that."

"Don't give up on it," Brace told her. "Who knows? Maybe soon, Haven will be so full of people, there will always be *someone* who needs *something*. You and Ronin will be so busy, you won't know what to do."

Tassie grinned. "Maybe." She sighed, stepping closer to Brace and taking his hand again. "Just how much of the morning did you let me sleep away?" she asked lightly.

"Not too terribly much," he replied. "I think we're halfway to midday. Why?"

"Maybe we could go over to the lake. Eat our meal there, and just spend the day in the sunlight. Does that sound all right?"

"That sounds great." Brace gently pulled Tassie into his arms and they held each other tightly. He began to wonder if Tassie would ever let him go, when a faint sound reached his ears. He frowned over the top of Tassie's head, listening as the sound grew louder and he recognized it for what it was.

"Tassie," he said, holding her at arm's length. "I hear the gate opening."

"Do you need to go and meet it?" she asked dejectedly.

Brace shook his head. "I don't, but I'm sure it's Gavin and the search mission coming home. I should go to the meeting, though, find out how things went. I think we'll need to wait and go to the lake for our evening meal. Do you mind waiting until then?"

"That will be all right."

"Will you go to the meeting with me?"

Tassie paused, then shook her head. "I'd rather not."

"That's no trouble. I'll tell you about it when I get back. I'm sure Eridan will be eager to see you again."

Tassie smiled. "I've missed her."

Brace breathed in the fragrance of baking bread. "I don't know if that bread will be done before I need to leave," he commented.

"We can eat it later."

"Of course." Brace glanced toward the door. "I should go. They're probably heading for the Main Hall by now. I'll get back as soon as I can."

"All right," Tassie replied. "And Brace? If anyone needs anything, send them to Ronin, will you? I know I said I wanted to help, but I feel like I just need peace for today."

"Of course I will. I understand. Just wait here for me. I'll be back soon."

Tassie nodded and sat at the table, facing the hearth fire. Brace hesitated for a moment, wanting to stay with her. But he was a member of the gate watch, after all, and it would be irresponsible of him to ignore both the opening of the gate *and* the meeting. So, without another word, he hurried out through the door and down the street, where he met up with Ben-Rickard.

"Off to the Main Hall?" Ben greeted him.

"Of course," Brace replied. "You?"

Ben nodded. "About time they came back, isn't it?"

"They get back when they get back," Brace told him bluntly. "There are things beyond their control."

Ben-Rickard eyed Brace as they went along. "Is everything all right?" he asked. "You seem a bit out of sorts."

"I'm sorry," Brace replied. "Everything's all right, or it will be. Don't take it to heart."

"It's fine. If you ever need a listening ear, I'm here for you."

"Thanks."

Ben nodded as they joined up with others making their way toward the Main Hall. Ovard and Jair wasted no time in calling the meeting to order, and everyone grew quiet, taking their seats. The returning party and the newcomers who had joined them gathered around the front of the room, freed at last from their heavy packs, looking at least partly refreshed from their long journey.

"Thank you for coming, everyone!" Ovard spoke up, Jair busily conversing with Gavin. "Another successful search mission has returned. We will make this brief, with some introductions, and get an idea of how things went. Are they ready, Jair?"

"Yes, they're ready," he replied. "Gavin, will you introduce everyone?"

"I will." Gavin pulled himself up from his seat and gestured toward the unfamiliar faces who were gathered behind him.

"This," he began, "is Noora and Lida Hayes, the first people we met in Pran's Helm." He smiled a tired smile. "They were the quickest of anyone I've ever met to want to come back with us."

The young dark-haired woman at Gavin's side smiled at his comment.

"And these are their friends," Gavin went on, "Mica, Eaton, and Drayus. Then there are Timur and Bress, and Kalder, who we met a few days later."

"It's good to meet you all," Jair told them.

"What happened to your hand?" young Shale asked bluntly from the front row of seats, his eyes on Eaton.

"Don't be rude," Farris scolded him, but Eaton shook his head. "It's all right," he said quietly, looking at the boy. "Do you mean my missing fingers?" he asked, and Shale nodded. "It happened two years ago," Eaton explained. He seemed overwhelmed, being in an unfamiliar place, surrounded by so many new faces. "My hand got stepped on by a big, heavy work horse." He shrugged. "I've learned to get by. It's no trouble for me now."

"Eaton was working at a blacksmith's shop," Gavin went on. "Noora and Lida introduced us to Drayus, Mica, and Eaton. We met Timur and Bress at the market, and they spread the word to Kalder, who is a friend of theirs."

"There was another," Eridan joined in. "His name is Corben. But," she said, glancing at the others, "he had too much of a reason to stay behind."

Drayus put an arm around Noora's shoulders.

"Well, it's wonderful to have all of you here with us," Ovard told the newcomers, some of whom smiled awkwardly in reply.

"This is your home now," Jair added. "You can get settled in today. There are empty homes ready for you to move right into."

"There is more we have to tell you," Stanner spoke up. "I'm sorry, but we can't end the meeting quite yet."

"What is it?" Jair asked.

"Well, it isn't good news at all. For one, the night screamers are getting more bold. We heard them, right there in Pran's Helm, every night we were there."

Fearful whispers filled the Main Hall as Gavin joined in the conversation. "That's right. And with the days getting shorter, it gives the screamers more time to be out. I don't know if that's why they're getting closer to the cities, or if…"

"What?" Jair prompted him. "If *what?*"

"Well, it's like Ovard's been telling us. The prophecies seem to show that now is the time of a great return to Haven. *We* are here, after all, and there will be more. If it's time for people to come to the city of light, maybe the darkness is working harder to stop them."

Brace noticed Ben-Rickard tense up beside him.

"You all right?" Brace asked him quietly, and he nodded, though his expression was unsettled.

Brace felt a strange sense of heaviness settle over him. The whole world, going dark, and there was no way for anyone to stop it. It was true enough, the world had never been kind to him, but it had for so long been his home, in a manner of speaking. All the places he'd been, all the people whose paths he'd crossed, they all came to his mind now. What would happen, in the end? How far could it all go? Would there be a time when the sun's light could no longer be seen at all? What would happen *out there* then, if it ever came to that?

"That isn't all of it," Halyard added, catching everyone's attention. "It seems – from what we've been told, and from what we've seen ourselves – that, well, the *people* are getting worse, too."

"What do you mean?" a woman named Belina asked fearfully.

Gavin looked over at Eaton, who nodded, turning to speak into the room.

"Well," he began timidly, "the smith – the man I worked for – he's been so short of temper these past months. Once, he got so angry he threw something at me. I've worked for him for four years now, and he'd *never* done anything like that until recently."

"But that's only one person," Worley pointed out.

"I've lived in Pran's Helm all my life," Timur spoke up. "Near forty years. I remember early days, when the people there were kinder, more neighborly." He shook his head. "It's not so, now. Rarely does anyone there give so much as a smile to anyone else, unless they're paid to do it."

"This is all in the prophecies," Ovard spoke up, his gray eyebrows furrowed in concern. "It has been said that, along with the sky itself, men's hearts would grow darker as well. All that you've said, sadly, makes perfect sense."

"What can we do about it?" Persha's voice carried across the room, from where she stood in the back with Bahadur at her side, and several heads turned in her direction.

"I don't think there is anything we can do," Ovard told her, "other than what we have already been doing. Bring people here where they will be safe."

Jair's face, Brace noticed, reflected his own feelings of bitter frustration. It was true – what else was to be done? They couldn't make the sunlight grow stronger just because they wanted it to last.

Ovard, seeing the deep scowl on Jair's face, spoke to the crowd. "Please, everyone. Don't be troubled. Worrying over this won't help to solve anything. This news comes as no surprise. This is the very reason why we have all decided to come here, to our true home. We will do what we can to help those on the outside, but in the meantime, we are all safe here. Please, welcome our new friends. Enjoy one another's company. We will meet again soon. Thank you all for coming."

Brace stood along with the many others who began to drift out of the Main Hall. Ovard was right – this news was not new, but it was a discouraging reminder of what went on past the safety of Haven's high stone gate. He tried to shake it off – he'd had enough trouble of his own to face recently, even here in Haven, and it seemed to finally be letting up. He couldn't wear this discouragement on his face, going back to Tassie. This was their day together, just the two of them, and he wasn't going to let anything spoil it.

# ~ 9 ~

"The breaking day shines sweet and clear," Kendie hummed to herself as she ran a damp cloth over the thick glass of the window. "Bright to my eyes ..." She paused. Was that right?

"To my eyes and my heart..." She stopped, flustered. How should that part of the song go? She played out the tune in her head, trying to decide on the right words. It wasn't easy, creating a new song, but it was all the more difficult today.

She just couldn't forget the look on Jair's face during the meeting yesterday. So *discouraged*. The bad report about how the world was changing had affected everyone, but Jair most of all. He was driven, Kendie knew, by a strong desire to make things right. He couldn't possibly do everything, though. What was there to be done to stop the darkness? It was impossible. Only here in the city of light did things remain as they were meant to be.

Kendie had wanted to stay and try to cheer Jair's mood after the meeting, but he had stayed at the Main Hall with Ovard and his other advisors. It wasn't her place to hang around.

"Sing, sissie!" Denira called out, and Kendie turned in her direction.

"I'm sorry, Denira, I don't know all of the words yet."

"No sing?"

"No, I can't sing right now. Sorry."

Denira sat quietly on the cushioned window seat, her silky blonde hair hanging in loose curls around her face, while Leandra washed the windows beside her.

"Maybe tomorrow I'll know all the words," Kendie went on. "I just don't know."

Denira made no response, only staring off into the room, her eyes glazed over. Kendie frowned. "Leandra? Look at Denira. Is something wrong?"

Slightly alarmed, Leandra stepped away from the window and looked at Denira's face for a moment. Zorix scurried over, sniffing at Denira, the bright orange of his fur showing his worry.

"Denira?" Leandra asked, her voice heavy with concern, resting her hand on the top of her head. Denira looked up at her, blinked, then grinned.

"Hi, mammy."

"Are you all right? Do you feel well?"

"Not sick," Denira replied, confused.

"Were you just thinking about things?" Leandra guessed. Kendie came closer, while Zorix's color began to return to normal.

"*Finking?*" Denira asked, rubbing the side of her face. "Finking," she replied.

Leandra stood up straight, the cleaning rag hanging limply in her hand. She and Kendie watched as Denira turned back to her toys, singing to herself as she played.

"That was strange," Kendie said quietly.

"It was."

"Has she ever done anything like that before?"

"Not exactly," Leandra replied.

"What do you mean?"

"Well," Leandra began, going back to the windows, "sometimes she does things that I can't really explain. Like … the other day at dinner, when Brace and Tassie were here, and she said 'fire'. Do you remember that?"

"Of course I do. It frightened me a little. Why do you think she said that?"

"I really don't know," Leandra replied, shaking her head. "Maybe … maybe she only imagines things that aren't really there? Maybe she's mixing up memories with what's actually happening now. I don't think we need to worry over it."

Kendie pondered Leandra's words. *Don't worry.* Easy to say, not so easy to do. But Denira certainly didn't *look* ill. Maybe it was nothing to fret over.

"How is your new song coming along?" Leandra asked, changing the subject.

"I'm a little stuck just now," Kendie admitted. "I know what I want it to be about, and what I want it to sound like. I just need to get the words right."

*And it's hard to concentrate*, she added to herself, *when most of my mind is still on Jair.*

"Well, I think the front windows are clean enough," Leandra commented. "Why don't you go out for a while? Getting outside always seems to help you gather your thoughts."

"Nothing else needs to be done?"

Leandra smiled playfully. "Not today."

"Well … If you're sure it's all right."

"Go on. Get your song worked out. Denira and I would love to hear it, and Arden as well."

"All right," Kendie replied, setting her rag down in the basin. "I'll go. Thank you."

Leandra smiled. "I'll see you later, then."

Denira waved, completely herself once again, calling out "bye, sissie!" as Kendie left the house.

*Strange*, Kendie thought to herself, but she tried to shake it off, the way Denira had been staring out at nothing, along with the image of Jair's scowling, worried face from yesterday's meeting.

"The song," she said aloud to keep herself focused, wandering beside the road leading toward the Fountain Court. "Just work on the song. Forget about everything else."

The mid-spring air was heavy with the scent of blossoming flowers, Kendie noticed. They were everywhere – in the orchard, on the vines in the courtyard, as well as in large clay pots that were scattered around in the public places, planted by Nerissa.

The scent was wonderful, and the bees were drawn to it. Eridan's bees had gone on with their daily activity of gathering pollen and making honey, and Kendie believed they hadn't even noticed Eridan's absence while she'd been in Pran's Helm.

"The breaking day shines sweet and clear," she sang as she walked, passing by the clinic and turning onto the wide, stone-paved road. "To my eyes … and my heart, just as bright."

Yes, that felt right, she thought as the lightstone walls opened before her into the wide, round courtyard. She smiled at the sight of the tall burbling fountain, sunlight reflecting off the white, churning cascades of water flowing down over the rims of the stone bowls. What a change from the days when it had stood dry and empty!

"The breaking day shines sweet and clear," Kendie sang out loudly, seeing no one else in the open courtyard. "To my eyes and my heart it is just as bright! Come, everyone, and gather near, and leave behind you the sadness of night!"

She stopped and stood up on one of the old stone benches surrounding the base of the fountain, holding out her palms to feel the gentle spray of water.

"Broken …"

She searched for more words to the song. "Broken lives… can be made new… and…"

She stopped, full of joy at the words she'd put together, at feeling the cool water on her hands, the warm sunlight on her face, and at hearing the birds twitter as they darted around the courtyard.

"That sounds like a nice song," a voice said unexpectedly, startling Kendie so that she nearly fell into the fountain head first.

Fortunately, she quickly recovered her balance and turned to see Jair, who wore a concerned expression.

"Are you all right?" he asked. "I didn't mean to scare you."

"No, I'm all right," Kendie replied, her heartbeat returning to normal. "I just, well, I thought I was alone," she explained, stepping down onto level ground. "I don't mind if you want to stay," she added quickly. "It's good to see you. I mean, it's good to see you, not frowning. Yesterday, after the meeting, you just looked so bothered by the news they'd brought back, and everything. You look better now."

Jair grinned. "I'm all right. It was just a reminder of what it's really like out there, you know? Living here where everything is safe and peaceful, you could almost forget, couldn't you?"

"Almost," Kendie replied. She felt herself falling back into wanting to attract Jair's attention, and she scolded herself inwardly.

*Forget all of that. Just be who you are. Don't be ridiculous.*

"I've known for a long time," Jair went on, "what the prophecies said, about everything growing darker. I just didn't expect it to happen so fast. Knowing won't make things any easier for the search missions. It will only be more dangerous."

Kendie nodded, at a loss for words. How could anything be an encouragement when the dark truth was staring them in the face?

"Well," she finally spoke, "I know there's really nothing I can do, but I'm here, at least. If you just need someone to talk to, I can be there to listen."

"Thanks," Jair replied, to Kendie's relief. She had felt her face reddening with embarrassment, wondering how he might respond. "That's good to know. But I'm all right, really."

"Of course. Just remember I'm here if you need a friend?"

Jair smiled broadly. "Thank you, Kendie. I'm glad to hear you say that."

Kendie smiled back at him. Jair's words were soothing to the injury she'd felt when it had seemed he didn't even want her around. Her friendship mattered to Jair! He had said it himself, and Jair never lied, *that* she knew for certain. Kendie could put aside the idea of trying to make Jair think about loving her, as long as she knew that for now, they could be friends, and someday, maybe *someday*, they could be something more.

"What's this?" she asked him, noticing the tightly rolled papers Jair held in his hand. "Are you working on a new project?"

"Oh – yes. Well, not a new one. I'm actually meeting Gavin here. We're going to keep up with the mapping we've started."

"The map of Haven?"

"Yes. The city is so much larger than we'd ever guessed. There are other courtyards, Kendie, other fountains, other Main Halls. This is just one small part of the city, here where we're all living."

"How many people could live here, do you think?"

"I don't know," Jair replied, shaking his head slowly. Turning toward the west, he pointed into the distance. "We've only gone that way, mapping as we went. It seems clear that this is the true center of the city, where we are, since it's closest to the gate. Gavin and I have gone on for almost three days toward the west, and we haven't come to the end of Haven."

"Wow," Kendie breathed. "Haven could hold hundreds of people, then."

"No," Jair told her. "It could hold *thousands*."

"That's amazing! What if there is no end to the city?"

Jair smiled. "That's what we want to find out."

The clattering of horses' hooves signaled Gavin's approach, and Kendie stepped back, suddenly aware of how close to one another she and Jair had been standing.

"You're going riding, then?" she asked nonchalantly.

"Yes, it's so much faster that way."

"Hello there!" Gavin called out from the back of his mare, leading another horse for Jair. "Are you ready?"

"I'm ready," Jair replied. "I'm sorry, Kendie. I've got to go."

"Of course," she answered. "Have fun exploring. Maybe some day you can show me what you've found?"

"Yes, I can do that," Jair told her, tying the scrolls securely to his saddle, then pulling himself up onto the horse's back. "Ready, Gavin?"

"Let's go."

"Goodbye, Kendie. I'll see you again soon."

"How far out are you going?"

"I'm not sure how far," he replied. "The last time, we traveled west for nearly three days before we turned back. We plan to go for four days this time. So we'll be back here in about a week."

"That's a long time! What will you do for food?"

"We're all loaded up," Gavin told her, patting one of the saddle bags. "We'll be all right."

"And Ovard and the advisors will take care of things while you're gone?" Kendie guessed, "just like the other times?"

"That's right. And there's no need to worry, Kendie," Jair added. "We're not leaving Haven, after all. We'll be safe."

"Of course. I'll see you next week then."

"'Bye, Kendie," Gavin said as he turned his horse away.

"Goodbye!"

Jair waved as he rode after Gavin. "Goodbye, Kendie. I'd like to hear the rest of your song when I get back."

"I'll have it finished by then, I'm sure of it. See you again soon!"

Jair and Gavin rode on in peaceful silence, the clapping of their horses' hooves on the cobblestones and the creaking of leather saddles the only sounds to be heard.

"I'm really glad you're back," Jair eventually commented.

"Are you?"

"Of course. Ovard won't let me go off on these mapping trips alone."

"And that's the only reason you wanted me to get back?" Gavin asked in mock dismay.

Jair laughed. "You know it isn't. You're the closest friend I have. It's not the same when you're gone."

"I'm glad to be back," Gavin replied. "And I know what you mean. I feel the same way."

"What was it really like, being out there? Everything you said at the meeting — was it so terrible? I haven't set foot outside Haven since we got here, not really. I haven't gone *anywhere*."

"It wasn't bad the entire time," Gavin told him. "There are still good people out there. But it was worse this time than it ever has been, for me. We hadn't heard the night screamers so close to any town until now."

Jair sighed and nodded, looking out at the empty homes as they passed them by. "There should be more people living here," he said, his voice heavy. "It's been three years, and there are still so many empty houses. If things keep getting worse out there, I wonder if it will be safe to keep sending search missions? I don't want anyone to get hurt."

"That's a chance we need to take," Gavin replied quickly. "We all know that something might go wrong, every time any of us leaves. But we're willing to risk it, Jair. We have a responsibility, don't we? If we don't go and tell people about Haven, those homes will never be filled, and the people out there will live in the dark for the rest of their lives. We can't just *not* go, and let that happen."

Jair looked over at Gavin in surprise.

"What?"

"I'm glad you're the one who's been leading the missions," Jair told him. "I remember how angry you were when I first chose you to go with Dursen. I thought you might never speak to me again."

Gavin chuckled. "People change."

"As long as it's for the better," Jair told him. "And you have changed for the better."

"So have you," Gavin told him. "Becoming Haven's leader. You are good at it, Jair. No matter how you might doubt yourself at times, you *are* a good leader. Just don't forget how to enjoy yourself."

"I don't think I need to worry about that," Jair remarked, "as long as I have you here to remind me."

"Do you remember that day," Gavin asked, laughing, "when you tried to build that small cart? You cut all those branches and then realized you didn't have any nails, so you tied them together with strips of leather …"

Jair laughed along with Gavin as he told the story.

"… and then you got the wheels on and had one of Hiller's dogs pull it, but when he started to run, the whole thing fell apart!"

"That was almost two years ago!" Jair protested while Gavin laughed. "It's still funny, though."

"You're right, it is funny," Jair had to admit. "But it's nothing compared to the time you drank an entire flagon of wine after your parents told you that you couldn't have *any*!"

Gavin groaned, and Jair laughed at him. "You were so sick!"

Gavin laughed along with Jair. "I could never forget that. You're right," he admitted, "Your story isn't near as bad as mine." His laughter settled into an amused chuckle. "Do you think you'll ever try to build another cart?"

"I don't know, maybe. If I have the time for it."

"Try to *make* time. You almost never attend any classes anymore; you can't possibly be busy *every* hour of *every* day."

"No," Jair replied. "But even when I'm not busy, my mind is. The city is almost always trying to tell me something."

"Like it is now?"

"Yes."

"What do you think it is?"

"I have no idea."

"Maybe you'll find out while we're out mapping," Gavin suggested.

"Maybe I will," Jair replied, trying not to have doubts. Things had become clear to him eventually, every other time Haven wanted him to know something. They would this time, too.

*Eventually.*

# ~ 10 ~

Brace shoved the large bed back against the far wall of the clinic, surprised at how heavy it was.

"Good, now push it over that way," Tassie directed.

Brace pushed.

"No, the other way," Tassie corrected. "Put the head against the wall by the window."

Brace sighed. "Right," he replied, looking over his shoulder at her. "Of course."

He wasn't about to begrudge Tassie his help in rearranging the main room of the clinic, if that was what she wanted. Of course he would help her. And he did *want* to help her. But that didn't make the work any easier.

Stepping around to the opposite end of the bed, he gathered his strength and leaned into it until it stopped, touching the far wall.

"Is that all right?" Brace asked.

Tassie smiled. "Perfect."

"Good," Brace replied, "because I don't think I have it in me to move it again."

"Now we just need to move this shelving," Tassie went on. She smiled at the surprised tilt of Brace's eyebrows. "I'll help you," she added with a laugh. "We can empty the shelves first, then it will be easier to move it around to the other wall."

Brace took a deep breath. "All right. This is the last of it, isn't it?"

"It is. Do you need some water?"

"No," Brace replied, shaking his head. "I'm all right. Let's just get it finished."

Tassie nodded and went straight to work, lifting the jars of glass or clay and setting them down on the nearby bed. Brace followed suit, trying to watch her closely without having her notice. She seemed determined. Determined to finish the changes she wanted made to the clinic, yes, but there seemed to be something more. A determination to go on with life as it had been, Brace assumed. She seemed to be more and more herself, and though Brace was pleased, he was afraid to let himself feel too much relief. This normalcy felt fragile, like ancient glass, and if he didn't handle it the right way, it could shatter.

The shelves were nearly empty when Brace heard a knock at the door just before it opened. He nudged Tassie's arm as Dursen entered the room, and she turned to look.

"Are you too busy now to see to someone?" Dursen asked.

"No," Tassie replied. "Of course not."

"Oh, I'm glad to hear it." Dursen turned and gently pulled Nerissa into the room, closing the door behind her.

"What's wrong?" Tassie asked, setting the clay jars she held back onto the shelf.

"Well, I just don't know, really," Dursen replied. "She's just been getting sick these past three days."

"Getting sick? Do you mean vomiting?"

"Yes," Nerissa answered. "I'm sorry to bother you about this, it's probably nothing. I just feel queasy. I haven't been eating anything out of the ordinary."

"Do you feel sick right now?"

"A little."

Brace watched as Tassie looked at Nerissa's hands, then peered at her face. It still amazed him that she could pick up on such subtle things to help her determine what might be ailing one of her patients.

"Have you been drinking enough water?"

"Yes, I think so."

Tassie stepped back and stood by pensively for a moment, then turned to look at Dursen. "Could … could she be pregnant?" she asked, and Brace felt himself tense up. He knew how those words must have stung for Tassie to say them.

"Well," Dursen replied as Nerissa's eyes widened in surprise, "surely she *could* be."

"You have ways of knowing for certain, don't you?" Nerissa asked, her voice unmistakably full of hope.

"I do," Tassie replied. "Come with me. It won't take long."

The women disappeared into the back room of the clinic, leaving Brace and Dursen behind. Brace glanced at the small jar he held in his hands, then set it down on the bed and leaned back against the wall.

"So, Nerissa might be pregnant?" Brace asked, and Dursen shrugged.

"It seems she might."

"Congratulations."

"Can't say that for sure just yet," Dursen pointed out, and Brace nodded.

"But if she is, I'll have been the first to say it."

Dursen grinned, then noticed the jars piled all over the bed. "What've you been doing here?"

"Oh," Brace replied nonchalantly, "just moving things around. Tassie thought the clinic needed a new look, or something."

"Right. Of course." Dursen glanced toward the side door distractedly.

"How are things going with the crops?" Brace asked, trying to keep Dursen's mind occupied.

"What? Oh – it's fine, o' course. Not too much work to be done, really. Planting, harvesting. Feeding the horses and such. Much easier farming here than it was out there."

"So you've been doing all right, then?"

"I have," Dursen replied with a smile. "*We* have. Thank you for asking. What about you and Tassie? I know she took it hard when old Lomar passed."

Brace nodded solemnly. "She's much better. Thank you."

"And y'are well enough?" Dursen went on. "Keeping the gate watch, and all?"

"Yes, I keep busy enough."

Dursen causally walked across the floor toward Brace, glancing back at the closed door.

"Do ya ever miss going out on search missions?" he asked, and Brace raised an eyebrow in thought.

"Maybe somewhat," he answered. "But I don't miss crossing the mountains, and I don't miss the worry about running into trouble. And I don't miss knowing I've left Tassie behind. What about you? Do you miss it?"

"Nah, not really," Dursen replied. "It's just sort of strange, being here while there are others coming here from someplace else, and not being a part of finding them."

"Hmm," Brace responded. "I guess I never thought about that. I've just been trying to figure out my own life, here with Tassie."

"Y'are doing all right there, aren't you? Truthfully, you've seemed a little down lately."

Brace lightly crossed his arms over his chest, wondering how he should answer. *Had* things been going well? They had seemed to be, until ... But no, he couldn't say anything about it, not until he'd made certain it was all right with Tassie first.

"I'm doing well enough," Brace finally replied with a tilted smile. "Thanks for asking."

The sound of the door opening drew the men's attention, and they both looked over to see Tassie and Nerissa entering the front room once again.

"Well?" Dursen asked, stepping up beside his wife. "Is she, or isn't she?"

"I'll be able to tell you in the morning," Tassie informed him kindly. "In the meantime, take this." Going to the near-empty shelf, she scanned it quickly, then turned to what had been placed on the bed. Finding what she wanted, she measured some crushed herbs into a small cloth envelope. "Make this into some tea," she directed, giving it to Nerissa. "It will help ease your sickness."

"Thank you again," Nerissa told her. "I'm sorry for the trouble, for interrupting your work."

"It's nothing," Tassie replied with a wave of her hand. "I'm here to help people first, not to organize the furniture."

Nerissa smiled as Dursen awkwardly shook Tassie's hand.

"Thank you so much, the both of you. Should I come around here first thing tomorrow to find out?"

"After breakfast," Tassie replied, amused at his enthusiasm.

"Right. Thank you again. I just been so worried, is all."

"Come on, Dursen," Nerissa interrupted, taking his arm. "You've thanked them enough. Let them work. We'll come back tomorrow and find out."

Dursen nodded, grinning, then waved to Brace. "See ya tomorrow, then."

"Take care of yourselves," Tassie called out after them as they left.

Brace stood unmoving, waiting for Tassie to say something before he assumed he knew what was on her mind. She had seemed so strong, and now *this*. Would another woman's pregnancy feel like a harsh reminder of her perceived failure to have a child, of her loss?

Tassie turned and half-smiled at Brace, wordlessly going back to work, emptying the shelves of their contents. Brace worked alongside her, and soon the shelf was empty. He easily pulled it around to the other wall, making sure that it was level and straight, sturdy on its footing, before beginning the task of putting away Tassie's collection of jars.

*Why didn't she say anything?* Brace wondered as she worked beside him. He did not want to upset her, but this silence left him with no idea whatsoever as to what she might be feeling. Wasn't she always the one who wanted *him* to share what was on his mind?

"That was unexpected," he commented when he knew she could see his face.

"It was," she replied, not missing a single step.

"Do you think," Brace went on, "it's likely that Nerissa *is* pregnant? And that's why she's been feeling ill?"

Tassie stopped, resting her hand on the shelf at her shoulder. "I think it is."

Brace nodded, unsure of what to say next. He could see that Tassie had been affected by Nerissa's visit, but she seemed more pensive than sorrowful.

"Are you all right?" he asked her, and she simply nodded.

"I think now is the right time to tell you what has been on my mind," she told him.

"What's that?" Brace asked tensely.

"I've been thinking about it for a while, but I wasn't sure when to bring it up. I think ... well, I think I'm ready for us to try again."

"Try again?" Brace asked. "To have a baby, you mean?"

"Yes."

"*Tassie.* Are you certain about this? All that time of nothing happening, and then losing the baby so early on? Are you sure you're willing to risk going through all of that again?"

"It did happen that way, once. That doesn't mean it will happen that way again. But yes, I am willing to take that chance."

"I'm not sure I am," Brace muttered.

"Brace," Tassie scolded lightly. "You know you need to speak more clearly than that."

"I'm not sure I am ready," Brace repeated. "I feel like I'm just starting to get you back. I don't want to lose you again."

"You never lost me."

"I feel like I did. You weren't yourself, Tassie, after we lost the baby. But how could you be? It was a terrible thing, what happened. I'm just afraid what it will be like for you if it happens again."

"I've thought about that too," she told him. "But how will we ever know if we don't try?"

"Are you sure you're not thinking about this just because of Nerissa being here?"

"No," she replied quietly. "It's been on my mind for some time. Do you think you could consider it, at least?"

Brace hesitated, moving more jars from the bed to the shelf. "I can do that much," he finally answered. "I'll think about it. I just want us to be happy, Tassie. Do you know that's all I really want?"

"I know. You do make me happy, Brace. There are times when we can get flustered with each other, I know. But I'm glad I have you for a husband. You do make me happy."

"And having a baby would make you happier?"

Tassie nodded slowly. "I'm sure it would."

Brace let out a breath. "All right," he said, wondering if Tassie could pick up on his hesitation. "I'm willing to try again if you are."

Tassie smiled thinly. "Thank you, Brace."

"Right," he replied. "Well, let's get this shelving filled, get these jars put up. Then," he added with a smirk, "you can tell me if you've got any more heavy furniture you want me to push around the room."

At last, they were four days' ride from the Fountain Court, and Jair stood in the empty road in a part of Haven that he had never seen until now.

This part of the city didn't look any different from the rest of it – the same wide, smooth streets, the same blue-gray stone of the houses. A bit farther on, he could see more lightstone walls indicating another round courtyard, with yet another fountain waiting to be filled with water.

With the horses loosely tied at the edge of an overgrown garden to graze, Gavin and Jair had stopped to refresh themselves and study their unfinished map.

"This is the road, right here," Gavin announced, pointing to their location. "This garden is the last thing we marked down when we came this way the last time."

"It is," Jair agreed. "See the courtyard, there?" he asked as Gavin began sketching with a charcoal pencil.

"I do," he replied, glancing up from his work.

"There should be more vine fruit growing inside it," Jair went on. "And ... and another Main Hall ... off to the right..."

Gavin looked up, frowning. "What's wrong?"

"I don't know," Jair muttered distractedly. "I think there's something over there."

"*Something?*" Gavin asked. "What are you talking about?"

Without another word, Jair went off at a quick pace toward the courtyard.

"Jair?" Gavin called out after him, then followed, almost running to keep up.

Jair stopped when he neared the center of the courtyard, looking all around it.

"What are you doing?" Gavin huffed, catching up with him, awkwardly clutching the map.

"I'm looking," Jair answered.

"For what?"

"I'm not sure."

"How will you know if you find it?"

Seeing nothing other than the quiet fountain and the red vine fruit growing along the walls of the courtyard, Jair went on again without answering, cutting away to the right.

"There's something out here," Jair said as he hurried along.

"How do you know that? We've never been out this far."

"I just feel it, all right? It's like all the other times when the city told me about something. I just know there's something up here that it wants me to find."

The boys hurried on through a grouping of long-empty homes toward what they expected to be another stretch of land that would be used for planting. Instead, the ground sloped upward steeply toward Haven's Woods, revealing the mouth of what appeared to be a small, rocky cavern.

Jair stopped suddenly and gazed at it in surprise.

"What is it?" Gavin asked, stopping beside him, catching his breath.

"I'm not sure," Jair answered quietly, continuing toward it slowly.

"How do you know it's safe?"

"This is *Haven*," Jair pointed out. "And the city drew me here to find it. It can't be anything dangerous."

Jair went on toward the cavern, and Gavin followed him, knowing he was right. Their boots crunched over small loose rocks strewn across the ground around the gaping mouth of the cavern, which rose several feet higher than their heads.

"How far back does it go?" Gavin asked.

"I can't tell. I'm going in."

"It's dark in there. You don't have any light."

Jair smiled. "No, but I know where to get some."

In a few moments, Jair had obtained a palm-sized piece of glowing lightstone, which Gavin knew the city had given him; that Jair had *asked* for it.

"Now I can see to go in," Jair commented cheerfully. "Will you follow me?"

"Sure," Gavin replied with a shrug. "Why not? If you're supposed to go in there, it must be worth seeing, right?"

"Right."

Jair held the lightstone out in front of him as he slowly progressed into the cavern. Rocks crunched under their feet as they went in, the roof of the cavern sloping gradually upward before them.

"I don't really see anything in here," Gavin commented. "There are just a lot of rocks."

"That's all I see, too," Jair agreed, disappointed. He wasn't certain what he had expected to find, but... rocks? Only rocks?

Catching a glimpse of the back of the cavern in the soft white light, Jair turned and started to leave, but abruptly stopped and looked around once again.

"Gavin, wait."

"Why?"

Jair didn't answer; he had that far-away look in his eyes. Gavin had seen it before, and he knew better than to try and talk to him at that moment. Instead, he followed him as he walked slowly, curiously, toward one side of the cavern.

Kneeling down, Jair picked up one of the loose rocks resting on the ground, and he studied it closely.

"These aren't just rocks," Jair stated, looking around again at the cavern walls.

The city was speaking to Jair again, Gavin knew.

"Fire?" Jair said quietly, surprise in his voice. "The rocks ... and fire? What does one have to do with the other?"

"Don't even try to ask me," Gavin told him. "I haven't the slightest idea."

"Come with me," Jair said as he quickly turned and headed out into the open. Setting down the lightstone and the mysterious, creamy-white rock, Jair pulled out his small knife and flint, striking them together just above the rock.

"What ..." Gavin began, but he stopped when a spark flew out and landed on the rough surface of the small, pale rock, and a flame enveloped it, flickering a bright yellow-orange.

"The rock catches fire?" Gavin asked in surprise as Jair looked up at him, smiling in amazement.

"The rocks burn," Jair announced. "It's a fuel source. And ... and they'll never burn up. They give off heat and flame, but they won't burn away to nothing. They just last and last." He shook his head, smiling. "We don't need to cut down any more trees. *This* is what we can use from now on, for cooking and for heat."

"How do you put the fire out when you're done?" Gavin asked him.

"Pour water on it," Jair replied simply. "When it's dry, it will light again."

"How do you know all of that?"

103

Jair shrugged. "I just know."

Gavin looked at the strange, burning rock, then at Jair, then back at the rock. "Well, that is … useful," he commented.

"Yes, it is," Jair agreed, pulling himself up onto his feet and unstopping his flask. Letting a stream of water pour out onto the stone, it hissed as the flame was extinguished, releasing a small cloud of steam.

"Come with me," Jair said to Gavin, stepping back toward the cavern.

"And do what?"

"Gather up a bunch of these rocks," he answered. "We'll take them back with us, and everyone can start using them!"

"What about the mapping?" Gavin called out as Jair ran back toward the cavern. "We just got out here, and you want to go back already?"

"This is more important," Jair replied, glancing back over his shoulder. "Come on!"

Gavin sighed and let his arms drop down to his sides, holding the map in one hand and the charcoal pencil in the other. "I can't believe it," he muttered.

"Are you coming?" Jair called out to him. Gavin tucked the pencil into the map and rolled it up tightly.

"Yes, Jair," he replied. "I'm coming."

# ~ 11 ~

Brace stepped out of the Main Hall into the sunlight, glad to be finished with another day's duty on the gate watch.

He shut the door of the building behind him, breathing in the scented air of springtime. The morning had been long and quiet; the only thing he'd seen approaching the gate was a group of curious deer who had looked on in interest for several moments before bounding off into the trees.

These uneventful days went by so slowly, making for a long morning spent in the solitude of the large white room. Gate watch days were quiet, yes, but they made up for the days when it seemed that everything in Haven was changing.

A week had passed now, since just such an event. Jair and Gavin had returned early from their mapping trek across the southern part of the city with unexpected news. Jair had discovered a new fuel source, and he had called for a spontaneous meeting in order to show everyone how it could be used, as well as providing each household with their own supply of the combustible stones they had brought back with them. This had been an important discovery, Brace had to agree. No longer was there a need to cut down any more trees to burn for fuel, which meant less work to do, and more sustainable forests.

Days of excitement, days of calm. Everything seemed to happen in circles, he thought as he made his way toward the clinic.

He and Tassie had come full circle as well. After the past year of failing to have a child, and suffering the loss that they had, they were now right back where they had started. Just one big circle.

Did all of life work that way? Brace wondered. When he had lived his years as a thief, everything had seemed to go just that way: finding a place to settle into, stealing when he had the chance, cheating at games of chips, flirting with attractive women. And whenever he felt he'd gotten in too deep, he would run and start all over again somewhere else. He'd done it so many times, there was no way he could remember them all.

He was grateful to have broken that cycle, but now he felt caught in the cycle of trying and failing, and the cycle of peace and upheaval that was life in Haven these days. Every time new people arrived in the city, things changed. Every time Jair made a new discovery, things changed. Then, as time went along, everything would settle back into the usual calm, and the days would pass by uneventfully.

Couldn't life be a forward path, Brace wondered, and not a circle? Why did he always feel caught, spinning around and around and not getting anywhere? He had thought, after making the decision to give up his old way of life, after deciding to settle down with Tassie, that everything would be different. Instead, he'd simply moved out of one cycle into another one. It made him wonder if he could really ever succeed at anything.

He had been good enough as a thief, but where had that gotten him? He had only been wasting his life, failing in the worst possible way. And now he was failing again, unable to father a child. He wasn't only failing himself this time, but Tassie as well. She had told him not to blame himself, but he couldn't help but wonder.

Here they were, two weeks into that cycle all over again, back to just *trying*.

And if life really was just one big circle, did that apply to Haven as well? Would the city become fully populated, as it should be, only to have everyone leave again in a thousand, two thousand years? Well, at least he wouldn't be around to see that happen.

Brace stepped up to the clinic and rapped his knuckles on the wooden door before entering, not for Tassie's sake – she wouldn't hear it – but for the benefit of any patient she might have. He could hear someone speaking inside, so Tassie wasn't alone.

"Come in, Brace!" she called out, and he stepped inside.

Kalen sat on the window seat in the newly-arranged clinic, and Tassie stood nearby, holding a small rolled bandage. The little smile that she gave

Brace brought back memories of when they'd first met, and it lifted his spirits. He smiled in return before she turned toward her patient.

"Hold your hand out," she directed Kalen, and he obeyed.

Tassie expertly wrapped Kalen's hand in the strip of cloth and tucked the end under snugly.

"What happened?" Brace asked lightly, leaning against the wall.

"An accident," Kalen replied sheepishly. "Fixing up one of the empty houses. I got careless, is all. Just a scratch, really."

"You should be fine in a few days," Tassie told him, and he nodded and stood to go.

"Thank you," he said. "Should I come back soon and have you take a look at it?"

"Yes, that would be wise. Come back in two days. And don't use your hand in the meantime."

"Yes ma'am," Kalen replied with a smile. "Good day, Brace."

"See you again soon," Brace replied as Kalen left the clinic. "How have things been today?" he asked Tassie.

"Well enough," she told him. "Not very busy, but that is a good thing."

"You're right there," Brace agreed.

"You didn't see anything at the gate, then?"

"No," Brace replied. "Nothing much at all going on right now, is there?"

Tassie shook her head. "That's all right, though. It could change at any time. And it will give our new friends the chance to see Haven as it really is. The ones who came from Pran's Helm," she added, seeing Brace's raised eyebrow.

"Ah, yes. They're settling in all right?"

"As far as I can tell," Tassie replied. She glanced at the small mess she'd piled on the table beside her. "Will you do something for me while I get this cleared away?"

"What's that?"

"I have some more of this tea," she told him, taking two packets down from the nearby shelf. "It's for Nerissa, to help with the nausea. And another that will help her and the baby stay healthy. She should just be running out of what I gave her last week."

"Sure," Brace replied, taking the packets of tea from Tassie. "I can take it to her. Will she be at the house?"

"I would think she'll be out at the gardens with Dursen. Try the northwestern one. They said they were going to start planting seeds there this week."

"All right," Brace agreed, giving her a quick kiss on the cheek, smiling when he noticed that she glanced toward the door out of habit, concerned that someone might be watching them. "I'll be back soon. Don't overwork yourself, all right?"

Tassie smiled. "I'll try not to."

～

Brace raised a hand to his eyes to shade them from the sun, peering out across the open stretch of farm land. Fortunately, he could see that there were several people working there; Tassie's guess had been correct.

He went on toward the garden, cutting across the smooth ground between the last two homes in that area of the city, making his way up to the first long, furrowed row of soil. People were scattered here and there, standing in the dirt, planting the seeds of the next crop. Brace spotted Dursen nearly halfway across the field, and though Nerissa was not with him at the moment, he was not alone. Coming closer, Brace could see a young girl with red-blonde hair working closely at Dursen's side, along with one of the young men who had recently arrived from Pran's Helm.

"Hello there!" Brace called out, and Dursen turned in his direction.

"Brace! What brings you out this way?"

"Tassie sent me on a little mission," he replied, squinting into the sun. "I've brought more tea for Nerissa. Tassie thought she might be running out."

"Thank you," Dursen replied. "She might be, I'm not certain o' that."

"Is she out here with you?" Brace asked, watching the girl push seeds into the soil.

"Yah," Dursen told him. "She's just gone up that way a bit. She'll be making her way back here soon enough."

"Mister Dursen, am I doing this right?" the girl asked, wiping dirt from her hands.

"Yes, Marit. Just remember not to bury the seeds too deep. They need to be able to feel the sunlight."

"What is it you're planting?" Brace asked the girl.

"Beans," she replied with a broad smile.

"Brace?" the young man asked, taking a tentative step forward. "Is that your name? Brace?"

"Yes, that's right. And you are … ?"

"Eaton," he replied, shaking Brace's hand.

"Oh yes, I remember," Brace told him, recalling his name from the introductions at the meeting, recalling that Shale had asked about his missing fingers. "Weren't you working as a blacksmith in Pran's Helm?"

"I was," Eaton replied softly. "I thought I'd try something new."

"This is a good place for that," Brace told him as a large, pale-colored spider dug its way out of the soil and scurried across the ground.

"Eek!" Marit exclaimed, chasing after it to try and squash it.

"Leave it be," Dursen told her. "Don't hurt it. It'll be good for the crops."

"But it might bite me," she protested.

Dursen smirked. "I've never seen a spider quite like that anywhere but here. If it's native to Haven, it'll do ya no harm."

"All right," Marit relented, stepping away from the crawling beast until it buried itself under the dirt once again.

"So, yah, it's true," Dursen addressed Brace. "Eaton here's doing a great thing, learning about our way of farming." He clapped Eaton on the shoulder, and the young man looked down shyly. "He'll catch on fast, I'm sure."

Eaton grinned doubtfully. "I'll try, at least."

"Not too much to worry about here," Dursen encouraged him. "Just plant the seeds right, and they should grow healthy on their own. They get quite a bit of water from under the ground, so we don't need to give them much extra."

"What if it rains?" Eaton asked him.

Dursen grinned. "It don't rain here."

"Ever?"

"Nah. There's no need for it. The crops near grow themselves, and the water in the lake never gets low. No need for rain."

"*Amazing.*"

"This place will never stop surprising you," Brace told Eaton. "Wait and see."

Eaton nodded, his eyes wide. "I'm sure you're right."

"Come on, Eaton," Marit spoke up. "Will you help me plant this row of seeds? We'll get done faster that way."

Eaton glanced at Dursen, who nodded. "Go on ahead."

"Sure, Marit," Eaton replied. "I'll help you."

Brace stood beside Dursen in the warm, dirt-scented air of spring as Eaton joined Marit, the two of them making their way down the long, straight row of soil.

"You've got quite a team out here," Brace commented, swinging his hand at a buzzing insect.

"I have," Dursen replied. "It's important work, keeping the crops growing. Plenty of folks want to help."

Dursen ran his fingers through his hair, then shook his head slowly, a smile growing on his face.

"Got something on your mind?" Brace asked him.

"Surely," Dursen replied. "I never thought I'd have anything like this in all my life. Being the lead of a team of workers on some farm, being married, expecting a little one…" His voice trailed off and he looked at Brace with a guilty expression. "I'm sorry I said that."

"It's all right," Brace told him. "Tassie and I are all right, really. Actually … she's decided she's ready to try again for a baby." He shrugged. "So we'll just see what happens."

Dursen smiled. "I wish the best for you."

"Thanks. How is Nerissa these days?"

"Much better. She don't feel too sick any more. That tea of Tassie's really seems to be helping."

"Good. Well, here's more of it," Brace added, handing the packets to Dursen.

"Thank you."

Brace watched along with Dursen as Marit and Eaton reached the end of the planting row, turning to start their way back toward them on the next, a gentle wind blowing their hair away from their faces.

"Brace!" Nerissa's voice broke though the quiet. "Hello! What brings you out this way?"

"I was just delivering your tea for Tassie," he replied as Nerissa came up and gave him a quick kiss on the cheek, her long, dark blue dress swishing against the dirt at her feet.

Ordinarily, Brace would have been caught off guard by her display of affection, but he had learned long ago that that was just her way.

"I got it here," Dursen told Nerissa, holding up the packets of tea for her to see.

"Thank you," she said, taking the tea in one hand and holding Dursen's hand with the other. "And thank Tassie for me."

"I will," Brace replied. He couldn't help but see how happy Nerissa was, how healthy. Her cheeks were full of color from spending her days in the sunlight, and her dark eyes shone with joy, Brace thought, with the knowledge that she was carrying a little one inside of her. They were so happy, the two of them. So why did Brace feel an edge of bitterness rising up suddenly? He should be sharing their joy, not resenting them their blessing, despite the fact that he and Tassie had been denied that blessing themselves.

"I should be getting back home," Brace told them, trying to keep his tone light.

"Thank you, Brace," Nerissa told him again. "Give Tassie a hug and a kiss for me, will you?"

Brace managed a smile. "I can do that."

Dursen lifted his hand to wave goodbye. "Have a nice evening."

"Thanks," Brace replied. "You too. And don't work your people too hard," he added with a teasing grin.

# ~ 12 ~

"Avi Penhallow," Jair spoke formally, "Will you take the vows as an advisor for the city of Haven, today, before all who have gathered here?"

"I will," the older man replied solemnly.

Jair couldn't help but smile. Avi would make a great addition to his small team of advisors, and Jair was truly glad that he had agreed to accept the position.

"Will you promise to share your wisdom with the other advisors, accepting their wisdom in return?"

"I will."

Jair lowered his eyes slightly as he continued. The next question always made him feel awkward.

"Will you promise to submit to the leadership of the overseer in all circumstances?"

"I will," Avi answered firmly.

Jair looked up at him. "Thank you," he said quietly, and Avi smiled, accentuating the creases at the corners of his eyes.

"Ovard?" Jair asked. "Will you lead the passing of the wine?"

"Certainly," Ovard replied, taking the ornately carved goblet from the table behind him. Taking a sip of the wine, he passed it on to Shayrie, who took a small drink herself, handing it off to her husband. When each of them had partaken of the wine, the goblet came to Avi, who held it a moment before taking a drink himself.

Signaling the closing of the ceremony, Avi turned and handed the goblet to Jair, who then took a drink, making it all official.

With a smile, Jair turned toward those who had gathered to witness the occasion. "Welcome Avi Penhallow, newest member of the advisors of Haven," he announced, and everyone began to applaud.

"Thank you all for coming," Jair continued. "Feel free to –"

"Wait!" Korian's wife Medarrie called out, hurrying toward the front of the room. "I'm sorry to interrupt," she apologized, seeing Jair's startled expression. "I – *we*," she went on, clutching a folded bundle of cloth in her hands, "Yara and Dorianne and I, we wanted to surprise you. I can see that we have," she added with a laugh.

"Surprise us?" Jair asked. "With what?"

"Ovard gave us permission to do this," Medarrie told him as she came closer. "But we didn't want you to know until now."

Jair glanced over his shoulder at Ovard, who was smiling along with the rest of the advisors, Avi included.

"What is it?" Jair asked as Medarrie held out the folded cloth.

"It's mainly for you," she told him, "but it's really for everyone. You'll see."

Confused, Jair accepted the gift, slowly lifting the corner of the white cloth. Larger and larger it grew each time he unfolded it, until finally it dropped open, and he held it up at the corners, while those gathered in the room reacted in surprise and delight.

The large white cloth bore an image, finely woven in blue thread – the frolicking deer which had been carved into the stone on the back wall of the meeting room, where they now stood.

"You made this?" Jair asked in awe, gathering the banner over his arm and running his hand over its surface.

"We did," Medarrie replied. "The three of us."

"How?"

Medarrie smiled. "Our secret."

"This is … *perfect*," Jair told her. "It doesn't seem like enough to say thank you."

Ovard came close and rested a hand on Jair's shoulder. "You've long said that Haven needed its own flag, its own crest. Well, now it does. All you've got to do is find a place to hang it up."

Jair couldn't stop smiling, gazing at the cloth banner in amazement.

"Thank you Medarrie, Yara, Dorianne. This is the best gift anyone has ever given me."

There was applause once again, the meeting over at last, as Jair's team of advisors – his *friends* – gathered close to admire Haven's flag along with him. Eventually, finally, Gavin was able to make his way to the front of the room, as Jair was reverently folding the flag away.

"Do you have any idea where you'll hang it?" he asked in greeting.

"I'm not sure," Jair replied. "Someplace where it will be seen as soon as anyone comes in through the gate. This is something I've wanted Haven to have for three years. I can't believe I'm actually holding it in my hands."

"That's really great," Gavin replied simply.

Jair smiled, once again at a loss for words.

"Well, my boy," Ovard said as the Main Hall began to empty, "where shall we keep our banner until it's decided where it will make itself at home?"

Jair considered the question. It had to be somewhere clean and safe…

"In the white room," he answered as soon as the idea came to him. "I think that's the perfect place. It shouldn't take long to decide where to hang it. I think it belongs in the white room until then."

"That is a fine idea," Ovard agreed, holding out his hands. "Would you like me to put it away for you, and allow you to spend a bit of time with your friend?"

"Well…" Jair began, but Gavin cut in.

"We can find a place to hang the banner permanently," he suggested. "We will plan it all out."

Jair looked again at the banner bearing Haven's crest before hesitantly handing it to Ovard. He had desired it for so long, he had a hard time putting it aside.

"All right," Jair told Gavin. "We do need to plan out where to hang it, knowing how big it is."

"I will make certain that it's kept safe," Ovard told Jair as he held the folded banner in his hands.

Jair managed a grin. "I know you will, Ovard. Thank you."

"I will be at the library," Ovard told Jair as he and Gavin left the Hall.

Jair was quiet, pensive, as he walked, while Gavin rambled on.

"That's really amazing," he commented. "They made that banner, just the three of them, and they *really* did manage to keep it a secret. You had no idea?"

"None."

"And Ovard knew," Gavin went on. "What a great gift. They couldn't have found a better time to present it, either."

Jair didn't answer; his eyes were fixed on the ground in front of him as he went along.

"*Could* they?" Gavin asked, testing him.

"What?" Jair asked.

Gavin smirked. "I said, they couldn't have found a better time to give you that banner, could they?"

"No, I suppose not."

"What's going on with you?" Gavin asked. "You were so glad in there when you saw the banner. You were so overwhelmed and excited, and now you're acting like you've just come from the dullest meeting of your life."

"No, I am glad," Jair told him. "I'm very glad. It's just that I haven't found out what it is that Haven is trying to tell me."

"But you *did*," Gavin replied. "You found those burning rocks. Have you forgotten?" he teased.

"No, I haven't forgotten. But that wasn't all of it, finding the rocks. There's something else the city is trying to tell me. It won't let up about it, either."

Gavin shrugged his shoulders. "It must be really important, then, huh?"

"It is. I can feel it. That's all it is, though. Just a feeling. It's not about any certain place, or any certain thing; I'm sure about that. Maybe it's about *someone*."

"Something bad?"

"I don't think so. I *will* find out what it is, somehow. I don't know how, but I'm not giving up on it."

"Just don't let it eat you up," Gavin half-teased.

"I'll try not to."

Making their way down the wide, smooth road from the Main Hall toward the Fountain Court, the sound of laughter reached their ears.

"That sounds like Ona," Gavin commented.

The curved walls surrounding the courtyard parted before them, and they had a clear view of the three-tiered fountain, rising solidly into the air.

They could also see, beside the fountain, Ona and Kendie were laughing, splashing one another with the water flowing down the lowest tier of the fountain.

"You were right," Jair commented, and Gavin smirked.

"Good morning, girls!" he called out, in a voice that Jair knew revealed the mischief that Gavin had on his mind.

Laughing, Ona turned in their direction. "Kendie!" she called out. "Look, it's Jair and Gavin."

Kendie straightened up from the fountain to look, the expression on her face taking Jair by surprise. Was she so surprised to see him there? Did she not *want* to see him?

"Jair!" she exclaimed, running her hands along her hair. "I thought you were at a special ceremony."

"It's over," he replied lightly.

Ona stood close beside Kendie, clutching her arm and laughing softly.

"Stop!" Kendie scolded, her cheeks reddening.

Ona laughed again, drying her hands on her dress.

Gavin nudged Jair with his elbow and winked. Jair raised an eyebrow, but Gavin was already sauntering toward the fountain. He reached out his hand, letting the cool water run through his fingers.

"Do you like getting wet?" he asked the girls.

"A little," Ona replied. "It's a warm enough day."

"A little?" Gavin asked, taking hold of Ona's arms and tugging her toward the fountain. "What about a *lot*?"

"No!" Ona exclaimed. "No, Gavin, no!" she laughed as she protested.

"Don't you dare!" Kendie joined in as Jair stood by, watching and laughing. He laughed harder still when Kendie splashed Gavin, flinging water at him by handfuls from the base of the fountain.

"All right, all right!" Gavin said as he released Ona, who immediately joined Kendie in soaking him.

"That's enough!" Gavin exclaimed with laughter in his voice. "I'm drenched! That's enough!"

Only when he was certain there was no more water flying around did Jair come over to join them. Gavin tried to dry his face with his damp sleeves. "I wasn't really going to throw you in, Ona. You got me twice as wet as yourself."

"Oh, poor thing," Ona replied in mock sympathy. "It's a warm day. You'll dry."

Gavin sat on one of the benches, smiling and flinging water from his hair.

"How did the ceremony go?" Kendie asked, looking at Jair.

"It was great, thanks."

"Did Medarrie give you the flag?"

"She did," Jair replied in surprise. "Am I the only person in Haven who didn't know about it?"

"Not the *only* one. Yara just showed it to us at the school yesterday. It was a good secret to keep though, wasn't it?"

"The *best* secret."

"Now we've got to find a place to hang it up," Gavin told her.

"Will it be here, in the Fountain Court?" Ona asked.

"I think this is the best place for it," Jair answered, looking around.

"I can't wait to see it up," Kendie thought aloud.

Jair nodded, absently rubbing at the side of his face.

He had been doing that more often lately, Kendie thought to herself. Was he wishing he didn't need to bear his markings any longer, or was he simply taking after Ovard, who often rubbed at his short gray beard when he was deep in thought?

"When are you going out on another mission?" Ona asked, sitting on a bench near Gavin's.

"Soon," he replied. "In another week, maybe."

"Where will you go?"

"We haven't ..." he began, but was cut short by Persha storming into the courtyard, wearing a deep scowl.

"Persha?" Gavin asked in surprise. "What's wrong?"

"Nothing," she snapped. "I'm going home."

"Something's wrong," Gavin challenged. "You're obviously angry. Did you have a fight with Bahadur again?"

"Ugh, don't even mention his name!" Persha blurted out in response. "I can't stand him! The stubborn ... clot-headed ... *ugh*!"

"Persha ..." Gavin began, but she waved him off.

"Forget it! I don't want to hear it!"

She marched her way out of the courtyard toward home, leaving the rest of them in shocked silence.

"Wow," Gavin finally spoke, after Persha had gone out of sight.

"It's just another one of their arguments," Ona said quietly. "Isn't it?"

"I don't know," Gavin replied. "I've never seen her that angry. She's never said she didn't want anyone to even say his *name*."

Kendie nervously chewed at a fingernail. She felt bad for Persha, and for Bahadur. She did hate to see them argue so much. She could never wish trouble on anyone. But she had to admit to herself that the main reason she wanted Persha to be with Bahadur was so Jair wouldn't be distracted by her. She thought she could see it in his face even now, that far-away look he always had when he was working something out in his mind.

Kendie had all but convinced herself that she could forget about trying to get Jair to notice her, and just be a friend to him. Now this had happened, and Kendie was right back where she'd started, full of jitters at the thought that Jair might pursue Persha instead of *her*.

Would this *never* end?

# ~ 13 ~

B race awoke to the loud twittering of birds outside the bedroom window. He stirred, lying on his stomach, and looked up blinking at the daylight. Stretching his arms, he thought it odd when his right hand felt only the bedcovering. Tassie was up already? She usually woke him in the morning.

Had she already gone to work at the clinic? Was she even scheduled to be there today, or was it Ronin?

Brace struggled to remember, rubbing his face in an attempt to wake himself up, pushing back his hair lazily. He closed his eyes and sighed. He wished, not for the first time, that he could call out Tassie's name and have her hear him from the front room. Some things would just be so much simpler if she could hear.

Well, she *couldn't*. She never could, and she never would. There had been a time when they had thought eating Haven's red vine fruit might restore her sense of hearing, as it had healed other wounds or illnesses, but nothing had ever come of it. It was no real loss, though. It simply meant life would carry on for Tassie the way it always had. Nothing more.

Brace finally pulled himself out of the bed, washed and dressed, and made his way into the kitchen, trying to stifle a yawn.

Tassie wasn't there; it must be her day to serve at the clinic after all. Well, he would stop by there to say good morning before heading out to see where he might be of some use for the day. Brace glanced around to see where Tassie might have set out his breakfast – usually a slice of bread and a mug of tea – but he didn't see it anywhere.

Odd.

A sense of uneasiness started forming in his stomach, and he tried to ignore it. *She doesn't need to set anything out for me,* he thought. *I'm perfectly capable...*

He had to go and check the front door to be certain. If Tassie was working at the clinic today, she would have hung the medic's crest on the door.

Brace felt his nerves grow tense as he crossed the front room of the house, pulling open the door.

It wasn't there. No medic insignia, no slice of bread, no Tassie.

This wasn't like her. In fact, it wasn't right. No, something was wrong. Brace felt the unease rise from his stomach to his chest as he left the house, pulling the door closed behind him.

He had to find her. The only place he could think where she would go so early was the clinic, so that was where Brace headed. With the quick pace he kept up, he was at the clinic door in a matter of minutes.

He wasted no time pushing open the door and stepping inside, surprised to see Ronin seated on the padded window ledge, holding a cup of water.

"Brace," he greeted him, his voice sounding tired and heavy.

"Where is Tassie?" Brace blurted out. "Have you seen her? I don't know where she's gone."

"She's here," Ronin told him, slowly standing and taking a step toward him. "She's in the back room."

"Oh," Brace let out a breath. "Thank you. I was starting to worry."

"*Brace,*" Ronin said heavily, coming closer and taking hold of his arm. "I'm sorry, Brace. She came to me early this morning because she was having trouble."

Brace felt his throat tighten. "What do you mean?" he managed.

"It happened again, Brace. I'm sorry. She just couldn't keep the baby."

"What?" Brace blurted out. "She was expecting? I don't understand."

"She didn't tell you?" Ronin asked, his eyebrows raised in alarm. "Brace, I'm sorry."

*Expecting?* Brace's mind whirled. *Couldn't keep the baby ... again?*

"Is she all right?" he managed.

"She will be," Ronin replied. "I'm terribly sorry," he apologized again. "I just assumed you knew she'd been pregnant again."

Brace shook his head, the fear building in his chest turning to anger. "No," he said shortly. "She never told me. How far along was she?"

"About a month, she thinks."

Brace took a breath. "How long ago did she get here?"

"Nearly two hours ago," Ronin told him. "She's just resting now."

Brace nodded slowly, the news of what had happened washing over him like a sheet of icy rain.

"Can I see her?"

"Yes," Ronin answered hesitantly. "But Brace…"

"What?" he asked, avoiding Ronin's eyes.

"She must have had her reasons for not telling you. I think that right now, she doesn't need anyone to say anything. Just be there at her side."

Brace nodded, struggling to keep his emotions in check. "I understand," he replied, and Ronin let him go.

"I will be out here if you need anything."

"Thank you."

Brace let his gaze settle on the door to the back room of the clinic. He *had* to go in there. He had to be there for her. He was beginning to feel like this was more trouble than he could bear, but he couldn't let himself run away from it.

No, he certainly could not. He took a long, slow breath before pulling open the door and stepping into the room.

Tassie lay on her side on the bed near the window, covered in a lightweight quilt. Her eyes were closed, and Brace thought she might be sleeping. He slowly crossed the floor and stood looking down at her for a moment. *How could this have happened? It just wasn't right!*

Brace slowly lowered himself to sit on the edge on the bed near Tassie's knees, and she opened her eyes. Her face instantly clouded over with worry at seeing him there, but he reached out and took her hand.

"Are you all right?" he asked.

Tassie nodded slightly. "Did Ronin tell you what happened?"

"Yes."

"Brace, I'm sorry," she said quietly.

"You don't need to tell me that, Tassie."

"No, I mean I'm sorry I didn't tell you. I was afraid this might happen again. I didn't want us both to get our hopes up only to … have this happen again."

"How long have you known?"

"Four weeks."

Brace sat quietly, taking a long, slow breath.

"I'm so sorry," Tassie whispered as a tear ran down her face.

"No," Brace replied. "*I'm* sorry. You should have told me. I could have been here for you."

Tassie nodded, wiping more tears from her cheeks. Brace tried to swallow, but it caught in his throat as he felt his own eyes grow damp.

"Tassie …" he began, but what could he possibly say?

"I will be all right," Tassie said, turning onto her back and resting a hand on his shoulder. "I'm just tired." She sniffed. "I just don't understand, Brace. Why is this happening to us?"

Brace smoothed her hair away from her face and kissed the top of her head. He knew the anger and confusion, and the sorrow she must be feeling, because he felt it right along with her, all over again.

When she finally looked up at him again, Brace had managed to get his emotions under control enough to respond.

"Please don't think about that right now," he told her. "Let's just stop. Stop thinking about it, and stop *trying*. This is too much, Tassie. It's too much for us to keep going through. We just need to stop."

Tassie nodded as her tears began to flow. Brace shook his head, but she had closed her eyes. He gently leaned over her to kiss her cheek, and she wrapped her arms around him tightly.

"Don't cry, Tassie," he said, though he felt his own tears escaping. There was nothing to say, nothing he could do but put his arms around her, so he did.

*We will get through this*, he told himself again and again as they grieved together. *We will get through this.*

⁓

This time, it was not kept a secret. There was no sense in keeping it to themselves, they had learned that much. What Arden had said had proved true – a burden was lighter when shared.

Brace broke the news first to Ovard, and reluctantly to Jair as well. He had, after all, been raised with Tassie as his sister. It would be wrong to keep it from him. Leandra and Arden were the next to be told, and by then Brace was drained. He had requested that Ronin inform their closest of friends after that, and he had honored Brace's request.

There was no pretending now, no trying to forget what had happened and just go on.

Tassie spent most of the three days that followed at home in bed, and Brace had been right beside her. Few words were spoken. They knew of one another's grief; there was no need to discuss it.

By the fourth day, Tassie had moved to the cushioned window seat, and she sat gazing out through the glass, her expression heavy with sorrow. Brace was grateful to be temporarily freed from his duty on the gate watch, and Ronin was keeping the clinic with help from Kendie and Ona. Arden and Leandra came bringing food, as did Eridan, Dursen and Nerissa, and Shayrie. Brace scarcely needed to leave the house.

No one asked any questions or made any attempt to be cheerful, a fact for which Brace was immensely grateful.

Brace was thankful for the hours he'd had to himself when Leandra came to sit with Tassie. He was thankful as well for brief visits from Arden, Ovard, and Ben-Rickard. He was thankful they had not felt much need to speak, only to be there, to sit with him on the bench outside the house or share a mug of tea at the kitchen table.

Arden had even given Brace a quick, strong embrace on his first visit, an unusual show of emotion for the tall, well-muscled archer.

By the fourth day, though Brace's emotions were still raw, he knew that he and Tassie were surrounded by many people who loved and cared for them, who shared their sorrow, and were willing to share their burden in whatever way they could.

Watching Tassie now as she sat beside the window wrapped in a blanket, he only wished he could do something to ease her sorrow. But if he had learned anything during their previous experience, it was that it would only take time. He had to be patient for the both of them.

A light knock at the door drew Brace out of his thoughts. Glancing again in Tassie's direction, he went to see who it was. Pulling open the door, he saw that Jair had come, for the second time since he'd been told what had happened.

"Hello," Jair greeted him softly.

"Hello, Jair."

"How are things?"

Brace shrugged slightly. "A little better, maybe. Tassie's out of bed, at least."

"That's good," Jair replied with obvious relief. "Can I see her?"

Brace looked back at Tassie, resting on the window seat. If she had realized that someone was at the door, she did not show it.

"I don't know," Brace answered. "I think… not right now. Maybe tomorrow."

Jair nodded. "All right. I just wanted to make sure she's okay."

"She is," Brace told him. "But tomorrow should be better. And bring Ovard, will you?"

"I will," Jair replied, nodding. He hesitated at the door before turning to leave. "How are you, Brace? Are *you* all right?"

Brace shrugged and nodded. "I think so."

"I wish I could do something to help."

"I know. None of us really knows what we're doing, though. We're just having to go through it."

Jair nodded, understanding.

"Come back tomorrow," Brace told him. "Knowing you're here is help enough."

"All right. Until tomorrow."

"Till tomorrow."

Jair waited until the door was fully closed before turning to walk down the smooth, stone-paved road toward home.

His heart was heavy – maybe heavier than it had ever been. When Ovard had first begun to tell him about Haven, that it was a wonderful, perfect place, he had been enchanted at the idea of its existence. When at last they had left Lidden to find it, he'd had mixed emotions, torn between anticipation and anxiety. But when they had found the city at last, he'd been overwhelmed with joy, feeling more strongly than he ever had in his life that he was truly where he was meant to be.

*This perfect place.* Never until now had Jair felt there was anything wrong with the way life worked, here in Haven. But now he was harboring doubts, even a hint of bitterness, and it frightened him. The city was alive, in some way or another, and Jair had built a kinship of sorts with it. Now he felt anger toward it, in a way that he imagined he would feel toward Ovard if he ever told Jair a lie.

Haven was a perfect place; wasn't life here supposed to be perfect as well?

Passing by the entrance to the Fountain Court, Jair glanced in, half expecting to see Kendie there, waiting to talk with him, but it was empty. So be it.

As he wandered the rest of the way home, Jair struggled with his thoughts. How could he harbor any anger toward this amazing city that had become his home, his calling, his purpose? Haven had never made the claim for itself, that life there would be without any unpleasantness. Others may have said it, but Haven itself never had.

Jair paused momentarily outside the door to the house, trying to shrug off some of his heaviness before going inside.

Ovard was home, as Jair had expected him to be. He was glad to see Ovard sitting on an old chair near the hearth, playing a flowing tune on his lyr flute; it always brought him contentment. He enjoyed the last few notes floating through the room before the tune faded away.

"Hello, son."

"Hello," Jair replied, joining Ovard in another empty chair.

"I was hoping you would be home soon."

"I stopped to see Tassie and Brace," he explained. "I think she's doing a little better. They want us to come again tomorrow."

"We will do that, then." Ovard's normally cheerful face was solemn. "In the meantime, there is something important I've been waiting to talk with you about."

"What's that?" Jair asked with a sense of unease.

"I've been meaning to bring this up for some time, but with everything that's been happening…" Ovard shrugged. "I just feel that it is my responsibility to prepare you for your future here, as the overseer. We don't know how long I will be here to help you."

"What are you getting at?" Jair asked fretfully, leaning forward in his chair. "Ovard, is something wrong?"

"No, no," Ovard replied, shaking his head. "I'm sorry, I didn't mean to worry you. I'm perfectly healthy, as far as I know."

Jair nodded, settling back into his seat.

"What I've been meaning to talk with you about," Ovard went on, rubbing thoughtfully at his short gray beard, "is that I have decided to, well, step down, in a way."

"Step down?"

"Yes," Ovard replied, smiling. "You have been doing so much on your own, it's true, as the overseer, and you have been doing it *very* well."

"Thank you."

"Yes, well, what I mean to say is that, since you *are* doing so well, leading meetings, keeping in touch with the various leaders and such, I feel that it's time to give you a bit more responsibility."

Jair raised his eyebrows in concern, and Ovard chuckled. "It isn't *much* more," he told him. "Nothing you can't handle."

"What is it?"

"Well," Ovard replied, settling comfortably in the creaky wooden chair, "As I said, I will be stepping down, or stepping back, rather. I won't be doing any more of the speaking at meetings, or search mission send-offs, that sort of thing. That will all be up to you now."

Jair nodded.

"From now on," Ovard continued, "I will simply be one of your advisors, nothing more. I will still be here for you if you need advice, and I will attend the meetings along with the rest of them. But as for leading the meetings, it will all be up to you."

Jair nodded gravely. "All right."

"You can do this, my boy," Ovard encouraged him cheerfully. "It won't really be too much more than what you've been doing already."

"I know that," Jair replied, looking down at his feet, stretched out in front of him.

"What is it, then? What's got you so down?"

"I just wish things didn't need to change," Jair told him. "Everything just starts to smooth out, and it works, and it makes sense, and then it changes."

"There will always be changes during our lives, Jair. Some will be good, some not. Don't let yourself be closed off to change. You could be missing something important. We can all learn from life's changes if we're open to them."

"All right," Jair replied, leaning his cheek against his fist.

"This isn't too overwhelming for you, is it?" Ovard asked with concern.

"No."

"Then tell me what's troubling you."

Jair shrugged, gazing at the hearth where they would later have a fire. "I just wish I could make things right for Tassie."

Ovard nodded somberly. "I agree with you wholeheartedly on that, my boy."

"It must have been hard for you," Jair began, recalling the fact that Ovard had once had a son, who had died in a fire along with his and Tassie's mothers. "When your family died, how long did it take you?"

"To do what?" Ovard asked, sounding tired.

"For you to really feel like you could go on again. I know it's only been four days for Tassie, but she just seems so weary."

"This isn't quite the same situation," Ovard answered, "but the heartache is much the same, I would think."

"So, how long?"

Ovard shook his head. "I didn't have the luxury of time to grieve. I had a little girl who needed me very much."

A sudden realization came to Jair, and he pulled his feet under him and sat up straighter. "Tassie's mother died when she was young," he thought aloud. "I wonder if she remembers her at all? If she wants to be a mother, the way her own mother was to her?"

Ovard smiled fondly at the memories. "My sister did the best that she could," he told Jair, "and yes, she loved Tassie very much. I'm sure that somewhere inside, Tassie remembers her mother's love. And I know that she will be able to give that love to a child of her own."

"Do you think she'll ever get the chance?"

Ovard sighed. "If only there was some way to know," he replied, then smiled ruefully. "I'm not a prophet. I can't say what will happen in the future; I can only read about what others have predicted."

Jair nodded. "I hope she will, someday. I know Tassie would be a good mother, and Brace would be a good father too."

"I do believe he would, Jair."

Jair sighed into the silence. "I'm not alone," he said quietly.

"Not alone?" Ovard asked. "No, of course you're not alone."

"Oh, it's just an idea I've been getting," Jair explained. "It's from Haven. I don't really know why it's been telling me that, or what it really means."

"Do you feel alone?"

Jair considered the question. "I don't think so. Sometimes I feel... *separated* from everyone else, sort of, being the overseer. Because everyone looks to me as their leader. But I have you, and Jayla and Shayrie, and the rest of them. And there's Gavin – he's a good friend. I know I'm not alone."

"Another mystery to be solved, eh?" Ovard asked with a smile.

"I suppose so."

"Well," Ovard commented, placing his hands on the armrests of the old chair and pushing himself to his feet. "I don't know of anyone who has the strength to solve any mystery on an empty stomach. Will you help me with our supper?"

Jair grinned. "Don't I always?"

Ovard chuckled as he perused the stone shelving on the wall where they had stored fresh fruits, vegetables, grain and eggs.

"Ovard?" Jair asked, standing beside him.

"Yes, son?"

"Just ... please don't get too old too fast, all right?"

Ovard laughed. "I certainly don't plan to, my boy."

# ~ 14 ~

B race settled himself onto the bench at the far side of the long, white table, near the viewing wall, allowing it to sense his presence and remain active.

With Tassie's condition slowly, steadily improving, Brace had come back to serving on the gate watch. This was his second day of service, the last one three days past. Eridan had volunteered to stay with Tassie for company, as she had done when Brace had last left her. Knowing that the two of them had enjoyed a day in the orchard had been quite a relief for Brace. It was far from over, he knew, the grieving - but things were beginning to look up.

Brace had begun to fear that some small part of Tassie would always remain wounded. Every time the thought came to him, he struggled to push it away – what good would it do to dwell on such a thing? All he and Tassie could do now was what they were already doing – taking each day as it came, finding strength in each other, as well as in those who had gathered around them.

Brace glanced up at the viewing screen, seeing nothing but the wide clearing and the trees beyond it. It was midsummer now, both in Haven and beyond, though Brace could see a difference in the sky outside the city. It wasn't only due to the slight distortion of the viewing wall, either, he knew. The sky outside of Haven was simply not as bright, even during the fullness of day. The others on the gate watch had noticed it as well, along with the members of the most recent search mission to the small town of Spire's Gate. They had only brought back one person, a middle-aged man named Ralston, but upon their return, they had shared the opinion that the sky looked as though the color was being drained out of it.

Brace tried not to let this news get to him, but he felt himself being pulled into a state of melancholy, and it was a struggle to get back out of it.

*Stay strong for Tassie*, he told himself, glancing back at the viewing wall.

Clearing, trees, sky.

*But wait …*

Brace looked again, getting to his feet. Did he see what he thought he saw?

Coming closer to the wall, Brace strained to look.

Yes! Someone was most definitely there, running out from the trees, across the clearing toward the gate.

"Someone is there!" he said aloud, to no one but himself. He looked back across the long white room toward the doors. The hallway beyond them was dark, and ordinarily he would light the tall, narrow candle he'd brought with him. But he couldn't take the time to do it, not now. They had to get to the gate!

Taking a breath and setting his jaw, Brace ran. He ran across the white flooring of the sacred room, pushed open the door and ran down the long, dark hallway, up the stairs, and shoved open the door at the top, pulling himself up into the Main Hall.

Ovard and Jair were there in the room, meeting with Arden and Persha, and all four of them looked up in surprise.

"Someone is at the gate!" Brace blurted out.

"What?" Jair exclaimed. "Who?"

"Who knows?" Brace replied. "I just saw someone running toward the gate from the forest."

"Let's go and meet them," Arden spoke up.

"I'm coming with you," Jair announced.

Arden and Persha turned to leave, followed by Jair and Ovard.

"Should I come or stay?" Brace asked.

"Come," Jair replied.

"All right," Brace said as he let the square door fall shut into the floor with a boom.

The five of them hurried down the wide road from the Main Hall, through the Fountain Court, and on toward the gate. Ovard struggled to keep up as Brace ran on toward the high wall of stone, with Arden just ahead of him.

Brace could hear a dull *thud, thud, thud* coming from outside the city, and a voice calling out to them.

"Let me in! Please, *please* let me in!"

The voice sounded frantic.

Persha hurried to press the plate of stone, triggering the gate to open with a loud groaning and creaking. Brace rushed out first into the clearing, not waiting for the gate to open completely.

"Be careful," Arden warned him, following behind him. "We don't know who is out here."

Brace glanced to the left and the right. "Where did they go?" he wondered aloud.

"Hello?" Jair called out, standing in the ankle-high grass of the clearing.

"There!" Brace noticed a lone figure crouching fearfully among the trees. "Are you all right?" he asked, stepping farther away from the city.

Looking up, the new arrival took in the sight of the open gate in a matter of seconds, then ran toward them.

It was a boy – a *young* boy, Brace noticed immediately, as the child ran to him and grabbed onto his shirt in desperation.

"Help!" the boy cried out. "Please help!"

"What's wrong?" Brace asked him.

"We've been trying to get to Haven," the boy gasped. "Is this Haven?"

"It is," Jair answered. "*We?* Are there others with you?"

"Yes," the boy replied, pointing out into the trees. "They're out there! Please help them!"

"Calm down a moment," Brace said, taking hold of the boy's arms. "Tell me what happened."

The child obediently took a breath, running his sleeve along his brown, freckled face and pushing his dark curly hair off of his forehead. "We're trying to find Haven," he repeated quickly. "My mam and dad and my uncle, and two others. We found our way through the mountains, but there are these black creatures flying all around. They were attacking us!" he exclaimed, his eyes widening at the thought. "They tried to fight them off. They told me to run ahead to find the city and get help. Will you help?"

"Of course we'll help," Arden replied without hesitation.

"Are there night screamers out there right *now*?" Jair asked.

"What are night screamers?" the boy asked in reply, clutching Brace's sleeve.

"I'm sorry," Jair replied quickly. "The black creatures. Are they out there now?"

"Yes!"

"It's nearly midday!" Persha protested.

"Jair," Arden spoke up. "We need lightstones. Quickly! We've got to get out there now and help them."

"Right," Jair agreed. He wasted no time in silently asking the city for another piece of lightstone, and having obtained it, he hurried back to Arden's side.

"I'm coming with you," he announced.

"Jair …" Ovard began to protest, but Jair shook his head firmly. "No, Ovard! I am going to help them. I have the lightstone; we will all be safe."

"Let's go then!" Arden exclaimed, giving Ovard no time to respond. He turned and ran across the clearing, with Persha right behind him. Jair only hesitated briefly before following after them.

"Stay here with Ovard," Brace told the young boy. "I'm going to try and help your family as well."

The child nodded as Brace passed him off to Ovard and hurried after the others.

Jair clutched the lightstone tightly in his grasp as the four of them hurried through the trees toward the rocky slope.

Brace was sure he could hear the faint sound of night screamers in the distance; that was not something he would ever be able to forget, having heard them so often. He had no fear of them now, as long as they had some of Haven's light to chase the creatures into the distance.

A steady summer wind flowed across the stony surface of the mountain as they climbed along the narrow pass, keeping watch for the boy's family.

Arden stopped halfway up the slope, securing his footing. "Hello!" he called out over the mountains. "Is anyone there?"

Brace waited in silence along with the rest of them, listening for any response. When none came, Arden continued on, and everyone followed.

"Where are they?" Jair panted.

"I don't know," Arden replied. "But if they were under attack by the screamers ..."

He left the words unspoken, though Brace knew along with the rest of them that if anyone had been injured, they would need the red vine fruit to heal them before it was too late.

"What if they've been bitten?" Persha asked. "I know that people have been healed after being bitten by one of those things, but what about a whole cloud of them?"

"Let's just find them," Arden spoke up, pushing on ahead.

Brace fought to keep up, grasping at the craggy mountainside and pulling himself along at Arden's back.

They reached the top of the first peak and stopped, the wind pushing at them unhindered, only the wide summer sky above them.

"There!" Arden exclaimed, pointing out across the downward slope of the peak. "I see them!"

"They aren't moving," Jair stated, his voice desperate and full of dread.

"Come on," Brace spoke up, pushing his way past Arden. "Let's just get to them and see what we can do." He had a sinking feeling in the pit of his stomach as he clumsily, hurriedly, worked his way downward, hearing the others following close behind him.

"We're coming!" he called out as the closed the gap between themselves and the people lying on the bare mountainside. "Can you hear us? Help is coming!"

There was no response, no movement. Brace could clearly see now that there were five people lying on the hard rock. *What if they were too late? The boy – what would they tell him?*

Brace slowed as he approached the man nearest him, lying on his front on the craggy surface of rock.

"I'm here," Brace said aloud, unsure whether the man could hear him. "I'm here to help you. Tell me if you can hear me."

There was no response, so Brace slowly, hesitantly crouched down and reached out to touch him. He grasped the man's shoulder and shook him gently, but he made no movement at all. He felt so heavy, so lifeless. Brace watched in dismay as Arden and Persha went on ahead of him, looking closely at the others who lay sprawled out on the rocks.

When they looked back, shaking their heads, Brace knew that his fears had come to pass. They were too late – there had been too many of the screamers. Taking a breath, he turned to look back at Jair, who stood only a few feet behind him. The boy's face was so full of grief that Brace felt himself flinch inwardly.

"Are they dead?" Jair asked, his voice strained.

"I'm afraid they are," Brace replied. "I'm sorry, Jair."

He hardly nodded in response, still clutching the piece of lightstone to his chest. Brace turned back toward Arden and Persha as they slowly picked their way back up the rocky slope. It was all too real, too eerie, Brace thought. How quiet it all was, with only the summer wind over the crags making any sound, and the way the people were lying there, as still as stone themselves, the only movement their lightweight cloaks flapping in the breeze.

Arden shook his head as he came to stand beside Brace. "There is nothing we can do," he told him.

Brace nodded, turning once again in Jair's direction.

"This should not have happened," Jair stated desperately. "They were so close to the city. They came all this way, almost in sight of Haven, only to die here." He shook his head. "This should *not* have happened!" Jair slowly went to his knees, his head bowed.

"There was nothing else we could have done, Jair," Brace told him. "We did all we could."

"Maybe I could have done more," Jair argued, looking up. "I should have been able to do more."

"What could you have done?" Arden challenged. "We cannot stop every wrong from happening, no matter how badly we may want to. You can't blame yourself for this."

Brace looked back out over the mountainside, catching a glimpse of Persha's sorrowful expression.

"Come on, Jair," he said, turning again in his direction. "There is one person who made it to Haven alive. We need to get back to him."

"We can't leave them!" Jair protested in desperation.

"We won't leave them," Arden replied firmly. "But we can't carry them all over the mountain ourselves. We will bring whoever is willing to help. We'll give them the only thing we can – a proper burial."

Jair nodded, sitting on the rocks with his feet under him, the large piece of lightstone on his lap. "I'm staying here," he announced quietly. "I won't leave them all alone."

"*Jair,*" Persha began, but Arden placed a hand on her shoulder.

"He will be all right," he told her. "No screamers will come back as long as Jair has the light. We won't be gone long."

Persha nodded assent as she followed Arden back toward the city.

"Come on, Brace," Arden spoke over his shoulder. "We'll need your help."

As Brace passed by the place where Jair sat slumped on the rock, he reached down and squeezed his shoulder. Jair looked up at him, his face full of anguish.

"Don't blame yourself," Brace told him softly, knowing full well that he did.

Jair only nodded slightly in response, and Brace left him to follow Persha and Arden back over the mountain ridge. As they approached the open gate once again, Brace could see that a small crowd had gathered there. Farris and Alban, two of the former members of King Oden's army, stood near the edge of the clearing, along with Ovard and the boy, accompanied by Bahadur, Gavin, and his parents, Shayrie and Nevin.

Brace could see the young boy, who stood beside Ovard, look up as they approached. As soon as he spotted them, he ran across the clearing and stopped an arm's length in front of Brace.

"Did you find them?" he asked, his eyes wide.

Brace nodded slightly. "We did, but..." How could he tell him such terrible news?

Arden stepped up beside Brace and rested his hand on the boy's arm.

"I'm sorry," Arden told him gently. "We were too late."

"They're dead?" the boy asked in surprise.

Arden nodded as Ovard's face clouded over. "Yes, I'm sorry."

"*All* of them?"

"Yes," Arden repeated. "All of them. I'm *very* sorry. We just didn't get there in time."

The boy's face fell, and he wrapped his arms around himself. Brace took a step closer to him. "I know your family didn't make it here," he told him gently, "but *you* did. And we will take care of you. I know it won't make you feel any better, but you do have a safe place to stay now."

He nodded wordlessly, his dark hair falling over his forehead.

"My name is Brace," he introduced himself. "What's yours?"

"Pavel Andrish," he replied quietly. "Where are my parents?"

"They're still out there," Arden told him as the small group stood around them in silence. "But they're not alone. Jair is with them. We'll bring them back here to have them laid to rest. We aren't going to leave them there."

Pavel nodded.

"How is Jair?" Ovard asked.

"Sad," Arden replied. "And angry."

Ovard glanced at Pavel, then off toward the mountains.

"You can go to him," Arden told Ovard. "We can find someone to look after the boy."

Pavel looked up, glanced around at each of them, then turned toward Brace and wrapped his arms tightly around his waist.

Brace looked down at him in surprise.

"Let me stay with you," Pavel spoke against Brace's shirt.

Brace was speechless, surprised at Pavel's words.

"Do you think that will work, Brace?" Ovard asked him. "Could you and Tassie watch over the boy until we know what we're doing?"

"I – I think so," Brace replied. How could he say no?

"Thank you," Ovard told him. "Right now, I'm going to find Jair."

"Be careful of your footing," Arden cautioned.

"I will."

Everyone stood in shocked silence as Ovard headed off through the clearing toward the trees.

"Well then," Arden went on at last, looking around at those gathered near the gate. "We have five … *people* who need to be brought into the city. Carried in. Are you all willing to help us?"

"I am willing," Bahadur replied without hesitation. Farris and Alban agreed, as well as Nevin, while Shayrie stood by looking helpless.

"Why don't you go on and find…" Arden paused, considering who would be best to help. "Find Stanner and Brodan, and Berrick. Ask if they are willing to … dig the graves."

"I will," Shayrie replied, then turned to leave, casting one last glance at Pavel, still with his arms wrapped tightly around Brace's middle.

"Should I leave the gate standing open?" Brace asked as everyone started off through the clearing.

"I think that would be best for now," Arden told him. "People will be coming and going for a time. Just watch over the boy, will you?"

"I will," Brace replied with a nod. "Come on then," he told Pavel, turning toward the city. "Come with me."

Pavel obeyed, only slightly loosening his grasp on Brace as he walked closely beside him. Brace gently reached out and put an arm around his shoulders. The boy was devastated – who wouldn't be? Should he try to say something comforting, or just let it be?

"How old are you, Pavel?"

"Ten years," he answered quietly.

"I'm taking you to my home," Brace told him. "My wife is there." Tassie's face immediately came to Brace's mind. She was still healing from her loss – how would it be for her, having someone in the house who needed to be cared for, even more than she still did herself? Would Brace need to emotionally divide himself between the two of them? *Could* he?

"You're safe now," Brace told Pavel, not knowing what else to say.

Eridan hurried out to meet them as they neared the house.

"Brace!" she exclaimed in surprise, seeing Pavel close at his side. "I heard the gate open, and I let Tassie know about it. What is going on?"

"Well ..." Brace began, "there were people coming over the pass to find Haven. There were night screamers," he added quietly. "Pavel made it here safely."

"The others?" Eridan asked, and Brace shook his head.

Sorrow filled Eridan's eyes, and she nodded.

"How is Tassie?" Brace asked.

"Well enough," Eridan replied. "Would you like me to stay?"

"No, that's all right. Jair is out there still, and Arden, and some others. I think they'll need more help than we will here."

"All right," Eridan replied. "Please come to me if you need *anything*."

"I will," Brace told her as she hurried off toward the gate.

"Come on, then," Brace told Pavel, guiding him inside. Tassie was coming toward the door just as they stepped into the room.

"Brace?" she asked, taking in the sight of the young boy clinging to his shirt. "What's going on?"

"This is Pavel," Brace replied simply, not wanting to repeat the story of what had happened for the boy to hear all over again.

"Paul?"

"*Pavel*," Brace repeated. "He's all alone. I…" *What?* Brace asked himself. *What can I do?*

"What happened?" Tassie asked, clearly confused.

"My family died," Pavel said quietly, and Brace looked down at him.

"What's that?" Tassie asked. "Brace, please tell me what's happening. Eridan said she heard the gate open. Did this boy come all the way here alone?"

"No," Brace answered, shaking his head. "*There were night screamers*," he mouthed the words. "*The rest of them didn't make it.*"

Tassie's eyes widened in alarm, then she looked down at Pavel, taking in the sight of his dark, shaggy hair, brown freckled face, and worn cottagers' clothing, dirty from travel.

When Tassie looked up, Brace tried to explain. "He needs a place to stay. He sort of … latched on to me. I didn't know what else to do but bring him back here."

Tassie nodded, her face betraying no emotion as she went down on one knee so that her face was level with Pavel's.

"Are you all right?" she asked him. "Are you hurt at all?"

"No," Pavel replied. "I'm not hurt."

"Are you hungry?"

Pavel shook his head.

"You must be thirsty, at least." Tassie slowly reached out and put her hand on his shoulder. "I am very sorry about your family. Will you let us help you?"

Pavel hesitated, then nodded.

"Good," Tassie replied. "I will get you some water."

Tassie rose to her feet, looked up at Brace momentarily, then turned to fill a mug for Pavel from the basin.

"Come and sit at the table," Brace told Pavel, who still had not released his grip on Brace's shirt. Sitting beside the boy, Brace gently pried his hand loose. "It's all right," he told him. "You're safe here."

Pavel nodded slightly, looking up when Tassie placed the water before him on the table.

"Thank you," Pavel whispered, wrapping his hands around the clay mug and taking a long, slow drink. Suddenly he set the mug down on the table, placed his hands in his lap, and sat quietly, his gaze lowered.

Brace looked over at Tassie, and she looked back at him. He shook his head and lifted his shoulders slightly. *What are we supposed to do now?* He wondered.

"Are my parents really dead?" Pavel asked in a small voice.

Brace sucked in a breath.

"I'm sorry," he told him, "but yes. They are. I saw them myself, all of them. We just didn't get to them in time."

Pavel nodded, his shoulders hunched forward as tears began to run down his face.

Brace looked at Tassie helplessly. "*What should we do?*" he mouthed.

"Let's get the bed set up in the extra room," she suggested. "He can at least have a place to stay for the night."

"All right," Brace agreed.

"I'll go to the clinic and get the extra bedding," Tassie volunteered. "I'll be back in a moment."

Tassie rose from the table and left, not giving Brace any time to respond. Before he had a chance to think about it, Brace was left alone in the house with the quietly sobbing boy. He wished he could tell him that everything would be all right, but how could he? How could he lie to him?

Searching for something – *anything* – to say, Brace came up empty. Instead, he simply put an arm around his shoulders and let him cry. Maybe that was all he needed for the moment.

It wasn't long before Tassie returned, her arms over-full of rolled bedding. She looked over at Brace and Pavel as she came into the house, heading for the unused side room. She paused, taking in the sight of them.

"You can bring him right in," she finally told Brace, going on ahead of them.

"Come on," Brace said to Pavel, gently pulling him off the bench. "We've got a room here you can use."

When they entered the room after Tassie, she had already unrolled the bedding and stood smoothing out the faded old quilt. She looked up at them, her expression difficult to read. Was she displeased that Brace had brought the boy here? What else could he have done? Brace knew that

Tassie was not the sort of person to turn anyone away who was in need, regardless of what she might be facing herself.

Brace led Pavel toward the bed, and he sat on the edge of it, wiping the tears from his eyes.

Tassie stood back a short distance as Brace sat beside Pavel.

"Pavel?" Brace asked hesitantly, and the boy looked up at him. "I know you've had a terrible day," he told him, fearing that his words were an enormous understatement. "I'm sorry about everything that happened, and I know everyone else here is, too. But I can at least tell you this much. You are in a safe place here in Haven, and with Tassie and me, at least for today."

Pavel nodded slightly, and Brace went on. "I think your family would be relieved to know that you got here safely, don't you?"

Again, Pavel nodded.

Tassie came closer and rested her hand on Pavel's shoulder. "You've had a long journey," she told him, "and I know you must be tired, inside and out. Please, try and get some rest. We will be here, Brace and I. We will be watching out for you."

"Did they bring my family back?" Pavel asked softly.

Tassie looked to Brace, clearly not having understood the question.

"I'm sure they have, or they nearly have. We won't leave them out there on the mountain, I promise you."

Pavel nodded, then turned and crawled onto the bed, facing the wall.

"*Come on,*" Brace mouthed to Tassie, and together, they left the room, leaving the boy alone with his sorrow.

"I'm sorry," Brace said quietly, standing in the front room. "I didn't know what else to do. He just couldn't seem to let go of me."

"You did right," Tassie replied. "The poor boy – I know what he's going through."

Brace nodded, avoiding Tassie's gaze until she rested a hand on his arm.

"You saw them?" she asked. "Pavel's family?"

"Yes."

"Killed by night screamers?"

"Yes."

Tassie took a long, slow breath. "Are you all right, Brace?" She asked intently.

"I'm fine," he replied with a wave of his hand. "I just don't know what any of us can possibly do to help Pavel. He wanted to come with me, Tass. Arden was there, and Ovard, but Pavel wanted to come with me. I'm sorry, I just didn't know what else to do."

"You did what was right," Tassie insisted, quiet but firm. "I know you wouldn't have turned him away."

"But you..."

"No," Tassie said, shaking her head. "It's all right. You know I'm here to help others, too. He's all right here for now. We can all decide what's best for him."

Brace looked back toward the room where Pavel lay grieving.

"What if he wants to stay here?" he asked Tassie. "I found him first, Tassie, at the gate. I'm not really saying that's what I want, but what if he doesn't want to go with anyone else? What if he wants to stay with me?"

Tassie paused, considering the possibility. "Well...I..."

"Maybe I shouldn't have asked."

"No, it's all right. I ... suppose we could look after him. I've never thought about anything like this."

"I don't know what to do for him," Brace protested.

"Neither do I," Tassie agreed. "Only to let him know he isn't alone."

"Can we do this?" Brace asked. "I mean, really?"

"Do you want to try?"

Brace considered Tassie's question. "I think I do," he told her. "I just don't know how he would take it if I told him to go stay somewhere else," Brace explained quickly. "But I also know you might not be ready for something like this. So I will let you decide."

Tassie's expression showed her conflicting thoughts. Finally, she nodded, more to herself than to Brace. "We can try," she told him. "If you're certain it's what you want, we can at least try."

"I am certain," he replied, taking her hand. "I just see myself in him, is all. I know how he must be feeling, suddenly being all alone."

Tassie nodded. "I know." She took another breath. "We can try to help him," she stated. "All we can do is try."

# ~ 15 ~

Pavel slept for nearly two hours, and when at last he woke and wandered into the front room of Brace and Tassie's home, he looked very lost and weary. Brace was seated at Tassie's side at the heavy wooden table, drinking warm tea when he noticed the boy standing just inside the doorway.

"Hello there," Brace greeted him softly as he came closer, stopping an arm's length away from the table. "How are you feeling?"

Slowly, slightly, Pavel raised his shoulders in a shrug.

Tassie rested her hand on top of Brace's. "Tell him," she said quietly, and Brace nodded.

"Pavel?" Brace asked. The boy looked up. "They brought your family back," he told him. "They are ready to have a funeral for them, but they're waiting for you to be there. It would... well, it would give you a chance to say goodbye. I don't know if it will help any, but it might. Will you come?"

A moment passed before Pavel nodded in reply.

"That's good," Brace told him. "If you'll come with me, we can go and tell Ovard that we're ready."

"Wait a moment," Tassie spoke up, rising from the table. Brace watched her as she found a small cloth, wetted it in the basin of clean water, and wrung it out. Crouching in front of Pavel, she waited until he looked her in the eye. "If your family were to see you there," she told him, "they would want you to look your best. Wouldn't they?"

Pavel nodded slightly.

"You're a bit dirty from traveling," Tassie went on. "May I wash your face?"

Again, Pavel nodded, standing still as Tassie ran the damp cloth along his face, over his dark mop of curly hair, then scrubbed at his hands.

"You look much better," she told him. "It always helps me feel a bit better when I'm clean."

Pavel made no reply, so Tassie rose and spread the cloth out to dry.

"Will you come with us?" Brace asked her, aware that Tassie might prefer to avoid the whole situation.

"Yes," she replied, to Brace's surprise. "I will. I will bring Arden with me. You said he helped bring them back – I know he would want to be there. You go straight on to Jair and Ovard. We can meet you at the burial ground."

"We will," Brace told her, then looked toward Pavel. "Are you ready? There is no reason to wait."

Pavel tugged nervously at the sleeves of his shirt, then nodded, his eyes on the floor.

"Have some water first," Tassie suggested, bringing Pavel the mug he had used earlier. Accepting it from her, he took two small sips, then gave it back.

"Right," Brace said, standing. "Let's go then."

Pavel fell into step beside Brace, who looked back at Tassie. "We'll see you there," he told her, and she nodded.

Brace led Pavel to Jair and Ovard's home, informing them that they were ready to hold the funeral.

"Good, then," Ovard replied gently. "We are ready here. Jair?"

"Yes," Jair answered heavily, coming to the door. "I'm ready."

"Tassie is coming," Brace went on, taking note of Jair's mood. "She is bringing Arden with her."

Ovard nodded, then leaned toward Pavel. "Son?" he asked softly. "We're going to remember your family. I want to let you decide how many people should come to the funeral. Should we let the others know, the ones who helped bring your family here? Or would you rather it be a small event?"

Pavel considered the question. "Small," he finally replied.

"That's fine," Ovard told him. "We will go on and wait for Tassie and Arden at the burial ground."

The three of them went on together in silence, a long, slow walk down the road with homes on both sides, past the outer walls of the Fountain Court, through more homes and beyond the northwestern garden. Partway there, Tassie joined them, accompanied by Arden and Persha. No words were spoken; their presence was acknowledged with a nod, as it was customary for the funeral-goers to remain silent before they stood graveside to say goodbye.

The full summer sun beamed down on them, and Brace felt its warmth on the top of his head, spilling over onto his shoulders. Pavel slunk along beside him, keeping his eyes on the ground at his feet. He did not cling to Brace now; he seemed to have withdrawn deeply within himself.

Brace felt the heavy reality of the situation once again, seeing the freshly filled-in graves as they approached them. Until now, only Lomar's body had been buried there. Now the flat, grassy stretch of land seemed more to Brace like a proper burial ground. It was a shame that such a thing was needed in Haven.

He waited at the edge of the row of graves with Pavel on his right and Tassie on his left. He expected Ovard to speak at any moment. Brace watched the older man from the corner of his eye, but he did not seem to be preparing himself to lead. Instead, he leaned in toward Jair, speaking quietly, and Jair shook his head.

Brace continued watching them as Ovard placed his hand on Jair's shoulder and nodded, gesturing unobtrusively toward the graves. Finally, with obvious reluctance, Jair stepped forward. He stood in silence for a moment, gazing down at the freshly-dug graves as though he had personally known those who had died and were buried there.

"This is a very sad day," Jair said at last, almost to himself. "A black day. We can't forget what happened. But at least we know it can't happen again. Not like this." He looked back at the small group gathered behind him.

"Pavel?" he asked quietly. "Will you say their names for us? So we can all say farewell?"

Brace could see that Pavel was fighting, trying not to cry, hesitating for fear that speaking the names aloud would bring his tears to the surface. It would mean having to admit to himself that they really were gone, and were never coming back.

At last, Brace could see the boy steel himself against the sorrow.

"Mam... Kya," he began, "Dad ... Nolin. Uncle Erhan, Ransen and Kanna." He swallowed and let out a breath. "Farewell."

"Farewell," Brace repeated, and the others echoed the word, then all was silent. A moment passed before Jair spoke again.

"You will not be forgotten."

Brace looked down at Pavel, but he found it difficult to bear the deep sadness the boy wore on his face.

"They won't be forgotten," Brace repeated, resting a hand on Pavel's shoulder.

"We will mark their names here very soon," Jair announced. "They will always be part of Haven now." He shook his head. "I'm sorry, Pavel. I'm so very sorry."

"Why don't we all head home?" Ovard suggested. "Our hearts are heavy. We all need our time to grieve," he added for Pavel's benefit. "We can leave things as they are for today. Brace, Tassie? May I speak with you privately for a moment?"

Brace glanced at Tassie, then nodded.

"Good. Pavel? Will you stay here with Arden and Persha for a moment? We won't be long."

Pavel looked over at the tall, broad-shouldered man, reluctance in his eyes.

"It's all right," Brace told him. "He's a good friend of mine. You're safe with him."

Pavel finally nodded and stood by awkwardly as Brace took Tassie's hand, moving a short distance away to join Ovard and Jair.

"We must decide where the boy will stay," Ovard wasted no time in saying. "He needs to be able to settle in somewhere, to give his heart time to heal. How has he been with you?"

"Very quiet," Brace replied. "He slept most of the time."

"He has taken a liking to Brace," Tassie added. "I think he feels safe with him."

"I had noticed that myself," Ovard told her. "I was beginning to wonder..." he paused, stroking his bearded chin in thought.

"You were thinking he could just stay with us," Brace stated.

"I was. But, it is a big decision to make. What are your thoughts?"

"Well …" Tassie began hesitantly. "He already has a room with us, a place to sleep. He knows he is safe there."

"Looking after him will not be an easy thing," Ovard cautioned.

Tassie nodded. "He's really taken a liking to Brace. If we decided to keep him with us, I know we wouldn't be in it alone. There are so many people here who could help us."

"Of course," Ovard agreed.

"I feel like it's the right thing for us to do," Brace spoke up, "keeping him with us." He paused, suddenly realizing that their lives were about to change completely.

"As long as we're not it in alone," he went on. "I don't know how to …" he hesitated, the words stuck in his throat.

"How to what?" Ovard asked.

"How to be a father."

"You are not alone," Ovard told him. "You can come to me any time you have need to. I'm certain Arden would say the same, as well as many others."

Brace could hear the relief in Ovard's voice, as it seemed the decision had been made. He looked over at Jair, but the boy's mind appeared to be elsewhere, his expression troubled.

"You mustn't keep blaming yourself for this, Jair," Brace told him abruptly, and Jair looked at him.

"They shouldn't have died," he stated plainly.

"No," Ovard agreed, "but we can take comfort in knowing this will not happen again, not on the pass at least."

"How can you know that?" Brace asked.

"Jair had another idea come to him while we were out on the mountain," Ovard explained. "The light stones keep the screamers away from the city, and when we take the stones with us, they keep us safe anywhere we go. So the lightstones would make the pass a safe place, where no night screamers would be able to trouble anyone. Jair was able to mount three bits of lightstone along the pass permanently."

"How?" Brace asked again.

Ovard looked to Jair, who explained further. "The lightstones attached themselves onto the rocks on the mountain. It sort of became a part of it. No one can ever take them off."

"Because of you," Brace pointed out. "The lightstones did that because you asked them to, didn't they? You're the only one who can talk to them. The pass is a safe place now because of you."

"But it could have been safe before," Jair argued. "I could have thought of this before now. This didn't have to happen."

"No one can think of everything," Ovard admonished. "Sometimes things need to happen; we need to see that there is a problem in order to provide a solution. I am just as disheartened about this as you are, son, but you cannot blame yourself."

"What if Pavel blames me?" Jair asked quietly.

"I'm sure he doesn't," Brace told him. "He isn't angry, he is saddened. If anything, I'm sure he would blame the night screamers, not you."

Jair nodded, but Brace knew it would take time for him to get beyond the way he was feeling.

"So it's decided, then?" Ovard asked. "Brace, Tassie? You will let Pavel stay with you?"

Brace and Tassie looked at one another, and Brace could see in Tassie's eyes that she was willing to try.

"Yes," Brace answered for the both of them. "Pavel can stay with us."

"Very good. Thank you for taking him in. I know that times have been hard for you as of late…"

"It's all right," Brace cut in quickly. "We'll make due. And it's good to know we will have help if we need it."

"You will," Ovard agreed. "Let us go, then, and tell Pavel the news."

Brace walked the few steps back, holding Tassie's hand tightly. Pavel looked up when they came close, his expression weary.

"Well, son," Ovard addressed him, "it has been decided that you can continue to stay with Brace and Tassie in their home. Is that something you would like?"

Pavel looked up at Brace; his eyes seemed to be searching for a glimpse into Brace's heart.

Brace grinned awkwardly. "You're welcome to stay with us if you would like to," he told him.

Pavel nodded slowly, looking first at Brace, then at Ovard.

"Very good. I'm glad that's taken care of. You are safe here, Pavel. Everyone in Haven can be your family now."

Pavel's gaze shifted to the ground at his feet.

"Well," Ovard went on, "I think that Jair and I ought to be heading home. The day is drawing on. Tomorrow is a new day. We will just start over every morning, won't we? Each day will get just a little bit easier."

Pavel did not even attempt to respond, and Jair's expression was still heavy with regret. Brace could see it plainly, and Tassie could as well. She slipped her hand out of Brace's and stepped up in front of Jair, lightly taking his face in her hands.

"You've done all you can to make this right," she told him gently. "Your heart is so big, Jair, and so open. Don't let it stay hurt, or it will break, and it will be that much harder to find hope again."

Jair nodded, then Tassie pulled him into a tight embrace.

"Arden?" Ovard asked. "Will you take care of the rest of it for me?"

"I will."

"The rest?" Brace asked as Tassie joined him once again.

"Their things," Arden explained. "We brought their things to my home after … after we brought them into Haven. It all belongs to Pavel now. It's the only right thing to do with all of it."

Pavel looked up at Arden's face, again seeming to be searching beyond what was easily seen on the surface. He seemed to desperately want to know the people around him more deeply, to know who they truly were. Brace realized how completely lost he must be feeling.

"Let's go, then," he said, looking straight at Pavel. "Let's go with Arden. I'm sure there are some things your parents would have wanted you to have."

Pavel nodded and stepped up close beside Brace.

"I think I will go then," Persha spoke up. "If that's all right. I don't think there is anything more I can do here."

"That's fine," Ovard told her after glancing at Jair, giving him a chance to answer her.

"Tomorrow?" Persha asked Arden, and he nodded.

"Yes, tomorrow."

"Goodbye, then, everyone. I hope your evening is restful, at least."

"Thank you, Persha," Tassie replied, having read her lips. "Yours as well."

Persha gave a quick nod, then turned and went on her way, not looking back.

"I believe we will need to hold a meeting tomorrow," Ovard commented. "Jair?"

"Hmm?"

"I said, we will need to hold a meeting tomorrow. We will need to set things straight about exactly what happened here today. The people need to hear it from *you*."

Jair nodded. "You're right. I know."

"Will you be prepared to tell them?" he asked firmly.

"I will."

"Good," Ovard replied, his voice softening.

"Right, then," Arden spoke up. "Brace, Tassie, let's go and get the boy's things."

Arden seemed as weary as the rest of them, ready for this day to come to a close.

A few brief goodbyes later, the four of them went on their way toward Arden and Leandra's home near the front of the city. Arden's expression was strained, and Brace was sure it was anger that the archer felt just beneath the surface. It was the kind of anger that burns at the thought of another's sorrow, at the terrible injustice they have had to suffer. Brace knew it— he felt it as well, though Arden, being a man of *harbrost*, lived a life driven by the desire for the *right* to prevail in every circumstance. Where was the *right* in this, for Pavel?

"Arden?" Brace asked, drawing him out of his thoughts. The archer's sharp blue eyes turned in his direction.

"Yes?"

"Can you tell us what it is you've got for Pavel?"

Arden's expression softened a degree, and he looked down at the boy, who only slightly looked up in his direction.

"We have their packs," Arden told Pavel. "Each of them. And we have their cloaks. We thought you might want to keep them, your father's in particular. And a few things they had with them, things that we thought shouldn't be buried."

"We?" Pavel asked quietly.

"My wife and I," Arden replied. "We kept the things at our home for you until you were ready to have them. My daughters are there as well," he went on, not wanting Pavel to face any surprises. "You are all welcome to stay and eat with us. I *insist*," he added, seeing Brace's hesitation.

"You want us to stay and eat with you?" Tassie asked.

"Yes," Arden replied. "We've made extra. You've been through quite a lot today, all three of you. Let us help you however we can."

"I would be glad to stay," Tassie replied. "I would be grateful."

"Good, then," Arden said as they neared the house at last. "Here we are."

Arden knocked twice on the wooden door to signal his arrival, then pushed it open and gestured for the rest of them to enter ahead of him.

Brace gently guided Pavel in through the doorway, and he and Tassie followed. The scent of food roasting over the hearth fire of ever-burning stones enveloped them as Arden stepped inside and closed the door.

Leandra stood nearby, looking tall and strong as she leaned against the wall near the hearth, sipping from a carved stone mug.

"Dadda!" Denira was the first to speak, calling out from the far side of the room where she played, with Kendie beside her. The little girl ran across the room and into Arden's arms, oblivious of the heaviness that hung in the room like smoke.

"Hi, Dadda!" Denira said as she kissed Arden's face.

"Hello, little bug," Arden replied softly. "Let Dadda help Pavel now, all right?"

Denira looked around until she noticed the boy standing nearby.

"Come with Mammy," Leandra suggested, setting down her stone mug and holding out her hands. Denira went into Leandra's arms, popping her thumb into her mouth.

Brace noticed Kendie watching them in silence as Arden gestured to the wall at the side of the room.

"Here it is," he said. "The five packs of supplies."

Pavel stood by and looked at them.

"Here," Arden said helpfully, reaching for what lay across the top of the nearest pack. "We think this was your father's cloak. Is it?"

"Yes," Pavel replied, reaching out slowly, gathering it into his arms.

"Thank you," he whispered.

Arden waited for Pavel to make a move toward the packs to see what else they'd brought, but he stood still.

"We kept this as well," Arden went on, retrieving another item that Brace could hardly see. "Do you recognize it, don't you?"

It was a brooch of some sort, Brace realized, as Pavel reached out to accept it.

"Yes. Mam's. Our family crest."

"Those are the most important things, I think," Arden told him. "No one went through any of the packs, I promise you. Whatever is in them belongs to you now."

Pavel blinked, looking at the lined-up heap of dirt-coated leather travel packs leaning against the wall nearby.

Brace stepped up beside Pavel and crouched down to the boy's height. "Do you want them?" he asked gently. "If you want them, Tassie and I will help you carry them. We live in the next house over. We won't have to go far with them."

Pavel was silent for a long moment, as though considering the question.

"Not all of them," he finally answered in a quiet voice. "Keep Ransen and Kanna's. I don't need them."

"Do you want me to hold them here for you for a time?" Arden asked.

"No," Pavel replied. "You keep them."

"All right. If that's what you would like."

Pavel nodded.

"All right then," Brace said as he stood up straight. "That's settled, at least."

"Come and eat with us," Leandra suggested. "The food should be ready by now. Please, make yourselves comfortable."

The room was quiet as everyone gathered around the table. Denira sat between Leandra and Kendie, sucking her thumb.

"Please, help yourselves," Arden told Brace and Tassie, handing each of them a two-pronged fork.

"You need to eat, Denira," Leandra said, gently tugging the girl's thumb out of her mouth.

"Boy sad?" Denira asked innocently.

"Yes," Leandra replied. "The boy is sad."

"Why?"

"Just eat, please. Don't talk now. Eat."

Denira picked at her food, never taking her eyes off of Pavel as he sat at the table, clutching the brooch and the cloak.

"Try to eat something," Brace encouraged. "Keep your strength up."

"Is the meat all right for you to eat?" Leandra asked when Pavel only stared down at the plate. "There are carrots and turnips, and bread."

Pavel made no reply; he simply reached out and took a thin strip of roasted deer, taking a small bite.

"Not much of an appetite is all, I'm sure," Arden commented.

Leandra reached out across the table and rested her hand on Tassie's.

"We want to come alongside you in all of this," she told her. "You're not alone in caring for Pavel. We're here if you need anything."

Tassie nodded in reply. "Thank you," she told her. "That means so much to me."

"I know what it's like, Pavel," Kendie spoke up from near the end of the table, "being part of a new family. My parents are gone, too. I don't know if they died, but I haven't seen them in almost seven years."

Pavel took in Kendie's words, eyeing her from across the table. He silently took another bite of food and chewed it slowly.

Brace felt himself wondering what in the world they'd gotten themselves into. This wasn't something that would last a few days, or a few weeks. This could last for *years*, taking care of the boy until he was of age to care for himself. Who knew how long he would be grieving for his lost family? He and Tassie were still fighting through grief of their own. He felt no resentment toward Pavel – after all, this was no fault of his. No, he felt no resentment; he wanted to be there for him. But how on this earth were they going to manage it, even with help from friends? Of that, Brace had not the slightest idea.

In the quiet of the room, Brace could hear when Pavel began to sniff, and he looked down to see him wiping away tears. A wave of sympathy swept over him, recalling the fear and sorrow he himself had felt when his own mother had died.

"I think Pavel's had enough for today," Brace spoke up, catching Leandra's eye. "I think we should take him home. Thank you for the meal – it was delicious, as always."

"It's no trouble," Leandra replied.

"Let me help you," Arden offered, rising from the table.

Tassie looked around, confused. "What's going on?" she asked.

Brace tapped her arm and nodded in Pavel's direction.

"Oh," Tassie said quietly, seeing him fighting against his tears. "Are we leaving?"

"Yes," Brace replied, taking hold of Pavel's arm. "Come on," he told him gently. "We don't need to stay."

Pavel rose from the table wordlessly, clutching the things that were all he had left of his parents.

Brace took one of the packs as Arden grabbed another, leaving the lightest one for Tassie to carry.

"Take care of yourselves," Leandra called after them, standing. "Call on us again soon."

"We will," Brace replied. "Thank you."

Arden pulled open the door and the three of them stepped out into the evening light of summer. Within minutes they had reached Brace and Tassie's home, and were indoors once again. The three packs were laid down along the wall in the room now occupied by Pavel, and Arden shrugged his shoulders to loosen his muscles.

"It's been too long since I've needed to carry one of those," he commented. "Can't say I miss it."

Brace agreed with a nod as Pavel sat on the edge of the bed.

"Well," Arden went on, "if there's nothing more you need tonight, I'll leave you to it."

"I think we'll manage," Brace replied. "Thank you."

Arden nodded. "Good night, then. Our hearts are with you. No need to show me out," he added. "Rest well."

"Thank you," Brace said again as Arden left the room.

Tassie sat down beside Pavel on the bed and put an arm around his shoulders. "You must be so tired inside," she sympathized. "Try and get some sleep. Would you like me to help you out of your boots?"

Pavel shook his head, tears pouring down his face faster than he could wipe them away.

"Do you need some water?" Tassie offered. "It might help."

Again, Pavel shook his head.

Tassie looked up at Brace helplessly. He let out a quick sigh and joined them, sitting on the bed and putting his arms around Pavel, holding him close.

"I know you're heartbroken," Brace told him. "And no one expects you not to be. Do you know that?"

Pavel nodded, wrapping his arms tightly around Brace.

"You're here now, in Haven," Brace went on, "Where your parents wanted you to be. And we're going to do our best to take care of you. *All* of us."

Pavel only cried, and Brace noticed Tassie wipe away a tear of her own. He reached out and rested a hand on her knee, and she looked over at him.

"Why don't you bring Pavel some water?" he asked. "You're right, he should drink something."

Tassie nodded and left the room.

"I know it might seem like nothing will ever be all right again," Brace told Pavel over the sound of his sobs, "but they will. It will take a long time, and you'll always miss them, but if you let it, things will be all right again, someday."

Pavel went on crying.

"Do you believe me?" Brace asked him. "Do you believe me that things can be all right again someday?"

"Maybe," Pavel replied tearfully.

"Well, that's something," Brace told him. "At least that's something."

Tassie came back into the room and sat down at Pavel's side once again, holding out the mug of cool water. "Please drink it," she told him.

"Come on," Brace encouraged, pulling himself out of the boy's grasp. "You need it."

Pavel obediently turned toward Tassie, settling his father's cloak and his mother's brooch onto his lap before taking the mug in both hands. He emptied the mug in long, slow, steady gulps, his freckled face damp from his tears.

"That's better," Tassie said kindly as he handed the mug back to her.

"It's getting late," Brace commented, running his hands through his hair, trying to let off a bit of tension. "I'm worn out from this day, so I know you've got to be as well. Try and get some more sleep."

Pavel sniffed, then nodded.

"Do you have any other clothing?" Tassie asked him.

"In my mam's pack," he replied. "They're dirty."

"Well, I guess this will have to work for tonight. We can wash your things tomorrow."

Pavel nodded, slipping off his boots, gathering his treasures into his arms and sliding under the bed quilt.

Brace and Tassie exchanged a look; they were trekking blindly through the wilds, and neither of them knew the way.

"Rest well, Pavel," Brace said quietly, reaching for Tassie's hand. "The sun will shine again tomorrow, you'll see."

Pavel lay quietly, his face toward the wall, as Brace led Tassie out of the room.

"The poor boy," Tassie breathed as she lowered herself onto the padded window seat. Brace sat down heavily beside her, loosening the laces on his scuffed leather boots.

"I can't imagine having to go through all of this," he said quietly, facing Tassie.

She nodded in agreement. "What can we do to help him?"

Brace leaned back against the window, pushing his hair away from his face. "I really don't know, Tassie. All I know to do is just be here. He's been clinging to me ever since I met him at the gate. I couldn't *not* offer to help him. It would feel like I was turning my back on him, as though I didn't care about him at all."

"I understand that," Tassie agreed. She paused, running her fingers along the ends of her long brown curls. "Do you think we made a mistake, taking him in? Do you that someone else would be able to care for him better than we know how?"

Brace mulled the question over in his mind. "I don't know, Tassie. Maybe Ovard would be a better choice, but he has so much to do, helping Jair. I just don't know."

Tassie slowly shook her head. "I know this won't be easy. But in my heart, I feel like this is right, somehow. I feel like this is something we should be doing."

Brace slid his hand into Tassie's, their fingers lacing together. "We've been through a lot of confusing times together," he told her. "We've always made it through. We can do it again."

Tassie smiled a little, her eyes full of hope and determination. "You don't ever give up, do you?"

"Well," Brace replied, "I'm not sure about that. I wouldn't say *never*."

Tassie's smile faded, though her eyes still shone with an inner strength. "Promise me you won't give up on this?" she asked.

Brace chewed at the inside of his lip. "I promise you. I'll do the best I know how. It might not be good enough."

"Remember, we're not alone," Tassie reminded him. "There are so many people here who can help us."

"Right."

Tassie sighed and leaned against Brace, resting her chin on his shoulder. "I've heard it said that nothing worth doing is ever really easy," she commented, then looked up at his face.

"Sounds about right to me," Brace agreed. "This is definitely one of those things."

Tassie nodded and nestled herself against Brace's side once again.

Brace enjoyed the quiet. He enjoyed the moment alone with Tassie. As the summer sun began to sink lower toward the horizon, setting the sky ablaze outside the window at their backs, Brace wondered when another moment like this one would happen again. The future was uncertain now, though hadn't it always been? He would gladly take moments like this whenever he was fortunate enough to have them given to him.

He was going to make this one last as long as he possibly could.

# ~ 16 ~

The two days following Pavel's arrival felt to Brace like one very long, difficult day. Pavel hardly spoke; he picked at his food; he slept long hours and was constantly on the verge of tears. He was lost, confused and distraught.

Brace could do nothing but simply accept all of it, knowing that the boy needed time to mourn. The only thing he and Tassie were adamant about was that Pavel eat his meals and drink plenty of water.

Thanks to Jair's meeting, everyone in Haven now knew about the orphaned boy and the five new graves in the burial ground. They knew exactly what had happened. There would be no speculation, no rumors.

Many of Haven's citizens expressed their concern, wanting to know what they could do to provide for Pavel's needs, and to support Brace and Tassie in their efforts to care for him. Pavel had arrived with only two sets of clothing, so, with Pavel's permission, Noora and Medarrie had taken the clothing that had belonged to the boy's father and uncle, altering them so they would fit him.

Dursen and Nerissa had stopped by briefly, bringing extra grain, eggs, milk, and words of concern and good wishes from several of their friends.

It was not until the third day that Brace suggested emptying the packs. Pavel had agreed with a nod, and now sat watching Brace as he carefully searched every pocket.

Brace was surprised to find, at the top of one leather pack, a painted lyr flute. It was old, but sturdy, and seemed to be in good condition.

"Who did this belong to?" Brace asked Pavel, holding it up for him to see.

"Uncle Erhan," Pavel replied flatly.

"It's a nice one," Brace told him. "Do you know how to play it?"

Pavel shook his head.

"Well," Brace went on, "Ovard has one, and he plays it fairly often. He could teach you how to play, if it interests you."

Pavel chewed at his lower lip and shrugged slowly.

"Right," Brace replied, setting the flute aside. "When you're ready."

Brace did not want to seem insensitive to the boy's pain, but he wanted to try and draw him out of it somehow. He wanted Pavel to see that life was still going on all around him. It hadn't stopped, not for *him* at least, not in the slightest. He had been telling him about things in Haven, anything that came to him. About the walls of lightstone, about the Fountain Court. About Arden's hunting skills and living with *harbrost*. He told him about Tassie's deafness and the way she could see what people said. He told him to be sure and look at her when he spoke, and she would understand him.

Not that the boy ever said much of anything.

Brace felt weariness and tension building up inside. Hour after hour of Pavel's pained silence, of neither he nor Tassie knowing what to do, and not knowing when anything would change, was wearing on him.

It was a small relief, being invited to share a meal out of doors with Arden and his family.

Setting the flute aside, Brace asked, "Do you remember who Arden is?" He tried once again to draw words from the boy's mouth, but Pavel simply nodded.

Well, that would need to be good enough.

"We are meeting him and Leandra at the Fountain Court today," he went on. "We can finish going through these packs later."

He stood, and Pavel's eyes followed him.

"Come on, Pavel," Brace prodded. "Getting out into the summer air will be good for all of us."

Pavel wrapped his arms around himself nervously. Brace drew in a breath, then let it out slowly. He knelt down in front of Pavel, resting a hand on the boy's shoulder.

"I know you miss your family," he told him gently. "No one wants you to stop missing them, do you know that? We don't expect you to stop missing your family, or even to stop feeling bad about what happened. We just want to help you realize that *you* are still alive."

Pavel nodded slightly, letting his gaze fall to the floor.

"There is something else," Brace went on as Tassie entered the room, her long, cream-colored dress almost brushing the floor. "Did you know that everyone who comes to Haven is meant to be a part of it?" he asked, feeling Tassie's hand on his shoulder. "There is a reason you're here, Pavel. You are an important part of Haven now. You have a purpose here, something important that only *you* are meant to do. If you give up hope, you will never find out what that purpose is."

Pavel tipped his head to one side, lifting his eyes to meet Brace's gaze. *At last, a significant response!*

"You can find out what your purpose is," Brace went on, "and you will make your mam and dad so proud of you. And knowing they would be proud will do your own heart good as well."

Brace waited as the significance of his words settled into Pavel's mind, finally showing in his eyes.

"Right, then," Brace said, getting to his feet. "Let's go and share a meal with our friends, shall we?"

When the three of them approached the high, arched opening in the walls around the Fountain Court, Brace realized that this would be the first time Pavel would be setting foot inside it. He would be seeing for the first time the vine fruit growing along the walls; he would see the tall stone fountain and hear the melodic burbling of the flowing water. Would any of it matter to Pavel? Or would he still be too down-hearted to even notice?

Brace tried to imagine what it would be like, seeing it all for the first time, through Pavel's eyes. There it all was, spread out around them. The high stone walls; the large red fruit with its sweet fragrance lingering in the air; the peaceful sounds of the flowing fountain and of Denira's childish laughter.

Leandra waved when she noticed they had arrived, making their way slowly across the courtyard. Brace intentionally kept up an easy pace; there was no need to hurry. Let the boy take his time, take in as much of what lay around him as he wanted to.

And he *was* looking, Brace was pleased to notice.

"Hello, Tassie," Leandra greeted her with a long embrace. "I'm so glad you came," she went on, stepping back so Tassie could see her face.

"So am I," Tassie agreed, setting down her basket of food.

"How are things?" Arden asked.

"Well enough," Brace replied. "We're managing."

Pavel stood close at Brace's side, looking back toward the ornate fountain.

"It's nice, isn't it?" Arden asked him.

Pavel nodded, moving closer to Brace.

"You don't need to be afraid," Brace told him quietly. "Come and sit on one of these benches here. You'll have a straight-on view of the fountain from there, and you can admire it while we eat."

Pavel obeyed, sitting on one of the stone benches along the wall. Kendie smiled at him as he did so, and Denira eyed him with curiosity.

"We brought fresh bread," Tassie said as she began to pull things out of her basket.

"I love fresh bread," Kendie commented. "Don't you, Pavel?"

He nodded once in response. Kendie glanced over at Brace, and she caught his eye. Brace shrugged slightly. *No harm in trying.*

Tassie's bread and fruit spread were a perfect complement to Leandra's thick meat-and-vegetable stew, and it was a welcome change for Brace as they enjoyed sharing their meal together in the warmth of the summer sun. Arden ate three helpings himself, while Pavel at least finished off one bowlful without any prodding.

Denira, seated on one of the benches, swung her feet over the edge as she licked sticky fruit from her fingers and stared at Pavel openly.

"Are you holding up well?" Leandra asked Brace quietly as he reached for another bread roll.

"Well enough, I think."

"You look weary."

Brace smirked. "I *am* that." He leaned closer to Leandra, speaking softly so that Pavel wouldn't hear him over the splashing fountain and birdsong. "The boy's grief is so heavy, it feels like it's filling the whole house."

"I would imagine so," Leandra replied. "The two of you have already had your share of grief. Please don't try and do this alone. Come to us if you need *anything*, even if it's only time to yourselves. You still need that, Brace."

He nodded, biting into the bread, chewing and swallowing. "Thank you. Really, I won't forget your offer. I'm sure we'll be needing it soon enough."

Near-distant voices echoed off the high stone walls from the far side of the courtyard. Brace turned to look, along with the others, to see Yara and Noora entering through one of the arched entryways, obviously in good spirits. Strong, confident Noora in her smooth, gray dress, fitted in the bodice and flaring out down to the tops of her leather boots. Yara with her long, pleated skirt and lace-fronted top – she was by no means shy, but she still carried with her a sense of uncertainty. Brace knew of her doubts and fears as to whether her friendship would truly be sought out by others.

"I'm just so plain," she had told Brace once. "I'm not wise and beautiful like Tassie. I'm not naturally exuberant like Eridan, or strong and bold like Persha or Leandra. I'm only me."

The memory of Yara's words came back to Brace now, as he watched her and Noora chattering on at the far side of the fountain. She seemed perfectly happy today, and he was glad for her.

Noora happened to glance in their direction, and she startled a bit.

"Oh, I'm sorry!" she called out, grabbing hold of Yara's arm. "I didn't think anyone would be out here."

The two young women came toward them, Yara being pulled along by Noora's grasp.

"I hope we're not disturbing you."

"Of course not," Leandra replied. "The Fountain Court is for everyone. It isn't a place one comes to for privacy." She smiled.

"I'm glad," Noora sighed. "How are all of you?"

"Well and good, thank you," Arden replied. "And you? Are your friends from Pran's Helm finding life here to their liking?"

"Of course!" Noora replied, her dark eyes shining. "We're so grateful to be here, you have no idea! Especially Lida, and Eaton. My only regret is that Corben chose not to come with us."

Arden nodded in response.

"How are you, Brace?" Yara asked. "Tassie? And the boy – what is his name?"

"Pavel," Brace answered, glancing in his direction, seeing that he was listening to their conversation. "We're getting by," he told Yara. "Bit by bit, we are getting by."

"Good to hear it," Yara said with a brief half-smile. "Terrible thing, what happened."

Brace nodded, frowning. He suddenly found himself feeling protective of Pavel, not wanting anything to upset him. When had that change happened inside of him?

Noora looped her arm around Yara's. "Let's go and let them eat," she suggested. "Let's soak our feet in the stream."

Yara nodded, then turned toward the small group with a smile. "Enjoy your day," she said in parting.

"And you," Leandra replied as Noora and Yara crossed the courtyard, waving. Brace looked over his shoulder at Pavel, wondering if he'd been bothered by Yara's mention of what had happened to his family. The boy sat gazing into his empty soup bowl, his face the same blank slate that it had been for the past two days.

Tassie moved to sit on the bench beside Pavel, resting her hand on his. "Are you all through?" she asked gently.

Pavel handed over his bowl, nodding slightly. There was an awkward silence for a moment as no one spoke.

"Pavel?" Leandra asked, and he looked up at her. "Why don't you go on ahead and get a closer look at the fountain? You can feel the cool water pouring over the rim. It's very soothing."

Pavel peered at the burbling fountain, then glanced at Brace, who nodded encouragingly.

"I'll go with you," Kendie offered. "I always love seeing the fountain."

Slowly, noncommittally, Pavel rose from the bench and followed Kendie across the courtyard.

"*Pwaying?*" Denira asked, her blue eyes bright.

"Yes," Leandra told her. "They are playing, a little."

"Deniwa pway?"

Leandra hesitated. "Yes, you can play. But stay with sissie."

Denira smiled and slid off the bench, made certain she was steady on her feet, then hurried after them.

"He's a very quiet child," Arden remarked.

Brace nodded. "He is that. I think it's his sorrow that keeps him from saying much. He seems to feel that speaking takes too much effort. He seems like he feels ... empty."

"Has he told you any of this?" Leandra asked.

"No," Brace replied. "It's just so easy to see it."

"What *has* he said to you?" Arden asked.

"Nothing, really. He will answer questions, but it's usually with a nod or a shake of his head. I don't really know anything about him."

"We only know," Tassie joined in, "that he is a boy who aches for his family."

Brace let his gaze wander toward the fountain, where Kendie stood, one hand stretched out allowing a stream of water to slide through her fingers. Pavel reached out to feel the cool, rippling water that pooled in the basin, while Denira lingered nearby, eyeing him curiously.

"I wonder," Leandra thought aloud, "if it would be good for him to have more time around other children. It might help, giving him something to do, so he doesn't have as much time to sit around and think about things."

Tassie eyed Leandra closely, reading the words she had spoken.

"Do you mean sending him to school?" she asked. "It's so soon. His parents have only been gone three days."

"It wouldn't be for the learning," Leandra explained. "He seems to be doing well over there with Kendie. It could be good for him to get to know some of the other children, maybe make a new friend."

Brace watched Pavel from across the courtyard and considered Leandra's words. How well would it work, sending the boy to school? He hardly spoke ...

"What do you think, Brace?" Tassie asked him.

He let out a sigh as he turned toward her. "I suppose it's worth a try. It would give us some time to ourselves as well. Haven't you been missing that?"

"I have."

"You should talk to him about it," Leandra suggested. "See what he thinks."

"Right now?" Brace asked.

"Why not?" Arden pointed out.

Brace hesitated, then nodded. "All right. Pavel?" he called out, in his best attempt at sounding easygoing. Pavel looked up, and Brace waved him over. He slowly made his way back toward the benches, with Denira right at his heels.

"Pavel," Brace began gently as the boy eyed him with uncertainty. "I'd like to talk to you about something important. We've decided that it could be a good idea for you to start going to school here."

Pavel's eyebrows furrowed with uncertainty and surprise.

"We're not doing it because we expect you to keep up with your lessons," Brace explained. "It's just that it would give you something to do, going to the school, and it would give you a chance to meet the other children who live here in Haven."

Brace stopped, nearly holding his breath as he studied Pavel's face for any hint of what he thought about the idea.

Tassie reached out and took Pavel's hand. "How does this sound to you? Will you try it?"

Pavel hesitated, then shrugged.

"Just give it a chance." Brace tried to sound encouraging. "Will you?"

Again, Pavel shrugged, and though he would have preferred to hide it if he could, the disappointment showed on Brace's face.

"*Pway!*" Denira exclaimed suddenly, grabbing onto Pavel's arm. "*Pway!*"

"She wants you to play with her," Leandra told Pavel. "She likes you."

With one last glance at Brace and Tassie, Pavel allowed Denira to pull him back toward the fountain, where Kendie waited for them.

"I don't think he's too keen on the idea," Brace grumbled.

"Give it time," Leandra told him. "He may not really want to go, but it will be good for him. Believe me."

Brace nodded, looking over in her direction. Tassie moved closer to Brace and put her arm through his, resting her chin on his shoulder.

"Are you all right?" Brace asked her, concerned.

"Yes," she replied. "I'm a little weary, but it will pass. I just love being out here with you, Brace."

He managed a crooked smile. "So do I."

Denira's high-pitched laughter drew everyone's attention. The little girl stood with her hands stretched out, catching droplets of sun-lit water on her palms and flinging them into the air, some of them landing in every direction. Kendie laughed from where she stood, a few feet away.

Brace could see Pavel flinching slightly when drops of water splashed on his face, but he could also see – was it only in his own mind? – the slightest hint of a smile.

His spirits uplifted, Brace held Tassie close at his side. They were going to make it, the three of them. It would take time, he knew, but they would make it.

~

Denira protested stubbornly when Brace informed everyone it was time for them to leave. She had very much enjoyed showing off for Pavel – he was a new face, someone who hadn't seen a hundred times the cute or funny or – in Denira's mind at least – the amazing things she could do. He had been a captive audience, and she did *not* want him to leave.

"You will see Pavel again," Leandra told her firmly. "He lives here now, with Brace and Tassie. You can see him again soon."

Eventually, Denira was convinced, and they were able to leave without any fuss. Pavel went along as silently as ever, but Brace noticed that his eyes weren't stuck on the ground at his feet. He seemed to finally be looking around him, taking in the sight of Haven at last.

Brace let him be, not attempting to force any conversation. Instead, he held Tassie's hand as they went along at a stroll, enjoying the peaceful quiet of the summer evening.

It was *always* this quiet for Tassie, Brace reminded himself. *Quieter.* There were no far-off birds' songs echoing in her ears, no snatches of conversations leaking from the windows of nearby houses as they passed.

Gold shafts of sunlight angled in through the ancient glass windows when they came inside the house. Brace stood awkwardly in the middle of the room, but Pavel turned and immediately went into the small room that had become his own.

Brace exchanged a glance with Tassie, each of them sharing the same concern. Brace shrugged helplessly, but Tassie pulled in a breath and turned to follow after Pavel.

Brace watched from the doorway as Tassie entered the room and sat beside Pavel on the edge of the bed. He had once again gathered his father's lightweight gray cloak into his arms, onto which he had pinned his mother's golden brooch, and he sat staring down at it.

"I know you must miss them terribly," Tassie said softly. "This was your mother's?" she asked, touching the edge of the brooch, the gold band encircling a leafy branch. "Can you tell me about it? Does it mean something?"

"It's just Mam's," Pavel muttered, his head down.

"She can't hear you," Brace reminded him gently. "You need to face her when you talk to her."

Pavel looked up at Tassie. "It was just Mam's," he repeated.

"It must have been special to her," Tassie commented. "It reminds you of her, doesn't it?"

Pavel nodded.

"It's good to have things to remind us of people we've loved and lost," she told him, her eyes filling with sorrow.

Brace felt his stomach tighten with the realization that they had no such comfort to help ease the pain of their own loss.

Pavel nodded in response, and Tassie ran her hand over his hair. "Are you hungry?" she asked him. "Would you like anything to eat before you go to sleep?"

"Bread?" Pavel asked, to Brace's surprise. He hadn't thought the boy would want anything, the way he always picked at his food.

"With honey?" Tassie asked. "Do you like honey?"

Pavel nodded.

"Good. Come with me and we'll have a little bread with honey before we go to sleep."

Pavel ran his hand over his father's cloak, fingering the brooch momentarily before gently setting it down beside him and rising to follow Tassie.

Brace moved aside, allowing them to pass through the doorway. He caught Tassie's hand for a moment and winked encouragingly at her. She glanced into the main room at Pavel's back, then gave Brace a quick kiss on the cheek.

After eating a bit of bread with honey in the fading summer light, Pavel went off to bed almost without having to be told.

Brace wandered through the front room after trying to leave Pavel with a few words of comfort. Sweeping a sprinkling of bread crumbs from the table, he brushed them off onto the stone platter that still held several slices.

Wandering.

Wondering.

*What am I doing? What are we doing?*

He lingered in the doorway leading into his own bedroom, watching Tassie smooth out the skirt of her night dress. Lowering herself onto the bed, she pulled the lightweight blanket up to her waist and sat gazing into the distance, loosely braiding her hair. He smiled to himself as he sauntered into the room and slipped off his shirt. Tassie grinned flatly, letting her hair fall loose as Brace slid into the bed. He wrapped his arms around her, holding her close, her long brown curls soft against his face. She looked up at him, smiling a tired smile.

"Today was a bit easier, wasn't it?" Brace asked as they lowered their heads onto their pillows.

"It was," Tassie agreed. "I don't think Pavel really wants to start going to the school, though."

"I saw that," Brace commented regretfully. "We'll just wait and see how he feels about it tomorrow, and take it from there. I still think it would be a good thing for him."

Tassie nodded and let out a breath.

"Tired?" Brace asked.

"Yes. Aren't you?"

"A bit." Brace hesitated, considering whether to bring up the question that had entered his mind. "Tassie? Do you have any regrets about letting Pavel stay with us?"

"Regrets? No ..."

"You don't seem certain."

"I'm not sorry that we're taking care of Pavel," Tassie explained. "I just wish he felt more at ease around me. It's only with you, Brace, that he ever seems to feel comfortable."

She was right, Brace knew. Pavel followed Brace everywhere, his brown eyes showing his desperation for something that was, at the very least, familiar to him.

"He just needs more time," Brace told Tassie. "It's only been a few days."

"I don't know how to help him with his grief," Tassie responded. "He doesn't know us. He doesn't know anyone here. His whole life has become a tumbled, terrible mess. His family must have been so full of hope, wanting to come to Haven. All of that hope has turned into terrible, terrible grief. What can we possibly to do ease it?"

"I don't know," Brace had to admit. "Try and get some sleep yourself," Brace advised gently. "You'll feel better about things in the morning."

Tassie nodded, though her expression was doubtful. Brace ran his fingers through her hair, brushing it away from her face.

"You said you always wanted to take care of people," Brace reminded her. "You said you wanted to do something that really mattered. Isn't helping Pavel doing both of those things?"

"It is," Tassie replied.

"You never said you expected any of it to be easy," Brace pointed out.

"No," Tassie admitted, finally smiling a little. "I'm glad you're in this with me, Brace. I know I've had a hard time admitting that I can't do everything myself. But I am glad we're in this together."

"I'm always here for you, Tassie. Always."

Tassie smiled and kissed him, a real kiss, the one she only gave him when she was certain no one else could see them. "You sleep, too. I'll see you in the morning."

The room was dark, and it was quiet, and Tassie was soon asleep, her back tucked up snugly against Brace's side. He lay on his back for the longest time, listening to the sound of her breathing. Despite the encouragement he had given her, there was no way to be certain about the outcome of anything, and the longer Brace thought about that fact, the more doubt began to fill his mind.

He tossed and turned, pushing the thoughts into the back of his mind, and eventually he dozed off.

It seemed only moments later when he felt himself flinch, waking up in the full dark of night. It only took him a moment to realize why he had woken up so suddenly – he could hear Pavel crying all the way from the other room.

"Oh, blast," he muttered, shoving the covers aside and pulling himself out of bed. He stumbled through the house into Pavel's bedroom.

The pale blue moonlight was all Brace had to see by, but he could tell, looking at him, that the boy was crying out in his sleep, having a bad dream.

Brace sat down on the edge of the bed and gently shook Pavel until his eyes flew open in alarm.

"It's all right," Brace told him quickly. "It's me. You're safe. It was only a dream."

Pavel sat up, whimpering, clutching at the blankets, and leaned against Brace's side, hot tears running down his face.

"It's all right," Brace told him, putting an arm over him awkwardly. He sat silently as the sound of Pavel's crying slowly faded away. If only Tassie could hear what was happening and come to help! Brace was by no means as skilled at giving comfort as Tassie, that was certain.

"Are you all right?" Brace asked at last.

*Of course he's not all right!* Brace scolded himself. *He's lost everything!*

"Maybe I should get you some water," Brace suggested.

"No," Pavel muttered.

"All right, then. You're all right. It was only a dream. If you feel better, you should try and go back to sleep. The night is just getting started." He gently pushed the boy's tangled curls away from his face, surprised at how warm he felt. "Are you feeling sick at all?"

"I'm not sick," Pavel replied, putting his head back down on the pillow.

"Well, all right. If you need anything, you can come and wake me up. It's all right, I promise you."

Pavel nodded in the pale blue moonlight.

"I'm not far away," Brace reminded him as he rose to leave.

"Brace?" Pavel's voice sounded small and timid.

"Yes?"

"Why did they have to die?"

Brace lowered himself back onto the bed. "They didn't *have* to die, Pavel."

"Why did they, then?"

"It was the night screamers," Brace told him. "They want to stop people from getting to Haven."

"Why?"

"Because they are evil, and Haven is good," Brace replied simply. "I know you're very sad about losing them," he went on. "It's all right. We understand. You don't need to try and pretend you're all right if you're not. Okay?"

"Okay."

Brace sat in the pale darkness, gazing down at his hands, listening to Pavel's quiet breathing. "Can you sleep again?" he asked him.

"I think so."

"Good. Try and sleep. I'll see you in the morning."

"Brace?" Pavel asked again, just as Brace was reaching the doorway.

"Yes, Pavel?"

"I think I'm ready to try going to school," Pavel said quietly, much to Brace's surprise.

"Really?"

"Yes. But… what if I cry?"

"There at school, do you mean?" Brace asked. "What if the others see you?"

Pavel nodded.

"Don't worry over it," Brace told him kindly. "Everyone knows what happened. They'll understand. They know how sad you are."

There was silence as Pavel took in Brace's words.

"All right."

"You'll be fine, Pavel. I know you will. You're brave, I can see that. You'll be all right. Try and go back to sleep."

The room was silent but for Pavel turning over under the old quilt. With a tired sigh, Brace got back into his own bed at last, slowly, not wanting to wake Tassie. The air was quiet and dark, though without its usual feeling of peace. There was tension in the air, though Brace knew it was just *there*, not in all of Haven, but only inside the walls of the house.

He took a deep breath, then let it out and closed his eyes, matching the rhythm of his own breathing with Tassie's until he finally drifted off to sleep once again.

# ~ 17 ~

Brace sat at the heavy wooden table and watched Pavel nervously picking at his boiled egg. Steam from Brace's mug drifted up into his face, and he blew lightly on the surface of the tea. Readying herself for another day at the clinic, Tassie came into the room, tying her hair with a wide strip of gauzy white cloth.

"Aren't you hungry, Pavel?" she asked, seeing his half-eaten meal.

"A little," Pavel muttered.

Brace reached out and lightly tapped his arm. "Look at her when you talk, remember?"

Pavel's eyes widened, realizing he'd forgotten, then he looked up in her direction. "A little hungry," he repeated.

"Does it taste all right?" Tassie asked.

"I think his nerves are just getting to him," Brace told her when Pavel made no response.

Tassie gave Pavel an encouraging smile. "I'm sure you'll be all right. You've been to school already, haven't you?"

Pavel nodded, picking a piece off his egg and eating it slowly.

Brace drank from his mug of hot tea while Pavel ate, one small bite at a time.

"You'll be fine, then," Tassie went on. "There are not a lot of other children living here, but there are a few. You'll have a chance to make some new friends."

Pavel nodded again, eating the last of his egg and washing it down with a glass of water.

"Are you ready to go, then?" Brace asked, and Pavel looked at him in surprise.

"The others are all at the school by now," Brace explained. "They've probably already started. It's all right, though. Don't worry over it. It won't matter if you're not there right on time."

Pavel let out a little sigh.

"Are you ready?" Brace asked him again, and he nodded.

Brace rose from his seat and took one step toward the door. "Come on, then," he said, gesturing for Pavel to follow him. Brace had mixed feelings as Pavel slowly got to his feet, ran his hands along the front of his shirt, and moved away from the table.

Were they pushing him too hard, too quickly?

"I'll be back soon," Brace told Tassie, as she handed him the drawstring canvas bag holding Pavel's lunch. "Will you be here, or at the clinic, when I come back?"

"Most likely at the clinic," she replied. "Try and have a good day, Pavel."

The boy looked back at her, a troubled expression on his young face.

"Come on," Brace told him gently, resting one hand on his shoulder. "Let's go. Tassie and I will be here waiting for you when you're done for the day."

Pavel simply nodded in response as they went out through the door, a gesture that Brace was by now all too familiar with.

After walking to the school house in silence. Brace could hear children's voices coming from inside, and Pavel must have heard them too; he stopped suddenly and looked up at Brace, his eyes full of uncertainty.

"I will walk you all the way inside," Brace told him, gently prodding him forward. "Do you remember Kendie?" he asked. "At the picnic we had in the courtyard, by the fountain?"

"Yes."

"Good. Well, she will be here at the school, today. That's one familiar face at least."

Pavel made no response as Brace pulled open the school house door. Nine pairs of eyes turned toward them almost as one, and Brace felt Pavel lean against him as though for protection.

"Good morning, Brace," Yara greeted him quickly, crossing the room. "This is the new boy ... Pavel, is it?"

Brace nodded, relieved that Yara was acting as though they simply had a new student, and not a grieving boy who had lost his entire family less than a week past.

"Hello, Pavel," Yara said, smiling down at him.

"Hello."

"We're glad you're here, Pavel," Dorianne joined in. "We're just getting ready to start our day. There are a lot of places where you can sit. Would you like to choose, or should I give you a place?"

Pavel peered into the room, and at the other children, as though he were being asked where he would like to sit in a forest full of wild bearcats.

"He can sit with me," Kendie called out from the far corner.

"Would you like to sit with Kendie?" Yara asked, as Brace gave Kendie a grateful smile.

Pavel nodded.

"Here is his food for later," Brace said as he held out the canvas bag for Dorianne.

"Oh, good. I'll go and put it with the others."

Dorianne took the bag, and Brace smiled awkwardly at Yara.

"Here, Pavel," she said, tearing her gaze away from Brace, "go ahead and sit down there with Kendie and we will start soon."

Pavel looked up at Brace nervously.

"You're all right. Try not to worry about anything. Try and make a friend."

Pavel took a deep breath and slowly made his way toward the far table, where Kendie sat smiling a welcoming smile.

"How is he?" Yara asked quietly.

"Well enough," Brace replied. "I don't know how things will work out for him here, today. He doesn't talk much."

Yara smiled. "That will be a welcome change from Shale and Trystan!"

Brace chuckled.

"I think Pavel will be all right today," Yara told him. "We will watch out for him."

"Thank you," Brace replied. "I'll be out around the city today, helping with some projects. Tassie will be at the clinic if…" Brace shrugged. "If things don't go well."

"Thanks." Yara smiled awkwardly.

"Well, I'll go and let you get started," Brace said as he ran his fingers through his hair.

"Right. Good. Tell Tassie hello for me," Yara replied, taking a step back.

"I will."

Brace gave Pavel one last glance before he turned to leave.

Yara turned toward the center of the room and caught Dorianne's eye, nodding.

"All right, everyone," Dorianne announced. "Let's start."

The room was already near silent, as the seven students were trying to unobtrusively watch Pavel, curious about the boy they had heard about, but for the most part never seen.

"Class, this is Pavel," Dorianne introduced him. "Pavel, my name is Dorianne, and this is Yara. We work together to teach everyone here." Getting no response, Dorianne went on. "Right. Well, why don't all of you tell Pavel your name and how old you are?"

Pavel watched and listened as he learned that Ona and Kendie were both fourteen, Hoden was twelve; Marit, nine, Aneerah and Trystan were eight years, and Shale, seven.

"How old are you, Pavel?" Dorianne asked.

"Ten years."

"Well, it's good to have you here," she told him, and his gaze fell to the table in front of him.

"Well," Dorianne said once again, "let's begin our day with the words we know in Haven's language. Who wants to start?"

There was silence for a moment, until Marit spoke up.

"I will."

"Thank you, Marit."

"*Ev* is house, *opok* is tree, *burkus* is bird and *cuva* is water."

"That's very good," Dorianne told her, "but remember, water is *suva*, not *cuva*."

"Right," Marit replied sheepishly.

Dorianne looked around the room. "Anyone else?"

"I remember some," Hoden announced softly, sitting at Pavel's right. "*Ishaya* is light and *ranik* is dark."

Dorianne smiled. "Thank you. Anyone else?"

"I'll say something," Kendie volunteered. "*Amat, rakkan*. It means 'welcome, friend'," she added, looking over at Pavel.

He merely blinked in response.

"That was perfect, Kendie," Yara spoke up. "Anyone else?"

Shale coughed, but no one volunteered any more words.

"All right, then," Dorianne began, "let's write down all of those words and see if we can think of any more words that go along with them. If Yara and I don't know how to say them in Haven's language, we will find out and we'll learn them together next time we meet."

Pavel watched as the other students began their work.

"Here, Pavel," Kendie said, sitting beside him. "I have an extra sheet of paper. You can have it. And you can use my pencil," she added, handing him the shaft of pressed charcoal wrapped tightly in a narrow strip of cloth.

Pavel ran his fingertips along the blank surface of the thick, soft paper.

"Do you know how to write?" Kendie asked him.

"Yes."

"Good. Now, this is a new language. Did you know that Haven has its own language?"

"No."

"Not until today," Ona pointed out, grinning.

Kendie laughed. "Right. Here, you can see what I've already written," she told him, pulling out another sheet of paper. "I'll help you if you need it."

Pavel followed Kendie's direction, slowly writing each word on the fresh paper. He noticed the boy on his right eyeing him curiously, and he could feel the occasional glances of the others as well.

He flinched, startled, when the door to the schoolhouse opened and a young woman entered, wearing a deep red dress and fringed sky–blue sash around her waist. Her long brown hair was pulled back in a loose braid, and she smiled broadly.

"Hello, class," she greeted them cheerfully.

"Hello, Eridan," Dorianne replied. "I'm glad you could come today."

"It's no trouble," Eridan told her with a wave of her hand. "I love sharing poetry."

"All right then, everyone," Dorianne addressed the class, "let's put our words away for now and hear some poetry from Eridan."

The rustling of paper filled the room, as at least most of the students were eager for anything that gave them less writing to do.

"Thank you for coming," Yara told Eridan, standing beside her as Pavel watched with curiosity. "This is your last day here for a time, isn't it?"

"Yes," Eridan replied. "We're leaving tomorrow for Larkswell."

"I'm glad you could spare a little time."

"Oh, I would *make* the time for this! I've been told music and poetry run through my blood, and I have no reason to doubt that it's true! In fact," she added, looking out through the window, "poetry is always so much more inspiring when heard outdoors. Would it be all right if we took the children outside for this?"

Eridan looked from Yara to Dorianne.

"Yes," Dorianne replied. "We've taught them outside before. That would be fine. Come outside, everyone," she told the class. "Let's all gather outside in the sunshine."

Pavel watched as the other students pushed away from the tables, leaving their papers behind.

"Come on, Pavel," the boy beside him urged. "Come with us."

Pavel obeyed, following the slightly taller boy toward the doors, glancing behind him to see Kendie smile at him kindly. Outside, Pavel could hear the splashing water in the fountain, but couldn't see it. He realized, as he stood in the small open area outside the school, that the fountain must be on the other side of the high wall behind him. Sitting on the paved ground with the rest of them, even the teachers, he found himself wondering which side road led back to Brace's house – he couldn't remember. He hugged his knees to his chest and tried to pay attention.

"Well," Eridan began, facing the small group of students, "I would like to share with you another one of my favorite poems. Are you all ready to hear it?"

"Yes!" Marit exclaimed enthusiastically.

Eridan laughed. "All right." She closed her eyes and breathed in deeply before beginning.

"The fair mists drifting o'er the land
Rising in dampness, covering the trees.
The clouds in the skies break open,
And once again my heart believes.
The rain sings a gentle song
Brought in by wind from o'er the seas.
Puddles dancing in the dirt,
Water pooling among the leaves.
The thirsty earth drinks its fill
And the soil no longer grieves."

Eridan settled into a contented silence, looking out over the students gathered close around her, and she smiled. "What do you think of that one?" she asked expectantly.

"It sounds hopeful," Ona replied. "I liked it."

"I'm glad!"

"But I thought rain was a bad thing," Trystan questioned. "That's why it doesn't rain here."

"I don't think rain is a bad thing," Eridan told him. "We just don't need it here. Haven gives us water from the ground up, not from the sky down."

"Did you know that?" the boy seated beside Pavel leaned over and asked him. "Did you know it never rains here?"

Pavel shook his head.

"Do all poems need to rhyme?" Shale asked, his voice heavy with complaint.

"No," Eridan replied. "They don't need to. But I like the rhythm of it when they do."

"People don't talk that way."

"That's true. But that's why it's called a poem." Eridan smiled, and Shale accepted her explanation with silence.

"The main thing with poetry," Eridan went on, "is to put words together so it makes a picture in your mind, or gives you a certain feeling. *Any* feeling."

"I like poems," Marit spoke up.

"I'm glad." Eridan smiled. "Why don't you try and make up some of your own poems? I think each of you should create just two lines of your own."

"Does it need to rhyme?" Shale asked petulantly.

Eridan laughed, and Dorianne scowled over her shoulder at the boy. "No, just make sure it paints a picture in your mind. I know you can do it."

Pavel looked around as the others sat, apparently deep in thought, trying to put words together. But Pavel didn't even try; he simply stared at the tops of his worn leather boots and hoped the teacher wouldn't ask him to speak.

~

When all of the newly created lines of poetry had been shared, some of which were actually very good, Eridan told the class how much she had truly enjoyed the time she had spent with them, encouraging them to keep using their imaginations. After she had left to ready her things for the trip to Larkswell, the students were all brought back inside to finish writing their words and sentences in Haven's language, and then there was mathematics.

Pavel already knew much of what was being taught on that particular subject, and he only half listened while everyone worked and asked the teachers their questions.

When the students were told they could go outside again to eat their meals and have an hour of sport, Pavel sat on one of the farthest benches, hoping he would be left alone. It didn't last long, though; the boy who had sat beside him in class quickly spotted him and came over to join him.

"Can I sit here with you?" he asked.

"Yes," Pavel replied hesitantly.

"My name is Hoden," the boy told Pavel. "In case you forgot."

Pavel nodded. He had forgotten, but he was not about to tell him that.

There was silence for a time as Pavel took a large bite of bread and chewed slowly. Hoden started in on what he'd brought with him as well – Pavel couldn't be sure, but it looked to him rather like rice mixed with corn.

"Is …" Hoden began hesitantly, "is it really true, what happened to your parents?"

Pavel had just been ready to take another bite of bread, but he stopped and lowered his hand.

"Yes."

"I'm sorry. I won't ever talk about it again, either. I promise," Hoden added, seeing Pavel turn his face away slightly.

The boys ate in silence. Pavel had the feeling that Hoden wanted to say more, but he was uncertain of himself. That was well enough – Pavel did not feel like talking.

They were nearly down to their last bite when two younger boys ran up, one of them clutching an old leather ball stuffed with leaves. The ball had been opened up, re-stuffed, and closed up again so many times that there were more holes in the leather than stitches.

"Let's play kickball!" the boy exclaimed.

Hoden looked over at Pavel. "Will you play?" he asked. Pavel hesitated. "At least *try*?"

Pavel slowly chewed the last of his bread, then stood.

"You'll play?" the younger boy asked hopefully.

Pavel shrugged.

"Come on," Hoden encouraged. "You'll have fun."

"What's this?" the smaller of the two girls exclaimed when the boys joined them. "*Another* boy to play? Now it's *four* against two. We'll *never* win!"

"Hush yourself, Aneerah," Hoden scolded her. "He's new here. We have to let him play."

"It isn't fair," Aneerah insisted, crossing her arms over her chest while Marit smiled at Pavel.

Hoden sighed. "All right, all right. Since I'm the biggest, what if I play on the girls' team? Would that be fair?"

Marit and Aneerah exchanged a glance.

"Yes," Aneerah replied firmly, apparently very satisfied with the outcome.

"All right," Hoden said in a firm voice. "Shale, Trystan and Pavel against me, Marit and Aneerah. Boys on that side," he said, pointing, "and girls over there." He turned toward Pavel. "If one team kicks the ball past the other team, past the edge of the courtyard, they win a point. We play to make as many points as we can until we run out of time."

Pavel looked around, taking note of the large, square area outside the front of the school. His eyes fell on Kendie and Ona, who stood at the far side of the school house, sharing in a private conversation. Hoden noticed the question in Pavel's eyes and smirked.

"Those girls say they're too grown to play. They probably won't even come to classes next year at all."

Pavel shifted his shoulders, almost a shrug.

"Let's play!" Trystan called out impatiently.

"Right," Hoden agreed. "Pavel, your team is over there. Try to kick the ball past us."

Pavel followed the younger boys as the two teams put distance between themselves.

Copper-haired Shale dropped the ball on the ground with a heavy *thump*. "All in!" he shouted, then kicked the ball with everything he had in him. The leather mass skidded and rolled across the courtyard as everyone rushed toward it.

Pavel had played games like this many times, and he recalled how it felt to strive for your team, to keep the other side from getting through at any cost. It felt strange to him now, though. What had once felt so important seemed pointless to him now. He felt heavy, and trembly inside. Every time he blinked, he could see those black, wingless creatures darting through puffs of thick smoke, diving at them, baring their teeth, their eyes glowing like points of flame ...

"Pavel, watch out!" a girl's voice shouted, but he hardly had time to react before the large leather ball came flying up off the ground and smacked him right on the side of his face.

He cried out in pain and surprise as he felt the sharp sting against his cheek, and felt the heat rising to the surface as he pressed his hand against his face.

"I'm sorry, Pavel!" Marit exclaimed, rushing to his side. "Are you all right?"

Pavel felt tears pooling in his eyes. He was all right – he knew he would be, of course. His emotions were raw, though, and he was frustrated, embarrassed, angry and sorrowful all at the same time. He turned away from the others, not wanting them to see him cry.

"What happened?" Kendie exclaimed as she ran to Pavel's side.

"The ball hit him on his face," Marit explained. "I kicked it. It was an accident. I'm sorry, Pavel!"

Pavel wanted to tell Marit that it was nothing, only part of the game, that he would be fine, but he couldn't bring himself to utter a single word. Waves of pin-pricks radiated across his hot face, and he could feel the tears escaping from his eyes.

"Pavel," Kendie said as she bent to look him in the eye. "Are you all right? Do you want me to take you to Tassie at the clinic?"

Pavel swallowed, then nodded.

"All right. Ona, will you tell Dorianne and Yara what happened, and where we're going?"

"I will," Ona replied, hurrying into the schoolhouse.

"Come with me," Kendie said gently as she put an arm around Pavel's shoulders and led him away. "You'll be all right. Tassie will help you feel better."

*Feel better?* Pavel wondered. Would he ever feel better? His face would, soon enough, that much he knew. But *inside*? Inside, he ached for the loss of his father, his mother, his uncle. Even Ransen and Kanna, who he'd hardly known. Inside, he was full of fear. He couldn't get rid of the pictures in his mind – those terrible creatures. He was plagued with worry that they would come after him again, though everyone here assured him it wasn't possible.

He just wanted someone to hold him close, with their arms around him, to feel like nothing in the world could harm him.

Would he ever be able to feel that way again?

# ~ 18 ~

The pure water of the orchard stream ran down hill, glinting in the sunlight, as Jair strode across the smooth grassy hill sloping up toward the center of the shady orchard, his small pack slung over his shoulders. The stream made a peaceful sound, a sleepy sound, and Jair let out a contented breath. He let the cool air of the orchard settle over him, a relief after his fast-paced walk through the streets. The day's meetings were over at last! Since Ovard had informed Jair that he alone was responsible for leading things, Jair had felt an added strain of responsibility.

Today he'd had several meetings, including the one with Hyman and Nadira about their pottery supplies and their kiln – they were in need of more clay to keep up with the requests they had been getting for drinking vessels, plates and bowls. Thankfully, the pale burning stones that Haven had led Jair to discover were keeping their kiln burning well, and they no longer had any need for firewood.

Jair trudged farther up the hillside, trying to put out of his mind the list of things people had said they needed. He had written everything down, and he couldn't possibly provide any of those things today. *Let it rest*, he told himself. Let it rest, and let his own mind rest as well. Goodness knows it had been working more than hard enough over the past week.

Shrugging out of his pack, Jair lowered himself onto the grass and stretched out under a short, sprawling fruit tree, lying on his back on the soft green grass and looking up at the blue patch of sky overhead. He flexed every muscle in his arms as he reached out, the blades of grass brushing against his hands.

So much had happened – Pavel's arrival, the funeral for his family, placing the lightstones along the mountain pass, dealing with self-blame. Gavin was leading another search mission now; they had been gone four days, and Jair was missing his friend. Gavin had tried, as had so many others, to convince Jair that he was not to blame for the recent deaths inflicted by the night screamers. Jair had grown tired of hearing it, and was relieved when Gavin had taken to simply starting meaningless conversations with him, or sitting quietly by his side. It was nice to just have his company.

Jair still felt a twinge of guilt whenever he saw Pavel. What could he say to him that hadn't already been said? He was so silent, Pavel was, Jair thought to himself. Even now, after having been in Haven six days, he hardly spoke. He'd been going to the school, Jair had been told, but he couldn't imagine how that could possibly be working out.

He pushed himself up with a sigh and leaned against the solid base of the fruit tree. He pulled his pack closer and untied the strings, tugging it open. He had tossed his carving knife into the bag, along with a new block of gnarled wood. He was intent on carving a statue of Haven's frolicking deer, though now that the banner bearing Haven's crest hung proudly at the front of the Fountain Court for all to see, he wasn't sure why. It was a challenge; perhaps it was as simple as that. Jair had given up on the first piece of wood when he realized that the proportions hadn't been right.

But *this* one – this one should work. Jair was confident that he could even make use of the twisty burl of wood as part of the design. Now he just needed to start.

He held the block of wood in one hand and his knife in the other, feeling the weight of it. Studying the shape of the wood, he pictured the finished project in his mind. Carefully, he pressed the short, sharp blade against one edge and began to carve off curling slivers of wood, letting them fall into the grass around his feet.

Over the last few days, the ache of what had happened to Pavel's family, though it still remained, had been replaced with the familiar nagging sensation that Haven was trying to tell him something. It was as though someone was tapping him on the shoulder, though it was in his mind that he felt it, and not on his skin.

Why couldn't he understand? Nothing that Haven had wanted to tell him had been clear at first, that was true, but he had always understood eventually. It had never taken this long, either. He was stubbornly hanging on to that truth, believing that whatever this was would come to him as well.

*Not alone …*

He thought he could see brief flashes of pictures in his mind, but he couldn't make himself hold on to them.

*Fire …*

The burning rocks? Yes …

*Laughter … Sunlight …*

Jair frowned, trying now to put the thoughts aside. *Later*, he told himself. *I'll try again later.* Right now, all he wanted to do was carve on the gnarled piece of wood and try to make an image of his own take shape in his hand.

He carefully planned out every cut he made, keeping the picture of the frolicking deer at the front of his thoughts. The top right edge of the wooden piece was starting to take a recognizable shape when Jair caught sight of movement among the trees.

He paused in his work to look up. It was Kendie, coming up the hill carrying a large basket.

*Oh, what is she doing out here?* Jair wondered, bristling. Picking fruit, of course, but of all the people in Haven, why did it need to be Kendie? Jair's mind was flustered enough already! He had come out here to calm his thoughts, but he felt them getting stirred up again.

The whole terrible mess about Pavel's family, the mysterious message that Haven was trying to communicate to him, and now *Kendie.*

Ordinarily, Jair would have enjoyed her company. It was true, they had been friends for so long, and lately Jair had begun to feel more than friendship toward her. His heart would jump in his chest, a strange sensation that he had never felt before, except perhaps about Persha, but it didn't feel quite the same. With Persha, he would often feel nervous and insecure, his palms sweating. But with Kendie … he just wanted to be near her. To hear her laugh or sing, to tell her things, deep things, and have her do the same.

Jair had thought she felt the same way about him, but lately she had seemed to be avoiding him. It was all too confusing, and now Jair had no idea what to do, what to say to her.

Jair watched her picking fruit for a moment, some distance away. Her long black hair was loose, not braided, and it fell around her shoulders and down her back in soft, dark waves. There was no wind today, Jair noted, no breeze to toss her hair around.

Kendie was pretty in her own way, Jair thought to himself. She must be fourteen years now, and Jair would be sixteen soon enough.

He smiled to himself.

*Kendie!* She so loved life! Jair loved to hear her sing, or even just try to make up songs. He loved the way she was determined to learn new things – anything and everything from archery to medic skills to reading Haven's language. He loved the way she still seemed so innocent, so hopeful, so open about caring for others, even before she really knew them. She was just so *good*.

He watched as she continued picking from the same tree, her basket nearly half full. He should let her know he was there. If she turned and came upon him suddenly, she would get startled. He whistled slowly, a low sound, mimicking the birds that often nested in the orchard. Kendie continued picking, so he whistled again. She stopped and looked out toward the sound. Jair whistled a third time, a high sharp whistle, and he waved as Kendie looked in his direction. She smiled a little, leaving the heavy basket at the base of the tree to come slowly toward him.

"Hello, Jair," she said as she came closer. "Nice afternoon, isn't it?"

"It is," he replied. "Will you be making a pie with all that you're picking?"

"Maybe. Something like that."

Jair nodded. He thought he noticed a slight edge to her voice – or had he only imagined it?

"How is everyone?" he asked, wanting to keep the conversation going. "How is Denira?"

"She's very well," Kendie replied, softening. "As full of laughter as ever, and just as lively. She's getting better at running around, and she wears me out sometimes. Zorix, too." Kendie laughed. "Sometimes he climbs up onto the shelves so Denira can't reach him to pester him."

"I don't blame him for that," Jair commented, grinning.

"What's that you're working on?" Kendie asked, her gaze falling on the block of wood.

"Well," Jair explained, "it's the deer. Haven's deer. I gave up on the other piece. It wasn't the right shape. I think this one will work out a lot better."

"That's good."

Jair shrugged.

"No, it really is. If it's something you want to do, don't give up on it."

Jair smiled. "I'm not sure if that sounds more like Ovard or Arden."

Kendie laughed softly. "I've decided it sounds like *me*. That's going to be my advice to others. Don't give up."

"It's good advice."

Kendie nodded, pushing her hair away from her face.

"How is Pavel these days?" Jair asked. "He has been going to school, right?"

"He has," Kendie told him. "He's doing all right, I think. He doesn't say much. No one's really worried about making him keep up with school work for now, of course."

"Right."

"I feel so bad for him," Kendie went on. "I want to be a friend to him, but I don't know if he's thinking about having friends, since he's still missing his family so much."

"Did you tell him not to give up?" Jair asked quietly.

"Not exactly," Kendie replied. "I just want him to know I care about him."

"That's good," Jair told her. "That's really important."

"You're not still blaming yourself?" Kendie asked. "For what happened on the mountain?"

Jair hesitated. "Not so much."

"Good," Kendie said firmly. "Because it was *not* your fault. Not at all. You know it's true."

Jair nodded, setting the gnarled piece of wood down in the grass.

"I'm sorry," Kendie said abruptly. "You were working on your project. I'll go."

"You don't need to," Jair told her.

"No, I should," she replied, some of the edge returning to her voice. "Leandra will be waiting for me to bring the fruit back."

"Do you need help?" Jair asked her. "It's going to be heavy, isn't it?"

"Not too heavy," Kendie replied. "It's fine. I can do it."

"You're sure?"

"Yes. I have enough fruit already. I don't need to fill the basket all the way. You stay and work on your carving." She smiled a little. "I'd like to see it when it's done."

"I haven't forgotten that," Jair told her. "I'll make sure you see it. I hope it will come out the way I expect it to."

"It will," Kendie replied. "I'd better go, Jair. I'll see you again soon."

"All right. See you soon." Jair tried to keep the surprise out of his voice due to Kendie's rush to leave. What had happened to the times when she used to seek him out, always seeming to want to stay near him longer?

Kendie waved and turned away, traipsing back down the grassy hillside to her basket. Jair watched as she hefted it up, balancing it on her hip, before heading back toward the city.

Jair groaned and lay down again on the ground. He did not need any more confusion, any more frustration, any more questions! He needed answers!

The bright blue sky spread out over him, over everything in every direction, as far as he could see. He felt a bit dizzy, lying on his back and staring up at it.

He hadn't set foot outside of Haven in three years – did the sky look as bright and full of summer out there as it did here? Likely not. Things were darker out there, Jair reminded himself.

Suddenly, a thought came to him. The dark, the light, the night screamers – and the hope and peace that Haven provided. Wasn't all of *that* the most important thing? Wasn't that the purpose he had dedicated himself to? Helping people come to live in Haven, and restoring it to everything it had once been, thousands of years ago? Making it everything it was meant to be, and helping people live lives they were meant to live here? Why should he burden himself with anything beyond that? How could he have let himself become so distracted from his calling, from his purpose, the purpose that Haven itself had chosen for him? Everything else would work itself out, wouldn't it? As long as he stayed true to his purpose as overseer. Jair felt it in his heart – a rekindling of passion about why he was here, why he had been marked with the way to Haven, why he was alive!

He gazed up at the sky, seeing it with new eyes. He had been taking the sunlight for granted. He had to remember the darkness that ruled beyond the safety of Haven's gate. He could never let himself forget there were still so many people who needed to be rescued. So many people were relying on him.

He watched the streaks of white clouds sailing by overhead, and his heart felt strengthened, lightened. Sitting up again, he gazed at the choppy, gnarled block of wood, picked up his knife, and went back to work.

# ~ 19 ~

Brace watched Pavel, sitting at the table once again, picking at his breakfast.

*Again.*

He hoped the boy wasn't losing any weight; he didn't seem to be. He wished there was some way he could talk to the boy's father, as crazy as it might sound, and ask him what he could do to help him.

Pavel had taken to wearing his mother's brooch, pinned to the front of his shirt, and Brace was so familiar now with the image of the small leafy branch, it was as though he'd been seeing it for years instead of days. Pavel also slept covered with his father's cloak, Brace knew. The boy was still having nightmares, mostly about the screamers. It was always Brace who came to his room at night when he heard him crying, and Pavel always clung to him, desperate to feel safe. It was in those moments when Brace felt the most helpless, the most inadequate.

Sometimes Tassie woke when Brace got back into bed, sometimes not. When she did wake, her question was always the same. Was Pavel all right? Brace never knew what to say, so he always said the same thing. *It was just a bad dream.* Pavel had been plagued by the same frightening dream again the previous night, and now, sitting down to eat, he looked so tired. Brace was tired, too; he felt it in his foggy thoughts, in his gritty eyes and in his creaking joints. He had served on the gate watch again, once during the past week, and Tassie had gotten Pavel off to school herself that day. The boy's heart was not in it, Brace had been told, not in class or in an effort to make friends. Dorianne had shared, though, her belief that Pavel had intelligent eyes.

189

There were no classes today, however, and Brace was searching for ideas as to what to do, so Pavel wouldn't be sitting around the house brooding.

"Please eat your bread," Tassie told Pavel. "You need to start your day with a good meal. Would you like to put some honey on it?"

"All right." Brace heard Pavel's mumbled response, but the boy quickly realized that Tassie hadn't heard or seen it, and he looked up. "Yes, please," he repeated clearly.

Brace grinned crookedly. One thing for certain, Pavel always seemed to respect the fact that Tassie couldn't hear, and he was more than willing to make certain she could see his face, whenever he did happen to speak to her.

Tassie gladly pulled the jar of honey off the shelf, removed the lid, and dropped a spoon into it, setting it on the table in front of Pavel with an encouraging smile.

"Thank you," Pavel said softly as he reached for the handle of the slowly-sinking spoon.

Brace watched him as he let the sticky golden honey drizzle onto his rounded slice of warm buttered bread, as Pavel carefully replaced the spoon in the honey jar and took a bite.

Brace looked aside at Tassie, and she returned his gaze, forcing a smile. *At least he's eating*, her eyes seemed to say. Their days with Pavel seemed to be one day that repeated itself again and again – struggling to get him to eat in the morning, getting him off to school, Pavel silent and melancholy all the while. Brace and Tassie both had other matters to take care of, working at the clinic or helping with various projects around the city, and Pavel would come home from school as silent as ever. They tried to make light conversation, but his responses to their questions were usually comprised of one or two words, given out of a sense of respect, not wanting to be rude, but not wanting to talk about anything.

And then at night, there was Pavel's nightmare. Brace would always awaken and go to him, trying to soothe him, telling him that everything was all right and he was safe.

Whenever Brace began to wonder if Pavel even wanted to stay with them, he had only to remember the way Pavel would cling to him so tightly every night when he came to comfort him. He had only to see the look in the boy's eyes – desperation mixed with gratitude.

It made Brace's insides churn, knowing that Pavel looked to him for safety, for security, and for something in his world to make some sense. When Pavel looked at Brace after he'd had his nightmare, it was as though he was pleading with him to tell him why this had happened, or that everything really *would* be all right, as everyone kept saying it would be.

Brace couldn't do it, though. He couldn't say that to Pavel, not again. They'd done all they could, Brace, Tassie, Jair, Arden, even Medarrie and Noora. Now it was up to Pavel himself to make the rest of it work. It would take time, Brace knew, for the nightmares to stop and the pain of loss to ease.

A light knocking sound drew Brace out of his thoughts.

"Someone is at the door," he told Tassie, looking in her direction. She started to get up from the table, but he gestured for her to stay.

"I'll see who it is."

He pulled open the door, not having the faintest idea of who to expect on the other side. Would it be Arden?

No, it was not Arden. It was Adivan, who had come from Roshwan two years earlier. He stood just outside the door, with his family beside him.

"Good morning," he greeted Brace. "I hope we're not disturbing you, coming early as we are."

"It's no trouble," Brace told him. "What brings you here?"

"It's Hoden," Adivan replied, resting his hand on his son's shoulder. "We're going out to the southeast garden to pick some berries, and Hoden thought Pavel might like to join us."

"Oh," Brace said in surprise. "Well ... sure, I'll ask him. I hope he will," he added quietly. "I'm glad you came by. It will be good for him to get out, and go somewhere other than just to the schoolhouse."

Adivan nodded as Hoden smiled shyly, Vania and Aneerah waiting nearby, carrying extra baskets.

"Do you mind waiting here for just a few minutes?" Brace asked.

"No, of course not," Adivan replied.

"Great. Thank you. I'll be back." Brace gently closed the door and turned back toward the room, Tassie and Pavel both eyeing him with curiosity.

"It's Adivan and Vania," Brace explained. "And the kids. They're going to pick berries and thought Pavel might like to come along."

Tassie nodded, looking over at Pavel.

"You know Hoden from school, don't you?" Brace asked. "He's inviting you to pick berries. Why don't you go with them? See if you can get a full basket."

Pavel chewed thoughtfully at his lip.

"Has Hoden been kind to you at school?" Tassie asked, and Pavel nodded. "Why don't you go, then? You could have some fun."

Brace watched Pavel for a moment, then came back to the table, sitting beside him, laying his hand over Pavel's where it rested on the table.

"Listen, Pavel," he began gently. "I can see that you're not overly *wanting* to go, and I understand why. But I also see that Hoden wants to be a friend to you. In the long stretch of things, I'm sure you will regret it if you don't go with him today. So I want you to go. I'm telling you to go. You understand why, don't you?"

"Yes."

"Good," Brace replied, feeling relieved at Pavel's response. "Then let's get you a basket and you can go. Hoden is waiting for you."

Tassie quickly located an empty basket and held it out for Pavel, who accepted it.

Brace gave Tassie a quick kiss on the cheek and ushered Pavel toward the door.

"Oh, good, you're coming," Adivan greeted them as the door opened.

"Hello, Pavel," Hoden said shyly. "I'm glad you're coming with us. I – I'm sorry about what happened the other day while we were playing ball."

Pavel nodded.

"He's all right," Brace spoke up. "Thank you. But you're not the one who kicked the ball, are you? Wasn't it one of the girls?"

"Yes, it was Marit. But I'm still sorry. I'm the one who talked him into playing."

Brace grinned, then shook his head and looked up at Adivan. "How long do you think you'll be out?"

"We should have him home for lunch," he replied. "Is that all right?"

"That's perfect," Brace told him. He rested his hand on Pavel's shoulder and gave it a light squeeze. "Try and have some fun," he said, but Pavel only nodded.

Brace shrugged apologetically, but Adivan shook his head. "We will have a good time, I'm sure."

"Goodbye, Pavel," Tassie spoke from the doorway.

Pavel blinked, shifting his shoulders, almost a shrug. Brace watched as Hoden walked beside Pavel, telling him about the different types of berries they would be gathering, and how each of them tasted.

When the high lightstone wall at the edge of the road blocked them from view, Brace turned back toward Tassie. She stood with her arms crossed lightly, leaning her shoulder against the doorframe. Her long, pale blue dress draped over her loosely, down to her sandaled feet. She had that free-spirited look to herself now, the one Brace loved, with her wavy brown hair was pulled back and loosely tucked up in a twist at the base of her neck, a few strands escaping and falling around her face. He focused in on her green eyes and grinned.

"I think Pavel will have a good day today," he commented lightly.

"If he will let himself," Tassie replied.

Brace nodded in agreement, standing at the other side of the doorway. "You know, this is the first time we've really been alone together in a while. You're not going to the clinic today, are you?"

Tassie smiled. "Not unless I'm asked for."

"I like that."

Tassie's smile widened. "And what, exactly, did you have it in your mind to do?"

"Anything you want," Brace replied earnestly.

Tassie glanced out at the road passing between their house and the next. She looked at Brace again before going inside, not speaking a word. Confused, Brace followed her, closing the door behind him.

"I'm glad it's just the two of us again, at least for a little while," she told him, taking his hand in hers. "I miss *us*."

Brace nodded, a thought forming in his mind. "So do I … but Tassie, it wouldn't have been just the two of us anymore, if we *had* been able to have a child of our own …"

Tassie frowned slightly, but she held his hands tightly. "You know it wouldn't be the same," she told him, "not like it is now. There would be a *baby*, Brace. Just a little baby, our own flesh, not this boy, who we know nothing about, other than his pain of having lost his family. It wouldn't have been the same at all."

"You're right, I'm sorry," Brace apologized, instantly feeling heavy regret at having spoken his mind. "It would not have been the same. I just meant about us having time to ourselves, that's all."

Tassie pondered Brace's words for a moment, and eventually her eyes softened.

"I know," she said in a whisper, then turned away. When she did not turn back, Brace went to her, resting a hand on her arm.

"What's wrong?" he asked, and she shook her head.

"Tell me."

"It's just everything," she said with a sigh. "All of this with Pavel. I want to help him, but I can't. I can't even hear him cry at night, but it's you he wants, Brace. Always. I can't make any connection with him. I've tried and tried. And I still ache inside, Brace. I ache over…"

"The baby?" Brace asked softly.

"Yes."

"Why didn't you tell me?"

"How could I?" she asked. "How could I put more burden on you when you've got so much of one already, caring for Pavel?"

"I'm still here for you," he told her. "I want to be here for *you*."

"There are things, Brace, things I haven't been able to tell you, there hasn't been time since Pavel came to us. There's been so much happening, trying to help him, and we – I – haven't had time to work out our own troubles. I still feel that way. Don't you?"

Brace sighed. "I do. But I'm here, Tassie. I've been here all this time. If you had something you wanted to say to me, why didn't you?"

She shook her head. "It doesn't seem right. You have so much on you, with Pavel. He needs you. And I can't really do anything to help you."

"You *are* helping me," Brace told her. "I don't want *us* to suffer, Tassie. I care about Pavel, and I know you do too, but we can't forget about *us*. If you have something you want to tell me, please do it."

Tassie held Brace tightly. "No," she said softly. "No, it's all right. I just – I just need to let it be."

"Will you tell me when you feel you need to?" Brace asked her as she stepped back.

She nodded. "I will. I promise."

"Good."

"I still think we're doing the right thing," Tassie went on, "looking after Pavel."

"I'm glad," Brace replied. "So do I."

"He never seems to *want* to be any trouble," Tassie thought aloud, "to bring anyone down or be a burden to anyone."

"He doesn't," Brace agreed.

"He is good-natured, I mean. Don't you think so? He has a good heart."

Brace nodded. "I think so too. That, and his parents must have been good people. They have been raising him well."

"They must have been."

"Pavel just needs to be able to get through his grief," Brace went on. "We'll never see who he really is while he has all of this sadness hanging over him."

"I think he is getting a little better, isn't he? He agreed to go berry picking, after all. I was afraid he wouldn't want to leave your side."

"He's been doing all right, going to the schoolhouse," Brace pointed out.

"But he still won't talk," Tassie reminded him.

Brace let out a breath. "One day at a time," he told her. He smiled. "I thought this time was supposed to be about *us*, not Pavel."

"You're right," Tassie agreed with a smile. "We could use some more fresh water in our basin. Will you walk me out to the orchard stream?"

"That's what you want to do?" Brace asked her in surprise. "Go get more water?"

"It won't take us three hours to get water," Tassie scolded, again taking his hand in hers.

Brace smirked, hearing the teasing edge in her voice and seeing that familiar feisty expression, for so long vanished, swallowed up in sorrow.

But it was back, that look on Tassie's face. She was strong, she was brave; she believed the best about others, even if no one else did. She knew what she believed, and knew what she wanted her life to be. She was all of those things, and she was kind, and she was beautiful.

And she was his.

Brace took her other hand and marveled once again at the sight of their markings, flowing across one hand and onto the other, joining them together as one.

He looked up at her. "Why did you promise yourself to me?" he asked. "You could have had anyone. What made you want me?"

Tassie tipped her head slightly.

"I love you, Brace."

"But you didn't always. When we first met, you knew I was trouble. You even told me so yourself."

Tassie smiled softly at the memory.

"I could see the struggle inside of you," she told him. "I could see that you were fighting to make a choice. And so many times, you made the right choices. You surprised all of us. But that isn't why I fell in love with you."

"Why did you?"

Tassie stepped closer to him.

"Why does anyone?" she asked quietly. "My heart was touched by yours. It started something – I felt something inside that I'd never felt about any man I'd ever met. Like there was a little fire burning in my heart, and it flared up whenever I saw you."

"You never let on," Brace said with a slight frown. "For the longest time, I had no idea how you felt about me."

Tassie ducked her head slightly. "I know," she replied, looking up again. "I am too independent at times, aren't I?"

"Aren't we all," Brace agreed, slipping his hands out of hers and gently holding her face close to his own. "I love that you're independent," he went on, gazing into her eyes. "I love that fierce temper of yours that you keep so well hidden. I love that you always want to do the right thing. I love the feel of your hair against my face at night."

Tassie's breath caught in her throat, and Brace leaned closer. "I love you," he whispered, kissing her before she had a chance to respond.

Tassie returned the kiss, and Brace was caught up in it. It was just the two of them again, at last! "*Pavel might see us*" was no longer a possibility. At least for a little while ….

Pavel stood surrounded by leafy, knee-high bushes, feeling rather as though he was in the middle of a sweet-smelling jungle. Hoden, his sister, and his parents were all nearby, pulling ripe red berries from among the little explosions of leaves protruding in every direction.

They had already filled two large baskets with small, round, purple berries growing at the far side of that particular stretch of farmland, and now they were working on filling the smaller ones. Pavel's basket, the one Tassie had given him, was woven from wide plant fronds that creaked whenever he picked it up. It sat on the hard-packed dirt at his feet now, the bottom half full of purple berries, covered over with a growing layer of red ones.

"Aren't you picking any, Pavel?" Aneerah asked, squinting at him in the bright sunlight.

Pavel looked over at her, then down at his basket.

"We're not tiring you out, are we?" Hoden's mother asked.

"No," Pavel replied, though his arms were beginning to feel a bit weary.

He could see more people off in the distance with baskets of their own, wandering up and down the rows of bushes. He knelt on the ground once again, not wanting to be asked any more questions about how he was feeling. Pushing aside the wide, flat leaves, he searched for ripe pieces of fruit.

A shadow fell across him and he looked up. Hoden stood over him for a moment before kneeling at the other side of the long row of bushes.

"My basket is almost full," he said. "I can help you with yours."

Pavel nodded. "All right."

Hoden smiled as the two boys went to work, pulling free one palm-sized berry at a time and dropping them lightly into Pavel's basket.

*All right.* That's all he had said. He had wanted to say more, he just couldn't bring himself to do it. He wanted to tell Hoden thank you for wanting him to come with him today, thank you for wanting to be his friend. His heart hurt too much, though. Pavel felt that if he just went on as he always had, it would be as though he was denying the fact that his parents had died, and his uncle Erhan, and Ransen and Kanna. How could he do that to them? Just force himself to go on and act as though they had never lived, as though they hadn't been killed by those horrible black creatures?

He felt tears welling up in his eyes, but he did *not* want to cry. Not again. Crying only made people pity him, and he did not want to be pitied. Especially not by Hoden.

Pavel forced himself to focus on the big pieces of red fruit, turning to stare into the basket for a moment until he was sure his eyes were clear.

"Is it getting full?" Hoden asked.

Pavel simply nodded, not trusting his voice at all for the moment. He held his hands out flat in front of him, leaving a gap between them to show Hoden how much room was left in the basket.

Hoden smiled. "Come on," he said, standing and brushing the dirt from his knees. "If we move farther down the row, there will be more berries and we can fill it up faster."

Pavel stood, feeling a hint of Hoden's smile in his own heart as he grabbed the basket's handles and dragged it through the dirt. Finally, they stopped at a place where Pavel could see the red berries peeking out all over. "Let's finish up," Hoden said excitedly as he knelt on the ground once again. "As soon as we get home, we can eat them." He grinned mischievously. "Or *more* of them."

Pavel was silent as he knelt in the dirt and went back to picking.

"Haven't you eaten any?" Hoden asked.

Pavel shook his head.

"No? Not any? Not even *one?*"

Again, he shook his head.

"It's all right to do that, you know. It's all right to eat a few while we pick them. They're really good. Have you had this kind of berry before?"

"Yes."

"Then you know they taste good," Hoden went on, "but they taste even better here! Go ahead, eat one!"

Pavel glanced along the leafy bush and found the biggest one. He gently tugged, and it came away easily, so he knew it was ripe. He looked at it for a moment, then bit it in half. It was firm and soft at the same time, and sweet and tangy all at once. The flavor settled onto his tongue, growing bolder, stronger. Hoden was right, the berries *did* taste better here. How was that possible?

"Good, huh?" Hoden asked.

Pavel nodded, managing a bit of a smile before eating the rest of the large red berry.

Hoden smiled broadly as he grabbed more berries and tossed them into the basket. In another moment, the berries reached to the rim so that the last one Hoden had tossed into it rolled right back out again.

"We're done!" Hoden exclaimed. He glanced around, the full light of the summer sun glinting off his smooth black hair. "Can you run fast?" he asked. "I'll race you to the far end of the field and back!"

*Race?* Pavel felt a jolt at the thought of it. *Run?*

Hoden leapt to his feet. "Come on, let's go!" He bolted down along the row of bushes toward the edge of the field, laughing. "Come on, Pavel!"

*Run!*

Pavel jumped to his feet and ran without even thinking. He used to run all the time, with friends back home. He would run and laugh, just as Hoden was doing now. But now Pavel only felt fear squeezing him, not laughter. The sun was bright, and the air was warm, and the sweet smell of red berries hung in the air. It didn't fit, this feeling of panic welling up inside him, but there it was. Pavel looked back over his shoulder, suddenly remembering what he had seen the last time he'd been running.

Those black things. *Screamers.*

His eyes quickly scanned the blue sky above him. He didn't see any, but suddenly he could hear them echoing in his ears. He ran faster, for all he was worth, with everything he had in him. His heart beat faster, and though Hoden was taller, Pavel's urgency pushed him on and he quickly passed him.

"Hey!" Hoden exclaimed, laughing. "I didn't know you were that fast! You're winning!"

Pavel kept running, panic overtaking him, erasing every thought but one.

*Run! Run, Pavel! Go get help!*

The sound of the black creatures screeched in his ears, and for half a second, he was sure he could see one hovering in the sky above him, trailing a twisting curl of gray smoke behind it.

He reached the far end of the field, but kept running. Hoden was right behind him, panting heavily, struggling to keep up.

"Pavel! You can stop now, Pavel! You won!" He reached out and managed to grab hold of Pavel's elbow, but he yanked it out of his grasp with a frightened cry, stumbled forward a few steps, then crumpled to the ground, landing on his knees and covering his head with his arms.

"Pavel," Hoden panted, standing beside him. "Are you all right? What happened?"

Pavel made no answer, only hunched on the ground, breathing hard.

"Mam! Dad!" Hoden called out across the field, waving his arms frantically. "Help!"

Adivan ran easily across the rows of berry bushes, reaching the boys quickly. "What happened?" he asked in alarm.

"I don't know," Hoden replied. "We were racing, and he won, but he kept running. Now he's like *this*."

Adivan crouched beside Pavel and gently laid a hand on his shoulder, but he flinched and pulled away.

"Pavel, you're all right," Adivan told him gently. "You're safe. It's all right."

"Night screamers," Pavel muttered. "Night screamers, night screamers!"

"What's wrong with him?" Hoden asked fretfully.

"He's afraid," Adivan replied. "I think some bad memories have caught up with him." He moved closer to Pavel, putting an arm around him and holding him close until he felt the tension in his muscles ease off.

"Pavel," he said softly. "It's all right. Nothing here will hurt you. You're safe here, remember?"

Slowly, hesitantly, Pavel looked up, his eyes wide.

"That's right," Adivan encouraged. "It's all right. We were picking berries, Pavel. You've got a whole basket of them back there waiting for you to take them home with you."

Pavel swallowed, still shaking, and nodded.

"All right, then?" Adivan asked him, speaking slowly, calmly. "You're all right? We can go and get our berries now. We're all done here."

Pavel glanced around nervously at the sky overhead before slowly getting to his feet.

"You're all right?" Adivan asked him again, standing.

Pavel nodded, though he felt on the verge of tears.

"I'm sorry, Pavel," Hoden told him. "I didn't think anything like that would happen."

Pavel nodded again, sniffing and running his sleeve across his face.

"Come on, boys," Adivan told them. "Let's get our baskets and head for home."

~

Brace and Tassie had scarcely been home for half an hour and were fixing a midday meal when Brace heard the sound of someone knocking. He gave Tassie a little wave and pointed toward the door, and she nodded.

Brace was not surprised to see Adivan and his family, along with Pavel, all of them carrying baskets full of berries. He was surprised, however, to see that Pavel's face was streaked with tears.

"What happened?" were the first words out of Brace's mouth.

"Pavel had a bit of a scare," Adivan explained.

"It was *my* fault," Hoden announced glumly. "I'm the one who said we should race each other."

"It was an accident," Vania asserted.

Brace looked Pavel over quickly, from head to toe. "Pavel, are you hurt?"

"No," he replied meekly.

"What, then?" Brace was utterly confused.

"I think it was the running that did it," Adivan spoke up. "It was like he was running from the night screamers all over again. I know how frightening those things are, Pavel, believe me. I've seen them myself."

Pavel kept his gaze low, clutching the handles on the woven basket.

"Well..." Brace rubbed absently at the back of his head. "Thank you for bringing him home."

"I hope you'll be feeling better soon, Pavel," Vania told him.

"He'll be fine," Brace told her, leaning toward Pavel. "You'll be all right, won't you?"

Pavel nodded.

"Good. I'll take that basket for you. I'm sure you've carried it far enough by now, haven't you?"

Pavel gave no answer as Brace hefted the full basket into his arms.

"Thank you again for inviting him along," Brace said as he stepped out of the doorway, allowing Pavel to go inside. "Try again some time, will you?"

"We will," Vania replied.

"Don't be so hard on yourself," Brace told Hoden, seeing his downcast face. "Pavel just has things he needs to get over, and I think having friends will help."

Hoden nodded as everyone said their goodbyes, taking their heavily-laden baskets and heading for home. When Brace turned into the front room, pushing the door closed with his foot, Tassie was kneeling in front of Pavel, her eyes full of concern.

"What's wrong?" she asked him. "You've been crying. Didn't you enjoy having time outside with your new friend?"

Pavel stood silently as a tear ran down his face. Tassie wiped it away, then looked over at Brace.

"He picked a lot of berries," Brace told her, setting the basket down on the table. "But ... he had a sort of ... he was ..." Brace stammered, unsure what to say.

"I don't understand, Brace," Tassie told him with frustration in her voice. "What happened?"

"He got scared," Brace replied bluntly.

Tassie looked back at Pavel. "You're all right now," she told him. "Are you hungry at all?"

"I'm tired," Pavel replied.

"All right. Why don't you go ahead and rest for a bit? We will have lunch ready soon, and you can eat when you get up."

Pavel nodded, then turned without a backward glance and disappeared into his room.

Tassie stood up with a sigh.

"It's all right," Brace whispered, standing close beside her. "He just had a setback, that's all it is."

Tassie leaned against Brace for a moment. "I wish I knew how to help him."

"I know," Brace agreed. "Don't worry about it right now. Let him sleep if that's what he needs. Let's eat."

Tassie sighed, then nodded.

Their meal was a quiet one as they sat at the table, the basket of berries still sitting untouched at the far end of it. The whole house was quiet, in fact, until Brace heard the all-too-familiar sound coming from Pavel's room. He startled, and Tassie looked at him in surprise.

"What's wrong?"

"It's Pavel. He's having a bad dream again. Do ... do you want to go to him?"

Tassie shook her head. "No. You should. It's you he'll be expecting to see."

"All right," Brace replied, pushing away from the table and crossing the room. He hurried over to Pavel's bed and hesitated before taking hold of his arms to gently shake him awake.

"Pavel! Pavel!" he called out his name when the crying stopped. "I'm here, Pavel. I'm here, and you're all right."

Pavel opened his eyes, pushed himself up from the bed and threw his arms around Brace.

"It was only a dream," Brace told him, but Pavel shook his head.

"No," he sobbed. "It was those black things. They attacked us!"

Brace let out a breath, wrapping his arms around Pavel, hoping that somehow he could make him feel safe. "It's all over now," he said quietly.

"It's *not!*"

"It was real, I know," Brace told him, "what happened on the mountain. But it was only a dream, just now. It's over."

Pavel whimpered and held Brace tighter.

"It wasn't real, out there in berry field, either," Brace went on. "The screamers can *never* come into Haven. You're safe from them. It was only your fears and memories catching up with you today."

Pavel sniffed. "I miss my mam and dad."

"Of course you do," Brace replied. "You'll always miss them." Brace chewed at his lip. Surely he could think of something better to say than that?

He realized, as he sat holding Pavel close, that he knew so much more about the boy than Pavel did of him. He hadn't opened up to Pavel at all, not really. He hadn't told him anything about himself, about his life.

"I know how you must be feeling right now," Brace confided, "losing your parents. My ... my own mother died when I was young."

Pavel looked up, his dark eyes wide with surprise. "She did?"

"Yes. She just got ill. She died, and I was taken to live with a man who was very cruel to me. I know how it feels, to have your heart breaking when the only person on this earth you want to run to, the one you want to hold you, will never be there for you, not ever again." Brace paused, suddenly flooded with unpleasant memories. "I know how it feels to be afraid."

Pavel blinked up at him, saying nothing.

"I know we're not your family, Tassie and I," Brace went on, "and I know it isn't the same, but you're not alone the way I was when I was a boy. Tassie and I care about you, and we want the best for you. Do you know that?"

Pavel nodded, slipping lightly out of Brace's arms to sit back and look at him.

"I'm sorry your mam died," Pavel said softly.

"Thank you," Brace replied, surprised. "I'm all right now. It was a long time ago."

"Do you still miss her?"

"I do," Brace replied, running his fingers through his hair, a nervous habit, "sometimes I do. But I'm not alone anymore, and neither are you." Brace paused to take a breath, encouraged by the way Pavel was looking up at him, and by the way he was responding to Brace's honesty. "I was alone for a long time," he continued, "and I know how it feels to think you don't belong anywhere. But I really think you do belong here, Pavel. I know Tassie and I aren't your true family, but we want to be here for you. You're not alone here. This is your home now, Pavel, or it *can* be. Here with me and with Tassie, and with everyone else who knows you and cares about you."

Pavel nodded slowly, and Brace could see that he really was taking his words to heart.

"I cried again today," Pavel told him, his voice full of regret. "I cried in front of Hoden *again*."

"That's all right. Hoden is your friend. He knows what you're sad about."

Pavel tucked his knees to his chest and wrapped his arms around his legs, resting his chin on one knee.

"I don't want people to see me cry."

Brace nodded. "I feel the same way."

"Have you ever cried in front of anyone?" Pavel asked.

Brace felt himself holding his breath for a moment. That had to have been the longest set of words he had ever heard come out of Pavel's mouth!

"I have," Brace admitted. "I think everyone has cried in front of someone. But it's all right to cry, especially in front of people who love you. If they really do love you, they'll be there for you even when you're hurting."

Pavel nodded slowly.

"Hoden really wants to be your friend, I think," Brace told him. "And he blames himself for what happened to you today."

Pavel glanced down at the quilt that covered the bed. "I'm not angry at him."

"Well," Brace replied gently, "make sure you tell him that when you see him next, will you?"

"I will."

"Good. And remember," he added, "to just keep on going, keep on living, even when life is difficult. Even if it feels like too much, you've got to keep a little bit of hope in your heart, that things will be good again. Friends will help you hold on to hope. I want to help you hold on to hope, Pavel. So does Tassie, and so does Hoden, and so do a lot of other people here."

"You do help me," Pavel told him, almost in a whisper.

"I'm glad. And I think you are bringing some hope here too, for Tassie and me both."

Pavel raised an eyebrow questioningly.

"Never mind about that," Brace told him, suddenly feeling that he'd said just a bit too much. "You've got to be hungry," he said, redirecting the conversation. "Or did you eat heaps of berries while you were out picking them?"

"No," Pavel replied, shaking his head. "I only ate one."

"Well then, are you hungry for something more? There's some food out there just waiting for you to eat it."

"Thank you," Pavel replied, unfolding his legs and sliding to the edge of the bed, standing beside it. Brace joined him, gesturing for him to go on.

"Thank you, Brace," Pavel said again.

"For what?"

"For … everything," Pavel replied.

"It's no trouble at all," Brace told him. "Really, it isn't. I'm glad you're here."

As Brace followed Pavel into the front room, he felt a renewed sense of peace in his heart. He felt that a large piece of his burden of worry had been carted off and thrown away, so that he would never be able to pick it up again. He was glad that he had been open with Pavel, sharing about his past. It had truly seemed to make a difference. Brace recalled the time when he'd told himself that he would never share his story with anyone. Had he changed that much? Haven certainly did have a way of changing people for the best; he had seen that with his own eyes.

Brace had been given that chance to change, and bit by bit, he had accepted it, though it had been painful at times. But he'd done it, with encouragement from those closest to him. If he could make it here, so could Pavel, Brace was sure of that. He would never give up on him, either. It was just going to take time.

# ~ 20 ~

Light-hearted chatter filled the courtyard as bright sunlight shone off the glassy surfaces of the thick lightstone walls surrounding it. Clear, cool water cascaded down the fountain, and one or two of Haven's little white birds found themselves bold enough to come in for a drink despite the small crowd of people who had gathered there.

Brace enjoyed watching Tassie talking with Essa, and he tried to keep his mood as light as everyone else's seemed to be. He was feeling pensive, though, weighed down by unanswered questions and almost-realized hopes.

Tassie's heart was truly healing after everything she'd gone through, and for that Brace was grateful, relieved. Also, the things he'd been able to share with Pavel only a few days past had seemed to bring a change to the boy's overall disposition, though he clearly still bore a heavy burden, and kept his words few.

Now, though, when Pavel looked up at Brace, it was no longer with a sense of desperation; it seemed to be more a look of respect, clouded over with lingering sadness.

Brace was grateful, today, for Ben-Rickard's companionship. The two of them sat side by side on a stone bench, leaning back against the wall, drinking chilled tea laced with sweet juice from the orchard's orange-yellow fruit. Jordis stood beside them, leaning casually against the wall, watching the others with a look of pure contentment. Brace recalled the time when Jordis had considered leaving Haven, feeling, as Brace once had, that he did not deserve to live in such a perfect place. Brace still found himself awed by the fact that maybe the man was still here in Haven because of things that he himself had been able to say to him, letting him know that no matter what his past, he was *here* now, and he belonged here.

He would never have thought that he would have been capable of touching the lives of others with anything good, anything that could make such a difference. His memories of feeling lost, angry, hurt, and abandoned were like a damp fog in the back of his mind. All of the times he had lied, stolen and cheated others, not caring an ounce what came of anything he did, were now in his distant past.

How had he managed to become molded into the man he was today, a man who loved deeply, a man who considered others before taking action, a man whose words had brought hope to others, had helped them make the right choices for their own lives?

His heart warmed considerably at the thought that he had actually been able to be a real help to anyone, but it also left him with a strange feeling of being burdened to do more. He found it easy to read people's moods without even trying. He could see when they were joyful, or confused, or hesitant, or full of fear of sorrow. And he always felt something deep inside of him, something that wouldn't let him walk away if he thought there was something he could tell them, something helpful or encouraging. How did he always know the right thing to say to them?

It baffled him.

Maybe Jair was right. Maybe everyone who found their way to Haven *was* here for a reason, a purpose. Maybe there was some specific role for each person to play here, to do something that really mattered.

Could he have become some sort of an encourager? He, Brace, the former thief, the liar?

He smirked to himself. Odd, ironic, that Haven would choose a man who had found it so easy to live a life full of lies to now speak the truth into the lives of others.

It made him wonder about each and every person who now called Haven home. Jordis. Ben-Rickard. What purpose had they been chosen for? And the three who had just arrived with the team who had just returned from Larkswell? Tormas, Arto and Ilarie Joutsen, Jair had said their names were – what important part would they come to fulfill here?

Brace felt a nudge from Ben-Rickard's elbow, and he looked over at him.

"Your boy seems to be much improved," Ben commented.

Brace looked out across the courtyard to where Pavel stood gazing up at the top of the fountain, where a small white bird was hopping and flapping around, snatching beakfulls of water.

"Better, yes," Brace agreed. "I don't know if I would say *much*, but he does seem to have gained a bit of confidence. It seems to help him, wearing his father's cloak as he is. And a brooch of his mother's. It's his way of keeping them close. I never thought I'd see the day when he would wander more than two feet away from me."

Ben smiled. "He must feel safe with you."

Brace nodded. "I do want him to know that he is safe here."

Brace heard Arden laughing, a rare sound, a deep sound that demanded to be heard. He looked in his direction, where Arden sat beside Leandra, with Daris, Ovard and Jair standing close around them. Something amusing must have been said; they were all laughing now.

Brace's eyes traveled slightly away from the group to where Kendie sat at the next bench, keeping Denira entertained. She seemed content, but Brace couldn't help noticing the way she would glance up now and again. It had to be Jair she was looking at, Brace decided. He recalled that she had, years ago, confessed interest in Jair that went beyond friendship.

She had made Brace keep her secret, and of course he had told no one. It wasn't his place; it didn't concern him at all. Besides, they were *children* – weren't they?

Suddenly, Brace wasn't so sure. Looking over at Jair once again, he took in his height, which now matched Ovard's; he took in the hint of defined muscles that ran along his arms, peeking out from under the half-cut sleeves of his white linen shirt.

Looking back over at Kendie, Brace watched her pull her eyes away from Denira once again, her gaze unmistakably falling on Jair's face. Her long dark hair was clean and soft, and looked as though she had taken extra effort to tame its unruly curls. She was near fully grown! Odd that Brace hadn't noticed until now. She was *Kendie*, the skinny little girl from the Wolf and Dagger, wearing the threadbare dress, who liked to sing and prattle on. Wasn't she?

In Dunya, Brace knew, eighteen years was considered an acceptable age to be eligible for marriage, and Kendie was only four years shy of that herself now. It seemed obvious that her infatuation with Jair had not faded over the years, but rather it had grown deeper. Brace wondered if Jair knew anything about any of it? And if so, did he return Kendie's affections at all?

"Bwace, Bwace!" Denira's small voice called out as she hurried toward him, her blond hair flouncing around her ears.

"Hey there," Brace blurted out in surprise as Denira flung herself at his knees. He reached out to steady her, and she laughed.

Brace looked up as Kendie followed after Denira, carrying a clay platter of food. She held it out with a smile.

"Would you like some goat cheese?" she offered.

"Well …" Brace began hesitantly, as Denira pulled at his hand. "I'm sure I've eaten plenty, but I can't pass up some of Leandra's cheese. She made this, right?"

"Right," Kendie replied. "Well, Essa and I helped her."

Brace smiled and took a piece off the plate. "Perfect." It was amazing, Brace thought as he savored the taste of the soft white cheese. The handful of herbs that Leandra always tossed into her batches of goat cheese made such an unexpected difference in the flavor, and he could never pass up on it when he was offered a slice or two.

"Cheese?" Kendie offered, moving over to Ben-Rickard.

"Of course," he replied. "Thank you."

Kendie smiled.

"Up, Bwace!" Denira said firmly, still tugging at his free hand. "Up, up!"

Brace chuckled, swallowing the last bite of creamy cheese. "I thought your dadda was trying to teach you some manners," he commented, lifting Denira onto his lap.

"Cheese, sissie?" The girl asked, holding out a hand.

"Well," Kendie replied, sounding unsure. "Just one. I don't think Leandra will mind if you have *one* more."

Denira finished off the square of cheese in three bites, smiling contentedly as she chewed.

"How have you been lately?" Kendie asked Ben-Rickard, holding the platter so that the rim rested against her hip.

"I can honestly say I have nothing to complain about," he replied with a chuckle. "And what about yourself? Are you still training with Tassie?"

"I haven't been lately," Kendie told him. "She's been ... taking some time away from it."

"Right," Ben replied quietly. "How has she been this past week?" he asked, looking over at Brace. "She seems to be quite herself today."

Brace noticed the full smile on Tassie's face as she stood close by her friends, her family.

"Yes, she does," Brace agreed. "She's been much better, thank you. It hasn't been easy, with Pavel here. But she's been all right."

"*Wook, wook*, Bwace." Denira tugged at Brace's shirt and pointed.

"What?" he asked, looking where she pointed. Jordis was there, and Daris had joined him, the two men talking quietly. "What's over there? Jordis?"

"No," Denira replied. "*Wook*."

Brace chuckled. "I am looking. I don't really see anything. Was there a bird over there?"

"No."

"How is my little one?" Leandra asked, coming over. "Is she behaving herself?"

"She's fine," Brace replied. "She's never a bother, are you?"

Denira smiled.

"I gave her a bit of cheese," Kendie admitted.

"That's all right," Leandra replied.

"Mammy, *wook*!" Denira said again, pointing, just as Pavel wandered over to join them.

"What, sweet?"

"She was just telling me that," Brace told Leandra. "Right before you came over."

"*Wook*!"

"Look at what, sweet?"

Denira pointed, staring, then looked up at Leandra as if to say, "don't you see it?"

"The flowers?" Kendie asked.

"No, *no*!"

"I'm sorry, Denira," Leandra said in an exasperated tone. "We just don't know what you want us to see. Can you show us?"

Denira slipped down off Brace's lap and took a few steps, then stopped. Slowly, she turned back toward them.

"Is it gone?" Kendie asked.

"Gone."

"I'm sorry we didn't see," Leandra told her, confusion in her voice. "Why don't you go play with Pavel for a bit? Go have fun with Pavel."

Denira frowned, but only for a passing second. She looked up at Pavel, then smiled and pointed out toward the center of the courtyard.

"Pway?" she asked hopefully.

Pavel looked over at Brace, and he shrugged and nodded, encouraging him to go on, if he wanted to.

"I'll play," Pavel told Denira, and Brace smiled to himself.

"That was strange," Kendie commented as Pavel followed Denira farther into the courtyard.

"What's that?" asked Ben-Rickard.

"The way she kept saying 'look'," Kendie replied.

"Oh, I wouldn't worry over it," Ben told her. "She's at a curious age, is all."

Leandra nodded in agreement. "It's nice to see Pavel improving a bit," she commented, picking a piece of cheese off Kendie's platter. "You and Tassie must be so relieved, Brace."

"He is doing better," Brace agreed. "He still seems fearful, though. And…" *What was it exactly?*

"He's grieving," Leandra finished.

"Yes," Brace replied.

"I still feel bad for him," Kendie said softly as she turned in his direction. "But Denira seems to be cheering him up, at least a little. She can cheer anyone up, can't she?"

Denira had remembered the basket of fruit that Leandra had brought, and she was busy taking one fist-sized piece out at a time, going up to each person, saying "*hewe!*" and giving them a piece. Tassie, Essa, then Jair, Ovard, Daris and Jordis. She wasn't shy around any of them. They all needed a piece of fruit, and *she* needed to share it with them.

Denira went back to the basket, on her way to where Brace sat beside Ben-Rickard, when she stopped and looked up intently at Pavel, who stood nearby. She tipped her head in thought, then waved him closer.

Brace watched, his interest piqued, as Pavel stepped closer. Denira wasn't satisfied, however, and she gestured for him to come down to her level. Pavel hesitated, then crouched on the stone-paved ground right in front of her.

Denira looked at him closely for a moment, then her face broke into a wide smile. She reached out and pressed the tip of her finger on the end of his nose.

"Pup!" she said, giggling. "Pup, pup!"

Pavel's eyes grew wide, seemingly in surprise, then a smile slowly spread across his face.

Denira laughed her bubbly, childish laugh, pressed the ball of fruit into Pavel's hand, then went back to the basket for another one.

"Pup?" Kendie wondered aloud.

Leandra lifted one shoulder in a shrug. "Maybe she's trying to say 'Pavel'."

"Could be that," Brace replied as Denira ran up to him with a piece of fruit.

"*Hewe*, Bwace! *Fwoot!*"

Brace smiled. "Thank you. It looks delicious."

When she was satisfied that everyone had received their gift, Denira began to hum a tune to herself, skipping and dancing around the wide base of the fountain.

Brace watched her for a moment, then looked up at Kendie, who still stood nearby holding the platter of cheese. Kendie didn't notice him, though – her eyes were once again fixed on Jair, who was busy eating his piece of fruit and conversing with Arden.

Brace had to take a bite of fruit himself to hide his smile. He hoped someday Kendie would be brave enough to tell Jair how she felt about him.

~

Before another hour went by, Tassie wandered over to where Brace was seated and wrapped her arms around his shoulders.

"I think we should head for home," she spoke softly into his ear. "You have gate watch duty early in the morning, remember?"

"Right, of course," Brace replied, looking up at her.

She smiled. "I had a nice time," she told Leandra. "Thank you for inviting us."

"Of course," Leandra replied.

Tassie embraced Leandra briefly. "I hope you have a peaceful evening."

"And you," Leandra replied.

"Pavel," Brace called out, "We're leaving now."

Pavel heard and nodded from where he sat on a stone bench beneath the fountain, watching it with a hint of a smile on his face.

Everyone called out their goodbyes and well-wishes, then Brace took Tassie's hand in his, and the three of them began their walk toward home.

Brace squeezed Tassie's hand and smiled at her. He did not want to break the peaceful silence, but he wanted her to know how content he was.

"You must have enjoyed yourself," Tassie commented. "It was good for you to spend some time with Ben-Rickard. You don't often get that chance."

"No," Brace agreed. "You're right. That was a good thing. It's good to know he's doing well. He, and Jordis."

"Yes, Jordis has become so much more at ease here."

"Kendie, though," Brace went on. "Did you see how she couldn't take her eyes off Jair?"

"I thought I saw her watching him. She has strong feelings for him but she must not know what to do about it."

Brace noticed Pavel looking up at them, listening to their conversation, and he smiled down at him. "Kendie has liked Jair for a long time," he told him.

Pavel nodded, smiling a little. Brace rested a hand on his shoulder.

"You must have enjoyed yourself today too. Denira can be a bright spot in any darkness, can't she?"

"Yes," Pavel replied pensively, running his finger along the bridge of his nose.

It wasn't long before Brace pushed open the door of their home and grandly gestured for Tassie and Pavel to enter ahead of him. Tassie smiled warmly and stepped over the threshold, and Pavel followed her, an amused look on his face.

Brace was in such a joyous mood, and he felt a laugh rising up inside of him as he came in, closing the door behind him. He watched Tassie as she pulled a drinking cup down from the shelf and filled it with water from the basin. She stood near the window, taking a drink, her long wavy hair braided neatly down her back. Brace glanced aside and noticed that Pavel was watching her as well. *Really* watching her. Brace had never noticed him looking that intently at anyone or anything, but for the fountain, maybe.

Brace glanced back at Tassie, then let his eyes settle on Pavel. Yes, he was looking at her, studying her, it seemed. Tassie finished the water, then turned toward Pavel.

"Are you thirsty?" She asked him. "You can get a drink for yourself any time you'd like one."

"No thank you," Pavel replied, his voice sounding more clear than Brace remembered ever having heard it.

"What is it, then?" Tassie asked him. "Are you all right?"

"Yes," Pavel replied, sounding surprised at his own answer. A smile played at his lips, a faraway look in his eyes.

"Pavel," Brace said, sitting on a wooden bench beside the table, "there's something different about you. You seem ... happy," he stated, for lack of a better word. "Can you tell me why?"

Pavel bit his lip, looking from Brace to Tassie and back again.

"It was Denira," he answered softly. "It's what she did in the courtyard. It's what she said."

"What did she do?" Brace prodded as Tassie looked on, intrigued.

Pavel touched the end of his nose. "That," he replied.

"When she touched your nose?" Tassie asked, and Pavel nodded.

"My mam used to do that," Pavel said, almost in a whisper. "And ... my dad used to call me 'Pup'."

Brace raised his eyebrows in surprise.

"Pup?" Tassie asked.

"Yes," Brace replied. "Denira called Pavel 'pup' today, when we were in the fountain court."

*What had just happened?* Brace found himself wondering. "So ... those things Denira said and did ... it reminded you of your parents?"

Pavel nodded. "It's like she knew. Maybe ..." Pavel hesitated, taking a step closer to Brace. "Maybe they told her."

"What? Who?" Brace was bewildered.

"My parents," Pavel explained. "Maybe they told her what to say, or what to do. Maybe … well, maybe they are here too, somehow."

Brace looked over at Tassie to see if she had caught everything Pavel had said, and her surprised expression revealed that she had.

"Pavel …" Brace began, but he shook his head.

"I know they're not *really* here. I know … I know they died. But I felt a little like maybe they wanted to tell me something. I never even got to say goodbye to them."

Brace nodded. "I know. Everything happened so fast."

"Yes," Pavel agreed. "They were there, and then they weren't. And it wasn't right, not any of it. But now I don't feel like they're as *gone* as they used to be."

He looked at Brace and Tassie, one eyebrow raised as though asking if what he'd said made any sense to them.

"I understand just what you mean," Brace told him, still amazed at the whole idea. How had Denira been able to know those things? That Pavel's mother would touch the end of his nose, a tender, familiar gesture? How had she known that Pavel's father had called him *pup*?

"I still miss them," Pavel said quietly.

"Of course," Brace replied. "Of course you still miss them."

"I'm sorry I've been so sad."

"Oh, Pavel," Tassie said, coming to stand close beside him. "You don't need to be sorry for that."

"I'm glad you let me stay with you," he told them. "I'm glad you're nice people."

Brace smiled and gently ruffled Pavel's curly hair.

"Can I …" Pavel began.

"What?" Brace prompted. "Can you what?"

"Can we go back out to the graves? I think I'm brave enough to really say goodbye this time."

Brace looked over at Tassie, and their eyes met briefly. She nodded, a smile growing on her lips. Brace turned back toward Pavel.

"Of course we can go back," he told him. "I'm glad you want to do this. I think your parents would be so proud of you."

Pavel smiled for a moment, then his face grew solemn. "I don't know why they had to die," he said quietly. "But I'm glad it's you I'm staying with."

"I'm glad too, Pavel," Brace told him, and he was surprised to find that he really meant it.

Pavel came up to Brace and wrapped his arms around him, gently this time, almost unsure if he should; not at all like the other times when he'd clung to him out of desperation.

Brace held Pavel close. "This is your home now, Pavel," he told him as he felt Tassie join them, putting her arms around the both of them. "Maybe," Brace went on, "we can be a family."

# ~ 21 ~

Pavel did not have a nightmare that night.

Tassie and Brace, after sharing a breakfast with Pavel which he *ate* and did not pick at, went with him once again to the burial ground. He was truly able, this time, to say goodbye to his family, to speak their names and feel the sorrow of their absence. He was no longer in despair, feeling now that they had been able to tell him they knew he had been grieving, and they wanted him to know that everything would be all right.

Brace was torn between relief and utter amazement – how had Denira possibly been able to say what she had to Pavel? How had she known? He had been mulling it over the past two days, but hadn't questioned either Arden nor Leandra about it. Pavel was so much improved since his brief interaction with Denira, Brace did not want to do anything that would undo the good that had been done.

Brace watched Pavel now, weaving several long, thin strips of leather together in an intricate pattern, and he felt an unexpected rush of emotion. The boy was going to be all right! He looked over at Tassie, smiled and winked, nodding toward where Pavel sat hard at work. She smiled back and nodded. *Yes, I see. Very encouraging, isn't it?*

Brace wandered over to the table and sat across from Pavel, watching him concentrate on what he was doing.

"What is it you're working on, there?" Brace asked him.

Pavel looked up and smiled a bit. "You'll find out when it's done," he told him.

Brace laughed, something he had not done often enough lately, and he felt lighter. "Fair enough!"

Pavel grinned and went back to work. Turning away from the table, Brace waved to get Tassie's attention.

"Do we need more water?" he asked.

Tassie glanced aside at the basin. "Well, we are getting a bit low. It could wait until tomorrow."

Brace shook his head lightly. "I'll go for some now. My legs could use a good stretching."

"All right, then. If you're sure. Thank you."

Brace turned back toward Pavel. "I'll be back within the hour," he told him. "Will you be the man of the house while I'm gone?"

Pavel looked up at him. "All right," he replied, his voice serious.

"Don't worry," Brace told him as he stood, giving him a wink. "I was only joking. Mostly."

Brace smiled as he grabbed the bucket they used to carry water, giving Tassie a quick kiss on the cheek.

"I won't be long," he told her as he headed outside. He wandered along the high lightstone wall edging the main road into Haven until he came to the wide gap, then turned to cut across the paved road, the empty bucket bumping lightly against the side of his leg. He had nearly gotten halfway across the road when he heard a shout.

"Watch out!"

Brace spun quickly, jumping out of the way. Arden was hurrying toward him, followed by Jair and Gavin.

"What's wrong?" Brace asked as Arden approached.

"It's the gate," Arden replied, hurrying on. "Someone is there."

"Again?" Brace blurted out, following him.

"There are three of them," Jair huffed. "Arden was on gate watch and saw them."

Brace nodded in reply. The water could wait. This was more pressing, to say the least. A wave of worry swept over him as he ran along with the others. The last time there had been someone at the gate …

But that could not happen again, Brace reminded himself. Jair had set the lightstones along the pass. No, they would not have had trouble with night screamers. Not along the pass, at least.

"I've got the gate!" Gavin called out as they neared it.

"Right," Arden replied, catching his breath as Gavin ran to press the stone plate, setting the gate to swing open, creaking and lumbering.

A small crowd of curious onlookers was gathering behind them, Brace noticed, but he only glanced in their direction. He watched, with Arden, Jair, and Gavin, as the enormous stone gate swung open, leaving a flattened patch of high summer grass in its path.

Brace had no idea what to expect – no one did – and he startled slightly when three figures came into view, eyeing the opening in the gate with amazement.

"Hello!" Jair called out, moving toward them. "You've found Haven, and you are welcome here!"

"We made it at last!" One of the men called out in relief, gripping the other by the arm. The third was a woman, and all three of them were wide-eyed and brown from head to foot. Brown hair, brown cottagers' clothing, smudges of brown dirt on their hands and faces.

"Come in, come in," Arden invited them, waving them on. "You are welcome here."

Brace felt someone step up beside him, and he glanced over. It was Ovard, with Avi and Brannock just behind him. This was the first time, Brace realized, that Ovard hadn't been right beside Jair to welcome any newcomers. Instead, he hung back, waiting, with Jair's other advisors. Brace could see in Ovard's eyes the desire to come forward and speak, but he held back, watching Jair proudly.

Their eyes wide, the three newcomers slowly came closer, clinging to one another tightly.

"Haven," the woman breathed as she stepped in past the gate's opening.

"Tell me," Jair said gently as more people gathered behind him, "how did you come to know about Haven? How did you know it was here?"

"Everyone knows about it," the taller of the two men replied. "It's all the talk just now." His eyes were wide with amazement as he took in the sight of the smooth, stone-paved road leading into the city, and the high lightstone walls, brightly reflecting white sunlight in every direction.

"How is this possible?" he wondered aloud.

"How?" Jair repeated, grinning. "How, we don't know, I'm sorry to admit. There are still some things about Haven that are a mystery to us. We don't know *how*, we just know that it is."

"What do you mean, everyone is talking about Haven?" Gavin asked boldly. "Last time I was out, there were still people who didn't believe in it."

The two men exchanged glances as the woman slowly came further in, gazing at the lightstone walls in amazement.

The taller man shook his head. "All of Dunya knows of it now."

Brace frowned in thought. *Everyone?* He looked over at the woman, standing near the wall, who pressed her hand to her head and slumped forward, leaning against the wall for support.

"Kaisha!" The woman's companions hurried toward her. "Are you all right?"

"I – I'm fine," she replied.

Ronin pushed his way through the group of people who had gathered near the gate. "I am trained as a medic," he told the new arrivals. "I can help, if you'd like."

Kaisha nodded, and Ronin gently touched her face. "You do feel a bit warm," he told her. "You've come a long way without much rest, haven't you?"

"We have," one of the men replied. "We had to."

"I'm sure you'll be all right," Ronin told Kaisha. "You just need rest, and food and water."

Kaisha nodded in reply as Jair came closer, Gavin following right behind him, almost defensively.

"I'm sorry," Jair began. "I should have introduced myself already. My name is Jair. I'm glad you all made it here safely."

Brace heard the deep sincerity in Jair's voice, and he breathed out a breath of relief himself.

"Thank you," the taller man replied. "My name is Kem. This is Bareo. We're glad to be here ourselves."

"I need to ask you something," Jair went on. "You said that you had to travel long and hard to get here, without much rest. Why?"

"We were afraid someone would find us and stop us," Bareo replied.

"Who would try to stop you?" Jair asked.

"Anyone, really," Kem told him. "Some of King Oden's men, or anyone who'd been paid to come after us."

"I don't understand," Jair said, frustrated and confused. "Why would anyone try to stop you from coming to Haven?"

Kem and Bareo exchanged another look.

"You haven't heard, then," Kem said heavily.

Jair shook his head.

"It's King Oden," Kem explained. "He's declared the city of Haven to be an enemy of Dunya."

A gasp rushed through the crowd as Kem went on. "He's made it known all through Dunya that anyone trying to leave is considered a defector, a betrayer. He's even had some people thrown into prison."

Another staggered gasp was followed by murmurs of anger and surprise.

"Imprisoned?" Arden exclaimed. "He has no right to imprison anyone for simply wanting to find Haven."

Brace could almost feel Arden's anger, it was so plain on his face. He rested a hand on Arden's broad shoulder, hoping to calm him a bit, though he was angered himself at the news.

"He may not have the right," Kaisha spoke up, "but he's done it nonetheless."

"Where are they being held?" Farris wanted to know.

"In the dungeons of Glendor's Keep," Kem replied heavily.

Whispers of fear and concern filled the silence.

Jair's eyes flashed with indignation. "He can't do this!" he exclaimed. "I don't care if he is king of Dunya. It's wrong, and we can't let this happen."

"What can we do about it from here?" Lira asked.

Jair glanced at everyone who had gathered around him, and Brace could see a decision forming in his mind.

"We will go and rescue them," he declared. "We will get them out!"

At those words, Ovard stepped forward at last. "Come now, Jair," he said firmly. "Let's not decide such important matters here. Our new friends need to be cared for. We need to call a meeting. This must be discussed properly, and not rushed into."

The muscles along Jair's jaw tightened, but he ducked his head in assent.

"Come on, then, everyone," he said, with only slightly less intensity. "Go and spread the word, will you? There will be a very important meeting at the Main Hall in thirty minutes. Everyone should attend, if they can. It's *very* important."

Immediately, the crowd began to disperse.

"Come along," Ronin told Kaisha, gently taking her by the arm. "Come and refresh yourself. All of you," he added, looking up at Kem and Bareo. "Regain some of your strength. Jair will want you to be at the meeting, I'm certain."

Brace gave Arden's shoulder a squeeze as he heard Jair request Gavin to shut the gate.

"We will work this out," Brace told Arden when he finally looked over at him. "We need to trust Jair's guidance."

Arden nodded abruptly.

"You should go and get Leandra," Brace advised. "She won't want to miss the meeting."

Again, Arden nodded. "We will be there."

A short while later, though it seemed as though no time at all had passed, Brace sat beside Tassie and Pavel near the front of a very crowded Main Hall. The murmur of voices rippling through the large room was so loud, Brace could hardly think. He found himself once again envying Tassie her inability to hear.

Jair was doing his best, with help from his team of advisors, to keep things under control, but everyone was unsettled, understandably so.

The news that Kem, Kaisha and Bareo had brought from the outside had come as quite a shock, to say the least, and Brace could almost feel the anxiety in the air filling the meeting room.

"It is true," Jair spoke up above the noise, "King Oden has no right to pass such a law, to keep people from finding Haven for themselves. It seems that he is acting on his own anger at not having been able to take Haven for himself." Jair glanced aside at Farris, Alban, and Korian – the King's former soldiers, who had themselves left Dunya to come to Haven. The three of them had pulled together, seeming to draw strength from one another in the midst of the disturbance.

"And not only so," Jair continued, raising his voice, "not only has he passed this law, he has imprisoned some who were caught trying to leave."

There was a general uproar now, and Brace held tightly to Tassie's hand as Pavel leaned against his side. Tassie may not be able to hear, but Brace was certain that she felt the rising temper of the room, just as he did.

"This isn't right!" A voice called out above the din.

"What can we do about it?" another voice challenged. "he is the king *out there*. How can we possibly undo what he's done?"

Jair held his hands up, requesting silence, as his advisors, Ovard included, implored the people to quiet themselves.

"I am just as angry about all of this as you are," Jair spoke again when he knew he could be heard. "I want to do something about it. I don't just want to sit by as though we accept what's happened. I want to fight back. But …" Jair paused, taking a breath to steady himself. "But I want to know your thoughts. It wouldn't be right for me to make a decision that affects everyone here without your … *approval*. Your agreement."

"What is it you think we should do?" Ben-Rickard asked, from near the center of the room.

Everyone grew quieter then, wanting to hear what Jair's answer would be. Jair glanced at Ovard, who kept silent, only gesturing for Jair to go on. It was all up to him; he was the overseer.

"Well," Jair went on, looking out over the crowded room, "I think we should try and set them free. The King's prisoners. It may seem impossible, I don't know. Maybe we can somehow speak with King Oden, tell him what a terrible thing he's doing. But we've got to try something, somehow."

Whispers and murmurs filled the room once again, but Jair remained undaunted.

"Tell me your thoughts!" he called out boldly. "Tell me what you think of this plan!"

"I agree," Arden spoke up first. "I agree it's the right thing to do. We cannot sit idly by while anyone is wrongly imprisoned."

"Do we form a rescue mission, then?" Brodan asked. "Send our own people out after them?"

"I think we've got to try," Jair answered.

"How on this earth do we expect to break into Glendor's Keep?" Silas questioned, speaking the thoughts that Brace was sure were on everyone's mind.

"That, I don't know," Jair admitted.

"We would need to send someone who is familiar with Glendor's

Keep." Korian spoke up, standing. "Someone who would know the way into the dungeon."

Jair looked at Korian intently. "Do you know the way into the dungeon?" he asked.

"I do."

"Korian!" Medarrie exclaimed, standing beside her husband. "You cannot do this! You left – you defected from the King's service. If you are caught, you could be killed!"

Korian took hold of Medarrie's hand, but he shook his head.

"I can go," Alban spoke up. "I'm familiar with most of the castle myself."

Jair was encouraged, Brace could see; he almost smiled.

"It will be dangerous," Jair pointed out. "We'll need to have a plan set in place, a real plan so we know exactly what we're doing and what we're getting into." He paused and took a breath. "Does anyone think we should not send out a group to try and help?"

So many looks were shared, so many voices whispered. Brace found himself holding his breath. Was this wisdom on Jair's part, or foolishness? Thinking they could do anything, to go against the king himself?

"What's happening?" Tassie whispered in Brace's ear.

"Jair wants to know if we should send out a search party to help the people who've been imprisoned."

Tassie squeezed Brace's hand tightly.

"Don't worry," he told her quietly. "I'm not planning on going anywhere."

"I don't see how we can possibly do anything," Worley spoke up, "other than get ourselves into trouble, or come to harm."

"Nothing can harm us as long as we are here in Haven," Torren added. "We're only in danger if we go outside the gate. If we did send out a search mission, it would need to be only those who volunteered to go, who were willing to take the risk."

"I agree," Jair replied. "If no one has a firm objection to this, I think we should put together a team of volunteers and come up with a plan."

There was relative silence for a moment, in which no one stated any encouragements or any objections.

"I volunteer," Alban declared.

"I'm going with him," Alban's brother Landers added, standing beside him.

Jair nodded. "Thank you. Anyone else? We'll need as many people as possible, to help defend each other against the castle guards."

"I am willing to go," Berrick spoke up.

"As am I," Stanner added.

Brace was not surprised; the two men had been on so many search missions already.

"Eridan went the last time," Cayomah said, standing. "I will go with you."

"This won't be a normal search mission," Jair pointed out. "We don't know what will happen. It might be too dangerous."

Cayomah shook her head. "I want to come along. You all know I can do this. You won't need to take care of me. I want to help."

Jair's expression was a mixture of respect and worry as he nodded his assent.

"I feel that I must join you," Korian added, much to Medarrie's obvious dismay. "I have knowledge of the Keep's layout in my memory. It was my duty to know the location of every hallway, every door. I can easily find the door to the prison."

Brace couldn't help but look over at Arden, sitting at the far side of the room. He could see plainly on the archer's face that he would volunteer, a half second before he spoke.

"I will go."

"Arden, no!" Leandra exclaimed. "You *cannot* do this!"

"Please, Leandra," he said, turning toward her. "You know my skills with the bow. I can be a defense for everyone, even from afar. I can clear the way for them as need be."

"Arden," Leandra pleaded, "it's no less safe for you at Glendor's Keep than it is for Alban and Korian. You are all putting your lives at risk to even be seen near the castle!"

"We should be the ones to go," Alban stated heavily. "Since we've been in service to the king, we have knowledge that others would not. If anyone can help us get in and out safely, we could do it."

Farris nodded, seated beside the place where Alban now stood, his face full of anguish. Brace knew that the man must feel strongly that he should join them, but how could he? He not only had his wife Breyann, who sat clinging to him defensively, but he had three young children. How could he possibly leave them behind, not knowing if he would ever come back to them?

"Arden," Leandra pleaded, tightly grasping his arm with one hand and holding Denira with the other. "Don't leave us. They might need your help out there, but I need you too. Denira needs you."

"Dadda?" Denira asked, not understanding what was happening.

Arden let his eyes fall on Denira, and the pain on his face was easy to see. If anything happened to him, he would never see his little girl, ever again. Denira would grow up without her dadda.

Arden met Leandra's gaze once again, some silent understanding passing between them. Leandra let out a long, shaky breath. "If you go," she began, "I want you to promise me you'll not set foot inside the Keep. Promise me you'll do what you said you could do – protect the others from a distance. Watch out for them. From farther off, you will be able to see threats of danger that they would be blind to."

Arden hesitated, then nodded. "I promise you."

Leandra was fighting to be strong; Brace could see it easily. Her respect for Arden's decision to live by *harbrost* was equaled only by her love for him, and her desire to keep her family together.

"Arden is going?" Tassie whispered in Brace's ear, and he nodded, hearing the long, slow breath that Tassie let out in response.

"Is there anyone else?" Jair asked.

No one spoke, and Jair glanced momentarily in Ovard's direction. "I feel as though, since this was my own idea … I feel as though I should go, too."

Many voices reacted in surprise and alarm, and Ovard hurried to Jair's side.

"*No*, son," he told him firmly. "I respect your reason for wanting to go, but we need you *here*. We cannot have Haven's overseer leaving us, especially at a time like this. We need you to stay here, keep us going in the right direction. Every one of our hearts would break if anything happened to you. Do you understand? You can't possibly do this. Not at all."

There were several agreements called out from among the crowd. Jair hung his head, nodding.

"I understand," he muttered, and Brace breathed out in relief.

"I could go in his place," Gavin offered.

Jair looked up at his friend, considered the idea, then finally shook his head.

"I don't think that would be a good idea."

"I've been leading missions for two years!" Gavin argued. "You know I can do this!"

"I know you can," Jair replied. "But with Arden going, and Alban, and Korian, we need people to take their place here. They all have important jobs here. Gate watch, hunting parties … We need people who can take their positions while they're gone."

Gavin crossed his arms over his chest.

"I know how you feel, Gavin," Jair told him. "You've been coming and going from Haven for years, and I haven't been able to go out there at all. I know you want to be part of this, knowing how important it is. I do too, but Ovard is right. Some of us just need to stay here. We could do more to help if we just stayed here."

Slowly, Gavin relaxed his posture, letting his arms fall back down at his sides. "I know," he said quietly.

Jair took a step closer to him. "Thank you."

Gavin nodded.

"All right then," Arden spoke up. "Persha, you'll take my place leading the hunting parties."

"Right," she agreed, and Jair nodded, looking over at her. She was Arden's second-in-command, and there was no doubt she should take his place.

Arden stood close to the front of the room, and he turned to face Jair. He seemed to want to say more, but was hesitant, realizing that he had taken over Jair's authority to lead the meeting.

"It's all right, Arden," Jair told him. "You need two more people on gate watch, don't you? To replace yourself and Alban?"

"I do."

"Well, I'll let you decide. It's your team. I know you'll know who is best for it."

Arden nodded, then scanned the sea of faces. "Bahadur," he called out, and the tall warrior stepped forward. "I would like you to replace me on gate watch, if it suits you."

"I would be honored," Bahadur replied, standing behind Persha, who, Brace noticed, turned away from him slightly.

"Gavin," Arden continued. "I would like you to join the hunting parties."

Gavin nodded in ready agreement.

"Torren?" Arden asked, spotting him in crowd beside Zora. "Can you be spared from helping repair the thatching?"

Torren glanced over at Rudge, who nodded.

"I can," he replied.

"Good. I would like to have you on gate watch until we return."

Torren accepted Arden's request humbly. Brace felt Tassie squeeze his hand. "What's going on now?" she asked quietly.

"They've assigned new help for the gate watch," Brace whispered, as the room had quieted considerably. "I think they've put a team together to go on the rescue mission."

Tassie nodded solemnly.

The team had indeed been formed, and the meeting was ended only after Jair had made it official – Arden, Korian, Alban, Landers, Berrick, Stanner and Cayomah would leave in two short days. They would have just enough time to sketch out a map of Glendor's Keep from Korian's accurate memory, and to make a copy of Ovard's map of Dunya and pack enough food and supplies for the journey there and back.

Medarrie wept openly, and Leandra did all she could to try and comfort her, but both of their husbands would be leaving on this dangerous mission. No one could say whether they would succeed, either in rescuing the prisoners or in finding a way to speak with the king, to dare and confront him with the truth, of what a dreadful mistake he had made by passing such a law.

Everyone was worried, fearful, Brace included. There was fear, yes, but also an overwhelming sense that they *must* do this. They alone, as citizens of Haven, considered it their duty to try and right this wrong, to bring what light they could out into the ever-darkening world around them.

# ~ 22 ~

Arden tugged at his thick, heavy jerkin, running his hand down the front of the dark brown leather, smoothing it over his long-sleeved woven shirt. He was completely a royal archer once again, inside and out. He had not even considered cutting his hair this time, though the length of it would easily give him away.

He felt the familiar sense of urgency, of duty, that it was of utmost importance that he stay alert to defend his traveling companions. The fire had burned low, but it had not been extinguished. Arden felt it flaring up inside of him once again at last.

The dull thudding of horses' hooves on solid dirt filled the narrow valley between the high rocky mountain range and the smooth stone wall of Haven. The seven of them each rode a horse of their own; Arden, Berrick, Stanner, Korian, Alban, Landers and Cayomah. The animals were sturdy, strong and well-fed, which was fortunate, as each of them carried not only their rider, but food, bedding, weapons, and supplies, including the medicines that Ronin and Tassie had provided. If all went as planned, they would be gone nearly a month.

The goodbyes had been desperate ones earlier that morning; no one knew what would come of this mission. As well as they had been able to plan and prepare, there was no telling what unforeseen troubles they might encounter. Or, though Arden hated to think of it, if they would make it back at all.

Tall, straight evergreens stretched up into the sky on their right, a thick, dense wood, with the bare rock of the mountains jutting up beyond it, unbelievably high.

Past the mountains, all that could be seen was the sky itself, with the sun rising up from the eastern horizon, its rays of light visible as though looking at it through a thick, gauzy screen.

Arden frowned at the thought that the darkness had grown deeper these past three years, while he had remained hidden away in safety. How could he have done such a thing? He wondered now. Shouldn't he have been putting his skills to better use?

He had needed to be there for his family, there was no doubt about that, and he had no regrets when he allowed himself to think over the time he'd had to spend with Leandra, and Kendie, and Denira. Despite the strong sense that he was now doing just what he should be, he had a small ache in his heart at the thought of being apart from his family for so long. The ache would get bigger, he suspected, the longer he was away.

"It's an odd sight, isn't it?" Berrick's question cut into Arden's thoughts.

"What's that?" he asked.

"The sun. It doesn't quite look right, does it?"

Arden slowly shook his head. "It does not."

"It's been getting worse," Berrick went on. "Each trip I go out on, the sunlight gets dimmer and dimmer. And the dark of night – it comes so early, so heavy. I don't mean to bring anyone down, I only want to be sure you're prepared for it."

"Of course," Arden replied. "Thank you. You were right to bring it up. Any other advice you can give is welcome and appreciated."

Berrick nodded, half smiling.

Korian nudged his large black horse, Bishop, alongside of Arden, and he passed by at a steady pace, his expression somber, almost troubled. Arden noticed and looked over at Berrick, who made a half-hearted attempt to smile.

They both knew what was on Korian's mind. His thoughts were much the same as Arden's – a strong sense of duty told him this was right, but paired up with sorrow at having left his wife alone to worry over him.

There was nothing to be said, Arden knew, so he kept quiet, turning to glance down the row of horses to be sure everyone was keeping up. He let his hand slide across the band of lightstones that he wore at his neck. They were not particularly heavy, but he had never before worn them and was unused to the feeling of gentle pressure on his collarbone. In a day or two, he was certain, he would no longer notice them.

Berrick wore another set, one that Jair had made just the day before. There needed to be two people wearing lightstones, Jair had explained. In case they were separated.

Arden pushed down once again the feeling that they were riding into a firestorm or a line of archers ready to fire on them at any moment. He could not let it get the better of him, this feeling of dread. He needed to stay focused on the reality of this moment; of every moment, if he would be of any real use.

Cayomah's horse, Gideon, chuffed and nickered, and she patted his neck to calm him.

"Easy now, boy. Steady on."

"What's wrong?" Arden asked her.

"Nothing, I think," she replied. "He doesn't seem startled. Only anxious." She smiled. "It's as though he's eager for the journey. I think he wants to run. He's had it too easy in Haven. He wants to work hard. He wants some adventure."

"Are you sure it's the horse you're speaking for?" Alban asked, riding up beside her.

"And who else would I be speaking for?" she asked lightly, with mock indignance.

Alban grinned. "It seems you're speaking about yourself, not your horse."

Cayomah smiled and looked down at the horse's long, dark, flowing mane. "Well, I could be," she admitted. "At least a little."

Arden silently took note of the gleam in Alban's eyes as he spoke with Cayomah. He filed away in his mind as something to speak with Alban about when given the chance. It was not wise to allow any feelings Alban might have for Cayomah to distract him from their mission.

Arden looked closely at Cayomah for a moment. She had already been part of several search missions, but this was the first time Arden had ever worked with her. Though she was nowhere near what could be called *plump*, an appropriate way to describe her would be to use the word *soft*. She had soft, wavy hair, and soft features, and in appearance she was quite unlike Eridan, who had unquestionably bony elbows.

Cayomah was quite capable, Stanner had informed Arden the day before. She knew well how to get by, traveling long distances, either by the Road or through any wilds. In fact, Stanner had told him, she seemed to thrive on it. Arden had had no reason not to have complete faith in Stanner when he had said that Cayomah could handle herself as well as any of the rest of them.

"May I ask you something?" Arden said suddenly.

"Me?" Cayomah asked, and Arden nodded. "Ask me anything you'd like."

"Why did you so want to come on this mission?"

A flash of concern showed in Cayomah's eyes, but it quickly vanished. "I was thinking of the prisoners mostly," she explained. "I can't imagine what they might be going through. And I thought, some of them might be women. If I were in her place, I would feel much relief if one of my rescuers was a woman. I would feel more comforted after my ordeal."

Arden nodded in reply. "Very good thinking."

"I'm glad you approve," Cayomah told Arden, riding between him and Alban. "I was afraid you would be displeased."

"To have you along?"

"Yes."

Arden considered the situation, considered his thoughts on the matter. "Anyone who can hold their own is welcome, as far as I'm concerned," he told her. "I've been made to understand that you can hold your own quite will."

"I'm glad to hear it," Cayomah replied. "I won't let you down."

"I'm sure you won't."

Cayomah smiled as Landers' horse sprinted past them, its hooves thundering, gaining some distance past Korian at the head of the group until Landers slowed him to a walk.

"What is he doing?" Arden demanded to no one in particular.

"Could be he's getting impatient," Alban suggested. "Or he's just having a bit of sport."

"Your brother could get himself into trouble doing that," Arden warned.

"You're right," Alban agreed. "I'll talk to him about it."

Cayomah's horse swished his long tail in a wide arc, keeping the forest flies away. Arden let his gaze settle on the sky once again. It was no longer morning; the sun was nearly at its full height overhead, but the sky was pale. It was as though a thin layer of clouds covered everything, but there were no clouds. The sky was a soft, dusty blue, and Arden found that he could look directly at the sun itself without it hurting his eyes.

It wasn't right, it wasn't natural.

Arden kept his growing sense of apprehension to himself, aware that the others likely felt it too. He let himself settle into the rhythm of his horse's gait, only periodically glancing up at the sky beyond the trees.

"You've noticed it, I see," Cayomah commented.

Arden raised an eyebrow.

"The sky," she explained.

Arden grunted.

"Everything is getting darker," Cayomah went on. "Night screamers are everywhere. And ... the people. There is so much more cruelty that there used to be. At least from what I've seen."

Arden only nodded.

"How could King Oden do this?" Cayomah asked, almost to herself. "Pass a law to stop people from finding Haven?"

"You're surprised?" Arden asked her.

"You're not?"

"Not at all. He tried once to take Haven by force, remember, but he failed."

"Yes," Cayomah agreed. "I've heard the stories. I suppose he was humiliated by the way it all turned out."

"Or angered," Berrick commented from behind them.

"Both, I'm sure," Arden replied.

"And this is his way of seeking revenge," Berrick added.

"Revenge against Haven," Cayomah mused. "If it's the city of Haven he wants to seek revenge against, or the people in it, he is failing once again. It isn't Haven he's harming now, but his very own people."

"Isn't he harming us?" Arden spoke up. "We have all been grieved at the news of his proclamation. And haven't we left our homes, our families, behind?"

Cayomah nodded solemnly. "I suppose you're right."

"Suppose this was part of his plan?" Stanner asked. "Suppose he knew – or thought at least – that if news reached Haven about people being imprisoned for wanting to leave, some of us would come and try to free them? What if..." – his voice lowered to a whisper – "what if this is some sort of a trap we're being lured into?"

"Unlikely," Arden stated.

"Is it?"

"Oden would have no way of knowing when or even if Haven would get word of his laws. He would have no way of knowing anyone would attempt what we're attempting."

"I hope you're right," Cayomah told him.

Arden simply nodded, looking straight ahead. He hoped he was right as well.

"Oden wanted to claim rule over Haven," Alban mused. "When he couldn't have it, and he found out that people were leaving Dunya, he must have feared he was losing the loyalty of the kingdom he still had rule over."

"And how would he think to gain loyalty by having people put in chains?" Berrick wanted to know. "Does he think such actions are going to win over the hearts of his people?"

"He has been spreading word that Haven is a dangerous place for a long time," Arden pointed out. "If he can get people to believe that, if he can instill a hint of doubt or fear, people will err on the side of caution and stay in Dunya. I'm sure Oden knows this. But still, some have been leaving for Haven despite what he has said about it. Now he is trying to reinforce that fear. He is adding consequences of his own when anyone tries to leave."

"How do you know all of this?" Cayomah asked.

"I spoke with the latest arrivals," he admitted. "With Kem, Bareo and Kaisha. They were able to give me some added insight."

Cayomah nodded, looking far ahead to where Landers and Korian had turned their horses around and were heading back toward the rest of them.

"Is the way clear?" Arden called out as they approached.

"Very," Korian answered. "Clear and quiet. There were some signs of the presence of small animals or birds, but nothing else."

"That's a relief," Stanner commented.

Arden nodded in agreement. "It is a relief, that's true, but please – do not wander so far ahead. Berrick and I have the lightstones. What good would it do either of you, so far ahead of the group? No swords or bows can guarantee any protection against night screamers."

"Night screamers, at near midday?" Alban asked with an almost amused smile.

"They no longer seem to be ruled by the hours," Arden replied, his voice brought low by the anger that simmered under the surface of his temper. "Take nothing for granted. We are traveling near the border of Haven now," he explained, "but we will not be for much longer. The light from the city will not be there to keep the screamers away. We have only the small pieces of lightstones we are wearing. We must stay closer together. It is our only guarantee of safety."

Korian's eyes widened in alarm. "I had not realized the extremity of the situation," he replied. "Forgive me."

"All is well," Arden said with a nod.

Landers said nothing, but he had no need to. Arden could read on his face what he would say – that Arden, unlike himself or Cayomah, or Berrick, or Stanner – had never been on a search mission. Wouldn't Landers know better than Arden when things could become dangerous?

Cayomah let out a breath. "I'm glad we have the lightstones," she commented. "On all the journeys I've made to and from Haven, I've only ever heard the screamers, either from a distance or nearby. But I've never seen a single one. I can't imagine having to live out here now that those beasts have become so widespread."

"And so bold," Berrick added. "Even villas and cities aren't safe places, as far as the screamers are concerned."

"All the more reason to stay focused on the purpose of our mission," Arden spoke up. "We must find some way to get word to King Oden, inform him of the seriousness of the wrong he's done. The people deserve to have the chance to get away from the screamers. To get away from the darkness."

"I agree," Cayomah said, almost in a whisper.

Arden cleared his throat. "Right. So, how soon do we head east? How far is it we've got to travel north?"

"Just past this mountain range here," Berrick replied. "As soon as we're able, we will turn eastward. Northeast, to be exact."

"How long until then?"

"Should be tomorrow some time," Stanner answered.

"Good. Everyone keep together. We may be traveling in safety now, but that will not always be the case. Nothing can be taken for granted."

There were nods of agreement, and a familiar glance between Alban and Cayomah, as the group nudged their horses onward. Arden scanned the tree line, then allowed himself one last glance over his shoulder, toward the high stone gate in the distance.

Toward *home*.

## ~ 23 ~

Brace leaned back against the wall near the window, one ankle crossed lightly over the other. The clay mug in his hands was cool, pulling the chill out of the water it held inside. He took a sip as he watched Leandra push her straight blonde hair behind her ears, then pick up one of Denira's cloth toys from off the table and set it down on a nearby shelf.

She was tense. Worried. She was trying to cover it up, and failing. Brace could see it in her eyes and the set of her mouth. It was there in her posture, in the way she kept pushing her hair behind her ears.

He could feel it in the air; the room was filled with it. Kendie felt it, and Pavel as well, as they sat at the end of the table half-concentrating on their game, something to do with flat-bottomed marbles that Brace knew nothing about.

Zorix sat on the window seat, his wide black eyes focused intently on every move Leandra made, his large ears pressed forward at full height, his thick coat of fur holding steady at a deep orange color.

Even Denira had picked up on the tension. She sat near the edge of the window seat holding her doll, but not playing with it. She simply gazed across the room at Leandra, her pale eyes wide, trying to understand why everything felt different. Why everyone was so quiet. Why her dadda wasn't home.

Brace had come to the house, and brought Pavel with him, knowing that there was no real way he could be of any help. All he could do was be there for Leandra as she had so often been there for him.

She had thanked him for coming, offering him and Pavel both a cool drink of water or a bit of fresh fruit. All the time, she was considering the needs of her guests, though Brace had come with Leandra's needs in mind, not his own.

Arden's decision to leave Haven, to be part of the rescue mission, had come as quite a shock, to Leandra most of all. They all knew how strongly Arden was driven to live by *harbrost*, and none of them felt any inclination to try and change him. Even if it meant having him leave to go on dangerous missions.

Brace looked over toward the steady, intermittent *click click* of the marbles being played on the table. Kendie looked up at him, forcing a smile. He grinned back crookedly, then let his eyes rest on Leandra's weary, troubled face.

"Are you sure there is nothing you're in need of?" he asked.

She looked at him, thought a moment, then shook her head.

*No*, Brace thought to himself. *The only thing she needs is something I can't give her. She needs Arden to come home.*

Denira wandered over, clutching her doll tightly.

"Mammy?" she asked. "Where's Dadda?"

Leandra looked down at her and took a breath. "Dadda went on a journey, remember? Just like when he goes out hunting."

Denira frowned and looked toward the door.

"I know," Leandra sighed, almost to herself. "He's never gone this long when he's hunting, is he? He's going to be gone for a long time, this time."

"Why?" Denira asked.

"There are some people who need his help."

"*Why?*"

Leandra gazed at Denira, her expression soft, but full of longing, wishing she could somehow make Denira understand the situation.

"Sissie," Kendie called out, trying to help. "Why don't you come and help me play this game? I think Pavel might win."

Denira glanced at Kendie, then up at Leandra, and back toward Kendie. Finally, she made her way to the end of the table and crawled up onto the bench beside Kendie, pointing at the marbles in such a way that Brace knew she had no more idea how to play the game than he did.

Brace stepped closer to Leandra.

"Arden knows how to stay safe," he said quietly, and Leandra nodded. "He'll be fine."

"Will he?" Leandra whispered, then glanced toward the table to be sure the children hadn't heard.

Brace didn't answer her. How could he? Of course the answer everyone wanted to hear was that he most assuredly *would* be safe – they all would. But there was no way anyone could say what might happen.

"I won," Pavel announced, without much enthusiasm.

Brace pulled his gaze away from Leandra to look over at Pavel. He smiled.

"Fun game?"

Pavel nodded. "Sure."

"Would you like to play again?" Kendie asked.

When Pavel hesitated, Brace spoke up. "Actually, we should probably get going, if there's nothing I can do here to help."

Leandra stepped forward and rested a hand on Brace's arm.

"You *have* helped," she told him. "I'm glad you stopped by. I really do appreciate it, Brace. It means so much to me, knowing you're here for us."

Brace nodded as Pavel left the table to stand beside him. Kendie pulled Denira into her arms and stood at Leandra's side.

"Try not to worry," Brace said feebly.

Leandra nodded, tucking her hair behind her ears yet again. Brace had never seen her so unsure of herself. She seemed so vulnerable, more than Brace would have thought possible. She was so strong – stronger than anyone Brace had ever met. Strong-willed and independent, or so it had always seemed. Fear over losing someone she loved seemed to be her only weakness, and now that fear consumed her.

Brace set the near-empty mug down on the table and stepped closer to Leandra, feeling awkward. Zorix slunk out of the window seat and across the floor, stopping at Leandra's feet, his long tail wrapping around one of her ankles.

"Tassie and I are here if you need anything," Brace told Leandra. "Even if it's just someone to talk to."

"Thank you."

Brace nodded, feeling like the words were not enough. She needed more. But what could he do? He nervously pushed his hair back away from his face, clearing his throat. He stepped forward, putting his arms around Leandra to embrace her, feeling very self-conscious. Was this something she would want him to do? He never would have considered doing such a thing if she hadn't done the same for him on occasion.

Now, Leandra welcomed the comforting gesture, holding Brace tightly for a moment before letting him go.

"Take care of yourself," Brace told Leandra as she took a step back.

"Right," she said with a nod. "Thank you, Brace. Tell Tassie hello for me. Tell her we're holding up well, will you?"

Brace raised an eyebrow, unsure if it were true, but he nodded just the same. "I will."

"Goodbye, Pavel," Leandra said as the boy passed by toward the door. "It's good to see you."

"Thank you," Pavel replied, shifting nervously. *Was that what I should have said?* His eyes questioned as he looked up at Brace.

Brace grinned and tipped his head toward the door.

"Goodbye, Pavel. Goodbye, Brace," Kendie said with a wave.

"Bye, Bwace. Bye, Pawwel," Denira repeated.

Pavel smiled at Denira as they stepped outside over the doorstep.

"Will you let Tassie know I can come for medic lessons tomorrow?" Kendie called after them. "If she says it's all right," she added.

Brace nodded. "I'm sure she will, Kendie. Thank you."

His eyes met Leandra's once again before he turned away. "Don't lose hope," he told her quietly. "Arden is brave, but he isn't foolhardy. He wouldn't willingly go into a situation if he believed it meant taking himself away from you permanently."

Leandra shook her head, then nodded. "Thank you, Brace. I know it's true. Thank you. Come again soon?"

"I will."

Though Pavel was silent, Brace was aware of him walking close at his side. The boy had once been a source of tension in Brace's life, so recently, but now the tension was everywhere, and Brace felt comfort at having Pavel beside him. The rescue team had only left two days past; they would likely be gone another twenty at the least. How would everyone get by, waiting, wondering, without any word from any of them, not knowing whether anything had happened to any of them?

Brace shifted his shoulders, the end of his sleeve brushing against the wide bracelet of woven leather that he now wore tied around his wrist.

Pavel had given it to him; he had made it, along with another nearly identical one, which he had given to Tassie. They were gifts of thanks, Pavel had explained, but they were also gifts from his heart. They were a symbol, Brace knew, of the depth of feeling he had in his heart for the both of them. His new family.

Brace looked down to see that Pavel was looking up at him, concern written all over his face.

"What's wrong?"

Pavel shrugged. "Everyone is worried."

Brace nodded. "And we can't really do anything to help, can we?"

Pavel shook his head. "Are you worried?"

Brace thought a moment before answering. "I am. But I've been worried for a long time, about a lot of different things. I think I've gotten used to worrying."

"About me?"

"Yes," Brace replied. "I've been worried about you. But I had worries before you came."

"About what?"

Brace absently rubbed at the back of his neck. Pavel hadn't been told about any of it, about the trying times Brace and Tassie had been going through. Brace wasn't certain if Pavel should be told at all, and he was not about to say anything without Tassie's permission.

"Just life," Brace replied, resting a hand on Pavel's shoulder. "Haven is a wonderful place, there's no questioning that fact, but life is never without troubles, I've learned. No matter where we go, it can never be *perfect*."

Pavel nodded solemnly.

"My point is," Brace went on, "is that we've gotten through hard times before, and we can do it again."

They were outside the clinic now, and the front door stood open lazily, allowing a cool draft of air to flow into the building. Brace nodded toward the door.

"I'll follow you in."

Pavel smiled – it was a small smile, but it was there – and pushed his way inside. Brace went in behind him, closing the door nearly all the way, leaving a narrow opening.

Tassie smiled as he entered the front room, with Pavel just in front of him. She slipped a bit of paper into the book she had propped open on the table in front of her, turning toward them.

"I'm glad you're back," she told them, looking from Pavel to Brace. "It's been slow these past few days. Only one sprained wrist today, nothing more. I'm beginning to feel like I'm not needed."

Brace picked up on the forced lightness in her tone of voice, but Pavel took her words seriously.

"I need you," he told her as she looked in his direction.

Her smile lessened slightly, her eyes full of emotion. "Thank you, Pavel. I'm glad to hear you say that."

Brace came close and took her hand in his. "I *always* need you."

Tassie smiled, her eyes fixed on his for a long moment. Then she abruptly turned toward Pavel. "I'm almost through for the day. Ronin will work the clinic tomorrow. What should we do then?"

"Leandra wants us to come back and see her again," Pavel replied, and Tassie nodded.

"We will, then."

"And ..." Pavel began hesitantly.

"And what?" Brace prodded.

"I would like to learn to play Uncle Erhan's flute. You said there was someone here who could teach me?"

"There is," Brace replied, surprised at Pavel's request.

"It would be wonderful if you learned to play," Tassie told him. "I'm sure my Uncle Ovard would love to teach you."

Pavel smiled for a moment. "But you wouldn't hear it," he pointed out.

"No." Tassie shook her head. "But I could watch you, and so many others could listen. You would make so many people so happy if you learned to play."

Pavel nodded, smiling shyly again.

"And you would make yourself happy too," Brace pointed out just as the clinic door was pushed open, and Pavel jumped out of the way.

Dursen and Worley entered, supporting a pale, weak Eaton between the two of them.

"Pardon our barging in here," Dursen apologized. "But Eaton's not well."

Tassie quickly left Brace's side. "What happened?" she asked, giving Eaton a quick once-over, then looking to Dursen for an answer.

"Can't say, really," he replied. "He just got weak in the legs, and can't seem to focus on anything anyone's sayin'."

Brace caught Pavel's sleeve, pulling him out of the way as Tassie directed the men to have Eaton sit down on the nearby bed.

Eaton pressed his hand to his forehead as Worley and Dursen moved aside.

"What's wrong?" Tassie asked him. "Can you tell me how you feel?"

"Dizzy," Eaton replied.

"Do you feel sick?"

Eaton nodded.

"How, exactly?"

"My stomach."

"Do you only *feel* sick, or did you *get* sick?" Tassie continued her questioning.

Eaton wobbled slightly, even sitting, and he steadied himself with his other hand.

Tassie looked over at Dursen. "Did he vomit at all?"

Dursen looked at Worley, who shook his head. "Not that I saw."

"No," Dursen answered.

Tassie reached up, holding Eaton's face in her hands. "He's very hot," she announced. "Was he working out in the fields today?"

"Yes," Dursen replied quickly.

"Eaton?" Tassie asked. "Have you been drinking enough water today?"

"I thought I was," he replied weakly. "Maybe I wasn't …"

Tassie nodded, then hurried across the room, filling a large clay cup with water from the basin. Brace was surprised when she thrust the cup into his hands and picked up the basin itself.

"He is overheated," Tassie declared, struggling with the weight of the basin. "It's from working in the sun and not drinking enough water."

She carried the nearly-full basin across the room, only sloshing out a few drops.

"I've got to cool him down. Eaton, I am going to pour this water over your head."

Eaton barely had time to nod in response before Tassie lifted the bowl higher, letting the water run in a wide stream over the top of Eaton's head, pressing his sand-colored hair down over his face.

He gasped and sputtered for a moment as Tassie returned the basin to its stand and took the drinking cup back from Brace.

"The bed is wet," Pavel stated softly.

"It's only water," Brace told him, giving his shoulder a squeeze. "It will dry."

"Here now," Tassie said to Eaton, helping him push his hair away from his eyes. "Drink this. Not too fast. Just one drink right after another. You need to cool off inside and out."

Eaton obeyed, taking the cup in his whole right hand and drinking slowly. His hair continued to drip onto his already-wet clothing as Worley and Dursen stood near the door, watching.

"Just sit there for a while," Tassie told Eaton. "You should be feeling better soon."

"Thank you," Eaton replied after swallowing a mouthful of water, blinking as his hair dripped onto his face. Tassie eyed him for a moment, assessing his condition, then pulled a small towel down from one of the shelves.

"You can dry your face," she told him, handing him the towel. "Only your face. Keep your head wet. It will cool you off more quickly."

Eaton nodded, running the towel across his face. He took a full breath. "I am feeling a bit better already," he told Tassie, peering up at her through wet clumps of hair hanging down over his forehead.

"Very good," Tassie replied. "Just rest there for a bit. Then stay indoors for the rest of the day. Drink plenty of water, and stay out of the sun, and you should be fine."

Eaton nodded, setting the damp wadded-up towel on the bed and flexing his fingers.

"Are you getting your strength back?" Tassie asked.

"I'm starting to," Eaton replied. "I feel foolish."

"You don't need to."

"I should have known better."

"So should I have," Dursen spoke up.

Tassie started to reply, but Lida burst into the room at just that moment.

"Is Eaton here?" she asked as soon as she entered, then saw him sitting on the bed. "Are you all right?"

Tassie startled as Lida hurried over to the side of the bed.

"I'm sorry," Lida apologized. "I just heard that Eaton was ill, or something. Is he all right? Are you all right?"

"I'm fine," Eaton told her as Tassie nodded. "I just didn't drink enough water."

"It's called dehydration," Tassie added.

Lida looked at Tassie and nodded appreciatively. "Thank you for taking care of him."

Eaton drank the last of his water, then gave the cup to Tassie. Lida brushed his damp hair away from his face, taking his hand tightly in hers.

"What more does he need?" she asked. "I'd like to help, if I can."

Tassie looked closely at Eaton once again, resting her palm on the side of his face.

"He has cooled off considerably," she thought aloud. "Do you feel dizzy still?"

"Only a little," he replied meekly.

"I think he's all right to go home," Tassie told Lida. "I've told him to stay indoors for the rest of the day, and to drink plenty of water. Will you take him home and look after him? If he gets to feeling weaker, or gets sick, hurry to let me know."

"I will," Lida promised. She put an arm around Eaton's damp shoulders and kissed the side of his face. "I will make sure you take good care of yourself."

Eaton smiled, chagrined, as Lida took his arm to steady him as he got to his feet.

"You're sure you're all right?" Tassie asked him. "Do you feel steady enough to walk?"

"Yes," Eaton replied. "I'll walk slowly. I'll be all right. Thank you."

"It's my pleasure," Tassie said with a nod. "It's why I'm here."

"I'll take good care of him," Lida said once again as she clung to Eaton's arm, leading him toward the doorway.

"Get plenty of rest," Dursen advised as they left, and Eaton nodded in response.

Brace felt Pavel tug at his sleeve. "She likes him," he whispered, and Brace smiled.

"I think you're right."

"Well," Worley said with a sigh, "it's back to work, then?"

"Nah," Dursen replied. "We worked enough today, I say. Let's just go on home ourselves."

Worley nodded. "Good day," he addressed Brace and Tassie. "Sorry for all of the commotion."

Brace waved him off, and Tassie shook her head.

"That *is* why I'm here," she stated firmly. Worley nodded, smiled, and left the room, but Dursen lingered.

"How are you all these days?" he asked.

"Well enough, thank you," Tassie replied, setting the empty cup down on a shelf near the empty basin. "How are you? How is Nerissa?"

"Very well," Dursen answered. "Quite well. Thank you. She's … she's carrying the baby just fine." Dursen's eyes shone with joy and pride, but at the same time, his expression showed his concern that Nerissa's pregnancy might be salt in an open wound for Tassie.

"I'm so glad for the both of you," Tassie told him earnestly. "Please tell Nerissa she's welcome to come any time. In fact, I would like to see her here at the clinic soon. Just to make sure we're doing all we can to keep her and the baby healthy."

"Right," Dursen replied with a nod. "Sure. O'course. I'll tell her." He glanced toward the open door. "So Eaton's fine, then? That's all it was? Not drinking enough water?"

"Yes, I'm sure that's all it was."

Dursen shook his head. "He had his water skin there with him. I guess he just weren't drinking from it."

"He's not likely to make that mistake a second time," Brace spoke up from near the window.

Dursen glanced in his direction, shaking his head. "No, he's not likely to, is he?"

Tassie glanced toward Brace, then rested her hand on Dursen's arm. "You did well bringing him here so quickly. You did the very best you could for him, and I'm certain he'll be all right. Don't worry, and don't think any of this was your fault. He's young, but he's a grown man, and he is responsible for taking care of himself."

"Right," Dursen agreed. "O'course. Thanks again. I'll pass your message on to Nerissa. I'm sure she'll come to see you soon. Goodbye, Tassie, Brace. Pavel," Dursen added, seeing the boy standing at Brace's side.

"See you soon," Brace replied as Dursen left the clinic. Tassie closed the door slowly behind him, leaving it open just enough to keep the air flowing inside.

She sighed, running her fingers over the wet spots on the quilt covering the bed along the wall. "I should hang this up to dry," she commented.

Pavel looked up at Brace. "She sounds sad," he told him, knowing that Tassie wouldn't hear.

Brace nodded and went to Tassie's side. "Eaton will be all right, won't he?" he asked her.

"Yes," she replied. "I wouldn't have sent him home if I thought otherwise."

"What's wrong, then?"

Tassie shook her head slightly, briefly glancing in Pavel's direction.

"Is it what Dursen said? About Nerissa?"

"Maybe," Tassie admitted. "I'd thought I was over all of that. Maybe it's just everything. All of this trouble with King Oden, and everyone who's left Haven. Worrying about them. About Arden. About Leandra. Just everything."

Brace felt Tassie's frustrations, her fears.

"Everything will work out," he told her.

"Will it?" she asked, studying his face.

"I have to believe it will," Brace told her. "We just have to believe the best. How can we go on the way we should if we expect the worst of things?"

Tassie shook her head. Pavel came and stood where Brace could see him out of the corner of his eye.

"Is Tassie okay?" he asked, concerned.

"Pavel is worried over you," Brace informed Tassie.

"I'm all right, Pavel," she told him gently. "Just so much catching up with me. Things… things I thought wouldn't hurt anymore."

Pavel looked at the both of them in silence.

"We'll be all right," Brace told the boy, pulling the quilt off the bed. "We'll take the quilt home and hang it up to dry."

Brace suddenly felt tired. Tired of all the fear and the worry and the emotional upheaval. He felt an unexpected rush of anger and frustration.

*Why couldn't things be simple again?*

What wouldn't he give to have some of the problems they'd once had to deal with? Questions about Haven's mysteries. How to fix the roofs of the old stone houses. How to fix the fountain. What kinds of crops should they plant?

Oh, for the days when that was all that worried them! But there could be no looking back. No matter how much any of them had suffered, no matter how much Brace had had to give of himself to comfort others, life kept going on. Kept throwing things at them that they weren't certain they were ready to handle.

If the city of Haven was alive, as Jair was so certain it was, couldn't it see that they all needed some peace? Some rest? Couldn't Haven's light *do* something about all of this trouble they were having?

Maybe those were ridiculous questions to be asking, Brace thought as he rolled the quilt into a ball. He lifted his gaze from the floor and let his eyes meet Tassie's. She looked at him, and Brace knew she had picked up on his anger. He could see it in her eyes that she suspected *she* was the source of at least some of that anger; or if not *herself* directly, her lingering sorrow had caused his temper to flare up. Not that he was angry about her grief; only that he was powerless to do anything to alleviate it.

"Let's go home," Brace said, trying to keep his voice steady. "Can you close up here for the day?"

"Yes," Tassie answered slowly. "The basin is empty. I'll need to go over and let Ronin know that it will need filling in the morning."

Brace nodded, the heat of his anger beginning to cool slightly. He turned in Pavel's direction.

"Come on," he told him. "Let's go home."

Pavel took one step, then stopped.

"It's all right," Brace said to him, holding out a hand. "Don't be upset. It's all right."

Pavel joined them, slowly, and Brace rested a hand on his shoulder as they walked. One hand on Pavel's shoulder, one arm holding the wet, rolled-up quilt, Tassie walking beside him. Everyone in Haven was troubled now, Brace reminded himself. It was not just the three of them. Everyone was concerned about the lives and safety of their loved ones, the ones who had so unselfishly volunteered for the intended rescue mission. Everyone had to deal with their own fears or concerns.

Had Brace made things worse for Tassie, for Pavel, by revealing his own frustrations? Wasn't he the one they should be able to look to for security, for stability, for strength? He should be able to help them, not make things worse.

Brace took a deep breath to steady his nerves. He gently bumped Tassie with his elbow.

"I'm sorry," he told her. "I'm sorry about what happened back there. I didn't mean to upset anyone."

He looked down at Pavel, who slowly looked up to meet his gaze.

"I'm okay."

Brace managed a half-smile, then looked up at Tassie again. She nodded, gently taking the quilt from him and leaning against his side lightly as they walked.

"We will be all right," she told him. "We can give each other strength."

Brace put an arm around Tassie and held her close, letting his hand slide off of Pavel's shoulder. He hoped he still had some strength to give her.

Unexpectedly, Pavel reached up and took Brace's hand. Why did that feel so strange? Brace wondered. He'd told Pavel that they could be a family, the three of them, and he had honestly meant it. Why did it feel strange to have Pavel hold his hand? Had Brace *ever* had a child hold his hand?

*Only Denira*, he thought.

He held Pavel's hand tighter, becoming used to the feeling of the boy's smaller hand in his own. They really *were* becoming a family, weren't they, the three of them?

*Strange*, Brace thought. Strange, the way life could twist and turn, take you in so many unexpected directions, like a wild river, bringing you toward – what destination? Only the river knew.

But they were a family now. There was no denying it. Brace felt it in his heart to be true.

"We will be all right," Brace echoed Tassie's words. "If we all pull together, somehow we will make it through this. No matter what has happened or what will happen, if we're together, we can help each other through."

Tassie smiled at him, her eyes shining with pleasure. "I'm so proud of you, Brace. I'm proud of who you are. I'm glad we belong to each other."

Brace returned Tassie's smile. How had he managed so many years alone? Convincing himself that he didn't need anyone? That he was better off alone?

The thought of it made him feel tight inside. No Tassie. No one to come home to every night, the same person every night, someone who knew him deeply and loved him just the same. Opening his heart up to let others in had also let in the pain that he had for so long been trying to shut out. But he had expected that, at least to a degree. What he hadn't expected was that even new pain, pain he felt because his life had become so intimately involved with others, was more quickly eased by their very presence as well. Alone, he had closed himself inside a hard, cold shell where no pain could get in, but neither could it get out. He was trapped, with heartache and bitterness for constant companions.

Now, Brace was no longer alone and cold inside. He felt warmed all the way through, like coming in from the snow and drinking a mug of hot cider.

He felt a laugh rise to the surface, and with it a new sense of determination to keep going, with Tassie, with Pavel, to bring his family through hard times the best that he could. He felt so much more capable than he ever had in his life, and he let that feeling carry him all the way back home.

# ~24~

"We are nearing the Road," Berrick announced.

Insects buzzed and zipped all around them, drawn in by the horses. Overhead, though the air felt warm on their skin, the sky was painted over with a sheet of gray, while deep clouds gathered along the horizon.

The trees were thick all around them, obscuring their view, but Arden trusted Berrick's observations. He had traveled this way many times, while Arden only knew the path over the mountains and through Spire's Gate.

"How long until we reach it?" Korian asked.

"I would say early evening," Berrick replied.

"Sounds right," Stanner agreed.

"What is it you're going by?" Arden wanted to know.

"The lake, there," Stanner replied, pointing toward the eastern horizon.

"That's Wayside Lake," Cayomah added, and Arden nodded. From where they rode, Wayside Lake seemed much smaller than it actually was; their view of it was from the narrow end. Arden knew that it spread out to be much longer than it was wide.

"What will we do when we come near the Road?" Alban wondered aloud.

Arden hesitated to respond, though he wanted to. He wanted to be certain everyone took proper precautions, but he was reluctant to establish himself as a leader. He had only come to provide protection, after all. Cayomah, Stanner and Berrick outranked him now, as far as he was concerned. They had experience in going on search missions; Arden did not.

Cayomah glanced at Stanner, her expression grim.

"This feels different," she commented. "We've come to the Road this way before, but it doesn't feel the same."

"It doesn't," Berrick agreed heavily.

"Come on now," Stanner chided lightly. "Don't go on that way. You're giving me the shivers! It's the Road, same as always. It never changes."

Landers shifted impatiently in the saddle. "Don't worry so much. We won't be traveling *down* the Road," he pointed out. "We're only crossing it."

"That is true," Arden spoke up. "We are only crossing it. But though the Road never changes, we can never know who we will encounter there. That always changes. We must be cautious."

Arden knew that caution was by no means one of Landers' strengths, but he reminded himself that the young man had long been part of the search mission teams, and he tried to address him respectfully despite his irritation at his reckless attitude.

"I agree," Korian said in response to Arden's advice. "Times have changed. Oden's proclamation has tainted things. The people out here are not the same. They can't be. Oden has made people suspicious of one another. He's turned people against each other. No one can know that we have come from Haven." He paused, his expression grave. "Or we could well end up inside the dungeon ourselves."

For a moment no one spoke. There was no need. They all knew that Korian was right enough. They knew it was a very real possibility, that they would be imprisoned if the mission failed. Imprisoned, or killed.

"Right." Cayomah's voice was just above a whisper. "So we'll tell no one. Alban and Korian can pass for guardians of the Keep, and Arden for a Royal Archer. Are we on official business, then? Scouting? What about the rest of us?"

"It's no one's place to ask," Alban replied. "They'll know we've been in the king's service, or assume we still are. They'll know their place, if they've got any intelligence. They won't question us."

"And if they haven't?" Landers asked. "What if they haven't got intelligence?"

Stanner chuckled. "That's a good question. It is best to have an answer, if we are asked what we're about. Better to be prepared."

"What is it, then? What is it we're doing out here?" Landers pressed.

Arden looked around at each of them, taking in their appearances, their clothing. Three of them were dressed as King's Men ...

"It is a training mission," he decided. "Korian, Alban and I are training new recruits. Showing them the lay of the land and seeing how they'll handle difficult situations."

Landers had been in training, after all. He had become quite skilled in archery, Arden knew, and had been letting his hair grow in anticipation of joining in the king's service. It was long still, reaching down over his shoulders. He kept it pulled back out of the way, but not cut short on the sides. It would likely never be cut in that way now, as long as he remained a citizen of Haven. That was reserved for Royal Archers alone.

Arden hesitated, chewing at the inside of his lip. "We're going through the towns to see if there has been any trouble, any talk of Haven."

"We have made ourselves into the enemy," Korian stated darkly, but no one refuted Arden's plan; it only made sense.

"What about Cayomah?" Landers asked.

"She is my wife," Alban answered quickly. "We're newly married. I wouldn't leave her behind."

Cayomah smiled, blushing slightly.

"Right, then," Arden said with a nod. "That is our story. Everyone stick to it. This is only if we are asked," he added. "We will volunteer no information otherwise."

Berrick's horse tossed its head, its long mane whipping out, chasing away insects buzzing at its face.

"All settled, then," Korian stated. "Let's keep moving on. Our beasts are suffering here with all of these flying pests."

Landers led them on, the hooves of their horses thudding dully on the thick layer of fallen needles beneath them. Arden looked up at the high trees all around them. There were few saplings, thin and scraggly. What a change from the thick, full trees growing in Haven's Woods! Everything there was so green, so alive. The trees here seemed half dead. The long thin needles protruding along the branches were dull in color, the tips of them turning a rusty brown.

Perhaps it was due to the dryness of summer? Had it not been raining out here? Even if it had been dry, Arden knew that the trees would still not have been affected this drastically. No, it was not for lack of water that the trees were suffering. It was for lack of sunlight. He was as sure of that as anything. Even now, in late summer, the sky overhead was more suited for a damp day in autumn.

Arden glanced up at the sky once again, but it had not changed. Likely it wouldn't either, unless it grew worse. He scanned the area of land around them, looking for any signs of danger.

He would not allow himself to become complacent, no matter how safe anything seemed. So much was riding on his shoulders. He was sure that he would never be able to forgive himself if anything happened to anyone, if he was somehow able to prevent it. At least Landers was staying with the rest of them, and not running on ahead as he had been, even after Arden had warned him not to. No, for the time being, Landers was showing restraint, though he looked none too pleased at doing so.

Arden set his jaw firmly. Well, he would take what he could get. Obedience with displeasure was still obedience.

~

Midday had long come and gone by the time the Royal Road came into view. Though no one said anything, or gave any spoken direction, each of them stopped some distance away, even Landers.

The Road was wide, flat, and very dry. Lazy billows of dirt hung in the air, stirred up by the passing of a large, heavy cart, which could be seen continuing westward.

Berrick coughed at the dust spreading out and drifting over them.

"We've reached the Road at last," Cayomah commented, almost to herself.

"Quite an endearing sight, huh?" Stanner asked with a chuckle.

Arden made no response. He looked up and down the Road and saw no one else approaching. Peering through the lingering cloud of dirt, he thought he could make out large shape off among the trees.

"Are we going on, then?" Landers asked.

"Wait," Arden replied.

"What for?"

"Reign yourself in already," Berrick snapped. "There's no sense rushing into anything."

Landers scowled and looked away as the dust cloud dissipated further into the air.

"I see something out there," Arden said at last.

"What is it?" Cayomah asked.

"There, among the trees on the other side of the Road," Arden replied, pointing.

"Wagons?" Korian asked.

"I believe so."

"Why are they just sitting there, on the side of the Road?" Alban wondered aloud. "Do you think they've had trouble? Broken a wheel, or some such thing?"

"Can't say from here," Arden replied. "The wagons look level to me. None of the wheels appear to be broken."

"If they are having trouble, we might be able to help them," Cayomah suggested.

Arden nodded, though he made no move forward.

"They are merchant's wagons," Stanner thought aloud. "We have no reason to fear them ..."

"Not if we stay true to our story," Arden finished. "Just remember what was decided. Remember who we are, on this journey."

"Right," Cayomah stated, smoothing out her hooded light blue cloak. "Alban is my husband. He works for the king. We are part of a training mission. A scouting mission."

"Exactly," Arden replied. He glanced right and left, then nudged Storm onward, onto the dirt surface of the Road. The others followed after him as Arden remembered the lightstones he wore around his neck. He stopped abruptly, pulling his horse around to face the other direction.

"What's wrong?" Korian asked in alarm.

"The lightstones," Arden said quietly. "We can't let them be seen." He quickly set about untying the thin rope around his neck, and Berrick did the same with his own. Stashing them inside the leather bags attached to their horses' saddles, they took a moment to breathe, to calm their frayed nerves. How could they have forgotten about the lightstones?

But it was all right – no one had seen them. The lightstones would not need to be hidden away for long, as it was unlikely they would encounter many others once they left the Road behind them and headed off into the wildlands.

"All right?" Arden asked Berrick. "Do we go on?"

Berrick nodded, slightly shaken. "I'm all right."

Arden gave a quick nod, turning Storm around in the right direction. It was easy to see now that there were two wagons nestled among the trees on the far side of the Road, with a small group of travelers gathered around a fire, ringed by sharp gray stones.

"We will simply pass them on our way," Korian spoke up.

"What if they are in need of help?" Cayomah asked, concerned.

"We will do what we can," Arden replied. "But we must keep up appearances. People will need to believe that we are who we say we are."

As they neared the wagons, they could see that there were horses tethered among the trees, grazing on low-growing feathery brush. The sound of their approach drew their attention, and they looked up, their ears flicking with curiosity.

The people sitting around the fire heard them as well, and in a moment four more pairs of eyes were fixed on them.

"Hello there," a man called out, standing and raising a hand in greeting.

"Hello," Landers replied. "Are you all well? Having trouble at all, are you?"

"No, no trouble," the man replied, smiling disarmingly. "Just making camp for the night." He shrugged. "It's as good a place as any, what with the dark falling fast."

Arden glanced at the four of them, seated around the low, snapping flames. The man who had greeted them was accompanied by a woman, seated so close to him that Arden assumed she must be his wife. A closer look through the gathering darkness revealed their matching tattoos decorating the backs of their hands. A simple design, indicating they hadn't much extra money to spend.

There was also a young girl, who peered at them through unruly blonde hair. The fourth was another man, a bit older, who looked at them with a frown.

"You're not going on, are you, sirs?" the younger man asked. "It'll be dark as ink out there soon enough. Why don't you join us? There's plenty of room for King's Men around my fire, any time."

Arden tried to hide his dislike for the whole situation. This was the last thing he'd expected, being invited to camp alongside the merchants and their wagons. But it was about to get dark, there was no denying it. He held his tongue, waiting for anyone else to answer.

"You're certain we wouldn't be a bother to you?" Korian asked politely.

"No, not at all," came the reply, though the deepening scowl on the older man's face told Arden that *he* did not quite agree.

Korian looked at the others. "Well?" he asked quietly. "What do you say? Shall we camp here tonight? We don't want to be caught out in the dark, do we?"

Cayomah shook her head. "It might be better to stop here," she suggested. "But … are these people trustworthy?"

"My thoughts exactly," Berrick added. "They appear to be traveling merchants. They could be honest folk. But one can never tell. They could be thieves."

"Arden?" Korian asked. "What are your thoughts?"

Arden quickly weighed their options, putting his thoughts together. He could not give any order, but he could make a suggestion.

"We camp here," he said quietly. "It's only for one night. We will stay awake in turns, to keep an eye on things. Is everyone agreed?"

"Agreed," Stanner spoke first.

"Agreed," Cayomah replied.

There were no statements to the contrary, so Arden nodded. "We would like to join you," he answered the man's question, though he felt that his words were only partially true.

"All well and good," the man replied with a smile. He remained standing as everyone dismounted and led the horses into the trees.

"My name is Bremis," he introduced himself, shaking hands with Korian. "This is my wife, Sirah," he went on, "and my daughter, Elsoran. And …" he paused, turning toward the older man. "Forgive me. What did you say your name was?"

"Harnan," he replied, his voice tight. He only looked up for a moment, his eyes like stone, before returning his gaze to the fire.

"Oh, you've only just met?" Landers asked, stroking Flecks' muzzle. "I had assumed you were traveling together."

"We met on the Road earlier today," Bremis explained. "Just decided to stop at the same time. It *is* safer than traveling alone."

Bremis never seemed to be without a smile, Arden noticed, and it irked him. Finding a way to keep in high spirits was one thing, but the man seemed unnaturally chipper given the heaviness of the early evening sky overhead, along with the recent passing of Oden's new law, a constant threat to their lives.

How much did this Bremis know about all of it? The last three people who had come to Haven had said that *everyone* knew. News of Oden's law had been spread all across Dunya, to every city and villa.

Arden lingered in the shadows as the others began to gather around the fire. They had brought out some of their own food to add to what was already cooking, the aroma of it lingering in the air. Arden couldn't shake the feeling that this was utter foolishness, stopping for the night alongside these travelers. They knew nothing of them! Could these people pose any risk of danger for them?

Cayomah stood close at Alban's side, taking his hand in hers. Was she playing a part? Arden wondered. She and Alban *were* posing as husband and wife. It seemed so natural for the two of them, though, twining their gloved fingers together as they were. It didn't take any effort at all.

The older man, Harnan, hadn't looked up since the introductions. He scowled into the low flames as though he wished this lot of new arrivals would just be on their way.

"Have you got enough to eat, there?" Sirah asked, her tone friendly, though decidedly more forced than her husband's. Her long, fair hair was pulled back into a messy braid, and her dark green cottagers' dress was patched, but for the most part clean.

"I'm sure we'll manage," Korian replied. "Thank you. We need to make it last."

The look on Korian's face after he'd spoken told Arden that he feared he shouldn't have said what he had. Did it fit in with their supposed identities? Korian glanced in Arden's direction, but he looked away, avoiding eye contact, shrugging his broad shoulders and crossing his arms over his chest.

"You needn't stand as sentinel," Bremis told Arden, grinning crookedly. "It's near full dark now. Shouldn't be anyone out on the Road for the rest of the night."

Arden only slightly acknowledged Bremis, giving him a nod and glancing around as though he'd heard something.

"He'll not budge until he's ready," Berrick told Bremis. "He's sworn to protect us, and he takes his duty seriously."

"Does he now? Tall, strong archer, he is. What's he got to protect you all from? King's Men, are you? I should think you'll find no trouble along your way. No one wishes to incur the king's wrath on their heads by troubling any of his men."

Harnan glanced up, over at Arden, then quickly looked down at the fire.

*What was that look?* Arden wondered. Did he harbor some malice in his mind? Was he in agreement with Bremis, or did he feel just the opposite? He seemed to dislike them immensely. Was it because he believed them to be King's Men? Well, there was no law stating that people could not hold to their own opinions. Arden would not begrudge Harnan this one.

Cayomah dropped her travel blanket onto the ground a short distance from the fire and sat close beside Alban. Everyone seemed well enough at ease, Arden noticed. Berrick hung back a bit, with Korian at his side, but they were all eating and drinking from their skin flasks, smiling or nodding appreciatively at Bremis and his family, eyeing Harnan warily.

Surveying the now pitch-dark forest on three sides and the Road on one, Arden could pick up on no obvious signs of trouble. The hair along the back of his neck stood on end when he heard the far-distant, yet unmistakable, sound of a night screamer's cry.

The young girl's eyes opened wide in alarm, and she moved as near to the flames as possible without singeing her tan floral dress.

"There they are again," Bremis commented, his smile fading at last. "Quite a lot of noise those creatures make. I trust you've encountered them in your travels as well?"

"We have," Landers replied.

"They shouldn't come too close, so long as we keep the fire strong," Bremis went on. "We had a close run-in with them just two nights past."

"You did?" Cayomah asked in surprise. "No one was injured?"

"No, thankfully," Bremis replied. "Sirah and I had to wave burning branches at them to keep them off. They must have finally got tired of fighting, so they eventually gave up."

"That must have been frightening," Cayomah sympathized.

"It certainly was," Sirah replied. "I thought they'd never leave."

"But you had a fire going?" Arden asked, speaking again at last.

"We did," Bremis told him. "A small one."

"They came close, even though you had a fire?"

Bremis frowned slightly, arching one eyebrow. "Sure they did. Do you know something about those creatures that I don't?"

Arden hesitated, not wanting to say too much.

"The fire used to always keep them away," Cayomah answered for him. "I've done a fair bit of traveling myself. I've seen those creatures before – screamers, I call them – but they've never come close when I've had a fire. *Any* fire."

Bremis shook his head. "I haven't seen them along the Road myself until recently. They've gotten bold, haven't they?"

That seemed to Bremis to be the end of the conversation, at least on the subject of the screamers. He turned the rough wooden spit over the fire, juice dripping from what appeared to be a skinned rabbit, almost fully cooked.

Arden glanced around at the others, willing them to remember the identities they had chosen to hide behind, hoping they would refrain from saying anything that would give them away. Bremis seemed friendly enough, but Arden knew all too well that first impressions could be deceiving.

"I wonder if the…" Landers began, but he stopped himself at the same instant that Arden quickly turned a harsh look in his direction. Landers caught the warning in Arden's eyes before he looked down at the ground, his expression shifting from guilt-ridden to fearful.

"Wonder if what?" Sirah asked, warming her hands over the fire and staring off into the dark sky.

"I wonder if the fire we've got here is enough to keep the screamers away," he replied lamely.

Harnan looked up at Landers for a brief moment, noticing how quickly the words had come spilling out of his mouth.

Arden cringed inwardly. It had been obvious to him that Landers was covering up what he'd really wondered – whether the lightstones would be able to keep the night screamers away, even from deep within their saddlebags.

"Well," Korian spoke up, "if it is not large enough, we will simply pull branches down from the trees and light them, if need be."

Bremis let out a chuckle. "That should do it."

Elsoran shivered. "I hate those creatures. Why do they have to bother us?"

"Don't keep thinking on them, Sor," her mother told her. "We've got King's Men with us tonight. They will protect us."

Alban gave her a half-hearted grin. "We will certainly do our best."

"I must say," Bremis began, the wide smile returning on his face, "I am honored to have you here. I never thought in all my days I'd be sharing my fire with any of King Oden's men."

There was silence for a moment as Bremis' words settled over them. Harnan glanced up, his eyes meeting Arden's briefly before he looked down again, popping a bite of dry bread into his mouth.

"You certainly do hold us in high regard," Korian commented as Arden slowly made his way toward the warmth of the flames, keeping his eyes on Harnan.

"And why shouldn't I?" Bremis asked jovially. "What would our country be without men like yourselves keeping the peace? Upright men of the law? What with people trying to desert right and left?"

"Desert?" Cayomah asked innocently.

"Of course," Bremis replied. "Surely you must be aware of the talk of that 'Haven' place. It got so King Oden had to pass a law against it. People would have started defecting from our country! It would have created chaos."

Arden and Korian exchanged a knowing glance. Now they knew where the merchant stood – on the side of King Oden. They most assuredly could not let on who they really were. Not now. Arden sat stiffly by the fire, willing Landers to keep his mouth shut.

Everyone was looking at them now; Bremis and his family out of curiosity, wondering whether they were indeed aware of the dire straits their country apparently *could* have been in. Harnan eyed them as well, his expression unreadable.

"Yes, of course," Korian replied. "Certainly. That is partially the reason we are on this mission. Training new recruits, and keeping an eye on things in the villas. Making certain everyone is abiding by the law."

Bremis' smile returned. "I'm glad to hear it."

The long, low wail of a night screamer pierced through the dark, wooded area, and everyone startled. Elsoran clung to her mother's arm.

"Try not to worry yourself, miss," Stanner told her kindly. "I don't think we'll have any trouble with those beasts tonight. Your father has built a good, strong fire. I'm sure it will be enough to keep them away."

"Do you think so?" Elsoran asked, her eyes pleading.

"I do," Stanner replied.

"Can we keep it going all night?" she asked.

"We can," Korian replied, then turned toward Bremis. "I would like to offer our services. My men and I will take the night watch in turns, so that you and your family can rest in safety. It would be an honor," he added, seeing that Bremis was ready to protest.

"Well," he responded, scratching at the stubble on his chin, "I wouldn't want to deprive you of any honor. I'm truly thankful for your offer. I accept."

"And you'll keep the fire going all night?" Elsoran pressed.

"Don't be a bother to them," Bremis scolded, but Korian nodded.

"We will keep up the fire. I promise you that."

The girl finally showed a bit of relief, though the screamers kept up their caterwauling in the distance.

"That being settled," Alban spoke up, "I think we'd all best turn in for the night. We've got a long way to go in the morning."

"I will take the first watch," Arden volunteered.

Korian nodded. "Thank you. Let's ... let's check over the horses before we bed down, get them set for the night."

"Right, then," Stanner agreed as Sirah pulled her daughter off toward their wagon. Bremis thanked them once again as everyone split up, wandering away from the circle of orange firelight to secure their animals and retrieve their bedding.

Arden tried to look nonchalant as he made his way toward Korian and Stanner.

"We've gotten ourselves in deep," Korian stated quietly as Arden stood nearby.

"It couldn't be helped," Arden replied. "We will keep watch, feed the fire, and keep an eye on our supplies. We'll be on our way again in the morning."

Korian nodded heavily. "I will take second watch."

"I'll take the third," Stanner offered.

"All well and good," Arden replied, when the snap of a twig underfoot drew his attention.

All three turned to see Harnan, of all people, cautiously approaching. He ran his fingers through his shaggy graying hair, his eyes guarded, stern and wary. He nodded politely as everyone turned to look at him.

"Good evening, friend," Korian greeted him. "May we be of any help to you?"

Harnan glanced at each of them, then gestured toward the horses.

"Fine animals you've got," he commented, drawing near. He held out his palm so the horses could gather his scent.

"You know horses?" Stanner asked.

"I do," Harnan replied. "Worked with them all my life."

"Then I truly do value your opinion," Stanner told him. Harnan glanced up at him, running his palms along the muzzles of the two horses, who had come right up to him.

"Do they have names?" Harnan asked.

Arden and Korian exchanged a wary glance.

"Bishop and Gilly," Korian replied. "And yours?"

"Stout," Harnan replied. "He is old, but sturdy. He has served me well."

The sighing breaths of the horses filled the silence as no one spoke. Harnan glanced back toward the fire before going on.

"I've seen you before," he stated, looking directly at Stanner. "But not with any of the others here. You had a lad with you. A young man. Dark hair."

Stanner caught Arden's eye for a moment.

A young man? With dark hair ….

*Gavin.*

Harnan must have seen them on one of the search missions.

"I know you're not King's Men," Harnan said quietly. "Or at least, you don't seem to be."

Arden tensed. This was a dangerous moment. If Harnan knew they had come out here on Haven's business and not King Oden's …

But it was a dangerous moment for Harnan as well, Arden realized. He had just accused them of lying, of impersonating King's Men. He had taken an enormous risk in saying anything. If he'd been wrong, they could have thrown him in prison. But even if he had risked saying anything, feeling certain he was right, how did he know they wouldn't kill him to keep him from revealing their secrets?

"You – you've seen me?" Stanner asked.

Harnan nodded. "In Pran's Helm." He lowered his voice to a whisper. "You were telling people about Haven."

Arden stood by, unmoving, unsure what to do or say. Stanner swallowed visibly while Korian scratched at the elbow of his sleeve.

Harnan glanced back toward the fire once again, then whispered, "I believe you. I believe what you've said about Haven, that it's a safe place. I don't believe it's dangerous."

Stanner let out an audible breath of relief. "If you believed us, why didn't you come back with us then?"

Harnan shook his head slowly. "It wasn't me you were talking to at the time. I was overhearing. And that was a year ago. I wasn't as sure then as I am now where I stand."

"I'm glad to hear you say this," Arden told him after a moment had passed in silence. "I had feared you would be a danger to us, the look you had in your eyes."

Harnan shook his head, looking directly at Arden. "I feared you would be a danger to *me*."

Korian managed a smile.

"So then," Harnan went on in a low voice. "Are you going back to Haven soon? I … I would like to go back with you."

"I'm sorry, we're not," Stanner told him. "We have something important to do first. Where are you headed?"

"Larkswell. Bremis and I both."

Arden tugged at his tail of hair, deep in thought. "Go on to Larkswell," he advised. "When you've done your business there, go back to Meriton. Stay at the Wolf and Dagger Inn. If all goes according to plan, we should be coming back that way in two weeks' time."

"If it doesn't?" Harnan asked.

"If it doesn't," Arden replied, "we may not be coming back at all."

Harnan nodded solemnly.

"If we make it back," Stanner told him, "we will take you with us. If not …" he shrugged. "The best way I know to give you directions is to go south from Meriton to Mt. Spire, then turn west and go through the mountains. There is a pass, but it's not wise to take your horse that way. Best to go on foot."

Again, Harnan nodded. "Thank you. I will wait for you in Meriton, and pray you succeed in your mission."

"Many thanks," Korian replied. "If we don't make it back, will you tell everyone in Haven that we gave it all we had? Tell them that, though we've failed, we fought with honor, willing to give ourselves for what was right?"

Harnan raised an eyebrow, but he asked no questions. He simply nodded.

"I will tell them."

"Wait fourteen days from now," Arden repeated. "If we succeed, we will find you at the Wolf and Dagger."

"The Wolf and Dagger," Harnan repeated. "You'd best succeed on your mission," he told them. "I do want to see Haven, but I hate to be the bearer of bad news. And I'd hate to leave my horse behind. I've raised him from a colt."

"We will certainly do our best," Arden replied, turning back toward where the Road was swallowed up in thick, starless darkness, toward the southwest. Toward home.

"We will do our best," he repeated. "We want to see Haven again ourselves."

# ~ 25 ~

Jair kicked a loose pebble out of his path as he wandered aimlessly down the empty stone-paved road. A small flock of Haven's red birds darted overhead, chattering noisily.

The past seven days had been difficult ones. On the surface, life in Haven had been carrying on as it always did. Children went to school, crops were tended to, the clinic remained open, stonework was repaired. Two of the goats under Nerissa's care had recently birthed their young, and Kendie had claimed the brown speckled kid as her very own, visiting it almost daily until it was old enough to leave its mother.

Yes, on the surface, all was well. But no one needed to look very deeply to see the worry that everyone carried around with them, Jair included.

As Haven's overseer, Jair felt the burden of responsibility, as everyone looked to him to make decisions and provide for their needs. Jair still had to meet with the city's team or project leaders, and he had still needed to lead the meeting they'd held the day before. Everything carried on, but it all felt strained. Jair felt like it would not take much for the strong face everyone had put on to crumble; only the slightest hint of any more trouble, and it would all shatter like thin glass struck by a rock.

Jair felt like he was on the edge of breaking as well. All of the tension that he sensed in others around him was being stored up in his own muscles, and his neck and shoulders ached.

Gavin had become his nearly constant companion, by his side whenever possible. Gavin's nearness was Jair's only comfort these days, and he was glad to have at his side now, as he made his way past newly-repaired, yet still empty homes.

Jair was frustrated and overwhelmed. Gavin knew that better than almost anyone. During so much of these past days, Jair's mind had been *out there* beyond Haven's gate, with Arden and the rescue mission; part of him still wished that he could have gone with them. Jair was also burdened, Gavin knew, with Haven's continued attempts to speak with him. There was something important that the city wanted him to know, and for a long time, Jair had been struggling to understand Haven's cryptic messages.

They were stronger now, the flashes of images or ideas that interrupted his thoughts, and Jair could not escape them, day or night. They infiltrated his dreams, or came to him while he was speaking at meetings. But their meaning was still unclear to him.

He wanted to know what it was that Haven was trying to tell him, but he also wanted to be left alone. He was tired – tired of the worry, tired of simply pressing on under the weight of his burden, tired of Haven's relentless attempts to speak to him.

Regardless of his exhaustion, Haven did not let up, even now. Jair walked with his head bowed. Gavin was close at his side, his thumbs looped carelessly over his belt, but his posture was straight. His eyes were alert, making up for Jair's distracted state of mind.

"You don't need to do that," Jair told him, looking up.

"Do what?" Gavin asked.

"Protect me."

Gavin raised an eyebrow.

"I can tell that's what you're doing," Jair told him. "The way you're looking all around. Nothing can hurt me here. You know that."

Gavin smiled crookedly, though his eyes held no humor. "You just don't look like you can take much more right now," he pointed out.

Jair sighed. "You're right. I can't." He stopped and looked up into the late summer sky. Thin streaks of white clouds drifted past, pushed along by a wind that flowed by far overhead.

*You are not alone.*

The words were clear in Jair's mind; he'd heard them countless times. But what they meant – that was a mystery to him. His eyes met Gavin's and he sighed again.

"What's wrong?" Gavin asked.

Jair shook his head.

"Same thing?" Gavin guessed. "Haven's trying to talk to you?"

"Yes," Jair replied.

Gavin grinned sympathetically. "I wish I could help you figure it all out."

"So do I," Jair replied. "I'm just glad you're here with me."

An image flashed through Jair's mind – sunlight reflecting off a lightstone wall, and he flinched, though he must have seen it a dozen times. Agitated, he moved aside and sat down hard on a low stone wall beside one of the empty houses.

"Are you sure you're all right?" Gavin asked, joining him.

"It just won't stop," Jair complained. "The things Haven is telling me, or showing me. They're always the same. I don't understand what they mean!"

Jair leaned his head in his hands and felt his elbow brush up against Gavin's knee.

"Should I try to distract you?" Gavin asked.

"You can try," Jair replied.

"I can't think of any funny stories at the moment."

"I've heard them all," Jair replied glumly.

Gavin chuckled. "Of course you have." He sat silently for a moment, trying to find the right thing to say.

"Have you seen the girls lately?"

"Girls?" Jair asked, looking up.

Gavin smirked. "Ona and Kendie," he replied.

"Have I seen them? Yes, of course I've seen them."

"I don't mean seen them. I mean *seen* them. Gone to see Kendie. Gone to talk to her. I *know* you like her."

Jair managed a smile. "I do," he admitted. "And you and Ona, right? Have you told her?"

"Not with words," Gavin replied. "I think she knows what I think of her. I'm going to tell her soon."

"Good."

Gavin crossed his arms over his chest and stretched out his legs. "So, when are you going to tell Kendie?"

"I don't know," Jair replied. "With everything that's happened, I …"

Jair was interrupted by another image flashing across his mind.

The Light Beings. The ones that had risen up from the lightstone walls to protect the city.

*She sees.*

The words were loud and clear in Jair's thoughts, unheard by anyone else. Jair quickly got to his feet. "Why can't you stop?!" he exclaimed, startling Gavin. "I don't understand what you're trying to tell me! Don't you see that?"

"Jair," Gavin said, concerned, standing beside him.

"It keeps telling me the same things over and over," Jair complained. "Please leave me alone!" he cried out, facing the wide, empty street.

"Jair, please calm down," Gain pleaded. "You're starting to scare me."

*You are not alone.*

"I know I'm not alone!" Jair shouted. "There are people all around me who are counting on me to lead them! What are you trying to tell me?" Jair rushed toward the nearest lightstone wall and pounded his palms against the high, flat surface. "Why don't you just come right out and tell me?" he demanded. "Why are you giving me all of these pieces of things? I don't know what they mean! I don't know what they *mean.* Why don't you just *tell* me?"

Jair felt suddenly drained, and he pressed his hands against the wall and leaned his head against it. Frustrated and exhausted, he was only vaguely aware of Gavin standing helplessly nearby as tears began to pool in his eyes.

"Why can't you just tell me?"

His voice was little more than a whisper now, full of desperation.

*You are not alone.*

Haven's words had so much more clarity as they spoke to him once again. So much depth, like a real voice, but almost musical, pure, majestic.

*You are not alone. She will help you.*

Jair felt himself calming, all other thoughts fading away, his whole mind filling with Haven's voice. The familiar image of sunlight reflecting off lightstone walls flooded over him. Sunlight reflecting off pale, golden hair. He could hear the sound of laughter.

*You are not alone. She understands.*

A new image came to him, as though he were high above the city looking down into it. He could see everything, every face of every person living within Haven's walls. He could see their joy, their sorrow, their confusion, their deep bonds of family, of friendship.

*She hears.*

Several images flashed through his mind.

The red vine fruit. The clear, clean water of the stream. The newly planted crops growing to full height right before his eyes. The lost key to the white room. The burning stones in the cavern.

*She sees.*

The Light Beings, dressed in long, flowing robes, their faces hooded, arms outstretched as they rose up from the lightstone walls.

*She sees.*

A face. A familiar, smiling face.

Jair saw. He understood. It all came pouring over him. He felt the warmth from the lightstones flowing through him, and with it, the answer to every question he'd for so long wanted to ask, not knowing how to do it. It all made sense now. What Haven had been trying to tell him – it all made sense.

Jair breathed out, a long, slow breath, as he felt himself being released, his own thoughts returning. His mind was quiet.

He stood up away from the wall, slowly letting his hands fall to his sides. He turned toward Gavin, who stood staring at him, his eyes wide in alarm.

"Jair?" he asked. "I was calling and calling to you, but you didn't answer. It was like ... you couldn't hear me."

Jair shook his head. "I'm all right now. I understand everything. Haven told me everything!" He stiffened, feeling a sense of urgency. "It's about Denira!" he blurted out.

"Denira?" Gavin asked. "What?"

Jair smiled broadly. "We have to go tell Leandra. Now!"

⁓

Jair and Gavin hurried through the streets of Haven, Jair driven by a strong sense of purpose, and Gavin following blindly. Jair ignored all of Gavin's questions, his focus only on one thing. He did not want to lose one ounce of clarity concerning the things Haven had told him. He did not speak another word until they reached the front of Leandra's house and he pounded on the door.

A brief moment passed as Jair and Gavin caught their breath, then Leandra pulled open the door, looking back and forth between the two of them in alarm.

"What is it?" she asked. "Is everything all right?"

"It's fine," Jair panted. "I have something important to tell you. *Very* important. Can we come in?"

"Of course," Leandra replied, stepping aside for them to enter. Inside, Kendie stood near the far wall, Denira clinging to her dress, both of them clearly startled.

"It's okay," Jair told them. "I didn't mean to scare anyone. I just have something to tell you. It's about Denira."

"Denira?" Leandra asked, scooping her daughter up in her arms. "What about Denira?"

Jair paused to catch his breath, falling onto the bench beside the table.

"Kendie, go get them some water, will you?" Leandra asked.

Kendie quickly obeyed, bringing two full glasses over and placing them directly into Jair and Gavin's hands.

Jair took a long drink before going on, trying to speak calmly.

"Haven has been trying to tell me something for a long time," he began. "I haven't understood what it was until today. But now I know – it's all so clear. I had to tell you before it starts to fade away. Haven has been telling me that I'm not alone, that there is someone who can help me. It kept showing me pictures of sunlight, and I would hear laughter, and get this feeling of happiness. All the pieces fit together now!"

He stopped to take a breath, and everyone's eyes were on him, including Denira's.

"Today there was something new," Jair went on. "Today, Haven said to me, "she understands, she hears, she sees! It's all about Denira! All this time, Haven has been trying to tell me that Denira can talk to the city just like I can! Well, not exactly, but she can hear things from Haven just like I can. Haven tells her things, about the vine fruit, and the stream water, and the fire stones."

"*Fiew!*" Denira exclaimed gleefully.

"Yes, fire," Jair replied, smiling. "The burning stones that I found – Haven tried to tell her about them too, but she didn't know how to tell us. I bet she would have known right where to go if we'd asked her to show us where they were."

Leandra pulled her gaze away from Jair to stare at Denira in amazement.

"*Fiew*, Mammy! I tell you about *fiew*!"

"You did," Leandra managed to reply.

"She can hear what Haven wants to tell her," Jair went on, "but there's more. She can feel what other people are feeling. Haven knows what we're feeling, all the time, and it shares these feelings with Denira. It wants her to know. And it tells her things that it knows are going to happen before they happen."

"Like a prophet?" Kendie asked.

"Not exactly," Jair replied. "She only knows what Haven tells her."

Jair paused, gathering his thoughts. "Denira is supposed to help me lead Haven," he said, in awe of the idea himself. "When she's old enough, of course. That's what Haven meant when it kept telling me that I wasn't alone. Denira can help me lead Haven too."

Leandra looked intently at Jair for a moment before turning back toward Denira, who laughed gleefully.

"Haven is happy!" she exclaimed. "Mammy happy?"

"I – I'm amazed," Leandra replied. "I don't know what to say. I don't know what to think."

Jair stood and rested a hand on Leandra's shoulder.

"Haven has chosen Denira," he told her. "Just like it chose me. It's chosen everyone for some purpose. This is Denira's." Jair smirked, struck by a new thought. "Denira is more in touch with the city than I am."

Kendie came closer, standing at Leandra's side. "It's because she was born here," she said quietly. "Haven is all she's ever known."

Leandra gazed at Denira's face for a long, quiet moment, running her hand over her pale blond curls.

"Be happy, Mammy," Denira insisted.

Leandra managed a smile, then looked at Jair again.

"You're certain about all of this?" she asked him.

"I am," Jair replied quickly. "I finally am. It was all so real, what Haven was telling me. I feel … peaceful. All that worrying and wondering what Haven was trying to say – it's all gone."

Leandra nodded. "I know," she said softly. "I know, you must be right, Jair. Denira has said things, done things, that didn't make sense to me. But I can see it now, so clearly." She paused to kiss Denira's forehead. "My little girl," she whispered in awe. "Chosen by Haven … Wait until Dadda finds out."

"I miss Dadda," Denira said as she leaned her head on Leandra's shoulder.

"So do I."

The room fell silent, as each of them felt the weight of worry over the team's safe return. Jair took a breath, still exhilarated at having discovered the secret at last. He looked over at Gavin for the first time since they'd entered the house, and smiled.

"I'm sorry I scared you."

Gavin stared at him in awe for a moment before he shook his head and smiled proudly.

Jair turned back toward Leandra. "Can we tell the others?" he asked. "About Denira, what she's able to do?"

Leandra hesitated, considering the question. "Not everyone," she replied. "Only your advisors, and Ovard, Brace and Tassie. Our closest friends. I want Denira to have as normal a childhood as possible. I don't want everyone thinking differently of her, treating her differently. When she's old enough to take her place, we can have a special ceremony. Everyone can know then. For now, I want her to laugh. I want her to play."

Jair nodded. "Of course. I want that for her too."

Leandra smiled now as though she truly meant it, pulling Jair close with her free hand to embrace him tightly.

"You truly are a blessing, Jair. Do you know that? Do you know how you have touched my heart today?"

Jair stood back and grinned sheepishly. "I'm only doing what I should be, that's all."

Leandra playfully tugged at his hair. "You are the truest leader Haven could ever have. Thank you for coming to tell me about Denira. This is something that I never could have expected, in all my life."

Jair gazed at Denira, snug in her mother's arms. She was no longer simply the lively little girl he'd always seen her as. Now, in his eyes, she had changed. She was someone destined to someday come alongside him to help lead Haven's people. She had a gift, she had a calling. Who knew what the future held for her, for them? How long would it be until she could take on the role that Haven had chosen for her? And what great changes would come about when she did?

# ~ 26 ~

Arden sat in the low, dry grass, his elbows propped on his knees, seething with anger. The sound of Fury's frightened, whinnying scream still echoed in his ears. Stanner sat beside him in an attempt to be a calming presence, but he himself was still shaken. He recalled the wave of fear that had run down his spine when Landers' horse had reared up at the sight of the coiled, hissing snake, throwing its rider down onto the sparse patch of bramble bushes they had been picking their way through.

Fury, true to his name, had quickly recovered from his fright and had rushed at the snake, trampling it and killing it. He was fortunate not to have been bitten.

Landers had not been so fortunate. His back and arms were now covered with scratches and puncture wounds from landing on the thick, thorned vines.

Everyone had been quick to regroup after the unexpected mishap, which, Arden had by no means forgotten, had been caused by Landers' going on ahead of the group yet *again*, something that he had been advised several times *not* to do.

The horses' tether rods had all been pounded into the dry ground, as everyone decided this would be a good time to stop for a rest and have a bit to eat.

Landers sat away from the rest of the group, his shirt a crumpled heap on the dirt beside him. Cayomah worked at removing bits of thorns from his scratches and dabbing at his skin with a rag soaked in medically treated water.

Alban wandered from Landers and Cayomah toward the rest of them, then turned and wandered back again. He had been doing just that since they had settled down near the edge of the dry, sandy desert, with narrow, trickling rivers half a day's ride to the west and east of them.

Korian ran his fingers through his hair, taking in the view of the land around them while Alban paced across the dry, grassy soil.

"Ouch," Landers muttered, and Stanner glanced in his direction.

Arden would not look at him. The whole mess was his own fault; at least he had been the only one to suffer any injury. He could have run into *any* kind of trouble, going on ahead of the rest of them. Why couldn't he just listen?

"I'm glad we have the chance to take a rest, at any rate," Stanner commented. "And I'm glad we've got the sunlight."

Arden nodded stiffly. The darkness of the previous night had lasted so long, they had all become disoriented. Arden was so accustomed to rising with the sun, and he always awakened at the same time every morning. When he had awakened that morning, however, it was not with cheery sunlight in his eyes. No, the sky had still been very dark, and it wasn't until everyone had risen, made a fire, and eaten breakfast that the sun's light had finally become visible.

Bremis had been friendly, though sleepy, and Harnan had taken up his quiet, distant role once again, eyeing Arden and the others from across the fire. They had then parted ways, when it grew light enough for travel, and the team had headed off into the wildlands while the merchants traveled east along the Road.

Arden resented the fact that they had needed to stop now, as late as they'd had to wait to go on. Landers. Of course it would be Landers, preventing them from making good time. He was guilty, yes, but he was also injured, and Arden could not begrudge him the time he needed to have his wounds tended to.

"Ouch," Landers moaned. "Ouch!"

"Are you all right?" Stanner asked, looking back at him over his shoulder.

"No," Landers replied. "That hurts."

"Stop your fussing now," Cayomah told him, picking up his shirt and dropping it onto his lap. "I've finished. You'll be all right." She grinned at him, pushing his hair away from his face as she stood, rejoining the team.

She passed Alban as she went, and he reached out briefly to take her hand in his.

Arden sighed under his breath. He wondered for a moment if there were other snakes close by, but they had likely been warned off by all of the commotion and stamping of horses' hooves. Despite his anger, he needed to stay focused. He was tired and discouraged, but he had to stay alert in every situation.

Alban's shadow fell across Arden's face, and he looked up. His expression was flat, but his arms were crossed tightly across his chest; even with Cayomah beside him, he was tense. Displeased. Arden pulled himself to his feet just as Landers wandered over, letting his shirt fall into place over his throbbing back.

"Now do you see what I've been warning you about?" Arden blurted out, and Landers' face instantly hardened. "Rushing on ahead of everyone? I warned you, more than once. Now do you see?"

"I am sorry about what happened with the snake," Landers bit back, "but I haven't put anyone in danger, all these past seven days. I would not endanger anyone."

"Not intentionally," Arden replied. "But your reckless behavior has gotten you injured now. And it could well get others injured, or into trouble, the closer we get to Glendor's Keep."

"He's all right," Cayomah spoke up. "It's only a few scratches."

"This time," Arden grumbled.

"We're all tired," Stanner commented. "Let's just rest up a while before we go on again."

Arden took a step toward Landers, and Alban unfolded his arms, standing just at his brother's back.

"No more going on ahead of the rest," Arden told Landers in a low voice. "Stay with the group from now on."

"I know more about going on search missions than you do!" Landers retorted. "You've never been on a single one!" he went on, ignoring the fire in Arden's eyes.

"That may well be," Arden replied, "but I know what it takes to keep everyone safe. That duty has been given to me many times, and again here, with all of us. It is a duty that I take very seriously. So far on this journey, *you* have been the biggest threat to our safety!"

"That's enough now," Korian said, standing.

"Arden is right," Berrick spoke up. "I'm sorry, my friend, but you have been a bit careless. Your desire for adventure is overriding your good sense."

"No one has been hurt by anything I've done," Landers argued, "no one but myself!"

"That may not always be the case!" Arden returned, his voice growing louder.

"All right now," Korian said forcefully. "We've all said our peace, and it has gone far enough. Let it settle."

"We're all in bad tempers," Stanner joined in. "The long stretch of dark has us all troubled. Let's not take it out on each other."

"We need to work together," Cayomah agreed. "We can't be tearing each other apart."

Alban rested his hand on Landers' shoulder. "I'm sorry, brother. I'm sorry you ran into that snake, and I'm sorry you were thrown from your horse. I'm sorry about your pains." He stopped and took a breath. "I'm also sorry to say that I can see Arden's point in all of this. You really do need to reign yourself in. I don't want *anyone* to get hurt, and that includes you."

Landers took a step back, Alban's hand sliding off his shoulder. "All right, then," he said stiffly. "I will keep to the back from now on. Forgive me for being a burden."

He turned and walked away, the wind pushing his hair out behind him and billowing his shirt as he went.

"Landers," Cayomah called out, but Korian held up a hand. "Let him go," he told her. "Give him time to calm himself, and come to the realization of the truth."

"What truth is that?" Alban asked wearily.

"That it is his *actions* that have displeased us," Korian replied, "and not he himself. That we do want him and need him here with us. Is that right, Arden?"

The muscle in Arden's jaw twitched, but he nodded. *Yes* was the answer Korian wanted to hear, what everyone wanted to hear. But right at this moment Arden was unsure whether that was how he truly felt. Maybe they would have less to worry about if Landers had stayed home?

"All right then," Korian addressed the group. "Rest your legs, rest your horses. Drink more water, make sure you've eaten your fill. We will be going on again soon enough, before the darkness catches up with us. Let us all be at our best when we go on once more."

Stanner nodded. "I'm all in agreement with you there," he told Korian.

Berrick went off alone to sit on the cloak he'd spread out on the ground, and the others began to drift over, joining him. Arden remained standing. He sensed a split forming in the group, and it worried him. They needed to be a strong unit if they hoped to accomplish their mission. Was he to blame? He felt as though he had started the argument. Should he have held his tongue? Would it have been better if he'd said nothing? The frustrations he and Berrick felt would have remained buried, but they would still be there. Now they were out in the open, but it had not helped to alleviate anything. Instead, all of their frustrations and irritations seemed to have gotten stronger. There were hurt feelings now, for the most part Landers', but Cayomah was grieved. Arden could see it. Alban was torn between loyalty to his brother and acknowledging the truth of Arden's words.

Somehow, things had to be mended. Arden felt a heavy responsibility to set things right, and soon. Should he apologize to Landers? Could he do so without lessening the sharp reprimand he'd given him? He had to learn his lesson, that much, at least, Arden was certain of.

Landers sat alone, away from the rest of the group, his back to them. Well, Arden thought, let it all rest for a time. Maybe it would be easier to mend things after tempers had cooled.

⁓

Within the hour, they were off again. Arden had tried to push down his hard feelings toward Landers, looking him in the eye and telling him he was glad that he was all right, that they did need him on the team, that he held an important place in the group.

Landers had listened, and simply nodded in response. It was only sewing patches on a shredded garment, Arden knew, but it was all that could be done for the time being. Landers now rode near the back of the group, as he had said he would, his face downcast. Alban and Cayomah stayed close beside him, Korian at the lead, Arden following behind him.

The Road was far behind them now, as they made their way deeper into the wild lands. A stretch of green at their right revealed where the narrow branch of river flowed eastward, and on their left, the land was flat and treeless. They could take no cover there, but it was likely they would have no need for it. Freely wearing the lightstones once again, they could at least be confident that the night screamers would keep their distance.

*Night screamers?* Arden found himself thinking. The flying, shrieking beasts were only seen or heard in the darkness, that was true, but the darkness had lingered so long that morning. If things continued on the way they had been, would there come a day with no sunlight at all, giving the screamers constant freedom to roam wherever they wanted, whenever they wanted?

Arden thought of what had happened to Pavel's family. The only place of safety away from the screamers was Haven itself, or the pass over the mountains leading up to the city's high stone gate. What would become of the people in Dunya if that day ever came? They couldn't possibly keep high fires burning every hour, without ceasing. How would they defend themselves from attack?

"Look, there," Stanner called out suddenly.

"What is it?" Korian asked him, and Arden pulled Storm to a halt.

"There," Stanner repeated, pointing toward the horizon, where gray clouds appeared to be gathering.

"What is it?" Cayomah asked.

"I'm not certain," Stanner replied. "I've never seen anything quite like it."

"Could it be fog?" Arden asked.

"Out here, where everything is so dry?" Alban questioned. "Unlikely."

"I don't like the look of it," Berrick commented, heavy with foreboding.

"Let's just keep going on," Korian suggested. "Whatever it is, it's there and we are here. We can't let it slow us down."

"Right," Arden agreed. "We will deal with whatever comes our way, but until then, we must keep gaining ground. We can't waste precious minutes."

Korian took a breath, then prodded his horse onward. The team was able to go on for nearly three hours more, all the while keeping watch on the gray mass spreading along the sky overhead. Soon enough, it became apparent that this was a sign of the early dark to come; shadows softened and the temperature cooled. Arden was bewildered; the position of the sun revealed that it was still early evening, but the daylight was fading fast.

How could it be that it was growing dark while the sun still shone?

Gideon nickered and pulled back, turning aside. Cayomah tried to encourage him, pulling him back toward the others, but he fought her.

"What's wrong with him?" Korian asked.

"I'm not sure," she replied. "He seems fearful. I don't see anything out there, do you?"

Arden quickly looked all around, but saw no movement among the low-growing brush. "Nothing," he reported. "It must be something he's sensing."

A few of the other horses flicked their ears back and forth and stomped their hooves, but still, Arden saw nothing approaching, not from any direction.

"It's the sky," Berrick stated plainly. "Everything changing the way it is — it's got the horses spooked. They know it's not natural."

"I'm sure you're right," Arden agreed. "We've got to keep going. From the look of things, we don't have long until it will be too dark to see. Let's get as far as we can before we're forced to stop."

Cayomah was able to soothe Gideon enough to get him going once again, and the ream rode on in tense silence. It wasn't long before a series of high, chattering yips broke through the air, startling the horses and their riders as well.

"What was that, now?" Korian asked, only partially able to hide his fear.

"Wild dogs," Landers replied, speaking again at last. "They're close."

Arden peered into the distance in every direction, at last spotting movement far off among the scrub brush. "I see something," he told the others. He pulled his bow free, readied an arrow, and waited. Dusk was falling fast, and so early; blue shadows weakened Arden's sharp eyesight. He lost track of the low, jerky movements for a moment, then picked them up again. He pulled back on his bowstring, aimed, and waited.

There! But that was no wild dog ….

Arden lowered his bow.

"It's a rabbit," he said aloud as the brown, furry creature bounded past them. In a moment, several others followed.

"Where are the wild dogs?" Stanner wondered.

"I don't hear them," Alban added. "Why would they stir up the rabbits and not chase after them?"

A new sound replaced the yipping barks – a long, shrieking wail of a night screamer as it zipped through the sky in a trail of gray smoke, its eyes glowing in the strange twilight sky. The gray that had begun at the horizon earlier now filled the sky, blocking out the golden rays of daylight. Night screamers appeared in the distance, much as the stars might have otherwise, on a clear night back in Haven.

"We need to stop here for the night," Korian told the others. "There's no sense in trying to go on today."

"Agreed," Arden replied without hesitating. He slid to the ground, pulling a tether rod from his saddle bag and beating it into the hard ground with a mallet. The others joined him, making quick work of it, as the horses were becoming agitated.

The night screamers made no attempt at coming closer, as Arden and Stanner both wore the lightstones, but they began crying out in desperate frustration.

"They can't hurt us," Alban stated, taking Cayomah's hand.

"No," she agreed.

"Do we put up the tents?" Berrick asked, "Or make a fire?"

"A fire would not be wise," Arden replied. "The brush is so dry; one loose spark and we'll have more flames than we can handle."

"The tents, then," Korian said as he wasted no time in pulling his own canvas dwelling down from Bishops' back.

"Put them in a ring," Arden advised, "with the doors facing inward."

All hands worked together, quickly pulling tents onto the ground, raising roofs and tying off ropes until they had formed a small round village of sorts, with the horses tethered all around them.

Everyone retrieved what was needed or wanted from their personal belongings, then sat in the doorways of their tents, gazing out at one another through the quickly deepening darkness.

"Everything is mixed up," Cayomah commented, pulling her blue hood up over her head.

"How's that?" Korian asked.

"We knew it would get dark fast," Landers told her.

"Yes, I expected it would," she replied. "But it's not just the sky. It's everywhere. Those wild dogs – I've heard them make that sound before, when they were on the hunt. They'd run up on some rabbits – we saw them – but they never chased them. Why not?"

"It could be we frightened them away," Arden suggested.

"I don't think so," Cayomah replied. "They are not easily deterred from making a catch."

Landers shrugged his shoulders deeper into his cloak. "Let's just not discuss it," he said. "We all know about the prophecies, about the darkness. We don't really need to talk it over, do we?"

Arden eyed Landers discreetly. He had heard fear in Landers' voice, for the first time since he'd met him, and it was unexpected. But he was right – there was no need to bring the subject up, again.

"I agree," Arden stated. "We all know what's going on out here in the world. That is why we're here, after all. Let's just stay focused on the task before us. We can't let ourselves become distracted by our fears."

Landers glanced up at Arden, a mixture of surprise and appreciation on his face. Arden nodded at him briefly, then turned into his tent.

"I'm turning in," he told the others. "We can get an early start in the morning, even if it is still dark out."

Some of the others followed suit; Arden could hear them moving around. But as he secured his tent flap and lay back on his blankets, his hands tucked under his head, his mind was settled on only one thing.

Would he ever get back to Leandra, to Denira, to Kendie?

Would he ever see home again?

# ~ 21 ~

Jair sat on the old stone bench along the wall and wrapped his arms around his legs, his knees tucked up to his chin. He was still so full of conflicting emotions, he wasn't certain which he felt more strongly – hope or despair. He had shared the news about Denira with Ovard and his advisors, instruction them to keep it to themselves until the time came when the little girl was ready to make her gift known. The thought of Denira knowing things would happen before they happened was so extraordinary, Jair couldn't help but imagine how things might play out in the future. His spirits were lifted by finally understanding what Haven had been trying to tell him, and his joy was squelched only by his worries over the rescue mission.

Were they safe? Had they reached Glendor's keep yet? What would happen if they did not succeed? So many hearts would be broken; so many lives would never be the same. And Haven – if the rescue team never returned, what would that mean for the city's future? If King Oden's law remained unchallenged, would anyone else ever arrive safely in Haven? What if, Jair couldn't help but wonder, the future generations, children and grandchildren of the people who were now living there, would be Haven's only hope for the future? What would happen when *they* grew old and died out? Would Haven once again be left empty for thousands more years, or even forever? What could they possibly do to keep that from happening?

Jair felt some small comfort at having his friends nearby, but they were just as plagued by worry. Ona and Kendie sat close to one another, their shoulders touching. Gavin was on the bench beside Jair, his arms crossed over his chest, gazing out across the courtyard.

How many times had the four of them gathered here, sharing light-hearted laughter? Everything had changed. Gavin's teasing, Kendie's songs, they were all gone, replaced by a heavy burden of uncertainty.

Jair let out a breath, trying to release some of his worry – what good would it do to hold onto it? He could in no way be of any help to the rescue team, not now, not here.

"You okay?" Gavin asked.

Jair nodded. "Sure," he replied, forcing a weak smile. "Just thinking too much, I guess."

"Right," Gavin sighed. "Aren't we all, these days?"

Jair leaned his head on his knees. "I wish there wasn't so much to think about," he muttered.

"I know," Gavin agreed. "But everything's not all bad. Don't forget about the good things."

Jair raised an eyebrow.

"Pavel is doing so much better," Gavin pointed out. "Ovard's teaching him to play the flute, isn't he? He never would have wanted to do that before."

"You're right," Jair agreed. "He is much better."

"Dursen and Nerissa are going to have a baby," Kendie added. "That's a *very* good thing."

Jair nodded. "It is."

Ona sighed and leaned her head on Kendie's shoulder. "Gavin, why don't you tell us one of your stories?"

"Like what?"

"I don't know. Something funny."

Gavin scratched the side of his head.

"Well …"

Jair looked up, knowing that Gavin wasn't exactly in the mood for humor. He was surprised when Gavin smiled.

"Did you all know Persha is terrified of insects?"

Ona laughed.

"Really?" Kendie asked. "I didn't think she was afraid of anything."

"Everyone is afraid of something," Gavin commented.

Jair chuckled. "Persha, afraid of insects?"

"Yes," Gavin replied with a grin. "Flying, crawling, it doesn't matter.

She'll keep as far away from them as she can. She says they give her the shivers."

The courtyard was momentarily filled with laughter.

"Don't say I told you," Gavin warned. "She'll whack me good if she finds out I made her seem squeamish."

"We won't tell," Jair replied. "We like your stories too much."

"Thanks," Gavin muttered.

Jair rested his chin on his knees while Kendie leaned back against the wall.

"Do you think Arden and everyone will reach Glendor's Keep soon?" She asked.

"They should," Jair replied. "Soon."

"I hope everyone's all right," Ona added. "I wish I was fully trained as a medic, so I could have gone with them."

"I wish I could have gone, too," Gavin replied.

"So do I," Jair agreed.

Things were quiet once again. Worry began to seep back into Jair's mind when Gavin elbowed him.

"Shhh," he said, pointing. "Look."

Through the gap in the walls around the Fountain Court, Jair could see the road leading east through the city. He sat forward for a better look, and Ona and Kendie did the same.

It was Persha, of all people. Did she have some sort of sense that told her when people were thinking about her or talking about her? How did she always manage to just show up?

But she wasn't alone. No, Bahadur was with her.

*Bahadur?* Hadn't she said she never wanted to see him again, to speak to him again?

But there they were, together. It was unmistakable, and four teens gathered in the courtyard shared knowing glances. They couldn't help but watch; couldn't tear their eyes away as Bahadur stood close to Persha, speaking to her so quietly they couldn't hear the words.

Persha did not pull away. In fact, she took a small step closer. Bahadur leaned in, reaching up to tuck her hair behind her ear. Jair watched all of it – he watched as Bahadur kissed Persha, once, twice. He watched as Persha kissed him in return, and they held each other close.

Was he holding his breath? Jair let it out, watching as the couple walked away, disappearing from sight around a corner.

"Wow," Ona said quietly.

"I thought she couldn't stand him," Kendie commented.

"It looks like she changed her mind," Jair replied.

"I'll say," Gavin agreed. He shook his head. "I just hope she doesn't *keep* changing her mind, or she'll wear out Bahadur's patience. If she wants to marry him, she's got to stop saying she's sick of him."

Jair nodded, saying nothing.

Kendie watched him, wondering what he was feeling. He always seemed to go off somewhere in his mind when something happened with Persha. He'd done it when Persha had said she didn't want to see Bahadur ever again. He didn't seem to be doing it now, not so much. He rested his cheek on his tucked-up knees and gazed down at the stony ground.

Was he just as tired of the mixed-up relationship as Kendie? Did it matter to him any longer? Did he ever get his hopes up that Persha could possibly think of him as more than just a *boy*, more than just a friend of her brother's?

Kendie hoped, now, that everything was finally settled. That Persha and Bahadur had made up for good. Maybe he had even asked her to marry him, and she had said yes. Jair would have to accept that that was that. She would eventually slip out of his thoughts altogether, and he would have more room in his mind and heart for Kendie.

If only.

# ~ 28 ~

"Stay back," Arden told the others. "Keep out of sight."

He made his way toward the far edge of the hillside, positioning himself behind the wide trunk of a tree. From there, he could peer out at the castle without fear of being seen.

"There are guards on the upper level," Arden reported. "Two of them."

"That's right," Korian replied. "They should move on in a moment, and it won't be long until another team comes around from the other side."

Arden watched in silence until the guards did, in fact, move on.

"Is that the door, there?" he asked, hardly moving.

Korian slowly, carefully, picked his way across to another tree. "That's it," he reported. "Guarded by one man. It's the rear door, hardly ever used. If we time it correctly, we can get down there as soon as one team of upper guards moves along, and be inside before the next arrives."

Arden nodded. "Now we decide who goes down and who stays here."

"You promised Leandra you wouldn't go in, didn't you?" Cayomah stood farther off among the trees, with Alban beside her and the horses tethered behind them.

"I did."

"You've got to keep your promise."

Arden took a breath. "I plan to."

"You'll be our eyes," Korian told him. "You'll have a wider view from here."

Arden nodded. What Korian said was true, he had to admit. He wasn't exactly pleased at the idea of waiting, hidden, while the rest of them went on into the thick of things. It was true, he could defend them quite well from the hilltop, but it was a small consolation for wondering whether he was doing all he should be.

"Someone should stay here with you," Stanner spoke up. "It wouldn't be a good idea to leave anyone up here alone."

Arden nodded in response. The one person who first came to mind gave him mixed feelings. An accomplished archer, he was without a doubt. But they had not exactly been on the best terms throughout the entire journey.

"Landers?" Arden asked, and the young man looked up. "Will you keep watch here with me? With both of our bows, we can provide better cover for the others going in."

Landers nodded slowly. "I will."

Cayomah rested her hand on his arm and smiled, but Landers' face remained solemn. His impetuous attitude seemed to have entirely vanished now that they were faced with completing the dangerous mission they had all volunteered for.

"All right, then," Korian said quietly. "Arden and Landers will keep watch here. Cayomah —"

"I'm going down there with you."

Korian started to object, but Cayomah held up her hand. "I've come all this way. I'm not stopping now. You know I haven't hindered you in any way. *This* is why I came, Korian. To help any of you, yes, but more so to help *them*. We don't know what shape the prisoners are in, or how many there are. We need as many hands as we can provide, to get them out of there quickly."

Alban gazed at Cayomah with a mixture of love and pride, but her expression was intense, determined.

"You'll need me down there."

Korian let out a breath. "You're right," he admitted. "We do need everyone in this. So. With Arden and Landers giving us cover, that makes five going in. The guard at the door will have the key. We'll need to get it from him so we can get inside."

"How will we get the key?" Stanner asked.

"Well," Korian replied, "he's not going to give it to us."

"We need to form a solid plan," Berrick declared. "Let's not rush into anything. We've gotten this far. The people have been in the prison this long. Let's not blow the whole thing by not being fully prepared."

"I agree entirely," Korian replied, waving for Arden to follow him back into the forest, where they would remain unseen.

The plan way finalized, though doing so brought no relief for Arden, nor for the rest of them. It only brought on deeper tension as they readied themselves for action.

Arden and Landers would keep watch from the hillside while the others made their way down the slope to the far right of the wall, where they would await Arden's signal – a single arrow shot into the ground at the base of the hill – telling them the upper level guards had moved out of sight. At that point, they would have six minutes at the most, as they had timed it, before another pair of guards made their way around the rear of the Keep.

They would overpower the guard at the door, take the key and get inside, locate the prisoners, and move them to just inside the door to wait for another signal, another arrow, telling them the way was clear and they should hurry back up the hillside.

Arden tested the string on his bow, checking the tension. Finally satisfied, he watched the others tightening their bootlaces or removing extra layers of clothing, which might be a hindrance. Cayomah wore a small leather bag strapped to her belt – medical supplies, Arden guessed – and Alban stood close at her side, protectively. Arden feared that his focus would be in the wrong place, but there was no time left to discuss it. Now was the time for action.

He carefully made his way to the crest of the hill, keeping out of sight, with Landers behind him and Korian joining him a bow's length away. They stood behind the trees once again and studied the scene before them.

"Is everyone ready?" Korian asked, turning his face back towards the woods.

"Ready," Berrick replied.

Korian took a breath. "This is it, then." He met Arden's gaze, and the tall archer nodded.

"You are a man of *harbrost*," Arden told him. "May it serve you well in this."

"May it serve us all," Korian replied as he turned and marched heavily down the hillside.

Everything grew quiet as the others moved into position. Landers took up watching from where Korian had stood behind the tall, thick evergreen.

Arden still sensed the tension between them now, as Landers seemed to be avoiding his gaze.

Arden cleared his throat, as quietly as possible, watching the guards slowly pacing the upper walk of Glendor's Keep.

"You're troubled," he commented.

Landers looked up. "I am. Aren't you?"

Arden nodded briefly. "I surely am, but not for the same reason you are, I think. Not entirely."

Landers shifted his shoulders. "Maybe not."

"What is it, then?"

Landers looked up, his eyes steadily meeting Arden's. "You don't think I'm a man of harbrost," he told him. "Do you? Not like Korian."

Arden considered Landers' question. "You do have courage," he replied. "It only needs to be tempered with wisdom."

Landers nodded. "Berrick feels the same. I admit, I could have avoided many of the scrapes I've gotten into."

*Scrapes, yes*, Arden thought. Landers' back was covered with them.

"How are your scratches?" he asked.

Landers raised an eyebrow. "They're fine," he replied. "They don't pain me any longer."

Arden nodded, keeping an eye on the guards. They were starting to move on at last.

"Landers?" Arden asked.

"Yes?"

"I know we've had our differences. But at this moment, I am truly glad it's you who is up here with me."

"You are?" Landers asked in surprise. "Why is that?"

"I trust your skill with a bow more than any of the others," Arden replied. "You are the best man for this task."

Landers managed a smile.

"Only second to yourself."

~

Korian led the others in single file along the base of the hill, with Glendor's Keep looming high above them on their right. Every step they took was planned, not making a sound. He waved them on toward a large cluster of reeds and bushes, where he knelt down to watch the prison door guard.

Everyone crowded in close, peering through the twisting, leafy branches.

"Is there still just the one guard?" Berrick whispered, and Korian nodded. "I see him clearly," he replied, then felt his heart miss a beat.

"What's wrong?" Cayomah asked, her voice scarcely heard.

Korian swallowed. "I know him," he replied. "The guard. That's Markham. I helped train him for service when he came on four years back."

"I'm sorry, but someone's got to take him down," Berrick pointed out.

Korian nodded. "I should be the one to do it."

"You won't need to kill him, will you?" Stanner asked.

Korian looked at him. "I hope not."

A sudden *whiss* and *thwack* alerted them all – it was Arden's signal arrow. The upper level guards had moved away. It was time to act.

Markham looked in the direction of the sound of the arrow as Korian rushed out from the brush, grabbing him from behind before he had the chance to see him. Markham tried to cry out, but Korian's arm was tight around his neck, a hand over his mouth.

"Don't fight me," Korian told him firmly.

Everyone stood by watching, holding their breath, as Markham tried to step down hard on Korian's feet, missed, then tried to kick back at his legs. He was too close to get any momentum, and Korian simply held him closer.

"Don't fight me," he said again, tightening his grip around Markham's neck as he pounded at Korian's arm with his armored fists, the blows strong at first, weakening as he went without air, fading into unconsciousness. Finally, he went limp and slumped to the ground. Korian stood over him, visibly shaken.

The others hurried over, Berrick grabbing the keys from Markham's belt and trying them in the lock, while Cayomah leaned over the fallen young guard.

She stood up, looking into Korian's eyes as Berrick pushed open the prison door. "He will live," she told him, and he nodded.

"Let's get him inside," Stanner told Korian. "Grab his arms. I'll get his legs. We'll need to tie him so when he wakes up he won't be able to run for help."

Cayomah hurried inside after the others while Korian and Stanner hefted Markham's limp form inside.

Alban shut the door behind them, and they were surrounded by torch-lit darkness and the smell of the moldy, soiled straw that covered the hard ground. Korian quickly located a coil of rope, cut it in half, and tied Markham's wrists and ankles securely. He ran a sleeve across his forehead, then grabbed a torch from the wall.

"Right, then. We're in. Let's find who we came to find and get out of here."

Alban took another torch, and they made their way into the rank darkness. They followed the wide hallway down the center of the prison, lined on both sides by large iron cages. They were all empty, going in. The cells would be filled from the inner door, working their way back. One by one, they were able to peer into the straw-lined cells as they approached them, quickly determining whether they were empty.

Cayomah startled when at last she caught sight of a pair of eyes looking out from the darkness. She grabbed onto Alban's sleeve and pointed.

"I see them," he replied.

*Them?* Cayomah looked again as the firelight spilled out across the cell.

"This has got to be who we're looking for," Korian breathed out in relief.

There were six of them huddled in the straw, eyes wide in alarm.

"It's all right," Berrick told them, his voice low as he tried the keys in the cell's iron lock. "We're here to get you out."

"Get us out?" One of the women asked.

"You were trying to get to Haven, weren't you?" Stanner asked.

"We were," a man replied. "How …"

"No time for that now," Berrick interrupted as the lock snapped open and he pushed his way inside. He waved everyone in after him, shutting the door nearly all the way.

"We've got to do this quickly," he advised in a whisper. "Let's take stock of the situation and get out of here. My name is Berrick, this is Korian, Stanner, Alban, and Cayomah. We're going to help you get to Haven, where we're from."

"My name is Breindel," the young woman replied. "We are Elias,

Ackley, Aurel, Paya, and," she added, gesturing off into the shadows, "that's Falk."

"What's wrong with him?" Cayomah asked, hurrying over to the man who sat against the wall, his arms wrapped around himself, dark circles under his eyes.

"He's been hurt," Elias replied.

"By the prison guards?" Stanner asked. "How?"

"I don't know what they did to him," Breindel replied.

"We didn't want to ask," Elias added.

"But why?" Cayomah asked. "Why would they hurt him?"

"They wanted him to tell them how we know the way to Haven," the man named Aurel explained. "They're trying to find all of us, everyone who wants to go to Haven. They want to stop us."

"They can't let anyone get away, can they?" Berrick mused. "If even one person leaves Dunya, Oden's authority will seem diminished."

"But he hasn't told them," the teenage boy, Ackley, commented, his eyes wide. "They keep trying to make him tell, but he won't do it."

Cayomah looked into Falk's tired eyes. "We're going to need to hurry to get out of here," she told him. "Will you be able to run?"

"I will," Falk replied with a nod.

"Good," Cayomah replied, smiling.

"Is anyone else injured?" Korian asked.

"No," Breindel replied.

"Is anyone chained?"

"No."

"Good. Then let's hurry out of here. Is this all of you?"

"It is," Elias replied, putting an arm around Falk to help him to his feet.

"Follow me," Korian instructed, pulling open the door and hurrying down the hallway.

"Just like that?" young Ackley asked. "What about the guards?"

"We've got a plan," Korian replied as everyone filed out into the dark hallway – all eleven of them. They quickly traveled down the hall, gathering at the rear door. Markham was beginning to stir, moaning under his breath, as Korian pulled open the heavy door.

"We wait here," he told everyone in a whisper. "No one make a sound.

We wait for the signal, for the shot of a single arrow, then we run up the hill into the woods."

"The arrow tells us that the upper guards have moved out of sight," Stanner explained.

Everyone nodded, waiting, hopeful, while Falk breathed heavily, leaning against Elias.

"Are you all right?" Cayomah whispered.

"I will be."

They waited and waited, listening to the sounds of their own breathing, their own heartbeats, and Markham's subconscious muttering in the straw just behind them.

Cayomah glanced back down the hallway, worried that another prison guard might come from the other end of the prison and find them there.

*Please, please*, she thought as Alban took her hand and held it tightly. *Please, guards, go on your way so we can all get out of here!*

～

Arden watched intently as the second set of guards made their way around the upper walk of Glendor's Keep. He could see Korian and Stanner in the darkened doorway, with the rest of them crowded in behind them. They had to have found the prisoners – so quickly!

The moments seemed to stand still, as though time had stopped altogether. The two guards at the top of the wall stood in place, sweeping their gaze back and forth across the wooded hillside. Neither Arden nor Landers dared move a muscle; they hardly dared to breathe. They could not allow themselves to be seen and destroy their hopes of completing their mission.

*Move on, move on*, Arden silently willed the guards. There is nothing to see here.

Another moment passed, and then it seemed as though the guards had heard him.

"Patience," Arden whispered as the armored men made their way around the corner. "Not too soon."

Landers had an arrow at the ready, should he need to provide cover for the others as they dashed through the outer prison door.

One … two … three … four …

Arden counted to himself after the guards disappeared from sight.

Satisfied that they had gone on far enough, Arden stepped out from behind his tree, pulled his bowstring tight, and loosed the arrow in flight down along the line of the hillside, where it struck firmly into the grass just at the bottom.

He could see Korian pointing at the arrow, then gesturing for everyone to hurry out through the door.

Arden let out a breath as he saw the large group come pouring out into daylight, rushing out across the flat stretch of land toward the base of the hill.

"Have we done it?" he dared ask.

"Arden, look!" Landers exclaimed, and Arden quickly followed his line of sight. A single armed and armored guard was making his way around the corner, slowly, carelessly.

The changing of the guard.

The prison door guard.

The man stopped, instantly taking in the unexpected sight, and cried out, "escape! Escape! The prisoners are escaping!"

Everything changed in an instant. The rescue team and the newly freed prisoners ran on faster as the upper level guards rushed back in response to the shouting. Two more appeared from somewhere inside the Keep, quickly unfurling rope ladders down over the wall and climbing down.

Landers took aim and fired, striking the new guard on duty and knocking him to the ground.

Arden readied an arrow as Landers did the same.

"Hold your bow!" Arden shouted. "Only strike when necessary. We've got the lead on them."

Landers obeyed, even as they watched the four guards drop to their feet and aim their own weapons at the large group fleeing before them.

Arden let out a frustrated growl as Stanner stopped, turning to face the attackers, his sword drawn.

His sword would be no match for the arrow aimed straight at his head!

Arden took careful aim himself, his arrow flying to strike the castle guard through the arm. He cried out in pain and surprise, momentarily drawing the attention of the three others.

But it wasn't long enough. Stanner stood his ground to keep the guards away as the others hurried on, and in an instant, three arrows were aimed at him.

"Drop your sword!" Arden heard the shout.

"Blast," Arden swore as he quickly readied another arrow.

"Stop," Landers warned, and when he looked up, Arden could see that Stanner had lowered his blade and was instantly grabbed by the guards. Arden swore again when Korian hurried over to help.

"I can't get a shot!" Landers exclaimed. "I'm afraid I'll hit the wrong person."

Arden pulled on his bowstring, sighting along the length of his arrow. "I can't either," he said, letting up on the string.

"What should we do?" Landers asked.

Arden glanced back and forth from the fleeing prisoners and their own captured men.

"Nothing," Arden replied.

"Nothing?"

Arden shook his head, looking down the sloping hillside. The group was scrambling straight up from the Keep instead of winding around the side. They would be at the top with them any moment; they needed to be ready for them.

An arrow whizzed past Arden's head, and he snapped his attention on the guards below. One stood clutching his wounded arm, while two others bound Stanner and Korian. The fourth aimed his longbow right at the group climbing up the hillside.

"Stop!" Arden called out.

An arrow flew, and Arden heard someone cry out before he readied an arrow of his own and let it fly, piercing through the guard's hand as he tried once again to arm his bow.

"Cover me," Arden told Landers as he flung his bow aside to help pull up the people climbing the hillside.

The guards down below were momentarily torn between firing at the escaping prisoners, dealing with Stanner and Korian, or tending to their wounded men. The third option finally won out, and soon enough, Arden had pulled the last man up to the top of the hill.

"Follow us!" he called out Landers. The group ran on, farther into the thick woods to where the horses were tied.

They made good speed, loading everyone on horseback, the larger horses carrying two, and raced away from the Keep where they could regroup in safety before deciding what to do next.

When they finally stopped, the horses were lathered and breathless, anxiously chewing at their bits.

"We rest here," Arden announced, sliding off Storm's back. "Is anyone injured?"

"Here," a woman called out. "This man – he's bleeding."

Arden strode over to where Alban sat on his horse's back, with the young woman behind him. The lower leg of Alban's trousers was soaked with blood, his face pale.

"What happened?" Arden asked.

"An arrow," Alban replied in a low voice. "I pulled it out."

"Get down," Arden ordered, and the young woman slid easily down to the ground. Landers was at Arden's side in an instant, helping Alban out of the saddle.

"I'll be all right," Alban muttered as he sat down on the dirt. Cayomah hurried over to him.

"Let me have a look at it," she said as Arden glanced around at the others.

"Anyone else?" he asked. "Is anyone else injured?"

"Falk just needs to rest," one of the older men reported. "He's been worked over by the prison guards."

Arden nodded. "Everyone drink some water," he instructed as Cayomah tore away the bottom of Alban's trouser leg.

"What are we going to do about Korian and Stanner?" Berrick asked.

Arden's jaw tightened. Now that they had all but gotten away from Glendor's Keep with the prisoners, there was no way they could rush back to help the others. The entire castle would be on high alert. They would need to wait for things to settle down, but by then …

"We do nothing," Arden said quietly.

"Nothing?!" Landers exclaimed. "You want to just leave them there?"

"I want to do no such thing," Arden snapped. "Think about it. If we try to go back for them, we will be running straight to our deaths."

"We can't just leave them to theirs," Landers argued, his voice desperate.

Arden ducked his head. "It isn't a decision I've made lightly," he said, then looked up. All eyes were on him. Cayomah paused in wrapping a cloth bandage around Alban's leg.

"We all knew the risk involved," Arden went on, his voice heavy. "We were all willing to take the risk."

He looked away, unable to bear everyone's pained expressions. He had been willing to take the risk, just as much as any of them, yet here he was, safe and unharmed. What would he tell Medarrie? Korian's wife had been just as distraught about him leaving as Leandra had about Arden. Why did he deserve to come home, and not Korian? And Stanner – he was a friend to everyone.

Any loss was heartbreaking.

Cayomah stifled a cry, and Alban, injured though he was, tried to comfort her.

Arden sighed and turned away, looking back toward the Keep, unseen in the distance. How could he make everyone accept what had happened, when he could scarcely accept it himself?

~

Stanner and Korian went along without a fight, pushed down the wide hallway with their hands tied behind their backs. They were in a heap of trouble, to put it lightly, and they both knew it all too well.

The castle guards had firm grips on their arms or shoulders, stopping them only when they reached two large, ornately carved doors, with yet more guards standing before them.

"Requesting permission to see the king," one of the men announced gruffly. "Reporting on trouble at the prison. These men broke in and freed some of the prisoners."

The man guarding the door in front of them grew wide-eyed, then pulled open the door and hurried into the room. In a short moment he returned, gesturing for them to enter. The captives were pushed inside, brought before the king.

"Kneel," the guard at Korian's back demanded, and he obeyed. He had been here before, though not under quite the same circumstances. Stanner knelt beside him as Korian kept his eyes on the floor.

"What is this I hear?" King Oden demanded. "Breaking into the prison? Speak up!"

"Aye, sir," Korian replied. "It is true."

"Some of our men were injured," the guard behind Stanner spoke up. "And Lowen is dead."

The king took in a sharp breath, then all was silent. "Should I know you?" He finally asked.

Korian swallowed nervously as the king stepped down from his throne and came closer. He was looking right at him. "I have seen you before."

"Yes, sir."

"You worked for me."

"Yes, sir. Nearly three years past."

There was a bit of commotion as the doors behind them opened again, and hurried footsteps approached.

"We found this one, my king," came the announcement, and Korian looked aside enough to see Markham being forced to his knees, looking rather disheveled with straw clinging to his hair, his eyes bleary.

"He was on duty, guarding the outer door," the guard reported. "He was there when they broke in, and six of the prisoners escaped."

Korian swallowed, working up his courage to speak.

"Don't be too hard on him, sir. He put up a good fight to try and stop us."

"We will deal with him later," the king replied impatiently. "What I want to know is *what* you were doing breaking traitors out of my prison!"

"Traitors?" Korian asked.

Stanner took a breath, giving Korian a look that said '*What are you doing?*'

"Those people weren't traitors," Korian went on, undaunted. "They were innocent people."

"Innocent?" Oden challenged. "They knew the law, yet they chose to try and sneak out right under my nose. I would not call that *innocent*."

"The law you've created is absurd!" Korian exclaimed, suddenly growing bold. "How can you think to create a law forbidding people from leaving to find Haven?"

The guard nearest Korian grabbed a fistful of his hair. "Shall I get rid of him, Your Majesty?"

"Not just yet," Oden replied, returning to his throne, looking smug and amused. "I would like to hear his opinion on the matter."

On either side of him, Markham and Stanner were all but trembling in fear, but Korian was beginning to burn with anger. The guard released Korian's hair, and he dared to look straight ahead, facing the king.

"The people who leave Dunya to find Haven," he went on, "are not doing so with traitorous hearts. They only want to find a better place."

"Better?!" King Oden exclaimed. "This 'Haven' is better, you say? You know yourself what happened to my men when they tried to enter the city. You know how they were destroyed – you were there! Oh, yes, I know who you are. You are a traitor yourself!"

"You are wrong!" Korian challenged. "Haven destroyed those men because they had hearts to obey you – what the city perceived as wicked intent. Haven is not a dangerous place, not for anyone who desires to live in safety within its walls. Haven is in fact, the very last place of true safety left on this earth. Surely you haven't been blind to the increasing darkness all around us? Even you, hidden within the walls of the Keep? The dark is in the sky, it is in the hearts of men, it is in the screeching beasts who come out at night! Surely you can't have been blind to their existence! Do you ever listen to the complaints of your people? They need protection, and only Haven can give them what they need!"

"*My* people," King Oden retorted. "They are *my* people, not Haven's! I will not lose them to this strange, ancient city."

"You are already losing them," Stanner joined in. "Their hearts are no longer with you. And this is your own doing, trying to control them, to forbid them their right, to control their every move."

"You live here in Glendor's Keep," Korian continued. "*Glendor's* Keep, named for the greatest king Dunya has ever known. You know as well as I that the name was kept so that every king after him would be challenged to rule as he did, with uprightness and honesty. And now you have turned away from both of those things, choosing instead to follow lies and manipulation!"

Oden's scowl deepened the longer he listened, but Korian could not stop himself. If he was to die for what he'd done, he knew he must go on.

He had to say what was on his mind, on his heart. King Oden might never hear it otherwise.

Korian took a breath, gathering his resolve. "What you have done," he said in a steady, even voice, "in creating this law, forbidding anyone passage to Haven, is what you have called 'right' for your own selfish ends. But the reality is, this law is the single most terrible wrong that has ever been done to the people here in Dunya."

"The land is falling under darkness that cannot be stopped," Stanner joined in once again. "The dark is growing, and the deadly beasts who thrive in the shadows are becoming more and more rampant."

"There is no law," Korian went on, "no force on this earth, that can stop them. People are already dying because of them. Haven is the last place of refuge, the only city of light. Soon, this land may very well be swallowed up in darkness, with no light left at all."

"Who will help you then," Stanner asked, "when all of your people have perished? Who will stop the night screamers from coming after you next?"

Korian shook his head. "This is a terrible thing that you have done. You are a disgrace to Glendor's name."

The king sat on his high, golden throne, frowning, staring out toward the high, painted windows. The guards seemed to be holding their breath, waiting, wondering how he would respond.

Korian risked a glance at Stanner, who looked at him with eyes full of respect mixed with sorrow at what would surely be their fate. Korian turned to face young Markham, who gazed at him in utter amazement.

When he heard footsteps, Korian looked ahead. The sound was from Oden's boots on the steps as he came toward them, his face an unreadable mask.

# ~ 29 ~

Ovard kept a well-trained ear on the notes flowing out of Pavel's flute. It was a simple tune he'd been learning, and he had mastered it quite well. Ovard nearly chuckled aloud at the look of intense concentration on the boy's face, but he did not want to throw off his rhythm.

When the last note faded away, Pavel let out a breath and smiled tentatively.

"Was that good?"

"Very good," Ovard replied. "I think it's time you learned another tune, for a bit more of a challenge."

Pavel's eyebrows lifted. "Really?"

"Yes," Ovard replied with a smile. "I think you're ready for it."

Pavel looked over at Brace, who nodded in agreement. "It sounded perfectly fine to me, and I trust Ovard's judgment."

Ovard smiled in Brace's direction. He laughed.

"What?" Pavel asked. "What's funny?"

"Oh, lad," Ovard said with a smile. "I think I will let Brace tell you all about his trusting my judgment."

Brace ducked his head and laughed regretfully. "There was a time," he explained, looking up, "when I trusted no one's judgment. It took me some time before I realized just how much wisdom was behind the advice Ovard had to give me. That's quite a story."

"Ah," Ovard spoke up, "but then, you're not much for telling your story, are you?"

Brace's smile faded. "You've been talking to Tassie," he guessed.

"No need to, son," Ovard replied, resting a hand on Brace's shoulder. "No need to."

"Well," Brace sighed, "some stories *might* be worth the telling."

"I'd like to hear them," Pavel said meekly.

"And you've got wisdom of your own to share," Ovard told him. "You have come so, so far."

Brace nodded. "Is it far enough, I wonder?"

Ovard gave him a strong pat on the back, then turned toward Pavel. "You have come quite far yourself, my boy. You've surprised us all."

"Do you think my Uncle Erhan would like how I play his flute?"

"Very much so," Ovard replied.

"You've learned fast," Brace added.

Pavel smiled, a small smile. "I miss them. Sometimes I imagine them all listening to my playing."

"I'm sure they would like knowing you do that," Brace told him.

"I wonder if they do," Pavel commented. "I wonder if they know."

"Know you imagine them listening to your playing?" Ovard asked.

"Yes. Remember when Denira knew what my mam used to do, what my dad used to call me? Somehow, she knew. I think somehow, my parents must have told her."

Brace rubbed at the back of his head as he exchanged a glance with Ovard They knew now about Denira's gift, being able to communicate with the life residing within Haven's walls. Pavel's family no longer lived, that much was certain – there was no way *they* could have told Denira anything. Haven, on the other hand, had ways of knowing things that were impossible for any of the them to comprehend. Haven had ways of knowing about Pavel's family, and had decided to share those things with Denira.

"Well," Brace began, "however it all happened, I'm glad Denira did what she did. She gave you just what your heart needed so you could go on."

Pavel nodded. "I wish she was older, so I could ask her all about it."

"She will grow," Brace told him. "I'm sure some day she'll be able to tell us how she hears what Haven wants to say to her."

"There's Tassie," Pavel commented, pointing, and Brace turned to look.

"Oh, her day at the clinic must be over. Perfect timing, hey?" Brace waved at Tassie, and she smiled, giving Ovard a quick kiss on the cheek before letting Brace hug her tightly.

"Not too tightly," she told him. "You'll squash me."

"I just missed you," Brace told her, and she smiled again.

"I missed you, too. And Pavel," she added, looking in his direction. "How were your classes today?"

"All right," he replied. "I learned a new word in Haven's language. It's *hayat*. It means *life*."

"That's a wonderful word to learn," Tassie replied earnestly.

"The boy has brought life back into his uncle's flute," Ovard declared. "The next time you come, I will have chosen another tune for you to learn."

"I'll be ready," Pavel replied.

"I have no doubt of that."

Tassie hugged Ovard as they all said their farewells. Brace walked along, holding Tassie's hand, as Pavel went on just ahead of them.

"Feeling all right?" Brace asked Tassie.

"I am," she replied. "A bit tired, though. I've been on my feet quite a bit today."

"Many patients?"

"Only two. Nerissa, to get checked over, and little Amalya. She had a bit of a cough, is all. She'll be fine. I gave her parents a bottle of vine fruit juice."

"Cures everything," Brace commented.

"It does."

"Brace?" Pavel asked after a moment, looking back. "When do you think Arden and everyone will get back from the rescue mission?"

Brace felt his heart miss a beat. *When, indeed?*

"I can't be sure," he replied honestly. "They've been gone – what, fifteen days now? I should think another week, maybe sooner. If …"

He glanced at Tassie, and her green eyes met his.

"If?" Pavel asked.

"If all goes as planned," Brace finished.

"Do you think they're safe?" Pavel asked in a small voice.

"I certainly hope so," Brace replied.

Tassie held his hand tightly, and he knew she was as worried as any of them.

"Arden knows how to watch out for others," Brace told her, and she nodded.

"He needs to come home to Leandra," Pavel stated. "And to Denira."

"He will," Brace replied. "As soon as they finish their mission, he will come home."

Tassie leaned in closer to Brace as Pavel nodded in response.

*Arden, you've got to come home*, Brace thought. *What will any of us do here without you?*

There was silence as they made their way back to the house. Silence, until Brace heard a young voice calling out in their direction.

"Pavel! Pavel!"

Hoden hurried toward them, waving and smiling. Trystan and Shale were right behind him, followed by Adivan and Farris.

"Hoden?" Pavel asked, clutching his flute.

"Hello, Mister Brace," Hoden greeted him. "We're going to the lake to swim. Can Pavel come with us?"

It immediately came to Brace's mind that the last time Hoden had invited Pavel along, it had not ended well. He still remembered Pavel's fear, and his tears.

Pavel remembered them too, Brace could see that. But he had come so far – surely such a thing wouldn't happen again.

Brace leaned forward, looking Pavel in the eye.

"Do you want to go with the other boys?" he asked, hoping not to sway him in one way or another.

Pavel chewed at his lip. "Yes," he said quietly.

"Yes?" Brace asked. "Are you sure of that?"

Pavel smiled. "*Yes.*"

Brace winked at him, holding out his hand to take the flute. "Go on, then."

Pavel smiled broadly as he handed over the flute and turned back toward Hoden. "I'm coming," he announced joyfully.

"We'll watch out for him," Adivan told Brace and Tassie. "He will be all right."

"Of course he will be," Tassie replied with a smile.

Brace held her hand tightly as they watched Pavel join the others, heading off toward the lake, the group talking and laughing as they went.

"Pavel will be all right today," Tassie commented after they'd gone out of sight.

"He will," Brace agreed.

"Will you?"

"What?" Brace asked. "Will *I* be all right?"

Tassie nodded. "Things are changing for us, again. Pavel is not so much in need of comfort any longer. He will be in need of a father now."

"And a mother," Brace pointed out.

"Can we be those things for him?"

"Haven't we been?" Brace asked. "As best we can, at least?"

"Maybe," Tassie replied.

Brace smiled and kissed Tassie's cheek.

"What is that for?"

"Do I need a reason to kiss you?" he asked, smirking.

Tassie shook her head and smiled. "If you ever needed a reason, I'm sure you could come up with one."

Brace kissed her again. "Really, though. I think you've been a good mother to Pavel."

"Sometimes I feel cut off from him," Tassie commented. "He seems to not know how to act around me. It's like he doesn't want to draw attention to my deafness, but he can't ignore it either. He wants to find a way to treat me like he would anyone else, but he feels awkward trying."

"I think that will just take time," Brace replied, putting an arm around her.

Tassie nodded, gazing off into the distance. Brace was all too familiar with that habit of hers. He had seen her retreat into her own thoughts often enough during their years together. It seemed the best way she knew to handle a situation that was overwhelming for her. Early on, Brace had tried to bring her out of it by joking around, but she had never really appreciated such tactics. No, Brace had found that what Tassie appreciated most in such moments was simply to have him hold her close, or simply be by her side, as he was now.

Brace let a moment pass before taking her hand.

"Tassie?" he asked when she looked at him.

"What?"

"You know I love you."

She smiled. "Yes, Brace. I know it."

"We've been through so much. And we're still here. You and me. I'm ... Well, I'm happy here with you. And I'm happy with Pavel. Aren't you?"

Tassie nodded slowly. "I am."

"So," Brace went on, "I feel like, no matter what happens next week or next year, we can get through it together. Maybe not perfectly, but we can do it. We've been trying so hard to turn the two of us into a family. With Pavel, we *are* one. The three of us – we *are* a family."

Again, Tassie nodded, a slow, thoughtful nod. "We are, Brace. I know there were things I wanted, plans I've made, plans we've made. And not all of our plans have come through for us. Maybe they will, or maybe they won't. I think I've had to learn something. I can't keep wanting the life I *could* have. I just need to be here in the life I have right now. Because truly, Brace, I have no regrets. None at all."

"Really?" Brace asked, running his fingers through her hair.

"Really," she replied, her deep green eyes locked on his. "I will love you forever."

Brace smirked. "Well, I should hope so," he replied lightly. "Because if my stubbornness or tendency to mouth off hasn't driven you away by now, I would think nothing ever could."

Tassie laughed softly, a sound Brace loved to hear. He held her hand firmly, leading her away from the house.

"Come on," he told her. "I heard Nerissa planted a stretch of flowers in the southeast garden. Let's go see if we can't find some yellow ones."

# ~ 30 ~

Kendie ran her palm over the thick, soft fabric of Leandra's dress as she pulled it down from the laundry line, neatly folding it into thirds before placing it in her basket. The towels were also dry, as were Denira's tiny dresses. Most of them had come clean, surprisingly. Denira could be a sloppy eater, always getting food on her front.

The line was empty when Kendie hefted the basket to her hip and took it indoors.

"And what is this?" Leandra asked Denira as Kendie entered. She pointed to the simple image she'd drawn on the sheet of paper.

"Wabbit," Denira replied confidently.

"Good!" Leandra praised. "Maybe tomorrow we can go out to the woods again and look for real rabbits. Would you like that?"

"And biwds," Denira replied.

"And birds? You want to look for birds?"

"I wike biwds."

Leandra smiled. "So do I."

Kendie set the basket of laundry on the padded window seat and watched them.

"How about this one?" Leandra asked, drawing another small image on the paper.

Denira frowned at it.

"Sometimes they look like this," Leandra said as she sketched again. "I'll give you a hint. They are way up in the sky, higher than the birds. They are white."

"Cwouds!" Denira exclaimed, smiling broadly.

"She's getting better at reading pictures," Kendie commented, folding a large towel. "Soon enough she'll be able to read letters."

Leandra smiled. "I've already taught her one. Denira, what letter is this?"

"Dee!"

"Very good. And what is 'D' for?"

"Deniwa!"

Kendie laughed. "That's very good, sissie! You're so smart."

"I dwah?" Denira asked Leandra, reaching for the pencil.

"Yes, but only on the paper," Leandra replied. "Not on the table."

Denira began scribbling contentedly as Leandra came to help Kendie with the folding.

"And how are you today?" Leandra asked quietly. "Between your classes and medic lessons, and spending time with Ona, we haven't had much time to talk."

"I'm all right," Kendie replied vaguely. "Just worried, like everyone else." She glanced at Denira, then lowered her voice. "Shouldn't Arden and everyone have been back by now? They said they'd be gone about twenty-two days, and it's been twenty-four."

"No one ever knows exactly how long any journey will take," Leandra said without looking up.

"Aren't you afraid for them?"

Leandra let out a sigh. "I can't allow myself to be afraid," she answered. "I just can't. I need to be here for you and Denira. I can't let myself start to worry."

"Or you won't be able to stop?"

Leandra nodded, letting out a shaky breath. "I just can't …." Her voice trailed off, and she shook her head.

"I'm sorry," Kendie told her, beginning to feel dread creeping up her spine.

"Jaiw!" Denira called out happily.

"What, Denira?" Leandra asked, gathering her courage.

"Jaiw!" She repeated. "Jaiw is coming!"

Leandra glanced back at Kendie just as there was a knock at the door. Leandra's eyes widened.

"Jaiw! Jaiw!" Denira got down from her seat and hurried to the door, trying unsuccessfully to open it. Leandra crossed the room in three quick steps and pulled open the door.

"Jaiw!" Denira exclaimed, seeing him standing there, holding a lumpy cloth sack in one hand.

"Hi, Denira," Jair replied as she wrapped her arms around his legs. He looked up to see Leandra and Kendie staring at him in surprise. "What?" he asked. "Is something wrong?"

"No," Leandra replied. "Denira knew you were coming."

"Oh." Jair looked down at the little girl as she smiled up at him. "Well," he said, looking up again, "we know she could do that, didn't we?"

Leandra managed a bit of a smile. "We did," she replied. "It's still strange, though, when she does."

Jair nodded. "It is."

"I'm sorry," Leandra said, picking up Denira. "You must have had a reason for coming?"

"Oh, yes," Jair replied, suddenly looking awkward. "I just wondered … Kendie, if you're not busy, would you like to go for a walk with me? Not to anywhere in particular."

Kendie looked at Leandra.

"You're free to go, if you'd like."

"Well," Kendie replied, "I'm sure the laundry can wait, can't it?"

"Of course," Leandra said with a smile. "Go on ahead. It's all right." She gave Kendie a knowing look, and Kendie almost blushed in response as she went out to stand beside Jair.

"Bye-bye!" Denira called out, waving, as Leandra took her back inside the house.

"Bye," Kendie replied distractedly. "Going walking?" She asked Jair as the door closed behind her. "To nowhere in particular?"

"Sure," Jair replied. "Why not?"

Kendie shrugged. "All right."

She felt a strange sense of apprehension – or was it anticipation – as they meandered along the roadway. "Is everything all right?" She asked.

"As much as it can be," Jair replied. "What about with you?"

"It's fine."

"I haven't really heard you singing any of your songs for a while."

"Well, I know. I haven't really felt much like singing since Arden left."

Jair nodded, understanding.

They walked on in silence a ways, wandering out toward the southwestern garden, where Eridan kept her beehives.

"What have you got in the bag?" Kendie asked nonchalantly.

"Oh," Jair said as though he just remembered he'd been carrying it. "It's ... actually ... something I wanted to give you."

"Me? Why?"

"Because, really, you're the main reason I finished it."

They had just passed the school house, and Jair sat down on the low stone wall at the edge of its paved courtyard. He pulled open the drawstring bag and removed a figure carved in wood – Haven's frolicking deer.

"It's for you," he said, holding it out to Kendie.

Momentarily speechless, Kendie reached out to take it. It was beautiful, smooth, its long legs flowing down to the wooden base resembling a forest path.

"Jair," she said breathlessly. "It's perfect. I knew you could do it. But you don't need to give it to me. You should put it in the library, or keep it at the meeting hall, somewhere everyone can see it."

"I want you to have it," Jair replied, shaking his head. "It meant a lot to me when you told me not to give up on it. One the carving, or on anything. It was good advice."

"But, Jair, everyone tells you not to give up. Not just me."

Jair scratched at the back of his head. "Well..." he began uncertainly. "I guess I just want you to know how much I appreciate *you*. Not just what you said. You ... you mean a lot to me, Kendie. I want you to have the deer. It's not much, really. It's just something I knew you'd like."

Kendie gently fingered the deer's smooth, pointed ears. "Thank you," she replied. "I do love it, Jair. It's your best carving yet." She hesitated before going on. "I was beginning to worry you thought of me as a pest."

"A pest?" Jair asked, surprised. "No! I don't think you're a pest. Why would you think that?"

Kendie shrugged. "Well, you would always get quiet when I talked to you. Lately, at least. You seemed like you didn't really want me around." She dared to pull her gaze away from the carved figure in her hands, dared to see Jair's expression.

He shook his head. "I'm sorry, Kendie. I was just so distracted. There has been so much going on, with Haven trying to tell me about Denira, and I didn't understand. I just had so much on my mind."

"But you acted like you didn't really want to, when I said we could go walking in Haven's Woods."

Jair stood up. "Yes, I did want to," he told her. "I did. I *do*. Everything just kept happening, and I never got the chance to ask you. We could go right now, if you want."

"No," Kendie replied. "I mean, we don't need to go now. I just was afraid you wouldn't want to walk with *me*."

Jair shook his head slowly, a smile growing on his face. "I'm glad to have you around, Kendie. You've always been so … I don't know. Happy. Singing, and telling stories, and smiling. I'm glad to have you as a friend. And lately … well, lately I've been feeling like we could be *more* than friends."

"More?" Kendie repeated, her heart missing a beat. Was Jair really saying this to her, or was she only dreaming, like she had so many times before?

"Yes. I have strong feelings in my heart about you, Kendie. More than just like friendship."

"So, you don't love Persha?"

"No," Jair replied. "Maybe I did, in some way. But not anymore. And not like I feel about you."

Kendie stood reveling in Jair's words, feeling them flowing over her. He really had said it – hadn't he? He thought more of her than he did Persha!

Nervously, Jair took a step back. "I didn't mean to say anything that made you feel …"

"No," Kendie replied before he could think of a word. "I'm glad you told me, Jair, because – well, because I've felt the same way about you. For a long time."

"You have?" Jair asked, his eyes wide. "But you didn't tell me."

"I didn't think you were ready to hear it."

Jair breathed out a laugh and smiled awkwardly.

Kendie laughed. "Funny, isn't it?"

Jair only smiled.

"Actually," Kendie admitted, "there were times when I wanted to tell you, or I wanted to do something to try and make you notice me, but Leandra kept telling me to wait. She said I was too young. But that was even before Denira was born," she added quickly, not wanting to make Jair wonder if she was indeed too young.

"That long?" he asked.

"Yes," Kendie replied sheepishly.

Jair tentatively took a step closer. "Well, I don't think we're too young now, to know how we feel."

"Neither do I."

"So, what do you want to do?"

Kendie only considered the question briefly. She knew what she wanted, but if she waited, she would lose her nerve.

"Will you kiss me?" she asked.

"Kiss you?" Jair replied in surprise.

"Yes. I've never kissed a boy."

Jair cleared his throat. "I've never kissed a girl either."

"We can be each other's firsts."

"All right."

"Do you *want* to kiss me?"

"Yes," Jair replied, stepping closer. Another step, and the only thing between them was the frolicking deer in Kendie's hands. Jair leaned forward, and their lips briefly touched before he straightened up.

They both laughed nervously.

"Can I try again?" Jair asked, his face reddening.

"Yes."

He tried again, leaning forward more slowly this time, letting their lips touch gently. Kendie closed her eyes and held her breath. In another moment, the kiss was over, and she tingled from the top of her head all the way down to her toes. She smiled, feeling silly and childish, not knowing what else to do.

Jair smiled back at her, reaching out to hold her hand. Their eyes met, and though neither of them spoke, they knew what thoughts they shared.

*I'm glad you told me.*

*I liked the kiss.*

Kendie held Jair's hand snugly as they made their way back toward home. She felt like everyone would be able to see it on her face, that she and Jair had kissed.

And she didn't care in the slightest.

# ~ 31 ~

The crops grew high and plentiful, as they did after each planting. This time, there were peas, beans, and melons in abundance, recently picked and waiting at the food storage building for everyone to come and take what they needed.

The days of harvesting and gathering fresh crops had always been joyous times, when everyone brought baskets to fill with as much as their family had need of. Today, however, was not quite so joyous. It had been twenty-eight days since the rescue team had left Haven, and everyone had spent the last six wondering if *today* would be the day when they would return. There was an unspoken fear, an unspoken worry, hanging over each of them.

What if the mission had failed?

No one dared ask the question. They hardly wanted to think it. They would need to face it one day, but every day, it seemed, everyone silently pleaded *not today*. *Give them one more day.*

Brace continued to stuff down his own worry, for himself as much as for Tassie and Pavel. He could see Arden's face in his mind – his cold, hard stare or his amused smile. Would he ever see his friend again?

He held hands with Tassie as they headed toward the food storage, each of them carrying an empty basket. Worried or not, there was still a new harvest of crops, and today was the day of distribution. They had to eat.

A small crowd was gathered around the open doors of the food storage building, where Dursen, Nerissa, Worley and Essa were working to help load up everyone's bags or baskets.

316

Airell and Silas gave Brace and Tassie friendly nods as they passed by, heavily laden with fresh food.

"They are giving out so much," Tassie commented. "It seems like too much, doesn't it?"

Eaton looked up from where he stood nearby, with Lida and her sister Noora close beside him.

"They don't know what else to do with it," he told them, having overheard Tassie's comment.

"What do you mean by that?" Brace asked.

"Well," Eaton began, "there are ... less people here right now to take it. And, Dursen told me, they used to take the extra to Meriton to trade or sell it?"

"That's right."

Eaton glanced around, then lowered his voice. "They said Jair doesn't want anyone to leave the city just now. We don't know what's going on *out there*. It might not be safe to leave at all."

Lida stepped up closer to Eaton, leaning her cheek against his shoulder.

Brace nodded. "I know, you're right. It might not be safe."

"So," Eaton went on, "they're letting people take extra."

"They're only keeping what they need," Lida added, "to have seeds for the next planting."

"We can have extra melon?" Pavel asked, looking up at Brace, then quickly dropping his gaze.

"It's all right," Brace told him, resting a hand on his shoulder. "It's all right to want more melon. We don't want it to rot in storage, do we?"

Pavel looked up slowly and shook his head.

"Thank you, Eaton," Brace said before going on. "Thanks for filling us in on what's happening."

"No trouble," Eaton mumbled.

Noora forced a thin smile as they passed her. Tassie held Brace's hand tightly.

"I know," he said, turning to face her. "You don't need to say it."

Tassie's eyes filled with sorrow – the sorrow everyone in Haven felt at the thought that their loved ones might never return. Brace felt his own sadness rising to the surface, but he pushed it down again. No, he couldn't let himself go there. His own family needed him to be strong.

"Hello!" A friendly voice called out. It was Eridan, of course, smiling in genuine pleasure as she came forward to embrace Tassie. "And how *are* you?" she asked.

"Well enough," Tassie replied. "You?"

"Yes, I'm all right. Hello, Brace. Hello, Pavel. How are you all?"

"We're all right, thank you," Brace told her, putting an arm around Pavel's shoulders.

"Oh!" Eridan exclaimed suddenly, then turned to look behind her. "Dorn!" She called out. "Bring me a jar of honey, will you?"

The red-headed man nodded and turned toward a small wooden cart.

"We had a good batch of honey again last week," Eridan told them as Dorn brought her a large glass jar, shining golden in the afternoon sunlight.

"I want you to have this," she went on, accepting the jar from Dorn and holding it out for Tassie.

"Really," Tassie began to protest, "we still have some from the last time."

"No, no," Eridan said with a wave of her hand. "One can never have too much honey in their larders. It won't go bad, after all, if you store it properly."

"Thank you, then," Tassie replied, accepting the gift.

"Pavel likes honey. Don't you?" Eridan asked. "You look like a boy who likes honey."

"Yes, miss. I do like it."

"Oh, come now, call me Eridan, please. I'm not much for formalities."

"Yes, miss – er, Eridan."

Eridan smiled. On the surface, she seemed unaffected by the tension plaguing everyone else in the city, but Brace noticed the way she pulled her lacy shawl tighter around her shoulders and fiddled with the chain around her neck. She was uneasy, just like the rest of them. And why shouldn't she be? Cayomah, her dear friend, was out there somewhere, in that dark, unsafe world.

"Thank you for the honey," Tassie told Eridan. "It won't go to waste, you can be sure of that."

"Oh, I'm sure it won't."

"Well, we'd best get what we came for," Brace spoke up.

"Of course," Eridan replied. "Don't let me keep you."

"Come over for a visit," Tassie encouraged. "I would love to see you."

"I will," Eridan replied, giving Tassie another quick embrace. "I see Nadira coming," she added, looking past Brace. "I think I'll go and talk with her. I will come by the house this evening, I promise. I would love to spend more time with you."

"As would I," Tassie agreed as they went on toward the open doors of the food storage building. Kendie was just inside, chatting comfortably with Dursen and Nerissa, whose belly was beginning to show some roundness as the child within her grew. Brace held Tassie's hand tightly, but she only looked at him with ease.

"I hope you have an appetite for beans," she told him.

He chuckled.

"And melon," Pavel added.

"Well, we're going to have plenty of both," Brace replied.

Dursen looked over as they approached, greeting them with a friendly smile. "Afternoon."

"Same to you," Brace replied. "Busy day?"

"Just like any other distribution day," he said, then grinned ruefully.

No, it was not just like any other distribution. Everyone bore a heavy burden of worry, no matter how they tried to hide it.

"Well," Kendie spoke up, "I've got plenty here. I think I'll head back."

"Will you manage?" Dursen asked. "Two big baskets full – can you carry them to Leandra's?"

"Or drag them," Kendie replied.

"Why didn't Leandra come with you?" Tassie asked.

"Denira is napping," Kendie replied.

"Well, if you'll wait for us, we can help you," Brace told Kendie. "We've got two baskets, and there are four of us. We can each carry one. Pavel's got two strong hands, don't you, Pavel?"

"I do."

"Thank you, Brace. I'll wait."

Dursen and Nerissa helped them fill their baskets, melon on the bottom, beans and peas on the top. Brace could see Kendie as he worked, and he looked up to see her smiling off across the square paved yard. He glanced in the direction of her gaze to see Ovard and Jair talking with

Nevin and Shayrie. Jair was looking over in Brace's general direction, but past him.

Looking at Kendie.

What was that Brace saw in their eyes? It was no simple greeting of friendship. No, it went much farther than that. *That* was a spark. Brace had no doubt in his mind. Well, hadn't Kendie been waiting for years for Jair to notice her? Now it had finally happened. Well, he wished her all the best. Jair had grown into a young man worth waiting for, of that Brace was certain.

He kept it to himself, the fact that he'd noticed, and he, Tassie, and Pavel headed off for home, each of them carrying a full basket. He smiled to himself when he noticed Pavel eyeing the fresh melon with anticipation of tasting it.

*Soon enough*, he thought, finally arriving at Arden and Leandra's home.

"Why don't you come inside?" Kendie invited them. "I know Leandra would like to see you."

"Isn't Denira sleeping?" Tassie asked.

"It's all right," Kendie replied. "We won't be making so much noise."

"I would like to stay for a bit," Tassie told Brace.

"All right," he replied willingly. "We will. Here, Pavel. Let's leave our baskets outside here and get Kendie's into the house."

Brace never hesitated to check in on Leandra, now that Arden was gone. It was the least he could do.

Leandra looked up from her seat at the table when they entered. Brace noticed right away the weariness in her eyes. Where was Arden? How much longer would Leandra be able to hold up under her fears, her worries, over her beloved husband?

Zorix sat on top of the table, his eyes unswervingly fixed on Leandra's face, hardly reacting at all to the new arrivals. His fur was a bright red color, revealing his concern and worries over Leandra.

"I've brought back company," Kendie announced with forced cheerfulness.

"I see," Leandra replied, her voice quiet.

"I hope you don't mind."

"No," Leandra said with a smile as she stood to greet them. "I'm glad."

"How are you?" Tassie asked, coming inside.

Leandra held Tassie in a tight embrace, then released her. "I'm all right," she replied. "Thank you all for helping bring the baskets back. I would have gone, but I couldn't leave Denira."

"It was no trouble," Brace told her.

"We didn't mind at all," Tassie said at the same moment.

Leandra smiled. "Let me get you all some water."

Zorix scampered to the floor and lingered close to Leandra as she filled stone mugs, Kendie helping her. There was silence as everyone drank the refreshing water from haven's flowing stream, any trace of tiredness in their limbs diminishing almost instantly. If only the water could do the same for the tiredness in their spirits.

The silence began to feel awkward. Zorix noticed it as well, looking around from face to face.

Finally, Leandra spoke.

"How have you been, Pavel?"

"I'm all right."

"You've been learning to play the flute?"

"Yes."

"I'd like to hear you play some day."

"Yes, ma'am."

"Do you like to play?" Leandra asked, but Denira wandered into the front room at that moment.

"Mammy?" she asked, her eyes sleepy.

"Oh, Denira," Leandra said, turning in her direction. "Hello, sweet. Did we wake you up?"

"No, I wake."

Denira reached out her arms, and Leandra picked her up, holding her close. "You smell like sleep," she told her, her voice full of affection. Denira leaned her head on Leandra's shoulder, sucking on her fingers.

"She is growing so quickly," Tassie remarked. "And she is doing well, isn't she? Strong and healthy, and happy."

"She is," Leandra replied. "There is no better place than Haven for raising children."

"There is no better place," Pavel repeated quietly.

"What's that?" Brace asked, crouching beside him.

"There is no better place," Pavel said again. "That's what my parents told me before we left to come here. They said there wouldn't be anything else like it anywhere."

"Do you think they were right?" Brace asked him.

"Yes," Pavel replied. "I especially do now. When I first got here, I was so afraid, and so sad and hurt because my family wasn't here with me. I thought I would never really be happy again, not anywhere. But ... then Denira showed me that my parents knew how I felt, and Haven knew all about my parents, and about me. That's when I started to be all right. It was all because of Denira. I think she's going to be able to help a lot of people."

"I think you might be right," Leandra agreed, stroking Denira's tousled curls.

"That's what Jair thinks, too," Kendie spoke up. "He knows Denira will be able to help him lead Haven, when she's old enough."

Brace nodded, standing. He resisted the urge to say something, letting Kendie know that he knew about her and Jair. Maybe another time.

Leandra finally looked over the baskets of fresh produce.

"This is so much," she commented. "Can we eat this before it spoils? Maybe you and Tassie should take some of it."

"We've got more than enough," Tassie replied. "There won't be any trip into Meriton to sell the excess, not this time."

"We may need to loosen our belts a notch or two," Brace added with a chuckle.

Zorix sniffed at the beans, peas, and melons, then turned his gaze on Leandra.

"I know," she told him. "you want meat. Will fish be good enough for now? We can go to the lake later."

There was silence for a moment, then Leandra laughed softly.

"What's Zorix got to say?" Brace asked.

"He says fish is better than little green sticks."

The house was filled with laughter, for the first time in nearly a month.

"Mammy," Denira said when the laughter faded, "I want Dadda."

"I know you want Dadda," Leandra told her. "So do I. For now, why don't we eat some of this melon?"

Denira peered down at the basket full of round, yellow-green melons, and nodded, again sucking on her fingers.

Leandra invited all of them to stay, and they accepted. Leandra was sharing with them now, and Brace and Tassie knew they could do the same for her another day.

The melon was bright yellow inside, sweet and tangy all at once, and everyone savored their slices. Kendie cut a small chunk of it, offering it to Zorix, who sniffed at it suspiciously.

"Oh, come now, try it," Kendie coaxed him. "I think you will like it."

Reluctantly, Zorix reached out and grasped the piece of melon, gave it one last sniff, and shoved it into his mouth, chewing it with his short, sharply pointed teeth.

"Well?" Leandra asked.

Zorix swallowed and sat staring at the table for a moment before looking at Leandra.

"He says it's better than he expected," she remarked, wiping melon juice from Denira's face with a towel. "But not as good as fish."

Pavel smiled. "I like this better."

"Mammy, is Dadda coming?" Denira asked.

"Yes, my sweet. He is coming back. We just don't know when. We need to keep waiting for him."

Tassie and Leandra's eyes met, exchanging a fearful glance.

They *were* coming back, weren't they? All of them? Not just Arden.

"He's missing out on some great melon," Brace commented. "We'll need to plant it again when they get back, won't we?"

"We will," Leandra replied appreciatively. "Pavel, would you like some more?"

"No, thank you. We have a lot to take home with us too."

"Speaking of home," Brace spoke up, "we should probably head back, get this stored away. I've got gate watch in the morning."

"Yes," Tassie agreed. "We'll all be busy tomorrow. Thank you for inviting us in."

"Please, come over any time," Leandra insisted.

"Mammy, Mammy!" Denira called out.

"What is it, Denira?"

"I want Dadda!"

"I know you do," Leandra replied, frustration building in her voice, "but he isn't here. He isn't home yet."

Kendie stared down at the table, biting her lower lip. Tassie reached out and held her hand, giving her a comforting smile.

"We're here for you, Leandra," Brace told her, seeing her eyes cloud over with worry. "Don't forget that. You're not alone."

"Thank you," Leandra whispered, fighting her emotions. Zorix leaped nimbly onto the bench beside her, and she ran her fingers through his fur, finding at least some small comfort.

Brace let out a sigh. "I'd hate to leave you now, but we really should get our own food home. Come over later today, if you feel the need for it."

Leandra nodded. "Thank you, Brace. We might do that."

Zorix's ears tipped forward, turning to look toward the window. In a moment, Brace could hear voices outside. Excited voices.

"What's that, going on out there?" he asked.

"Dadda, Dadda!" Denira exclaimed, scrambling down from her seat and hurrying toward the door.

"Denira!" Leandra called out, exasperated, following her.

The voices outside grew louder as they approached, and an instant later, there was a familiar deep rumbling filling the air.

"The gate's opening!" Kendie shouted, jumping up from her seat.

Brace instinctively reached out and grabbed Tassie's hand.

"What, Brace?" she asked in alarm. "What's happening?"

"The gate is opening!" he replied, feeling his heart beat faster. "Could it be…?"

Leandra wasted no time. She picked up Denira, set her on her hip, and pulled open the door, hurrying out into the street.

"To the gate! To the gate!" Bahadur called out, a large group gathering behind him.

In an instant, the house emptied.

"Have they returned?" Brace asked. "The search mission? Is it them?"

"It is," Bahadur replied. "I recognized some familiar faces through the white wall. Alban, for one."

The road was filled with excited questions and exclamations as everyone hurried toward the opening gate, Jair and Gavin working their way to the front of the crowd.

"They are back, Tassie!" Brace told her, and her eyes widened.

"All of them?"

"I don't know. We can only find out if we go to the gate with everyone else. Come on, Pavel!"

Leandra and Kendie had already gone ahead by the time Tassie grabbed hold of Pavel's hand and the three of them fell in with the others.

Jair made no attempt to keep control as the gate opened wider and people began emerging into the city. He simply stood by, smiling boldly with relief.

Cayomah and Alban led their horses through first, and they were instantly surrounded by friends. Leandra fought to see through the sea of people.

Landers and Berrick came in next, and then –

"Dadda!" Denira called out, pointing. Leandra's heart leaped when she saw his face.

"Arden!" she shouted, but her voice was swallowed up in all the noise. She pushed her way to the front of the crowd. "Arden!"

He heard, and turned in her direction. Wasting no time, he released his grip on Storm's reins and ran to her, pulling her and Denira into his arms.

"You're back," Leandra breathed against his shoulder. "You're back!"

"I'm back," Arden replied, kissing her repeatedly.

"Dadda, Dadda!" Denira laughed as she wrapped her arms around his neck.

"My little one," Arden said as he managed to hold her and not let go of Leandra. "Dadda's home. I'm home." He pulled Leandra closer as Kendie wrapped her arms around him.

"Don't you dare leave again," Leandra told him. "Do you hear? Don't you dare leave again unless you take me with you."

"I don't plan to."

Leandra kissed him deeply, full of relief. "So, you're back?" she asked. "Your mission succeeded?"

"It did."

"Tell me about it."

Arden shook his head. "That can wait. We'll tell everyone about it at the meeting. There is a lot to tell."

# ~ 32 ~

There was indeed much to tell. If Brace had thought the Main Hall was full on other occasions, this time it was overflowing. The entire city's population was relieved to find that the rescue mission had returned. Not completely unharmed, but alive. And they'd brought eight people back with them, giving them a chance to rest and recover from the journey before holding the meeting on the following day, where they were introduced by name: the rescued prisoners, Aurel, Paya, Elias, Breindel, Falk, and Ackley; a traveling merchant named Harnan; and a young castle guard named Markham.

Jair gazed steadily at Arden and Korian as they went on to relate the tale of their journey. Everyone present at the meeting paid them their utmost attention, Jair most of all, so it seemed.

Their mission had gone as planned, they were told, up until the point when they had exited the dungeon with the freed prisoners. The changing of the guard had happened just at that moment, and Stanner and Korian had been captured.

"We were afraid we would need to leave them behind," Arden told them. "We saw no other options."

"And you would have been right," Korian agreed. He faced the room full of people, whose eyes were all on him. "We were taken before King Oden himself," he continued. "We were somehow made bold enough to confront him with the truth."

"*You* were," Stanner spoke up, grinning ruefully. "I only followed your lead."

Korian acknowledged him with a nod and a smile. "I must honestly say, we feared for our lives. I truly expected King Oden to have us killed that very day."

"Why didn't he?" A voice asked from the crowd. Drayus, from Pran's Helm, sat forward in his seat as he waited for the explanation.

"Why didn't he indeed?" Korian asked, smirking. "He could have. But he realized the truth of what we told him. We reminded him of the increasing darkness, and warned that it would increase all the more. We confronted him with the truth about the night screamers, who are becoming more of a threat to everyone's safety, *out there*. He knew it was all true. And he was losing the hearts of his people because of it. It's the one thing he can't bear to lose – the respect of his people, his kingdom. He wanted to know how to stop the darkness, how to stop the night screamers. We had to tell him there was no way to stop the darkness. And the only way to keep the night screamers away was with the lightstones. They are the only hope of keeping people alive.

"And so," Korian went on after taking a breath, "King Oden realized that he had to change his plans. If he had kept his law preventing people from leaving Dunya, he still would have lost his kingdom. The people would have started dying, more than they have been. Killed by screamers. And the king would have lost their loyalty. So, he changed his mind."

"Changed his mind?" Jayla asked.

"Yes," Korian replied. "He told us that he would allow people to come and go between Dunya and Haven as long as we swore to bring back lightstones, to be kept in the center of every city and villa in Dunya, to protect them from the screamers. For everyone who chooses to stay. He is waiting for us now, to come back with them. If we don't, he will simply go back to his previous law, forbidding anyone to leave. It's as simple as that."

Jair stared at Arden and Korian in amazement. "So," he began, "if we bring lightstones to the cities, King Oden will let people leave?"

"Yes," Arden replied. "Starting with Glendor's Keep."

"And the king just let you go?" Ovard asked Korian.

"Yes," he replied. "And Markham came with us. I don't think King Oden expected *that*."

A smile passed between Markham and Korian before he went on. "We found some horses and hurried to catch up with the others. We found them just north of Fool's March."

"It was quite the unexpected relief to see them," Arden commented.

"It was a relief to find you."

"But people truly *are* free to leave Dunya?" Jair asked. "No one will try to stop them?"

"I shouldn't think so," Korian told him. "Oden's men are spreading the word now." Korian's expression changed into a smirk. "All the people will know that their benevolent king has found a way to protect his beloved citizens from the night screamers, and that the strange city of Haven has opened its doors to them at last."

"Our doors were never closed!" Brodan protested.

"Of course not," Arden agreed. "But *they* don't know that."

"Everyone is free to come here!" Jair spoke up again. "We *will* take lightstones to the cities. And anyone will be able to come to Haven whenever they want!"

"They don't know the way," Gavin pointed out.

"We'll tell them!" Jair replied, undaunted. "We can tell anyone the way to Haven. Anyone who wants to come here — we can show them the way!"

"We can," Arden agreed hesitantly. "But we'll still need to use discretion. We don't need to draw any extra attention to ourselves. No sense bringing the king's anger down on us by being too blatant about it."

"It doesn't matter," Jair replied, smiling broadly, his eyes shining with excitement. "This is it! Don't you see? This is the victory for us! This will be the time of great return of people to Haven, after these thousands of years! Just like in the prophecies Ovard has told us about! Now everyone in Dunya knows about Haven, and there is nothing stopping them from coming! We need to celebrate this, and then we need to get back to work fixing things up! Our little area of Haven is getting so full, we'll need to get another one ready. Another Main Hall, more gardens to plant crops, another food storage building, and a group of leaders to move over there and get things started …"

"Hold on there, my boy," Ovard said with a laugh. "You are right about all of it, of course. But things have been so disheartening here for us for a long while, and we do need to celebrate this. Our people are home again, the prisoners have been freed, and Haven will be getting many new arrivals. I felt it in my bones. We need to lighten our hearts and revel in our joy!"

~

And so they did. There was no shortage of food to eat – fruits and vegetables, grain baked into bread and cakes, goat's milk and honey, fresh fish from the pure water of the lake, and plenty of game birds from the Woods.

Music from Eridan and Ovard's flutes filled the Fountain Court along with much joyful laughter, as well as a new song from Kendie, which she finally had the heart to sing.

"The breaking day shines sweet and clear
To my eyes and my heart, it's just as bright.
Come everyone, and gather near
And leave behind you the sadness of night.
Broken lives can be made new.
Rise up, rise up in the gladness of day!
Let our hearts come together to beat as one
See, the morning dawns so clear and true
Shining down on me and you
Nothing can ever block its light
As we live on for Haven's right!"

The courtyard filled with cheering and tears of joy, mingled with the chirping of birds and the burbling fountain, and the many aromas of delicious foods. Kendie blended into the crowd, feeling that now all-too-familiar tingling sensation when Jair snuck a quick kiss on her cheek.

Brace hugged Tassie tightly, relishing the sound of her laughter in his ear.

"Have we made it?" He asked her. "Everyone is truly free here now?"

"It seems so," Tassie replied, her eyes shining. "At last, yes!"

"Hello, old friend," Arden greeted Brace, giving him a firm slap on the back.

"So great to have you home," Brace told him. "We were so worried for all of you."

"Nothing will ever be the same," Arden commented.

"It will change for the better," Leandra joined in, holding Denira on her hip. "If more people arrive, we can start spreading out across the city. I don't know about anyone else, but things have gotten a bit crowded here for my liking."

Brace laughed. "The courtyard certainly is packed today," he agreed.

"Down, Mammy," Denira said, squirming. "Down, pwease!"

"Why?"

"Bwace, Mammy! Tassie!"

"You want to go to Brace and Tassie?"

"Yes."

"All right," Leandra said as she set Denira down on her feet. The little girl scampered over to Brace and stood staring up at him.

"Do you want me to pick you up?" he asked her.

She blinked, then looked at Tassie. She smiled, reaching up to rest her hand on Tassie's stomach.

"Baby," Denira stated confidently.

Brace felt his breath catch in his throat as he looked at Tassie, whose eyes were wide, her face flushed.

"Baby," Denira said again, confused at why everyone stood staring at her.

Leandra stepped forward and lifted Denira into her arms. "I think we'd better let Brace and Tassie talk among themselves just now," she commented. Arden eyed Brace with concern and wonder; Kendie smiled a nervous smile as Leandra gave Tassie a quick kiss on the cheek. "Pavel?" Leandra asked. "Why don't you come with us and get some of that bread?"

Pavel agreed, glancing back over his shoulder as he followed Arden, Leandra and Kendie across the courtyard.

Brace swallowed. "*Baby*?" he asked softly, and Tassie took in a breath.

"Yes, I ..." She began, then stopped, averting her eyes.

Brace reached out and took her hand. She looked up.

"You knew?"

"I did."

"Why didn't you say anything?"

"Because, Brace. Because of what happened before. I didn't want to tell you and then ... have it come to nothing."

Brace stepped closer to her. He glanced down at her middle, but there was no visible sign of any pregnancy.

"How long have you known?"

"Twelve weeks."

"Twelve?" Brace asked. "But the other times you only made it to six."

"I know." Tassie smiled a little.

Brace breathed out a laugh. "Tassie," he said, daring to let himself feel hope and relief. "We could go all the way this time. We could have our very own child."

"Yes," she replied. "I've been hoping for that ... and ..."

"And?"

"Denira knew, Brace. That means Haven told her. Haven knows. I think Haven is trying to tell us that it will all work out this time."

A smile broke across Brace's face, and he pulled Tassie into his arms.

"Don't draw attention," she scolded, pulling back, but she smiled along with him.

"Pavel will be a brother," Tassie commented, and Brace nodded. He was content to simply stand there, looking into Tassie's green eyes. Let tomorrow wait. Let everything wait. He just wanted to live in this moment, where everything was good. Everyone was safe, they were home, Haven was free from Oden's restrictive law, and they were going to have a child.

He felt like he could fly, his heart was so light.

Cheerful voices filled the air all around him, many of them voices he knew so well.

Friends.

Family.

Home.

More than he ever deserved, more than he'd ever asked for, or dared to dream he could have in his life. Remembering back to that day in the wilds when he'd been fleeing Dunya, heading for Danferron ... he'd been full of fear, anger, and hatred. If he hadn't run into Zorix, where would he be now? He'd never have met Leandra.

No Arden, no Ovard or Jair. No Tassie.

What had Ovard told him then? Maybe he was *meant* to meet them there. He could be part of some great plan. Part of restoring the city of light and beauty, part of bringing people there, within its walls of safety, health and peace. Part of life that was so much better, so much more complete, than he ever thought possible.

And who knew? It wasn't over, not in the slightest. He had Pavel to care for, and soon enough, a child of his own – what other pieces of this plan lay ahead of him, yet unfulfilled? If Haven had chosen him, then Haven knew what he was destined for. Maybe Denira would know, when she was older. Brace could ask her …

But no. He hadn't known what awaited him around any bend in the path. Every decision he'd made had brought him farther away from the life he'd once had, and closer to the one he lived now. But he hadn't been able to foresee anything. There was so much promise in the unknown.

And he could live with that.

# About the Author

Tia Austin lives in Northwest Washington, where she enjoys spending time outside, walking the forest trails and along the rocky beaches. She has been writing fiction and poetry from a young age, with some poems published in anthologies. Haven's Joy is her third published novel. Her favorite genres to write (and read!) are fantasy and historical fiction.

Printed in the United States
By Bookmasters